As Vatch neared the place of the fallen soldiers he thought he saw motion in the mist. He raised the flashlight high over his head and drew his sword.

Some soldiers carried bread or rolls of hard candy into battle. Some of these never ate their provisions. It was a repugnant task, this searching of dead men. But he continued to search. He was savagely hungry.

Motion in the mist again made him look up. Two shadows were coming toward him. They were much bigger than lopers . . . and manshaped.

Vatch stood up and called, "Hello?"

They came on, taking shape as they neared. A third blurred shadow congealed behind them. They had not answered. Annoyed, Vatch swung the flashlight beam toward them.

The light caught them full. Vatch held it steady, staring, not believing. Then, still not believing, he screamed and screamed.

ROBERT ADAMS

PHANTOM REGIMENTS

BAEN BOOKS

PHANTOM REGIMENTS

Copyright © 1990 by Robert Adams, Pamela Crippen Adams and Martin Harry Greenberg

A Baen Books Original

Baen Publishing Enterprises
260 Fifth Avenue
New York, N.Y. 10001

ISBN: 0-671-69862-1

Cover art by Ken Kelly

First printing, February 1990

Distributed by
SIMON & SCHUSTER
1230 Avenue of the Americas
New York, N.Y. 10020
Printed in the United States of America

Acknowledgements

"Larroes Catch Meddlers" by Manly Wade Wellman—Copyright © 1951 by Fantasy House, Inc. for *The Magazine of Fantasy and Science Fiction*. Reprinted by permission of Karl Edward Wagner, Literary Executor for the Estate of Manly Wade Wellman.

"The Spirit of Sergeant Davies" by Michael and Mollie Hardwick—Copyright © 1971 by Michael and Mollie Hardwick. Reprinted by permission of the authors.

"Death Holds the Post" by August Derleth—Copyright © 1936, renewed 1953 by August Derleth. Reprinted by permission of the Scott Meredith Literary Agency, Inc.

"Night on Mispec Moor" by Larry Niven—Copyright © 1974 by Larry Niven. Reprinted by permission of the author.

"The Spectre General" by Theodore R. Cogswell—Copyright © 1952 by Street and Smith Publications, Inc.; renewed © 1980 by Theodore R. Cogswell. Reprinted by permission of George Cogswell.

"The Bells of Shoredan" by Roger Zelazny—Copyright © 1966 by Roger Zelazny. Reprinted by permission of the author.

"Ghosts of the Mutiny"—Copyright © 1971 by Michael and Mollie Hardwick. Reprinted by permission of the authors.

"Commander in the Mist" by Sterling E. Lanier—Copyright © 1982 by Mercury Press, Inc.; copyright © 1986 by Sterling E. Lanier. First appeared in *The Magazine of Fantasy and Science Fiction*. Reprinted by permission of Curtis Brown, Ltd.

CONTENTS

Introduction

SKELETONS AT THE FEAST

David Drake

Old soldiers never die; they only fade away.
                              —Traditional

Well, of course old soldiers did die. They probably died with rather greater frequency than a population of old farmers, old shopkeepers—or old duchesses, for that matter.

It was possible for a citizen of Victorian England to think otherwise, though, because there was always a fresh crop of paid-off soldiers to replace the season's deaths. One old soldier was very like another, if you didn't care much; and most people didn't care at all.

The armies of classical Greece were (with a few very limited exceptions) composed of citizens. Occasionally the state might vote some form of relief to a man injured in its service, but that was neither expected nor, to a great degree, necessary. "Citizen" was itself a title of rank, implying the holder could meet a stringent property qualification and had supplied his own expensive military equipment. Such a soldier had resources on which he could draw if he were wounded in battle.

The Roman army originally recruited from a similar class, but the growing scope of Roman military operations forced a change. War was no longer limited to a fighting season roughly equivalent to the growing season: the period between when farmers sowed their

1

crops and the harvest. Instead, soldiers might have to serve year round in a garrison—and for a period of years. Furthermore, broader commitments—through conquest or alliance—meant longer borders. The pool of available manpower had not increased as rapidly as the need for it.

The Romans therefore opened the army to men who could not afford their own equipment and to whom the pay and loot of military service were more important factors than patriotism. The result was a professional, long-service army—and a body of retired veterans who had spent twenty or more years, their entire adult lives, as soldiers.

Men like that had no remaining links to civilian society; they had to be cared for by the state. Veterans were given grants of land, and frequently the government built cities for them.

This wasn't solely altruism. The great Roman generals —and the emperors who arose when great generals smashed the last vestiges of the Roman Republic— depended on the armies for their power and their very lives. No emperor dared show contempt for the veterans he no longer needed, since he slept surrounded by the swords of their comrades.

The Roman system died with the Empire, and it wasn't until the late 17th century that professional citizen armies of the later Roman type reappeared as a significant factor in Europe. Wars in the interim had been fought by nobles supplying their own equipment; lowly retainers, for whom the nobles were responsible; and mercenaries in the modern sense, fighters who sold their skills to the highest bidder.

In none of the above cases was the lot of the veteran a matter for the state's concern (and as for the mercenary armies of the Thirty Years War, recent studies have shown that there weren't enough surviving veterans to matter anyway).

> *You haven't an arm and you haven't a leg,*
> *You're an eyeless, boneless chickenless egg;*

You'll have to be put with a bowl to beg.
From *Johnnie We Hardly Knew Ye* (18th Century)

The British army of the 18th and 19th centuries was different. It was professional and highly trained (the "thin red line" was so called because the British, with two ranks, achieved a rate of fire comparable to that of Continental armies with twice the number of men per foot of front). In that it was similar to Caesar's legions.

But unlike Rome, the British needed their army only to fight. The state—the landholding citizenry which held political power—was quite stable. The men who enlisted in the army were the dregs of British society. They were regarded as pariahs, shunned in peace and scorned even in wartime.

If they died in service, they were buried. If they were maimed or somehow managed to survive until they were too old to be useful to their country, they were discharged with a pension of half the pittance they had earned on active duty.

The British army wasn't a large one, and the number of veterans who survived to return to England was smaller yet; but these men with no breeding or civilian skills were very visible. A few of them, wearing their medals, eked out a living as commissionaires for hotels and clubs—calling cabs and carrying letters for tips.

Some of them begged. Very many of them begged.

And when one beggar died, another crippled veteran of this or that imperial skirmish would be there to take his place on the sidewalk with a begging bowl.

Come and lose your eyes and limbs
For thirteen pence a day.
From *The Young Recruit* (ca. 1850)

World War II was in a real sense a national war in the United States. *Yachting Magazine* had a war correspondent on Guadalcanal because so many members of the Harvard Yacht Club had volunteered for dangerous duty in the PT Boat squadrons there.

By the time of our involvement in Viet Nam, things had changed. Selective Service selected disproportionately from the classes of society whose members didn't have the power to work the system—and work themselves out of it. The troops that fought in Nam were socially very similar to the underclasses filling the British army during the 18th and 19th centuries.

There's a Veterans Administration (left over from more popular wars, I'm afraid). The educational benefits available to Nam vets were a joke; but there are VA hospitals, and pensions at a somewhat higher relative level than those offered to Kipling's "Tommy Atkins." Things could be worse.

But remember that a soldier risks more than his life and limbs in a war zone.

And remember that the largest single group among the today's street people—the derelicts, the winos, the bums—are Viet Nam veterans.

THE LOST LEGION

Rudyard Kipling

When the Indian Mutiny broke out, and a little time before the siege of Delhi, a regiment of Native Irregular Horse was stationed at Peshawur on the frontier of India. That regiment caught what John Lawrence called at the time "the prevalent mania" and would have thrown in its lot with the mutineers, had it been allowed to do so. The chance never came, for, as the regiment swept off down south, it was headed off by a remnant of an English corps into the hills of Afghanistan, and there the newly conquered tribesmen turned against it as wolves turn against buck. It was hunted for the sake of its arms and accoutrements from hill to hill, from ravine to ravine, up and down the dried beds of rivers and round the shoulders of bluffs, till it disappeared as water sinks in the sand—this officerless rebel regiment. The only trace left of its existence to-day is a nominal roll drawn up in neat round hand and countersigned by an officer who called himself, "Adjutant, late—— Irregular Cavalry." The paper is yellow with years and dirt, but on the back of it you can still read a pencil-note by John Lawrence; to this effect: "See that the two native officers who remained loyal are not deprived of their estates.—J.L." Of six hundred and fifty sabres only two stood strain, and John Lawrence in the midst of all the agony of the first months of the Mutiny found time to think about their merits.

5

That was more than thirty years ago, and the tribesmen across the Afghan border who helped to annihilate the regiment are now old men. Sometimes a graybeard speaks of his share in the massacre. "They came," he will say, "across the border, very proud, calling upon us to rise and kill the English, and go down to the sack of Delhi. But we who had just been conquered by the same English knew that they were over bold, and that the Government could account easily for those down-country dogs. This Hindustani regiment, therefore, we treated with fair words, and kept standing in one place till the redcoats came after them very hot and angry. Then this regiment ran forward a little more into our hills to avoid the wrath of the English, and we lay upon their flanks watching from the sides of the hills till we were well assured that their path was lost behind them. Then we came down, for we desired their clothes, and their bridles, and their rifles, and their boots—more especially their boots. That was a great killing—done slowly." Here the old man will rub his nose, and shake his long snaky locks, and lick his bearded lips, and grin till the yellow tooth-stumps show. "Yea, we killed them because we needed their gear, and we knew that their lives had been forfeited to God on account of their sin—the sin of treachery to the salt which they had eaten. They rode up and down the valleys, stumbling and rocking in their saddles, and howling for mercy. We drove them slowly like cattle till they were all assembled in one place, the flat wide valley of Sheor Kôt. Many had died from want of water, but there still were many left, and they could not make any stand. We went among them pulling them down with our hands two at a time, and our boys killed them who were new to the sword. My share of the plunder was such and such—so many guns, and so many saddles. The guns were good in those days. Now we steal the Government rifles, and despise smooth barrels. Yes, beyond doubt we wiped that regiment from off the face of the earth, and even the memory of the deed is now dying. But men say—"

At this point the tale would stop abruptly, and it was impossible to find out what men said across the border. The Afghans were always a secretive race, and vastly preferred doing something wicked to saying anything at all. They would be quiet and well-behaved for months, till one night, without word or warning, they would rush a police-post, cut the throats of a constable or two, dash through a village, carry away three or four women, and withdraw, in the red glare of burning thatch, driving the cattle and goats before them to their own desolate hills. The Indian Government would become almost tearful on these occasions. First it would say, "Please be good and we'll forgive you." The tribe concerned in the latest depredation would collectively put its thumb to its nose and answer rudely. Then the Government would say: "Hadn't you better pay up a little money for those few corpses you left behind you the other night?" Here the tribe would temporise, and lie and bully, and some of the younger men, merely to show contempt of authority, would raid another police-post and fire into some frontier mud-fort, and, if lucky, kill a real English officer. Then the Government would say: "Observe; if you really persist in this line of conduct, you will be hurt." If the tribe knew exactly what was going on in India, it would apologise or be rude, according as it learned whether the Government was busy with other things or able to devote its full attention to their performances. Some of the tribes knew to one corpse how far to go. Others became excited, lost their heads, and told the Government to come on. With sorrow and tears, and one eye on the British taxpayer at home, who insisted on regarding these exercises as brutal wars of annexation, the Government would prepare an expensive little field-brigade and some guns, and send all up into the hills to chase the wicked tribe out of the valleys, where the corn grew, into the hill-tops where there was nothing to eat. The tribe would turn out in full strength and enjoy the campaign, for they knew that their women would never be touched, that their wounded would be nursed, not mutilated, and that as soon as each man's bag of corn was spent they could surrender and palaver with the English General as though they had been a real enemy. Afterwards, years afterwards, they would pay the blood-money, driblet by driblet, to the Government and tell their children how they had slain the redcoats by thousands. The only drawback to this kind of picnic-war was the weakness of the redcoats for solemnly blowing up with powder their fortified towers and keeps. This the tribes always considered mean.

Chief among the leaders of the smaller tribes—the little clans who knew to a penny the expense of moving white troops against them—was a priest-bandit-chief whom we will call the Gulla Kutta Mullah. His enthusiasm for Border murder as an art was almost dignified. He would cut down a mail-runner from pure wantonness, or bombard a mud fort with rifle-fire when he knew that our men needed to sleep. In his leisure moments he would go on circuit among his neighbours, and try to incite other tribes to devilry. Also, he kept a kind of hotel for fellow-outlaws in his own village, which lay in a valley called Bersund. Any respectable murderer on that section of the frontier was sure to lie up at Bersund, for it was reckoned an exceedingly safe place. The sole entry to it ran through a narrow gorge which could be converted into a deathtrap in five minutes. It was surrounded by high hills, reckoned inaccessible to all save born mountaineers, and here the Gulla Kutta Mullah lived in great state, the head of a colony of mud and stone huts, and in each mud hut hung some portion of a red uniform and the plunder of dead men. The Government particularly wished for his capture, and once invited him formally to come out and be hanged on account of the many murders in which he had taken a direct part. He replied:

"I am only twenty miles, as the crow flies, from your border. Come and fetch me."

"Some day we will come," said the Government, "and hanged you will be."

The Gulla Kutta Mullah let the matter from his mind.

He knew that the patience of the Government was as long as a summer day; but he did not realise that its arm was as long as a winter night. Months afterwards, when there was peace on the border, and all India was quiet, the Indian Government turned in its sleep and remembered the Gulla Kutta Mullah at Bersund, with his thirteen outlaws. The movement against him of one single regiment—which the telegrams would have translated as war—would have been highly impolitic. This was a time for silence and speed, and, above all, absence of bloodshed.

You must know that all along the north-west frontier of India there is spread a force of some thirty thousand foot and horse, whose duty it is to quietly and unostentatiously shepherd the tribes in front of them. They move up and down, and down and up, from one desolate little post to another; they are ready to take the field at ten minutes' notice; they are always half in and half out of a difficulty somewhere along the monotonous line; their lives are as hard as their own muscles, and the papers never say anything about them. It was from this force that the Government picked its men.

One night, at a station where the mounted Night Patrol fire as they challenge, and the wheat rolls in great blue-green waves under our cold northern moon, the officers were playing billiards in the mud-walled club-house, when orders came to them that they were to go on parade at once for a night-drill. They grumbled, and went to turn out their men—a hundred English troops, let us say, two hundred Goorkhas, and about a hundred cavalry of the finest native cavalry in the world.

When they were on the parade-ground, it was explained to them in whispers that they must set off at once across the hills to Bersund. The English troops were to post themselves round the hills at the side of the valley; the Goorkhas would command the gorge and the death-trap, and the cavalry would fetch a long march round and get to the back of the circle of hills, whence, if there were any difficulty, they could charge down on the Mullah's men. But orders were very strict that there should be no fighting and no noise. They were to return in the morning with every round of ammunition intact, and the Mullah and the thirteen outlaws bound in their midst. If they were successful, no one would know or care anything about their work; but failure meant probably a small border war, in which the Gulla Kutta Mullah would pose as a popular leader against a big bullying power, instead of a common Border murderer.

Then there was silence, broken only by the clicking of the compass-needles and snapping of watchcases, as the heads of columns compared bearings and made appointments for the rendezvous. Five minutes later the parade-ground was empty; the green coats of the Goorkhas and the overcoats of the English troops had faded into the darkness, and the cavalry were cantering away in the face of a blinding drizzle.

What the Goorkhas and the English did will be seen later on. The heavy work lay with the horses, for they had to go far and pick their way clear of habitations. Many of the troopers were natives of that part of the world, ready and anxious to fight against their kin, and some of the officers had made private and unofficial excursions into those hills before. They crossed the border, found a dried riverbed, cantered up that, walked through a stony gorge, risked crossing a low hill under cover of the darkness, skirted another hill, leaving their hoof-marks deep in some ploughed ground, felt their way along another water-course, ran over the neck of a spur praying that no one would hear their horses grunting, and so worked on in the rain and the darkness, till they had left Bersund and its crater of hills a little behind them, and to the left, and it was time to swing round. The ascent commanding the back of Bersund was steep, and they halted to draw breath in a broad level valley below the height. That is to say, the men reined up, but the horses, blown as they were, refused to halt. There was unchristian language, the worse for being delivered in a whisper, and you heard the saddles squeaking in the darkness as the horses plunged.

The subaltern at the rear of one troop turned in his saddle and said very softly:

"Carter, what the blessed heavens are you doing at the rear? Bring your men up, man."

There was no answer, till a trooper replied:

"Carter Sahib is forward—not here. There is nothing behind us."

"There is," said the subaltern. "The squadron's walking on its own tail."

Then the Major in command moved down to the rear swearing softly and asking for the blood of Lieutenant Halley—the subaltern w had just spoken.

"Look after your rearguard," said the Major. "Some of your infernal thieves have got lost. They're at the head of the squadron, and you're a several kinds of idiot."

"Shall I tell off my men, sir?" said the subaltern sulkily, for he was feeling wet and cold.

"Tell 'em off!" said the Major. "*Whip* 'em off, by Gad! You're squandering them all over the place. There's a troop behind you *now!*"

"So I was thinking," said the subaltern calmly. "I have all my men here, sir. Better speak to Carter."

"Carter Sahib sends salaam and wants to know why the regiment is stopping," said a trooper to Lieutenant Halley.

"Where under heaven *is* Carter?" said the Major.

"Forward with his troop," was the answer.

"Are we walking in a ring, then, or are we the centre of a blessed brigade?" said the Major.

By this time there was silence all along the column. The horses were still; but, through the drive of the fine rain, men could hear the feet of many horses moving over stony ground.

"We're being stalked," said Lieutenant Halley.

"They've no horses here. Besides they'd have fired before this," said the Major. "It's—it's villagers' ponies."

"Then our horses would have neighed and spoilt the

attack long ago. They must have been near us for half an hour," said the subaltern.

"Queer that we can't smell the horses," said the Major, damping his finger and rubbing it on his nose as he sniffed up wind.

"Well, it's a bad start," said the subaltern, shaking the wet from his overcoat. "What shall we do, sir?"

"Get on," said the Major. "We shall catch it tonight."

The column moved forward very gingerly for a few paces. Then there was an oath, a shower of blue sparks as shod hooves crashed on small stones, and a man rolled over with a jangle of accoutrements that would have waked the dead.

"Now we've gone and done it," said Lieutenant Halley. "All the hillside awake and all the hillside to climb in the face of musketry-fire! This comes of trying to do night-hawk work."

The trembling trooper picked himself up and tried to explain that his horse had fallen over one of the little cairns that are built of loose stones on the spot where a man has been murdered. There was no need to give reasons. The Major's big Australian charger blundered next, and the column came to a halt in what seemed to be a very graveyard of little cairns, all about two feet high. The manœuvres of the squadron are not reported. Men said that it felt like mounted quadrilles without training and without the music; but at last the horses, breaking rank and choosing their own way, walked clear of the cairns, till every man of the squadron reformed and drew rein a few yards up the slope of the hill. Then, according to Lieutenant Halley, there was another scene very like the one which has been described. The Major and Carter insisted that all the men had not joined rank, clicking and blundering among the dead men's cairns. Lieutenant Halley told off his own troopers again and resigned himself to wait. Later on he said to me:

"I didn't much know, and I didn't much care what was going on. The row of that trooper falling ought to have scared half the country, and I would take my oath that we were being stalked by a full regiment in the rear, and *they* were making row enough to rouse all Afghanistan. I sat tight, but nothing happened."

The mysterious part of the night's work was the silence on the hillside. Everybody knew that the Gulla Kutta Mullah had his outpost-huts on the reverse side of the hill, and everybody expected, by the time that the Major had sworn himself into quiet, that the watchmen there would open fire. When nothing happened, they said that the gusts of the rain had deadened the sound of the horses, and thanked Providence. At last the Major satisfied himself (a) that he had left no one behind among the cairns, and (b) that he was not being taken in the rear by a large and powerful body of cavalry. The men's tempers were thoroughly spoiled, the horses were lathered and unquiet, and one and all prayed for daylight.

They set themselves to climb up the hill, each man leading his mount carefully. Before they had covered the lower slopes or the breast-plates had begun to tighten, a thunderstorm came up behind, rolling across the low hills and drowning any noise less than that of cannon. The first flash of the lightning showed the bare ribs of the ascent, the hill-crest standing steely-blue against the black sky, the little falling lines of the rain, and, a few yards to their left flank, an Afghan watchtower, two-storied, built of stone, and entered by a ladder from the upper story. The ladder was up, and a man with a rifle was leaning from the window. The darkness and the thunder rolled down in an instant, and, when the lull followed, a voice from the watchtower cried, "Who goes there?"

The cavalry were very quiet, but each man gripped his carbine and stood beside his horse. Again the voice called, "Who goes there?" and in a louder key, "O, brothers, give the alarm!" Now, every man in the cavalry would have died in his long boots sooner than have asked for quarter, but it is a fact that the answer to the second call was a long wail of "Marf karo! Marf karo?"

which means, "Have mercy! Have mercy!" It came from the climbing regiment.

The cavalry stood dumbfounded, till the big troopers had time to whisper one to another: "Mir Khan, was that thy voice? Abdullah, didst *thou* call?" Lieutenant Halley stood beside his charger and waited. So long as no firing was going on he was content. Another flash of lightning showed the horses with heaving flanks and nodding heads; the men, white eye-balled, glaring beside them, and the stone watch-tower to the left. This time there was no head at the window, and the rude iron-clamped shutter that could turn a rifle bullet was closed.

"Go on, men," said the Major. "Get up to the top at any rate!" The squadron toiled forward, the horses wagging their tails and the men pulling at the bridles, the stones rolling down the hillside and the sparks flying. Lieutenant Halley declares that he never heard a squadron make so much noise in his life. They scrambled up, he said, as though each horse had eight legs and a spare horse to follow him. Even then there was no sound from the watchtower, and the men stopped exhausted on the ridge that overlooked the pit of darkness in which the village of Bersund lay. Girths were loosed, curb-chains shifted, and saddles adjusted, and the men dropped down among the stones. Whatever might happen now, they held the upper ground of any attack.

The thunder ceased, and with it the rain, and the soft thick darkness of a winter night before the dawn covered them all. Except for the sound of falling water among the ravines below, everything was still. They heard the shutter of the watchtower below them thrown back with a clang, and the voice of the watcher calling, "Oh, Hafiz Ullah!"

The echoes took up the call, "La-la-la!" and an answer came from the watchtower hidden round the curve of the hill, "What is it, Shahbaz Khan?"

Shahbaz Khan replied in the high-pitched voice of the mountaineer: "Hast thou seen?"

The answer came back: "Yes. God deliver us from all evil spirits!"

There was a pause, and then: "Hafiz Ullah, I am alone! Come to me."

"Shahbaz Khan, I am alone also; but I dare not leave my post!"

"That is a lie; thou art afraid."

A longer pause followed, and then: "I am afraid. Be silent! They are below us still. Pray to God and sleep."

The troopers listened and wondered, for they could not understand what save earth and stone could lie below the watchtowers.

Shahbaz Khan began to call again: "They are below us. I can see them! For the pity of God come over to me, Hafiz Ullah! My father slew ten of them. Come over!"

Hafiz Ullah answered in a very loud voice, "Mine was guiltless. Hear, ye Men of the Night, neither my father nor my blood had any part in that sin. Bear thou thine own punishment, Shahbaz Khan."

"Oh, some one ought to stop those two chaps crowing away like cocks there," said the Lieutenant shivering under his rock.

He had hardly turned round to expose a new side of him to the rain before a bearded, long-locked, evil-smelling Afghan rushed up the hill, and tumbled into his arms. Halley sat upon him, and thrust as much of a sword-hilt as could be spared down the man's gullet. "If you cry out, I kill you," he said cheerfully.

The man was beyond any expression of terror. He lay and quaked, gasping. When Halley took the sword-hilt from between his teeth, he was still inarticulate, but clung to Halley's arm, feeling it from elbow to wrist.

"The Rissala! The dead Rissala!" he gasped. "It is down there!"

"No; the Rissala, the very much alive Rissala. It is up here," said Halley, unshipping his watering-bridle, and fastening the man's hands. "Why were you in the towers so foolish as to let us pass?"

"The valley is full of the dead," said the Afghan. "It is

better to fall into the hands of the English than the hands of the dead. They march to and fro below there. I saw them in the lightning."

He recovered his composure after a little, and whispering, because Halley's pistol was at his stomach, said: "What is this? There is no war between us now, and the Mullah will kill me for not seeing you pass!"

"Rest easy," said Halley, "we are coming to kill the Mullah, if God please. His teeth have grown too long. No harm will come to thee unless the daylight shows thee as a face which is desired by the gallows for crime done. But what of the dead regiment?"

"I only kill within my own border," said the man, immensely relieved. "The Dead Regiment is below. The men must have passed through it on their journey— four hundred dead on horses, stumbling among their own graves, among the little heaps—dead men all, whom we slew."

"Whew!" said Halley. "That accounts for my cursing Carter and the Major cursing me. Four hundred sabres, eh? No wonder we thought there were a few extra men in the troop. Kurruk Shah," he whispered to a grizzled native officer that lay within a few feet of him, "Hast thou heard anything of a dead Rissala in these hills?"

"Assuredly," said Kurruk Shah with a grim chuckle. "Otherwise, why did I, who have served the Queen for seven and twenty years, and killed many hill-dogs, shout aloud for quarter when the lightning revealed us to the watchtowers? When I was a young man I saw the killing in the valley of Sheor Kôt there at our feet, and I know the tale that grew up therefrom. But how can the ghosts of unbelievers prevail against us who are of the Faith? Strap that dog's hands a little tighter, Sahib. An Afghan is like an eel."

"But a dead Rissala," said Halley, jerking his captive's wrist. "That is foolish talk, Kurruk Shah. The dead are dead. Hold still, *Sag!*" The Afghan wriggled.

"The dead are dead, and for that reason they walk at night. What need to talk? We be men; we have our eyes and ears. Thou canst both see and hear them down the hillside," said Kurruk Shah composedly.

Halley stared and listened long and intently. The valley was full of stifled noises, as every valley must be at night; but whether he saw or heard more than was natural Halley alone knows, and he does not choose to speak on the subject.

At last, and just before the dawn, a green rocket shot up from the far side of the valley of Bersund, at the head of the gorge, to show that the Goorkhas were in position. A red light from the infantry at left and right answered it, and the cavalry burnt a white flare. Afghans in winter are late sleepers, and it was not till full day that the Gulla Kutta Mullah's men began to straggle from their huts, rubbing their eyes. They saw men in green, and red, and brown uniforms, leaning on their arms, neatly arranged all round the crater of the village of Bersund, in a cordon that not even a wolf could have broken. They rubbed their eyes the more when a pink-faced young man, who was not even in the Army, but represented the Political Department, tripped down the hillside with two orderlies, rapped at the door of the Gulla Kutta Mullah's house, and told him quietly to step out and be tied up for safe transport. That same young man passed on through the huts, tapping here one cateran, and there another lightly with his cane; and as each was pointed out, so he was tied up, staring hopelessly at the crowned heights around where the English soldiers looked down with incurious eyes. Only the Mullah tried to carry it off with curses and high words, till a soldier who was tying his hands said:

"None o' your lip! Why didn't you come out when you was ordered, instead o' keeping us awake all night? You're no better than my own barrack-sweeper, you white-'eaded old polyanthus! Kim up!"

Half an hour later the troops had gone away with the Mullah and his thirteen friends. The dazed villagers were looking ruefully at a pile of broken muskets and snapped swords, and wondering how in the world they had come so to miscalculate the forbearance of the Indian Government.

It was a very neat little affair, neatly carried out, and the men concerned were unofficially thanked for their services.

Yet it seems to me that much credit is also due to another regiment whose name did not appear in brigade orders, and whose very existence is in danger of being forgotten.

THE SPELL OF THE SWORD

Frank Aubrey

"Yes, it is a curious-looking ornament, isn't it? And it has a curious history, too—at least, the sword had of which it once formed part," observed Clayton, with a gravity that was somewhat unusual with him.

"Tell me about it," I said. I am not inquisitive, as a rule; but, somehow, his manner impressed me.

He remained silent a short time. Then, looking at me very earnestly, he answered.

"Well, perhaps I may; though I would not tell it to many. Indeed, only two other people know the story. I hate—ah! more than I can convey to you—even to think about it. But to you it may be of special interest, for you are not one of those who thoughtlessly laugh at that which is out of the common, merely because it cannot be explained on ordinary grounds."

I began to grow interested. I scented something savoring of the mysterious, the supernatural. However, I replied quietly.

"You know that I regard all such matters from the point of view of a simple, unbiased inquirer. If one cannot always explain, one need not therefore ridicule."

"Just so, just so," he returned gloomily; and then lapsed into silence again. I said nothing; only pulled at my cigar, and patiently waited for what I saw was coming.

19

"Do you know—but no, of course you don't," he began presently. "But can you imagine how it can be, that a man may suddenly, unexpectedly, once in his life, feel like a would-be murderer? You have heard of men in the East who suddenly run 'amok,' as it is called? Well—what would you say if I tell you that *I*— even *I*—who sit now so soberly before you, whom you know to be ordinarily, a quiet, peaceably-disposed English gentleman—had once been on the verge of running 'amok'?"

"Temporary frenzy—a heat-stroke, probably," I suggested.

"You think so, *now;* but wait till you've heard my story. Then you'll be better able to judge." And he proceeded to unfold to me the following strange tale.

"When I said, just now, that I knew the history of the sword to which that curiously wrought silver death's-head belonged, I meant only its history since it came into the hands of a friend of mine named Knebworth. I suspect that many other histories or stories—and terrible ones—attach to it, if we could but trace them. But what I have to tell is quite gruesome enough, and I have no wish to learn anything more about it.

"You have heard that I fought in the Brazilian civil war of some years back. My friend, Jack Knebworth, and myself attached ourselves to the popular—and winning—party.

"We were given commissions, and fought almost side-by-side through nearly the whole term of the war.

"It was just before the close of the last campaign that I one day found Jack in possession of that sword. It had the most curiously worked hilt I ever saw: and that death's-head was fixed on to the end by a screw. You see, there are two emeralds in the eye-sockets of the skull. They are dull now; they seem, somehow, to have lost their luster; but, I tell you, their brightness formerly was something little short of marvelous. I have been told they are not very valuable, being scarcely, I believe, strictly speaking, emeralds at all. Some other stones of a similar color, perhaps. Anyway, they used to throw out greenish-yellow beams of so vivid and fiery a character that the thing made you sometimes jump when you looked at it. These beams, with the grinning jaws, gave the whole affair a most ghastly, yet strangely fascinating appearance—you almost thought it was alive, and was grinning and rolling its eyes at you!

"The rest of the hilt was curiously worked out with strange woods inlaid with silver, upon which were signs, or letters, or designs of which I could not guess the meaning. The blade was an old-fashioned rapier, of wonderfully tempered steel; and this also had on its four faces signs or characters which no one, however, professed to understand. There was a scabbard of leather, mounted with soft black velvet and silver; the latter with similar markings. It was probably of ancient Spanish manufacture; that was all we could guess at. Knebworth bought it of an Indian chief, we know, who, one day, came into the camp, and offered it at a ridiculously low price. That was all he could tell about it at that time.

"Well, two or three days after he bought it, his servant, a staunch, trustworthy old soldier, who had served him faithfully, and fought bravely, all through the war, 'ran amok,' as they say in India—I don't know how else to describe the affair—killed two of his own comrades, and then threw himself over a bridge into a mountain torrent, where he was dashed to pieces on the rocks. In one of the victims he left this sword; and, after the inquiry, it was returned to Knebworth.

"Then came the peace; and we were moved into one of the towns. There Jack obtained another servant; one strongly recommended by a brother officer who was packing up to leave the country. Two days afterward, this new servant disappeared; but, in one of the side streets, a man was found lying dead, with a wound through the heart; and, beside him, this sword! There was more fuss this time, and it was well for my chum that he could show a very clear and unassailable *alibi*. As it was, he had much trouble about the affair; and by the time it was over I was packing up and was nearly ready for my journey back to England. Knebworth was returning to the old country too, but not just then; he wished first to make a trip upon some matter of private business into the interior. He promised to follow me as soon as he could; and to look me up in London.

"Entering his room one day, I found him sitting on a packing-case with the sword lying across his knees. He told me he thought the thing was 'uncanny,' and that he was about to break it and throw the pieces away. After some talk I induced him to give it to me; I procured some sacking, and wrapped it up then and there, ready to pack in one of my chests. And that's how the thing came into my possession.

"I came back to England full of hope and expectations of happiness: for I was hastening to return to one I dearly loved, one who had long ago promised to be my wife. Her name was Mabel—Mabel Karslake—and she had been all the world to me for many long years. True, I had not heard from her of late; but I attributed that to the disorganized state of the country while the war was about. But alas! when I arrived here, I soon found that this silence had a different, and, for me, a more sinister, meaning; she was engaged to another; and that one, an old college friend of mine!

"That was a terrible blow! I do not wish to dwell upon it; it is best passed over; but for weeks—months—I lived in a sort of dazed condition, as one who has been stunned and has never fully recovered from the shock. It is a dreadful experience for any man to have to face such a thing. The terrible sense of loneliness that falls upon you as you realize that you have come back, not to the world you know, but to one that is new and altogether strange, where everybody is interested in himself and his own affairs alone; and you are—an outsider, a stranger!

"And then, above all, to be deserted by the one being you had believed would be true to you through everything; by the one you had lived for, worked for, fought for, risked your life for, again and again. Ah! think of it! But—let it pass. I go on now to other matters.

"I had taken some rooms in London, in Fitzroy Street. They were large, lofty, roomy apartments of the kind let out to artists as studios. They were, in fact, used for that purpose by an artist who was away for the summer and who was desirous of making a few pounds by letting them during his absence. I liked them better than the ordinary stuffy London lodgings; for, if poorly furnished and rather rough, they were airy, and there was plenty of room to move about, even after I had placed in them all my packages. Many of these I had never even taken the trouble to open since my return, so listless and miserable was my state of mind.

"I received a letter from Knebworth, written at Rio, saying he had nearly finished his business, and would come to England by the next boat. This letter contained a rather curious paragraph, which ran thus: 'By the way, I have a message for you from Macolo, the old Indian from whom I bought that unlucky ancient sword you took away with you. The beggar had been playing double, it seems; he got into mischief, and I was able to do him a good turn—about saved his life. By way of showing his appreciation, the rascal confessed that he sold the weapon to me in hope that it would get *me* into trouble—as it most certainly did. *Now*, he wants it back again, and offers quite a big sum for it.

" 'When I told him you had taken it away, he looked very anxious, said he had always liked you, and did not wish to bring you to harm. "Therefore," he said, "tell your white brother to avoid the sword as he would a rattlesnake. Tell him on no account to take the handle in his hand. There is a curse upon it; and those who come under its spell become lost." He did not use exactly those words, but that's the sum and substance of his information. Cheerful news, isn't it? Did I not say the thing was uncanny? In all seriousness, however, if you send the beastly thing back to him, he promises you "much gold" for it.'

"I smiled languidly at the strange message, and thought no more of it at the time. Later I had a note from Knebworth, saying he had arrived at Southampton; then one saying he was at Croydon. Finally, came a post-card, announcing that he would call upon me the following afternoon.

"Now that same afternoon, I was expecting a visit from Cyril Bellingham—the man who had won Mabel from me. He came to call upon me sometimes. I cannot say I was glad to see him; but he was, as I have told you, a college friend, and I did not like to appear so mean as to break off an old friendship because of what had occurred. Indeed, I was inclined to blame *her* rather than him; especially after the one interview I had with her. Her behavior then had seemed to me strange, inexplicable; her replies to my impassioned words were cold and stinging. Yet in her eyes was an expression I could not fathom. It seemed a mixture; there appeared to be doubt, surprise, and a look as of half fear, mingled with a sort of pathetic pity for myself. This last was so evident that I had no heart to upbraid her; and I left her without one word of reproach for what she had caused me to suffer.

"Jack Knebworth's expected visit had put me in mind, as I sat expecting him and Bellingham, of the old sword that lay packed away in one of my closets, but which belonged, properly, to him. I decided I would give it back to him, and let him do with it what seemed good in his own eyes. I therefore opened the chest, and began pulling out the contents till I found it wrapped in the sacking in which I had tied it up.

"Amongst other things I discovered, before coming to it, were two fencing foils, which were very old friends; I had had them many years. I laid these on the floor, took out the sword, and went and sat down by the table to undo the wrapper at my leisure. Soon the curious old rapier was unfolded, and I drew it from its scabbard to see if it had rusted. I found it quite bright; and, then, as my glance fell upon the hilt and the death's-head, I gave a great start. Never have I seen in any stones such gleams of lurid light as those that danced, and sparkled, and darted from the two eyes of that skull! I say 'lurid,' for, at times, the stones seemed to change to rubies and the scintillations took a blood-red hue, changing quickly again to a glittering green.

"As I gazed, the baleful glare of those fiery eyes seemed to grow and grow in intensity, and the eyes themselves to increase in size, till I felt as though I were enduring the mocking gaze of a mighty demon; and, verily, I half expected each moment to see appear before me some appalling, devilish shape from the under world. I took hold of the hilt with a half-conscious determination to see whether the thing was really alive; and also, as I believe, with the vague wish to shut out the sight of the hideous skull and its rolling, leering eyes.

"As my hand closed upon it, I felt at once an odd tingling in the fingers, that was not, however, at all unpleasant. Gradually it increased, and crept up my arm, and it seemed to bring a sensation as of great strength and power. I began to brandish the weapon, and to make lunges at an imaginary foe, thinking how easy it would be to bear down his guard, or wear out his defence, with such nerve and vigor as had suddenly come into the muscles of my arm.

"Then my thoughts took a fresh turn. I thought of Bellingham, and, for the first time, I felt toward him a fierce anger. *'He has stolen your loved one from you,'* seemed to be whispered into my ear. *'He has taken from you all you had worked for, striven for, risked your life for. There is, perhaps, treachery at the root of it all. Kill him, kill him,* KILL HIM! *Rid yourself and your loved one of him; then the road to happiness will lie open before you.'* And—God help me!—I listened to it all! I madly resolved I would kill my rival when he came in; and I knew that he might arrive at any moment.

"Meanwhile, the queer sensation grew till it had permeated my whole frame. I felt full of a rich, warm glow, that tingled and rushed through my veins like a fiery flood, and that seemed to give me the strength of a dozen men. Then I began to fancy I heard strange sounds—murmurings and voices; the room rocked and swayed, and one of its walls—that on my left—opened, and there, spread out before my eyes, I saw a wonderful scene. From the floor on which I stood I looked out on a wide tropical landscape—a great stretch of rolling pampas, that ended, in the distance, in a range of blue mountains.

"On each side, in long ranks, were numbers of people of almost all nations, dressed in the strangest garbs—costumes, for the most part, of those who had been dead and gone, for hundreds and hundreds of years. Some were men in flowing robes of various hues and shapes—Moors, Saracens, Arabs; many were in flashing armor or coats of mail; while others, again, were like unto the Incas and the priests of ancient South America. Mingled with them were Spaniards, Portuguese, Indians of many tribes; and some, again, of later times; even a few were of today. Never, not even on the stage in wildest pantomime, have I seen such a motley throng.

"Those on the left were grim, hard-visaged beings who gazed at me with an expression that was half-friendly, half-mocking. Their looks, however, filled me with aversion; for somehow, it was borne in on me that their friendliness was more to be dreaded than their most terrible enmity. They were nearly all men; though amongst them were a few women; and each held a sword—the exact counterpart of the one that was in my own hand! The figures on the right carried no swords; but here, each one showed some ghastly wound, apparently still fresh and bleeding. And there came upon me the knowledge that all these I saw before me were the forms of the wicked or unhappy beings who had fallen under the spell of the sword; those to the right being the victims, and those to the left their murderers.

"For a while we gazed at each other in silence, I looking from one to the other in ever-increasing wonder and awe. Then those that carried the swords, lifted them in the air toward me as in salute, and, at the same time, began a strange, wild singing or chanting, the words being sung first by a few, and then repeated by the remainder.

" 'Hail! Brother of the Sword!' was chanted by the first singers.

" 'Hail! Brother of the Sword!' came the response, so deep-toned and sonorous that it resembled a great wave that travels from afar, and falls, with its deep diapason, as from some grand ocean of sound, thundering upon the shore, rather than the melody of human voices.

" 'He is one of us!' was next chanted forth; and 'He is one of us!' came the deep response.

"But at this a great horror seized me; a feeling of loathing and repulsion of these weird figures. 'One of them? No! That I would never be.' And as these thoughts rushed through my mind, I tried fiercely to loose my grasp upon the fatal sword, and to cast it from me. But I could not; try as I would, I found myself utterly unable to let it go. And the figures before me, as though they read my thoughts and answered them, sang again; but this time there was a sound of mockery in their tones: 'He who takes up the sword cannot loose it! It is the spell of the Sword!' And the words were repeated, as the others had been.

"Still, however, I strove; I wrestled and fought strenuously against the dread power that kept the sword in my hand. Seeing this, the figures, as by one accord, lifted their swords, and pointed to the wall of the room in front of me. As I turned in the direction thus indicated, the wall there opened also, and I seemed to see the Mall in St. James's Park, and, walking toward me, my rival, Cyril Bellingham. He appeared to be looking at me; but I knew that, though he was thinking of me, he did not really see me. And, on his face, was an expression of such insolent triumph as stung me to fury again as I gazed. At once the voices chanted: '*He sees his enemy. He will kill him!*'

"But even as the sound of the response died away, the wall on my right hand opened, and there, gazing at me with a look of indescribable anguish and intreaty, I saw the face of Mabel—of my dear lost love.

" 'Shall the one I loved—*and love still*—become a murderer?' it seemed to say. I almost heard the whisper from the loved lips; and it fired me with sudden strength and resolve to throw off the spell.

" 'No! A thousand times No!' I cried resolutely. With my left hand I seized the blade, and, with a desperate effort, wrenched the hilt out of my right, and the sword fell with a clatter, on the floor. Then the voices burst out into mocking laughter.

" '*He thinks to escape! But the Sword shall be turned against him!*' they cried.

"But the sound grew dim, and soon died away in a low wail; the room rocked and swayed around and under me, the figures faded slowly from my sight, and the walls seemed to return to their places.

"Then, trembling, and feeling strangely weak, I went over to a sideboard, poured out a glass of brandy, drank it off, and dropped into a large armchair that was near. There I must either have fainted or fallen asleep, for I remember nothing more till I seemed to wake up suddenly and saw Cyril Bellingham standing before me. He was looking at me with the same cynical, triumphant smile that had so exasperated me a short time before. But it vanished as he saw me rouse up; and in its place came the usual look of cordial friendship.

" 'Having forty winks, eh?' he said, with a short laugh. 'What in the world are you doing with all these playthings scattered about?' He indicated the foils and the sword, and, picking up the latter, he laid it on the table.

"I watched the action in silence, and, until I saw him

put the weapon down, I made no reply. Then I said I felt tired, and out of sorts, and supposed that I had fallen asleep.

" 'I have something to tell you,' he went on, regarding me curiously. 'Mabel has been so good as to fix the happy day. We are to be married this day month. I want to know if you will be one of my groomsmen?'

"This was, I need not say, cruelly trying to me; but I still felt tired and listless, and only answered quietly.

" 'Thank you, but I shall not be in London. I am going away with Jack Knebworth. He is coming here this afternoon to arrange about it.'

" 'Ah! Mabel will be sorry,' he returned, but, I could see, with evident relief. Then he took up the sword, and began bending it with the point on the floor.

"Now, by that time, I had persuaded myself that I must have fallen asleep, and dreamed all that I have just told you. Therefore I did not trouble myself about his handling the thing. I rather welcomed it as a ready way of changing the conversation.

" 'It's good steel,' he went on.

"I picked up one of the foils, and bent it as he was bending the sword.

" 'Not better than this,' I said indifferently.

" 'Ah, I remember those foils,' he replied. 'You and I had many a bout with them years ago, hadn't we? I think I used to be the better fencer in those days. I wonder if I am so still?'

" 'I've learned more of fencing than I knew then,' I told him. 'And in a hard school too—where either you or your antagonist has to "curl up," as the Americans call it; and—it was not I that went under as you can see,' I finished rather grimly.

" 'H'm. Well that may be a good thing for you,' he answered musingly, 'because—'

" 'Because what?' I asked, as he seemed to hesitate.

" 'Because it's your only chance,' he exclaimed, suddenly springing up and lunging at me with the weapon he was holding, 'I mean to *kill* you!'

*   *   *

"It was fortunate for me that I held the foil in my hand; and still more fortunate that I was looking at him at the moment; otherwise the weapon would have passed through my heart. Something in his manner, however, had put me on the alert; and I parried the stroke.

" 'Great Heavens, Bellingham! What on earth's the matter with you? What are you thinking of?' I cried. 'Are you suddenly mad?'

" 'Aye,' he shouted, lunging again, 'mad for your life! And I mean to have it too, as you will soon find out!'

"Again I parried the thrust, and stepped back, looking at him in horror and astonishment. Then I saw that his eyes seemed to be blazing; he looked literally, unmistakably, a madman.

"Suddenly, the truth flashed upon me. What I had experienced had been no dream; it had all been true! And now *he* was under the spell of the sword, as I had been but a short time before!

" 'For the love of heaven, Bellingham,' I gasped out, 'throw that accursed sword down. Why should you wish to kill me?'

" 'Why,' he hissed out, making at me again, 'because I know that Mabel loves you still. She has never loved *me*. I told her lies about you—said you had a Creole wife and three children out in Brazil; showed her letters that made her believe it. And she *did* believe it—ha, ha! And became engaged to me. But I know she loves you all the time—and *that's* why I mean to kill you!'

" 'Great God!' I burst out. 'You infernal scoundrel! But—why do you tell me all this?'

" 'Why do I tell you, fool?' he almost screamed. 'Because I mean to kill you. You will never leave this room alive! Today I feel I have the strength of ten men—aye, of fifty! All your boasted swordsmanship will avail you nothing today, for I shall *kill* you. But I want you to die knowing that, had you lived, you could have won back Mabel from me. As it is, you will die with the knowledge that she will be *mine*.'

"He got all this out in incoherent gasps, attacking me fiercely the while; and I saw it was no time for reply or for bandying words. It was all I could do, in this one-sided encounter, to defend myself. As he had nothing to fear from my weapon, all the advantage, of course, lay on his side. He had no necessity to defend himself; all he needed to do was to try to pass my guards, or to tire me out.

"And when I remembered the feelings I had experienced while grasping that diabolical sword, my heart sank within me. I recalled the strange sensation of wonderful strength and vigor; my conviction that I could prevail against any, even the strongest, opponent. And now all that mysterious force and power were turned against myself—against *me,* when I had but a foil to defend myself with, and at the moment, too, when life seemed sweeter than ever it had before—when I knew that Mabel loved me!

"This thought nerved me to fight hard for my life; but it could not give me the advantage my antagonist held; nor equalize the chances. Still, I fought desperately. Round and round the studio—there was no table in the middle—to and fro—backwards and forwards, we went; sometimes stopping as by mutual consent, for a moment's breathing space, when we would stand and glare at one another like furious, watchful tigers. But, in the end, I knew my strength was gradually failing me. I felt a wild, mad despair creeping over me—the feeling of one struggling hopelessly in the toils and knowing he can, at best, only stave off death for a few moments longer.

"Twice, Bellingham, with a fierce, almost irresistible beat, nearly forced the foil out of my aching hand. I knew the end was near; I felt sick and staggered, when the door opened, and Jack Knebworth entered. He looked, in open-eyed astonishment, for a second, then, taking in the whole situation in that brief glance, he raised a heavy walking-stick he was carrying, and, with one slashing blow, knocked the sword out of Bellingham's hand. It was just in time, for Bellingham had seen him, and, expecting that he would interfere, evidently determined to finish me off first. He threw himself forward with his whole power, and, as his weapon was knocked up, he came on to the bottom of my foil with such force that it snapped off near the end, and the jagged blade entered his breast. He fell to the ground with a mad yell of disappointed fury, and then lay still, the blood flowing from the wound.

"I rested, panting, against the wall, and stared at Knebworth, who stared back at me.

" 'Well!' he exclaimed, 'this is a pretty business, truly! Lucky for you I came in when I did.'

" 'Lucky, indeed, old friend! Give me a drop of that brandy over there. Is he badly hurt—dead, do you think?'

" 'What does it matter?' he returned coolly, as he poured out the brandy. 'The infernal, murdering villain! To set on, with a sword, against a man armed only with a foil!'

" 'Ah! there's worse than that at the bottom of it all,' I said savagely. 'Deceit, treachery, devilry! But I'll tell you another time. What's to be done now?'

" 'Go for a doctor,' he said, 'and bring one as soon as you can; I'll see what I can do for him meanwhile. But first we'll have no more devil's tricks with this cursed plaything.' And, with that, he picked up the fatal sword, broke it into several parts over his knee, and threw all the pieces into the chest, shutting down the lid.

" 'Now, remember,' he went on, looking meaningly at me, 'you were fencing, in a friendly way, with those two foils; and there was an accident. I happened to see it, and can give all necessary explanations.'

"I gave him a nod of comprehension and assent, and hurried away for a medical man. Later on, Bellingham was carried, still unconscious, to the nearest hospital. His wound was a bad one; and for long it was not known whether he would live or die. In the end, however, he recovered, and went abroad.

"I took no steps against him, but let him go. I felt too

happy, and too well pleased with the world in general; for, by the time he was convalescent, Mabel and I were married.

"I unscrewed that death's-head from the hilt—handling it very gingerly the while, you may be sure—and, one day down at Brighton, Jack Knebworth and I threw all the rest of the weapon into the sea. We were determined that no other human creature should run even the faintest chance of coming under the influence of that terrible sword and its spell."

LARROES CATCH MEDDLERS

Manly Wade Wellman

The woods were thick and damp, swampy underfoot
and woven through with stealthy little noises, and under the branches the darkness of night seemed thick-
ened and concentrated. Here, at the edge of the last
belt of jack-oaks both men paused, gazing into the
dim-silvery wash of moonlight that fell around the jagged silhouette of the lonely old house in the open.

Purdy hunched his thick shoulders inside his denim
jumper, as though to make his big body smaller, smaller
even than Crofton's. "Tell me all that there stuff over
again," he begged in a half whisper. "About the half
million dollars worth of gold."

"I read you like a book, Purdy," muttered Crofton,
sourly scornful. "You need the smell of money to prop
you up. You're still scared to make yourself rich on a
dark night."

A cloud drifted over what moon there was and stayed
there for seconds.

"Tell me about it again," repeated Purdy. "I just
wanted to get it straight."

"All right." Crofton sounded like a disgusted adult
yielding to the importunities of a stupid child. "It's
what was left from the treasure of the Confederate
States of America. A ton of gold. All the truck yonder
can carry." He gestured to where, at the head of the

34

bumpy path through the woods, stood the battered pickup truck they had coaxed through the dark without headlights.

"A ton," repeated Purdy, as raptly as though he prayed.

"Jefferson Davis and his cabinet and family ran away from Richmond in April, 1865," Crofton ill-humoredly rehearsed the story once again. "They had wagons to carry the treasury funds, and there were sixty naval cadets to guard them, commanded by a naval captain named William Parker. They didn't bother to bring any Confederate paper money, it was already worthless. The wagons carried some silver, a hundred thousand dollars or so, and that was drawn to pay Davis' cavalry escort. The party got as far as Washington, Georgia, before it split up. Parker crossed his wagons and cadet detail back into South Carolina. He unloaded the gold in a warehouse at Abbeville. He drew forty dollars apiece for the sixty cadets and told them to scatter and go home. The rest of the gold was never heard of again."

"A ton of it." Purdy plainly loved the word.

"American double eagles," elaborated Crofton. "Mexican and English and other foreign money. Likewise nuggets and bars. Nobody ever got it."

"That's hard to believe, Crofton."

"Abbeville was stiff with Confederate bomb-proofs and deserters and stragglers who hoped to steal some of that gold in the warehouse," Crofton told him. "But up came the Federal troops, and drove them away. The Federals never got it either, though they'd heard of it—it was reported as high as thirteen million dollars in value. It vanished from the warehouse. Somebody carried it up from Abbeville to this part of the country."

"To that old house yonder," said Purdy, still rapt.

"Yes, that old house yonder. Larroes."

"Larroes," echoed Purdy, straining his eyes in the night. "You wouldn't know about that, Crofton, without I'd told you."

"Don't keep saying you told me," Crofton scolded him. "For years I've combed the Southern states, on the trail of clues to that Confederate treasury gold. All you contributed was that old family tale of yours, and half of that is superstitious guff. More than half. It wouldn't add up for a moment unless I knew everything else to go with it."

"I gave you the tale as it was give to me," Purdy said plaintively. He was timid in the darkness, in the presence of the smaller, sharper-tongued, more resolute Crofton. "My daddy got it from his daddy. They said two Confederate officers came to Larroes with something worth a lot—"

"There you are," broke in Crofton, half accusingly. "Something worth a lot. They never said it was the gold. I tied it in with what I know."

"Them two officers stored the stuff in the cellar," Purdy continued his share of the story. "The Larro family was in cahoots with them, part ways. And there was somebody who passed an old-time hoodoo spell—"

"Voodoo spell, you ignorant ape."

"No sir, it's hoodoo spell. Not voodoo, only kind of an alikely sound. Then in a few days the Yankees burned the house, like they burned most of the big houses here around, and later the Larro folks built another house on top of the foundations, without taking out what was shut up down there. And nobody's dared go look, though Larroes has standed unlived in since ever I remember."

"Well, I dare go look," said Crofton, "and don't stand there making silly faces. You're going with me."

"I just keep remembering that hoodoo charm account," said Purdy.

"Well, remember the half million dollars. A ton of gold. Lots of the coins worth much more than their face value to numismatists."

"To what?"

"Coin collectors, yokel. Now forget that voodoo or hoodoo or whatever you want to call it."

"Hoodoo," said Purdy. "No, sir, I won't forget it, I'll

remember it. That's why I got this here glory hand."
He fumbled in his breast pocket.

"Don't show me that spare part for a mummy again!"
Crofton warned him.

"Just wanted to be sure I hadn't lost it," said Purdy.
"I got it from old Mrs. Peddicoe. Costed me nine
dollars. She cut it off Lew Barr when them night riders
lynched him year before last."

"Leave it in your pocket," said Crofton.

"Well, you ain't doing everything about this job,"
Purdy insisted. "The glory hand is goin' to give us a
way to that treasure."

"Use it whatever way you think it'll help. Come on.
Never mind the truck, first we'll see how we get in
there."

Crofton put a hand into his own pocket, touched the
short-barrelled revolver he carried, and picked his way
out into the open, along a weed-grown path down a
gentle moonlit slope toward the quiet old house called
Larroes.

As he groped along, Crofton mentally cursed his
big, stupid partner for cowering before a dimly-remem-
bered legend of rural magic; Purdy had communicated
a sense of extra uneasiness to Crofton himself. Hoodoo
. . . so Southern country people still feared things like
that. Yet, if fear had guarded the treasure for so many
years, if the treasure was here where it must be, as
Crofton's money-hungry research insisted it must be
. . . well, they'd have it. Maybe even Purdy's glory
hand might help get it. Crofton felt magnanimous as he
granted some possible trifle of power to the thing. At
dawn tomorrow he'd sneer at Purdy's terrors, and bully
him into taking less than a half share.

"Larroes is a pure funny name," ventured Purdy,
tramping behind. "Never knew what for a sort of name
it was. Maybe foreigner."

"You said the name was Larro, not Larroes," re-
minded Crofton. "What's the difference? No Larro has
lived here for fifty years."

" 'Larroes catch meddlers,' " quoted Purdy softly. "The old folks used to say that when we was chaps, to keep us from playing 'round that old house."

Crofton cleared his throat over a grating laugh. "Larroes catch meddlers? That's an old saying everywhere, not just here around Larroes. I don't know what it means. Maybe it can be treed in some old quotation collection, or in Mencken's *American Language* book. I'm not worrying about it right now."

"Larroes catch meddlers," said Purdy again. "Names mean something. I heared once that Purdy was an old French name, means getting lost."

"*Perdu,*" supplied Crofton. "I'll keep you from getting lost."

"Glad we got the glory hand, anyway," said Purdy.

They were in the yard, among shadow-clotted old trees, rank of foliage. Their feet crunched the gravel of an untended path. Crofton approached the saggy big porch of the house, Purdy at his heels. Crofton heard the big man's worried, heavy breathing.

"Come on," said Crofton, and mounted the rickety planks. He saw the door, dimly sketched among the shadows cast by the ruined roof. Its glass pane was shattered. Crofton took hold of the knob, and the door yielded to his push with a slow, weary creak of rusty hinges. Stepping inside, he produced his flashlight from his other side pocket. Purdy entered behind him.

"Who's there?" croaked a voice, as rusty as the hinges.

Purdy squealed and darted out again, swift as a lizard for all his clumsy bulk. Crofton sprang against the wall inside the door. His right hand drew the revolver, his left snapped on the flashlight and stabbed its beam around.

"What are you doing in my house?" croaked the voice.

Crofton's light momentarily touched a face. It was pale, fringed with fluffy white hair and centered with two black eyes like ripe watermelon seeds. The face dodged out of the light, and Crofton probed for it again.

"Stay where you are," he cried shrilly, "or I'll shoot."

Again he trapped the face with his light, in a corner of a big, black room. He walked toward it. The black eyes hooded themselves in crinkled lids, a white hand lifted as though to gesture the blinding glare away.

"You're trespassing here," mildly accused the face.

Crofton saw a stooped shred of a man, in nondescript rags of garments. Long white hair banged the brow, the mouth and chin sprouted a heavy white beard. The pale face had deep, tight wrinkles, the narrow shoulders drooped beneath a burden of age.

"Who are you?" challenged Crofton.

"My name is Larro."

"That's a lie," Crofton growled. "There haven't been any Larro people here for decades."

"I have come back. I want to be alone here, quiet. What do you want?"

"Purdy!" yelled Crofton over his shoulder. "Come back in, it's all right. Nobody here but an old tramp."

"I'm not a tramp," gently argued the old man who called himself Larro. "I own Larroes. You're trespassing."

"I've got a gun." Crofton thrust it into the light of his flash. "Don't argue or try to run, or I'll shoot you."

"Very well." Larro seemed to grant the point for the sake of peace. "But what is it you want?"

Purdy came in, slowly and furtively. "Know this old rooster?" Crofton asked him.

Purdy looked. The whites of his eyes reflected the light. "No, sir," said Purdy, "never saw him in my life."

"I've been away so long," said Larro. "And I haven't shown myself to anyone hereabouts. I'm old. I just want to die here." His thin hand stroked his beard. "Once more, in all patience, what do you want?"

"Half a million dollars in gold," replied Crofton.

Larro sank noiselessly into an old chair. "Oh, you know about that."

"Hear that, Purdy?" cried Crofton in triumph. To

Larro he said, "Yes, I know all about it. And I want it."

"You won't get it, sir," said Larro gently. "How did you learn?"

"From American history. I took off from the point where the Confederate treasury disappeared and I've researched all the way to here." Crofton spoke with proud awareness of his own wit and industry. "And Purdy here supplied the old ghost story about this tumbledown house. I've winnowed his bushel of superstition down to the grain of truth. The gold's down cellar, under us."

"But you won't get it," said Larro, stroking his beard again.

Crofton laughed, dangerously mocking. "You think you can scare us with Purdy's hoodoo tale?"

"I'll leave you to find out for yourself."

"Tie him up," Crofton bade Purdy.

The big man produced a doubled hank of cord. Quickly he tied the small, unresisting old figure to the chair. Crofton turned his flash into Larro's face.

"Listen to me," he commanded. "You really came here to get that gold yourself, didn't you?"

"I wouldn't touch it," said Larro with the same gentle insistence. "It isn't mine. It isn't yours. I haven't long to live, anyway. And the gold belongs to the Confederate States of America."

"There aren't any Confederate States of America."

"That's why no one can have the money," said Larro. "It belongs to nobody."

Purdy gazed at Larro and breathed heavily. He was nervous.

"Listen, Purdy," said Crofton, "get back to the truck. Drive it as close up to the front door as you can get. Don't use anything but the parking lights."

Purdy left, plainly glad of the chance. Alone with Larro, with the darkness close around his flashlight beam, Crofton permitted himself another ugly laugh.

"You know how to find that money in the cellar?"

"The cellar's closed up." Larro might have been any serene old man politely answering questions for an interview. "My father, the last of the Larro brothers who owned the older house, built this second one on the foundations of the first. He left no cellar door."

Crofton quartered the floor with his beam. Dark broad squares of stone fitted together, with cracks as narrow as the strokes of a fine-pointed pen. He stamped. The floor sounded as solid as a paved street.

"All right," he said, "what the hell else do you know? What's this story about the hoodoo man who bewitched the treasure?"

"My uncles," said Larro, "brought upon themselves the spell you mention."

"Brought it on themselves?"

"They're down below us with the gold."

"Come off that!"

"You ask for the truth. My uncles were Major Micah Larro and Captain Nelson Larro. They brought the wagons with the treasure this far, and by then Jefferson Davis was captured and the last Confederate army had surrendered. In June, 1865, they proved themselves true to their lost country. They went to the cellar with the gold, said certain words that would shut it in there."

"And shut themselves in with it?" snarled Crofton.

"The door never opened to release them. They remain on guard."

"Fairy story!"

"No. My father was only a boy, but he remembered. He told me. He never lied in his life."

"Then you learned the habit somewhere else." Crofton shoved the gun muzzle into Larro's beard. "Where's the cellar door?"

"I've said that there is no cellar door?"

Turning, Crofton walked across the floor, examining it by flashlight. There was no opening or indication of one. The floor sounded as solid as pavement under his pacing feet. "I'll make you show me," he said to Larro at last.

Larro sat relaxed in his bonds. "My good fool, I came here—poor, friendless, weary, full of years—to die quietly in my old home. Hasten my dying process if you like, but I've told you the truth."

The truck rattled up outside. Then Purdy tramped in.

"I'm goin' to—" said Purdy, then broke off and struck a match.

Crofton watched. Purdy held something and touched the flame to it. For a moment the something looked like a twisted stub of root, with suckers attached. One of the protruding spikes ignited, then another and another—five, Purdy brought the light closer. Its several flames glared more brightly, Crofton fancied, than the flashlight.

"Like I said, I got it from old Mrs. Peddicoe," said Purdy. "She cut it off Lew Barr when they hung him, them night riders. Costed me nine—"

"Ah," said Larro appreciatively, "a hand of glory."

A sudden rank stench made Crofton wrinkle his nose. "Keep that thing from reeking in my face," he snapped.

"I think it must be one of the oldest of charms," contributed Larro. "A hand severed from a man who died by hanging, specially treated with its own fat so that the fingers serve as a sheaf of candles. By its light, one opens concealed ways, finds hidden valuables—"

"Get rid of it!" Crofton snatched at the thing, but Purdy held it out of his reach.

"Don't mess with my glory hand, now," argued Purdy, suddenly stubborn. "Old Mrs. Peddicoe swore it would work. Let it alone, and let's go down cellar."

He pointed to an opposite corner, and Crofton looked. In the light from the five burning fingers he saw what he must have overlooked.

A whole section of the floor was flung upward and back against the wall, like a hatchway, with open blackness exposed beneath.

"So you did lie about the cellar door," Crofton accused Larro.

"It opened when I lit this glory hand," said Purdy.

"He is right," said Larro. "You see, there is something in what you call superstition."

Crofton did not reply. He had run to the hole and was exploring its depths with the beam of his flashlight. Purdy followed him, lifting the blazing hand. The rank smell assailed Crofton's nose again, but the fivefold glare seemed to help the electric beam. Crofton saw stone steps, older and darker than the squares of the floor.

"Here we go," he said to Purdy, and descended carefully.

The air of the cellar lay heavy around and upon him, like a quiet cloud of dust. He was in a rectangular chamber with walls of rough old brick, a floor of flat, dry dirt. Almost at the foot of the steps huddled a pile of chests or trunks, dark and grubby. Beyond these stood something, stood two somethings.

Crofton levelled his ready pistol.

"Hands up!" he roared.

The two shapes stood as silent as hall trees.

Purdy was with him. Crofton could tell by the odor of Purdy's lights. The beams struck past Crofton, and he could see gray jackets, broad hats, faces as stiffly immobile as the carved faces of statues.

"Them's just dead folks," chattered Purdy.

"They are my uncles," came the muffled voice of Larro from above the stairs. "My uncles Micah and Nelson."

Gun poised, flashlight at waist level, Crofton moved around the stack of chests and confronted the nearest shape.

"This one's dead, all right," Crofton said to Purdy.

He examined the figure at close range. It was lean, of medium height, with long brown hair and a spike of tawny beard on the wood-stiff chin. It wore a snug gray jacket, buttoned back on either side from a tight vest and a black cravat. On the sleeve of each arm showed a tracery of gold braid. Gray pants with yellow stripes at the seams were stuck into black riding boots. A leather belt supported a long sheathed saber with a heavy curved guard of brass.

"Dead," said Crofton again.

"Look!" gasped Purdy. "Them beards! They're trimmed, neat-like. They ain't growed . . . like hair does on 'em when they're dead!"

"You *are* a fool," snapped Crofton. "Don't you know that's damned rare? Doesn't happen once in a thousand times!"

But Purdy came no closer. Crofton nudged a body's flank with his revolver. It was like prodding a tree trunk. Toward him stared eyes as bright and empty as fragments of stained glass. The hair looked rigid, like masses of fine wire.

"They got swords," said Purdy. "Old-time Confederate swords."

He moved toward the other figure, heavier bearded and a thought slimmer, but otherwise the twin of the one Crofton examined. Purdy caught the hilt of the second figure's sword and tugged. It did not stir in the sheath. Then Purdy straightened, his five-fingered light almost under the nose of the figure.

"Hark at that old man!" said Purdy.

"Uncle Nelson, Uncle Micah!" Larro was calling from the room above. "Isn't it time that the cellar should be closed again?"

Purdy sprang clear of the bearded shape with a stammered oath.

"What's the matter with you?" growled Crofton.

"That there dead fellow took and blowed out my glory hand," Purdy quavered.

The hand flared no more. Crofton moved away from the figure he confronted. He felt cold of hand and foot and brow.

"Nonsense!" he said. "A puff of wind."

"Ain't no wind down here," argued Purdy. He was groping in his pockets. "Where's a match?"

"Never mind that stinking thing of yours now. We came here after gold."

As Crofton spoke, he was back at the chests. He put away his gun and lifted a reluctant lid. Dust slid from it as he tilted it back. In one hand he gathered a palmful of the great heap of metal disks that gleamed dully inside.

"Hey," Purdy said as he joined Crofton, "what's happened to them stairs? They ain't there no more."

Crofton held out his palmful. It clinked. "Gold!" he said again.

"Is all them trunks full?" said Purdy. "They'll make all the load our truck will carry. Let's hustle them out of here. Where's the stairs, Crofton?"

"First of all," said Crofton, "we'll do our friend Larro a favor. Shoot him dead. Come up with me." He took a step toward the stairs.

There were no stairs. The wall of brick, ancient but solid, faced him.

"They're gone!" Purdy yammered. "Where's them stairs?"

Crofton turned his light along the wall. There was no opening.

"Dammit, they were right here, next to the stack of treasure chests," said Crofton. His throat seemed to be full of mud. "Purdy! That thing you call the glory hand—get it lighted up, quick!"

Purdy had found a match and struck it on the bricks. It flared away in a moment. He struck another. Shakily he kindled the five fingers.

"Now," he said. "But where's them stairs? Why ain't they there?"

Crofton was pounding at the bricks. They thudded, but did not stir.

"This glory hand worked once," Purdy was insisting. "You seen it work, like Mrs. Peddicoe said. It opened the way to the treasure."

Crofton whirled, and shrieked at Purdy.

"But it won't open the way from the treasure! It's no good!"

Purdy fell back a step. He blinked at Crofton. The

light of the glory hand was growing dim, as though it did not have enough air to burn strongly.

"We've got to get out," said Crofton. "Wait—those dead men. Those swords they wear, we can use those to pick out the bricks and—"

He heard a dry *phlop*. Purdy had dropped the hand. Then Crofton heard another sound: the swish of twin sabers sliding smoothly from their scabbards.

PHANTOM REGIMENT

James Grant

After many years of hard fighting in the old 26th, and after carrying a halbert in the kilted regiment of the Isles, Ewen Mac Ewen returned home to his native place, the great plain of Moray, a graver, and, in bearing, a sadder man than when he left it.

His first inquiry was for Meinie.

She had married a rival of his, twenty years ago.

"God's will be done," sighed Ewen, as he lifted his bonnet, and looked upwards.

He built himself a little cottage, in the old highland fashion, in his native strath, at a sunny spot, where the Uise Nairn—the Waters of Alders—flowed in front, and a wooded hill arose behind. He hung his knapsack above the fireplace; deposited his old and sorely thumbed regimental Bible (with the Cameronian star on its boards), and the tin case containing his colonel's letter recommending him to the minister, and the discharge, which gave sixpence per diem as the reward of sixteen battles— all on the shelf of the little window, which contained three panes of glass, with a yoke in the centre of each, and there he settled himself down in peace, to plant his own kail, knit his own hose, and to make his own kilts, a grave and thoughtful but contented old fellow, awaiting the time, as he said, "when the Lord would call him away."

Now it chanced that a poor widow, with several children, built herself a little thatched house on the opposite side of the drove road—an old Fingalian path—which ascended the pastoral glen; and the ready-handed veteran lent his aid to thatch it, and to sling her kail-pot on the cruicks, and was wont thereafter to drop in of an evening to smoke his pipe, to tell old stories of the storming of Ticonderoga, and to ask her little ones the catechism and biblical questions. Within a week or so, he discovered that the widow was Meinie—the ripe, blooming Meinie of other years—an old, a faded, and a sad-eyed woman now; and poor Ewen's lonely heart swelled within him, as he thought of all that had passed since last they met, and as he spake of what they were, and what they might have been, had fate been kind, or fortune proved more true.

We have heard much about the hidden and mysterious principle of affinity, and more about the sympathy and sacredness that belong to a first and early love; well, the heart of the tough old Cameronian felt these gentle impulses, and Meinie was no stranger to them. They were married, and for fifteen years, there was no happier couple on the banks of the Nairn. Strange to say, they died on the same day, and were interred in the ancient burying-ground of Dalcross, where now they lie, near the ruined walls of the old vicarage kirk of the Catholic times. God rest them in their humble highland graves! My father, who was the minister of Croy, acted as chief mourner, and gave the customary funeral prayer. But I am somewhat anticipating, and losing the thread of my own story in telling theirs.

In process of time the influx of French and English tourists who came to visit the country of the clans, and to view the plain of Culloden, after the publication of "Waverly" gave to all Britain, that which we name in Scotland "the tartan fever," and caused the old path which passed the cot of Ewen to become a turnpike road; a toll-bar—that most obnoxious of all impositions to a Celt—was placed across the mouth of the little glen, barring the way directly to the battlefield; and of this gate the old pensioner Ewen naturally became keeper; and during the summer season, when, perhaps, a hundred carriages per day rolled through, it became a source of revenue alike to him, and to the Lord of Cawdor and the Laird of Kilravock, the road trustees. And the chief pleasure of Ewen's existence was to sit on a thatched seat by the gate, for then he felt conscious of being in office—on duty—a species of sentinel; and it smacked of the old time when the Generale was beaten in the morning, and the drums rolled tattoo at night; when he had belts to pipe-clay, and boots to blackball; when there were wigs to frizzle and queues to tie, and to be all trim and in order to meet Monseigneur le Marquis de Montcalm, or General Washington "right early in the morning"; and there by the new barrier of the glen Ewen sat the live-long day, with spectacles on nose, and the Cameronian Bible on his knee, as he spelled his way through Deuteronomy and the tribes of Judah.

Slates in due time replaced the green thatch of his little cottage; then a diminutive additional story, with two small dormer windows, was added thereto, and the thrifty Meinie placed a paper in her window informing shepherds, the chance wayfarers, and the wandering deer-stalkers that she had a room to let; but summer passed away, the sportsman forsook the brown scorched mountains, the gay tourist ceased to come north, and the advertisement turned from white to yellow, and from yellow to flyblown green in her window; the winter snows descended on the hills, the pines stood in long and solemn ranks by the white frozen Nairn, but "the room upstairs" still remained without a tenant.

Anon the snow passed away; the river again flowed free, the flowers began to bloom; the young grass to sprout by the hedgerows, and the mavis to sing on the fauld-dykes, for spring was come again, and joyous summer soon would follow; and one night—it was the 26th of April—Ewen was exhibiting his penmanship in large text-hand by preparing the new announcement of "a room to let," when he paused, and looked up as a peal

of thunder rumbled across the sky; a red gleam of
lightning flashed in the darkness without, and then they
heard the roar of the deep broad Nairn, as its waters,
usually so sombre and so slow, swept down from the
wilds of Bade-noch, flooded with the melting snows of
the past winter.

A dreadful storm of thunder, rain, and wind came on,
and the little cottage rocked on its foundations; frequently the turf-fire upon the hearth was almost blown
about the clay-floor, by the downward gusts that bellowed in the chimney. The lightning gleamed inces-
santly, and seemed to play about the hill of Urchany
and the ruins of Caistel Fionlah; the woods groaned and
creaked, and the trees seemed to shriek as their strong
limbs were torn asunder by the gusts which in some
places laid side by side the green sapling of last summer, and the old oak that had stood for a thousand
years—that had seen Macbeth and Duncan ride from
Nairn, and had outlived the wars of the Comyns and
the Clanehattan.

The swollen Nairn tore down its banks, and swept
trees, rocks, and stones in wild confusion to the sea,
mingling the pines of Aberarder with the old oaks of
Cawdor; while the salt spray from the Moray Firth was
swept seven miles inland, where it encrusted with salt
the trees, the houses, and windows, and whatever it fell
on as it mingled with the ceaseless rain, while deep,
hoarse, and loud the incessant thunder rattled across
the sky, "as if all the cannon on earth," according to
Ewen, "were exchanging salvoes between Urchany and
the Hill of Geddes."

Meinie grew pale, and sat with a finger on her mouth,
and a startled expression in her eyes, listening to the
uproar without; four children, two of whom were Ewen's,
and her last addition to the clan, clung to her skirts.

Ewen had just completed the invariable prayer and
chapter for the night, and was solemnly depositing his
old regimental companions, with "Baxter's Saints' Rest,"
in a place of security, when a tremendous knock—a

knock that rang above the storm—shook the door of the cottage.

"Who can this be, and in such a night?" said Meinie.

"The Lord knoweth," responded Ewen, gravely; "but he knocks both loud and late."

"Inquire before you open," urged Meinie, seizing her husband's arm, as the impatient knock was renewed with treble violence.

"Who comes there?" demanded Ewen, in a soldierly tone.

"A friend," replied a strange voice without, and in the same manner.

"What do you want?"

"Fire and smoke!" cried the other, giving the door a tremendous kick; "do you ask that in such a devil of a night as this? You have a room to let, have you not?"

"Yes."

"Well; open the door, or blood and 'oons I'll bite your nose off!"

Ewen hastened to undo the door; and then, all wet and dripping as if he had just been fished up from the Moray Firth, there entered a strange-looking old fellow in a red coat; he stumped vigorously on a wooden leg, and carried on his shoulders a box, which he flung down with a crash that shook the dwelling, saying, "There—damn you—I have made good my billet at last."

"So it seems," said Ewen, reclosing the door in haste to exclude the tempest, lest his house should be unroofed and torn asunder.

"Harkee, comrade, what garrison or fortress is this," asked the visitor, "that peaceable folks are to be challenged in this fashion, and forced to give parole and countersign before they march in—eh?"

"It is my house, comrade; and so you had better keep a civil tongue in your head."

"Civil tongue? Fire and smoke, you mangy cur! I can be as civil as my neighbors; but get me a glass of grog, for I am as wet as we were the night before Minden."

"Where have you come from in such a storm as this?"

"Where you'd not like to go—so never mind; but, grog, I tell you—get me some grog, and a bit of tobacco; it is long since I tasted either."

Ewen hastened to get a large quaighful of stiff Glenlivat, which the veteran drained to his health, and that of Meinie; but first he gave them a most diabolical grin, and threw into the liquor some black stuff, saying, "I always mix my grog with gunpowder—it's a good tonic; I learned that of a comrade who fell at Minden on the glorious 1st of August, '59."

"You have been a solider, then?"

"Right! I was one of the 25th, or old Edinburgh Regiment; they enlisted me, though an Englishman, I believe; for my good old dam was a follower of the camp."

"Our number was the 26th—the old Cameronian Regiment—so we were near each other, you see, comrade."

"Nearer than you would quite like, mayhap," said Wooden-leg, with another grin and a dreadful oath.

"And you have served in Germany?" asked Ewen.

"Germany—aye, and marched over every foot of it, from Hanover to Hell, and back again. I have fought in Flanders, too."

"I wish you had come a wee while sooner," said Ewen gravely, for this discourse startled his sense of propriety.

"Sooner," snarled this shocking old fellow, who must have belonged to that army 'which swore so terribly in Flanders,' as good Uncle Toby says: "Sooner—for what?"

"To have heard me read a chapter, and to have joined us in prayer."

"Prayers be damned!" cried the other, with a shout of laughter, and a face expressive of fiendish mockery, as he gave his wooden leg a thundering blow on the floor; "fire and smoke—another glass of grog—and then we'll settle about my billet upstairs."

While getting another dram, which hospitality prevented him from refusing, Ewen scrutinised this strange visitor, whose aspect and attire were very remarkable;

but wholly careless of what any one thought, he sat by the hearth, wringing his wet wig, and drying it at the fire.

He was a little man, of a spare, but strong and active figure, which indicated great age; his face resembled that of a rat; behind it hung a long queue that waved about like a pendulum when he moved his head, which was quite bald, and smooth as a cricket-ball, save where a long and livid scar—evidently a sword cut—traversed it. This was visible while he sat drying his wig; but as that process was somewhat protracted, he uttered an oath, and thrust his cocked hat on one side of his head, and very much over his left eye, which was covered by a patch. This head-dress was the old military triple-cocked hat, bound with yellow braid, and having on one side the hideous black leather cockade of the House of Hanover, now happily disused in the British army, and retained as a badge of service by liverymen alone. His attire was an old threadbare red coat, faced with yellow, having square tails and deep cuffs, with braided holes; he wore knee-breeches on his spindle shanks, one of which terminated, as I have said, in a wooden pin; he carried a large knotted stick; and, in outline and aspect, very much resembled, as Ewen thought, Frederick the Great of Prussia, or an old Chelsea pensioner, or the soldiers he had seen delineated in antique prints of the Flemish wars. His solitary orb possessed a most diabolical leer, and, whichever way you turned, it seemed to regard you with the fixed glare of a basilisk.

"You are a stranger hereabout, I presume?" said Ewen drily.

"A stranger now, certainly; but I was pretty well known in this locality once. There are some bones buried hereabout that may remember me," he replied, with a grin that showed his fangless jaws.

"Bones!" reiterated Ewen, aghast.

"Yes, bones—Culloden Muir lies close by here, does it not?"

"It does—then you have travelled this road before?"

"Death and the Devil! I should think so, comrade; on

this very night sixty years ago I marched along this road, from Nairn to Culloden, with the army of His Royal Highness, the Great Duke of Cumberland, Captain-General of the British troops, in pursuit of the rebels under the Popish Pretender—"

"Under His Royal Highness Prince Charles, you mean, comrade," said Ewen, in whose breast—Cameronian though he was—a tempest of Highland wrath and loyalty swelled up at these words.

"Prince—ha! ha! ha!" laughed the other; "had you said as much then, the gallows had been your doom. Many a man I have shot, and many a boy I have brained with the butt end of my musket, for no other crime than wearing the tartan, even as you this night wear it."

Ewen made a forward stride as if he would have taken the wicked boaster by the throat; his anger was kindled to find himself in presence of a veritable soldier of the infamous "German Butcher," whose merciless massacre of the wounded clansmen and their defenceless families will never be forgotten in Scotland while oral tradition and written record exist; but Ewen paused, and said in his quiet way, "Blessed be the Lord! these times and things have passed away from the land, to return to it no more. We are both old men now; by your own reckoning, you must at least have numbered four-score years, and in that, you are by twenty my better man. You are my guest tonight, moreover, so we must not quarrel, comrade. My father was killed at Culloden."

"On which side?"

"The right one—for he fell by the side of old Keppoch, and his last words were, "Righ Hamish gu Bragh!"

"Fire and smoke!" laughed the old fellow, "I remember these things as if they only happened yesterday—mix me some more grog and put it in the bill—I was the company's butcher in those days—it suited my taste—so when I was not stabbing and slashing the sheep and cattle of the rascally commissary, I was cutting the throats of the Scots and French, for there were plenty of them, and Irish too, who fought against the king's troops in Flanders. We had hot work, that day at Culloden—hotter than at Minden, where we fought in heavy marching order, with our blankets, kettles, and provisions, on a broiling noon, when the battlefield was cracking under a blazing sun, and the whole country was sweltering like the oven of the Great Baker."

"Who is he?"

"What! you don't know him? Ha! ha! ha! Ho! ho! ho! come, that is good."

Ewen expostulated with the boisterous old fellow on this style of conversation, which, as you may easily conceive, was very revolting to the prejudices of a well-regulated Cameronian soldier.

"Come, come, you old devilskin," cried the other, stirring up the fire with his wooden leg, till the sparks flashed and gleamed like his solitary eye; "you may as well sing psalms to a dead horse, as preach to me. Hark how the thunder roars, like the great guns at Carthagena! More grog—put it in the bill—or, halt, damme! pay yourself," and he dashed on the table a handful of silver of the reigns of George II, and the Glencoe assassin, William of Orange.

He obtained more whiskey, and drank it raw, seasoning it from time to time with gunpowder, just as an Arab does his cold water with ginger.

"Where did you lose your eye, comrade?"

"At Culloden; but I found the fellow who pinked me, next day, as he lay bleeding on the field; he was a Cameron, in a green velvet jacket, all covered with silver; so I stripped off his lace, as I had seen my mother do, and then I brained him with the butt-end of brown-bess—and before his wife's eyes, too! What the deuce do you growl at, comrade? Such things will happen in war, and you know that orders must be obeyed. My eye was gone—but it was the left one, and I was saved the trouble of closing it when taking aim. This slash on the sconce I got at the battle of Preston Pans, from the Celt who slew Colonel Gardiner."

"That Celt was my father—the Miller of Invernahyle," said Meinie, proudly.

"Your father! fire and smoke! do you say so? His hand was a heavy one!" cried Wooden-leg, while his eye glowed like the orb of a hyena.

"And your leg?"

"I lost at Minden, in Kingsley's Brigade, comrade; aye, my leg—damn!—that was indeed a loss."

"A warning to repentance, I would say."

"Then you would say wrong. Ugh! I remember when the shot—a twelve-pounder—took me just as we were rushing with charged bayonets on the French cannoniers. Smash! my leg was gone, and I lay sprawling and bleeding in a ploughed field near the Weser, while my comrades swept over me with a wild hurrah! the colours waving, and drums beating a charge."

"And what did you do?"

"I lay there and swore, believe me."

"That would not restore your limb again."

"No; but a few hearty oaths relieve the mind; and the mind relieves the body; you understand me, comrade; so there I lay all night under a storm of rain like this, bleeding and sinking, afraid of the knives of the plundering death-hunters, for my mother had been one, and I remembered well how she looked after the wounded, and cured them of their agony."

"Was your mother one of those infer—" began Mac Ewen.

"Don't call her hard names now, comrade; she died on the day after the defeat at Val; with the Provost Marshal's cord round her neck—a cordon less ornamental than that of St Louis."

"And your father?"

"Was one of Howard's Regiment; but which the devil only knows, for it was a point on which the old lady, honest woman, had serious doubts herself."

"After the loss of your leg, of course you left the service?"

"No, I became the company's butcher; but, fire and smoke, get me another glass of grog; take a share yourself, and don't sit staring at me like a Dutch Souterkin conceived of a winter night over a 'pot de feu,' as all the world knows King William was. Dam! let us be merry together—ha, ha, ha! ho, ho, ho! and I'll sing you a song of the old whig times."

" 'O, brother Sandie, hear ye the news,
   Lillibulero, bullen a la!
An Army is coming sans breeches and shoes,
   Lillibulero, bullen a la!

" 'To arms! to arms! brave boys to arms!
   A true British cause for your courage doth ca';
Country and city against a kilted banditti,
   Lillibulero, bullen a la!' "

And while he continued to rant and sing the song (once so obnoxious to the Scottish Cavaliers), he beat time with his wooden leg, and endeavoured to outroar the stormy wind and the hiss of the drenching rain. Even Mac Ewen, though he was an old soldier, felt some uneasiness, and Meinie trembled in her heart, while the children clung to her skirts and hid their little faces, as if this singing, riot, and jollity were impious at such a time, when the awful thunder was ringing its solemn peals across the midnight sky.

Although this strange old man baffled or parried every inquiry of Ewen as to whence he had come, and how and why he wore that antiquated uniform, on his making a lucrative offer to take the upper room of the little toll-house for a year—exactly a year—when Ewen thought of his poor pension of sixpence per diem, of their numerous family, and Meinie now becoming old and requiring many little comforts, all scruples were overcome by the pressure of necessity, and the mysterious old soldier was duly installed in the attic, with his corded chest, scratch-wig, and wooden leg; moreover, he paid the first six months' rent in advance, dashing the money—which was all coin of the first and second

Georges, on the table with a bang and an oath, swearing that he disliked being indebted to any man.

The next morning was calm and serene; the green hills lifted their heads into the blue and placid sky. There was no mist on the mountains, nor rain in the valley. The flood in the Nairn had subsided, though its waters were still muddy and perturbed; but save this, and the broken branches that strewed the wayside—with an uprooted tree, or a paling laid flat on the ground, there was no trace of yesterday's hurricane, and Ewen heard Wooden-leg (he had no other name for his new lodger) stumping about overhead, as the old fellow left his bed betimes, and after trimming his queue and wig, pipe-claying his yellow facings, and beating them well with the brush, in a soldier-like way, he descended to breakfast, but, disdaining porridge and milk, broiled salmon and bannocks of barley-meal, he called for a can of stiff grog, mixed it with powder from his wide waistcoat pocket, and drank it off at a draught. Then he imperiously desired Ewen to take his bonnet and staff, and accompany him so far as Culloden, "because," said he, "I have come a long, long way to see the old place again."

Wooden-leg seemed to gather—what was quite unnecessary to him—new life, vigour, and energy—as they traversed the road that led to the battlefield, and felt the pure breeze of the spring morning blowing on their old and wrinkled faces.

The atmosphere was charmingly clear and serene. In the distance lay the spires of Inverness, and the shining waters of the Moray Firth, studded with sails, and the ramparts of Fort George were seen jutting out at the termination of a long and green peninsula. In the foreground stood the castle of Dalcross, raising its square outline above a wood, which terminates the eastern side of the landscape. The pine-clad summit of Dun Daviot incloses the west, while on every hand between, stretched the dreary moor of Drummossie—the Plain of Culloden—whilom drenched in the blood of Scotland's bravest hearts.

Amid the purple heath lie two or three grass-covered mounds.

These are the graves of the dead—the graves of the loyal Highlanders, who fell on that disastrous field, and of the wounded, who were so mercilessly murdered next day by an order of Cumberland, which he pencilled on the back of a card (the Nine of Diamonds); thus they were dispatched by platoons, stabbed by bayonets, slashed by swords and spontoons, or brained by the butt-end of musket and carbine; officers and men were to be seen emulating each other in this scene of cowardice and cold-blooded atrocity, which filled every camp and barrack in Continental Europe with scorn at the name of an English soldier.

Ewen was a Highlander, and his heart filled with such thoughts as these, when he stood by the grassy tombs where the fallen brave are buried with the hopes of the house they died for; he took off his bonnet and stood bare-headed, full of sad and silent contemplation; while his garrulous companion viewed the field with his single eye, that glowed like a hot coal, and pirouetted on his wooden pin in a very remarkable manner, as he surveyed on every side the scene of that terrible encounter, where, after enduring a long cannonade of round shot and grape, the Highland swordsmen, chief and gillie, the noble and the nameless, flung themselves with reckless valour on the ranks of those whom they had already routed in two pitched battles.

"It was an awful day," said Ewen, in a low voice, but with a gleam in his grey Celtic eye; "yonder my father fell wounded; the bullet went through his shield and pierced him here, just above the belt; he was living next day, when my mother—a poor wailing woman with a babe at her breast—found him; but an officer of Barrel's Regiment ran a sword twice through his body and killed him; for the orders of the German Duke were, 'that no quarter should be given.' This spring is named MacGillivray's Well, because here they butchered the dying chieftain who led the MacIntoshes—aye bayonetted him, next day at noon, in the arms of his bonnie young wife and his puir auld mother! The inhuman monsters! I have been a soldier," continued Ewen, "and I have fought for my country; but had I stood, that day on this Moor of Culloden, I would have shot the German Butcher, the coward who fled from Flanders—I would, by the God who hears me, though that moment had been my last!"

"Ha, ha ha! Ho, ho, ho!" rejoined his queer companion. "It seems like yesterday since I was here; I don't see many changes, except that the dead are all buried, whereas we left them to the crows, and a carriage-road has been cut across the field, just where we seized some women, who were looking among the dead for their husbands, and who—"

"Well?"

Wooden-leg whistled, and gave Ewen a diabolical leer with his snaky eye, as he resumed, "I see the ridge where the clans formed line—every tribe with its chief in front, and his colors in the centre, when we, hopeless of victory, and thinking only of defeat, approached them; and I can yet see standing the old stone wall which covered their right flank. Fire and smoke! It was against that wall we placed the wounded, when we fired at them by platoons next day. I finished some twenty rebels there myself."

Ewen's hand almost caught the haft of his skene-dhu, as he said, hoarsely, "Old man, do not call them rebels in my hearing, and least of all by the graves where they lie; they were good men and true; if they were in error, they have long since answered to God for it, even as we one day must answer; therefore let us treat their memory with respect, as soldiers should ever treat their brothers in arms who fall in war."

But Wooden-leg laughed with his strange eldritch yell, and then they returned together to the tollhouse in the glen; but Ewen felt strongly dissatisfied with his lodger, whose conversation was so calculated to shock alike his Jacobitical and his religious prejudices. Every day this sentiment grew stronger, and he soon learned to deplore in his inmost heart having ever accepted the rent, and longed for the time when he should be rid of him; but, at the end of the six months, Wooden-leg produced the rent for the remainder of the year, still in old silver of the two first Georges, with a few Spanish dollars, and swore he would set the house on fire, if Ewen made any more apologies about their inability to make him sufficiently comfortable and so forth; for his host and hostess had resorted to every pretence and expedient to rid themselves of him handsomely.

But Wooden-leg was inexorable.

He had bargained for his billet for a year; he had paid for it; and a year he would stay, though the Lord Justice General of Scotland himself should say nay!

Boisterous and authoritative, he awed every one by his terrible gimlet eye and the volleys of oaths with which he overwhelmed them on suffering the smallest contradiction; thus he became the terror of all; and shepherds crossed the hills by the most unfrequented routes rather than pass the toll-bar, where they vowed that his eye bewitched their sheep and cattle. To every whispered and stealthy inquiry as to where his lodger had come from, and how or why he had thrust himself upon this lonely tollhouse, Ewen could only groan and shrug his shoulders, or reply, "He came on the night of the hurricane, like a bird of evil omen; but on the twenty-sixth of April we will be rid of him, please Heaven! It is close at hand, and he shall march then, sure as my name is Ewen Mac Ewen!"

He seemed to be troubled in his conscience, too, or to have strange visitors; for often in stormy nights he was heard swearing and threatening, and expostulating; and once or twice, when listening at the foot of the stair, Ewen heard him shouting and conversing from his window with persons on the road, although the bar was shut, locked, and there was no one visible there.

On another windy night, Ewen and his wife were scared by hearing Wooden-leg engaged in a furious altercation with some one overhead.

"Dog, I'll blow out your brains!" yelled a strange voice.

"Fire and smoke! blow out the candle first—ha, ha, ha! ho, ho, ho!" cried Wooden-leg; then there ensued the explosion of a pistol, a dreadful stamping of feet, with the sound of several men swearing and fighting. To all this Ewen and his wife hearkened in fear and perplexity; at last something fell heavily on the floor, and then all became still, and not a sound was heard but the night wind sighing down the glen.

Betimes in the morning Ewen, weary and unslept, left his bed and ascended to the door of this terrible lodger and tapped gently.

"Come in; why the devil this fuss and ceremony, eh, comrade?" cried a hoarse voice, and there was old Wooden-leg, not lying dead on the floor as Ewen expected, or perhaps hoped; but stumping about in his shirt sleeves, pipe-claying his facings, and whistling the "Point of War."

On being questioned about the most unearthly "row" of last night, he only bade Ewen mind his own affairs, or uttered a volley of oaths, some of which were Spanish, and mixing a can of gunpowder grog drained it at a draught.

He was very quarrelsome, dictatorial, and scandalously irreligious; thus his military reminiscences were of so ferocious and blood-thirsty a nature, that they were sufficient to scare any quiet man out of his seven senses. But it was more particularly in relating the butcheries, murders, and ravages of Cumberland in the highlands, that he exulted, and there was always a terrible air of probability in all he said. On Ewen once asking of him if he had ever been punished for the many irregularities and cruelties he so freely acknowledged having committed.

"Punished? Fire and smoke, comrade, I should think so; I have been flogged till the bones of my back stood through the quivering flesh; I have been picquetted, tied neck and heels, or sent to ride the wooden horse, and to endure other punishments which are now abolished in the king's service. An officer once tied me neck and heels for eight and forty hours—ay, damme, till I lost my senses; but he lost his life soon after, a shot from the rear killed him; you understand me, comrade: ha, ha, ha! ho, ho, ho! a shot from the rear."

"You murdered him?" said Ewen, in a tone of horror.

"I did not say so," cried Wooden-leg with an oath, as he dealt his landlord a thwack across the shins with his stump; "but I'll tell you how it happened. I was on the Carthagena expedition in '41, and served amid all the horrors of that bombardment, which was rendered unsuccessful by the quarrels of the general and admiral; then the yellow fever broke out among the troops, who were crammed on board the ships of war like figs in a cask, or like the cargo of a slaver, so they died in scores—and in scores their putrid corpses lay round the hawsers of the shipping, which raked them up every day as they swung round with the tide; and from all the open gunports, where their hammocks were hung, our sick men saw the ground sharks gorging themselves on the dead, while they daily expected to follow. The air was black with flies, and the scorching sun seemed to have leagued with the infernal Spaniards against us. But, fire and smoke, mix me some more grog, I am forgetting my story!

"Our Grenadiers, with those of other regiments, under Colonel James Grant of Carron, were landed on the Island of Tierrabomba, which lies at the entrance of the harbor of Carthagena, where we stormed two small forts which our ships had cannonaded on the previous day.

" 'Grenadiers—open your pouches—handle grenades— blow your fuses!' cried Grant, 'forward.'

"And then we bayonetted the dons, or with the clubbed musket smashed their heads like ripe pumpkins, while our fleet, anchored with broadsides to the shore, threw shot and shell, grape, cannister, carcasses, and hand-grenades in showers among the batteries, booms, cables, chains, ships of war, gunboats, and the devil only knows what more.

"It was evening when we landed, and as the ramparts of San Luiz de Bocca Chica were within musket shot of our left flank, the lieutenant of our company was left with twelve grenadiers (of whom I was one) as a species of out-picquet to watch the Spaniards there, and to acquaint the officer in the captured forts if anything was essayed by way of sortie.

"About midnight I was posted as an advanced sentinel, and ordered to face La Bocca Chica with all my ears and eyes open. The night was close and sultry; there was not a breath of wind stirring on the land or waveless sea; and all was still save the cries of the wild animals that preyed upon the unburied dead, or the sullen splash caused by some half-shrouded corpse, as it was launched from a gun-port, for our ships were moored within pistol-shot of the place where I stood.

"Towards the west the sky was a deep and lurid red, as if the midnight sea was in flames at the horizon; and between me and this fiery glow, I could see the black and opaque outline of the masts, the yards, and the gigantic hulls of those floating charnel-houses our line-of-battle ships, and the dark solid ramparts of Sun Luiz de Bocca Chica.

"Suddenly I saw before me the head of a Spanish column!

"I cocked my musket, they seemed to be halted in close order, for I could see the white coats and black hats of a single company only. So I fired at them point blank, and fell back on the picquet, which stood to arms.

"The lieutenant of our grenadiers came hurrying towards me.

" 'Where are the dons?' said he.

" 'In our front, sir,' said I, pointing to the white line which seemed to waver before us in the gloom under the walls of San Luiz, and then it disappeared.

" 'They are advancing,' said I.

" 'They have vanished, fellow,' said the lieutenant, angrily.

" 'Because they have marched down into a hollow.'

"In a moment after, they reappeared, upon which the lieutenant brought up the picquet, and after firing

three volleys retired towards the principal fort where
Colonel Grant had all the troops under arms; but not a
Spaniard approached us, and what, think you, deceived
me and caused this alarm? Only a grove of trees, fire
and smoke! yes, it was a grove of manchineel trees,
which the Spaniards had cut down or burned to within
five feet of the ground; and as their bark is white it
resembled the Spanish uniform, while the black burned
tops easily passed for their grenadier caps to the
overstrained eyes of a poor anxious lad, who found
himself under the heavy responsibility of an advanced
sentinel for the first time in his life."

"And was this the end of it?" asked Ewen.

"Hell and Tommy?" roared Wooden-leg, "no—but
you shall hear. I was batooned by the lieutenant; then I
was tried at the drumhead for causing a false alarm, and
sentenced to be tied neck and heels, and lest you may
not know the fashion of this punishment I shall tell you
of it. I was placed on the ground; my firelock was put
under my hams, and another was placed over my neck;
then the two were drawn close together by two cartouch-
box straps; and in this situation doubled up as round as
a ball, I remained with my chin wedged between my
knees until the blood spouted out of my mouth, nose,
and ears, and I became insensible. When I recovered
my senses the troops were forming in column, prepara-
tory to assaulting Fort San Lazare; and though almost
blind, and both weak and trembling, I was forced to
take my place in the ranks; and I ground my teeth as I
handled my musket and saw the lieutenant of our company, in lace-ruffles and powdered wig, prepare to join
the forlorn hope, which was composed of six hundred
chosen grenadiers, under Colonel Grant, a brave Scottish
officer. I loaded my piece with a charmed bullet, cast in
a mould given to me by an Indian warrior, and marched
on with my section. The assault failed. Of the forlorn
hope I alone escaped, for Grant and his Grenadiers
perished to a man in the breach. There, too, lay our
lieutenant. A shot had pierced his head behind, just at

the queue. Queer, was it not? when I was his covering file?"

As he said this, Wooden-leg gave Ewen another of those diabolical leers, which always made his blood run cold, and continued, "I passed him as he lay dead, with his sword in his hand, his fine ruffled shirt and silk waistcoat drenched with blood—by the bye, there was a pretty girl's miniature, with powdered hair peeping out of it too. 'Ho, ho!' thought I, as I gave him a hearty kick; 'you will never again have me tied neck-and-heels for not wearing spectacles on sentry, or get me a hundred lashes, for not having my queue dressed straight to the seam of my coat.'"

"Horrible!" said Ewen.

"I will wager my wooden leg against your two of flesh and bone, that your officer would have been served in the same way, if he had given you the same provocation."

"Heaven forbid!" said Ewen.

"Ha, ha, ha! Ho, ho, ho!" cried Wooden-leg.

"You spoke of an Indian warrior," said Ewen, uneasily, as the atrocious anecdotes of this hideous old man excited his anger and repugnance; "then you have served, like myself, in the New World?"

"Fire and smoke! I should think so; but long before your day."

"Then you fought against the Cherokees?"

"Yes."

"At Warwomans Creek?"

"Yes; I was killed there."

"You were—what?" stammered Ewen.

"Killed there."

"Killed?"

"Yes, scalped by the Cherokees; dam! don't I speak plain enough?"

"He is mad," thought Ewen.

"I am not mad," said Wooden-leg gruffly.

"I never said so," urged Ewen.

"Thunder and blazes! but you thought it, which is all the same."

Ewen was petrified by this remark, and then Wooden-leg, while fixing his hyaena-like eye upon him, and mixing a fresh can of his peculiar grog, continued thus, "Yes, I served in the Warwomans Creek expedition in '60. In the proceeding year I had been taken prisoner at Fort Ninety-six, and was carried off by the Indians. They took me into the heart of their own country, where an old Sachem protected me, and adopted me in place of a son he had lost in battle. Now this old devil of a Sachem had a daughter—a graceful, pretty and gentle Indian girl, whom her tribe named the Queen of the Beaver dams. She was kind to me, and loved to call me her pale-faced brother. Ha, ha, ha! Ho, ho, ho! Fire and smoke! Do I now look like a man that could once attract a pretty girl's eye,—now, with my wooden-leg, patched face and riddled carcass? Well, she loved me, and I pretended to be in love too, though I did not care for her the value of an old snapper. She was graceful and round in every limb, as a beautiful statue. Her features were almost regular—her eyes black and soft; her hair hung nearly to her knees, while her smooth glossy skin, was no darker than a Spanish brunette's. Her words were like notes of music, for the language of the Cherokees, like that of the Iroquois, is full of the softest vowels. This Indian girl treated me with love and kindness, and I promised to become a Cherokee warrior, a thundering turtle and scalp-hunter for her sake—just as I would have promised anything to any other woman, and had done so a score of times before. I studied her gentle character in all its weak and delicate points, as a general views a fortress he is about to besiege, and I soon knew every avenue to the heart of the place. I made my approaches with modesty, for the mind of the Indian virgin was timid, and as pure as the new fallen snow. I drew my parallels and pushed on the trenches whenever the old Sachem was absent, smoking his pipe and drinking firewater at the council of the tribe; I soon reached the base of the glacis and stormed the breast-works—dam! I did, comrade.

"I promised her everything, if she would continue to love me, and swore by the Great Spirit to lay at her feet the scalp-lock of the white chief, General the Lord Amherst, K.C.B., and all that, with every other protestation that occurred to me at the time; and so she soon loved me—and me alone—as we wandered on the green slopes of Tennessee, when the flowering forest-trees, and the magnolias, the crimson strawberries, and the flaming azalea made the scenery beautiful; and where the shrill cry of the hawk, and the carol of the merry mocking-bird, filled the air with sounds of life and happiness.

"We were married in the fantastic fashion of the tribe, and the Indian girl was the happiest squaw in the Beaver dams. I hoed cotton and planted rice; I cut rushes that she might plait mats and baskets; I helped her to weave wampum, and built her a wig-wam, but I longed to be gone, for in six months I was wearied of her and the Cherokees too. In short, one night, I knocked the old Sachem on the head, and without perceiving that he still breathed, pocketed his valuables, such as they were, two necklaces of amber beads and two of Spanish dollars, and without informing my squaw of what I had done, I prevailed upon her to guide me far into the forest, on the skirts of which lay a British outpost, near the lower end of the vale, through which flows the Tennessee River. She was unable to accompany me more than a few miles, for she was weak, weary, and soon to become a mother; so I gave her the slip in the forest, and, leaving her to shift for herself, reached headquarters, just as the celebrated expedition from South Carolina was preparing to march against the Cherokees.

"Knowing well the localities, I offered myself as a guide, and was at once accepted—"

"Cruel and infamous!" exclaimed honest Ewen, whose chivalric Highland spirit fired with indignation at these heartless avowals; "and the poor girl you deceived—"

"Bah! I thought the wild beasts would soon dispose of her."

"But then the infamy of being a guide, even for your comrades, against those who had fed and fostered, loved and protected you! By my soul, this atrocity were worthy of King William and his Glencoe assassins!"

"Ho, ho, ho! fire and smoke! you shall hear.

"Well, we marched from New York in the early part of 1760. There were our regiment, with four hundred of the Scots Royals, and Montgomery's Highlanders. We landed at Charleston, and marched up the country to Fort Ninety-six on the frontier of the Cherokees. Our route was long and arduous, for the ways were wild and rough, so it was the first of June before we reached Twelve-mile River. I had been so long unaccustomed to carrying my knapsack, that its weight rendered me savage and ferocious, and I cursed the service and my own existence; for in addition to our muskets and accoutrements, our sixty rounds of ball cartridge per man, we carried our own tents, poles, and cooking utensils. Thunder and blazes! when we halted, which we did in a pleasant valley, where the great shady chestnuts and the flowering hickory made our camp alike cool and beautiful, my back and shoulders were nearly skinned; for as you must know well, comrade, the knapsack straps are passed so tightly under the armpits, that they stop the circulation of the blood, and press upon the lungs almost to suffocation. Scores of our men left the ranks on the march, threw themselves down in despair, and were soon tomahawked and scalped by the Indians.

"We marched forward next day, but without perceiving the smallest vestige of an Indian trail; thus we began to surmise that the Cherokees knew not that we were among them; but just as the sun was sinking behind the blue hills, we came upon a cluster of wigwams, which I knew well; they were the Beaver dams, situated on a river, among wild woods that never before had echoed to the drum or bugle.

"Bad and wicked as I was, some strange emotions rose within me at this moment. I thought of the Sachem's daughter—her beauty—her love for me, and the child that was under her bosom when I abandoned her in the vast forest through which we had just pene-

trated; but I stifled all regret, and heard with pleasure
the order to 'examine flints and priming.'

"Then the Cherokee warwhoop pierced the echoing
sky; a scattered fire was poured upon us from behind
the rocks and trees; the sharp steel tomahawks came
flashing and whirling through the air; bullets and ar-
rows whistled, and rifles rung, and in a moment we
found ourselves surrounded by a living sea of dark-
skinned and yelling Cherokees, with plumes on their
scalp locks, their fierce visages streaked with war paint,
and all their moccasins rattling.

"Fire and fury, such a time it was!

"We all fought like devils, but our men fell fast on
every side; the Royals lost two lieutenants, and several
soldiers whose scalps were torn from their bleeding
skulls in a moment. Our regiment, though steady under
fire as a battalion of stone statues, now fell into disorder, and the brown warriors, like fiends in aspect and
activity, pressed on with musket and war-club bran-
dished, and with such yells as never rang in mortal ears
elsewhere. The day was lost, until the Highlanders
came up, and then the savages were routed in an instant, and cut to pieces. 'Shoot and slash' was the
order; and there ensued such a scene of carnage as I
had not witnessed since Culloden, where His Royal
Highness, the fat Duke of Cumberland, galloped about
the field, overseeing the wholesale butchery of the
wounded.

"We destroyed their magazines of powder and provisions; we laid the wig-wams in ashes, and shot or
bayonetted every living thing, from the babe on its
mother's breast, to the hen that sat on the roost; for as I
had made our commander aware of all the avenues,
there was no escape for the poor devils of Cherokees.
Had the pious, glorious, and immortal King William
been there, he would have thought we had modelled
the whole affair after his own exploit at Glencoe.

"All was nearly over, and among the ashes of the
smoking wig-wams and the gashed corpses of king's soldiers and Indian warriors, I sat down beneath a great

chestnut to wipe my musket, for butt, barrel, and bayonet were clotted with blood and human hair—ouf, man, why do you shudder? it was only Cherokee wool;— all was nearly over, I have said, when a low fierce cry, like the hoarse hiss of a serpent, rang in my ear; a brown and bony hand clutched my throat as the fangs of a wolf would have done, and hurled me to the earth! A tomahawk flashed above me, and an aged Indian's face, whose expression, was like that of a fiend, came close to mine, and I felt his breath upon my cheek. It was the visage of the sachem, but hollow with suffering and almost green with fury, and he laughed like a hyaena, as he poised the uplifted axe.

"Another form intervened for a moment; it was that of the poor Indian girl I had so heartlessly deceived; she sought to stay the avenging hand of the frantic sachem; but he thrust her furiously aside, and in the next moment the glittering tomahawk was quivering in my brain—a knife swept round my head—my scalp was torn off, and I remember no more."

"A fortunate thing for you," said Ewen, drily; "memory such as yours were worse than a knapsack to carry; and so you were killed there?"

"Don't sneer, comrade," said Wooden-leg, with a diabolical gleam in his eye; "prithee, don't sneer; I was killed there, and, moreover, buried too, by the Scots Royals, when they interred the dead next day."

"Then how came you to be here?" said Ewen, not very much at ease, to find himself in company with one he deemed a lunatic.

"Here? That is my business—not yours," was the surly rejoinder.

Ewen was silent, but reckoned over that now there were but thirty days to run until the 26th of April, when the stipulated year would expire.

"Yes, comrade, just thirty days," said Wooden-leg, with an affirmative nod, divining the thoughts of Ewen; "and then I shall be off, bag and baggage, if my friends come."

"If not?"

"Then I shall remain where I am."

"The Lord forbid!" thought Ewen; "but I can apply to the sheriff."

"Death and fury! Thunder and blazes! I should like to see the rascal of a sheriff who would dare to meddle with me!" growled the old fellow, as his one eye shot fire, and, limping away, he ascended the stairs grumbling and swearing, leaving poor Ewen terrified even to think, on finding that his thoughts, although only half conceived, were at once divined and responded to by this strange inmate of his house.

"His friends," thought Ewen, "who may they be?"

Three heavy knocks rang on the floor overhead, as a reply.

It was the wooden leg of the Cherokee invader.

This queer old fellow (continued the quarter-master) was always in a state of great excitement, and used an extra number of oaths, and mixed his grog more thickly with gunpowder, when a stray red coat appeared far down the long green glen, which was crossed by Ewen's lonely toll-bar. Then he would get into a prodigious fuss and bustle, and was wont to pack and cord his trunk, to brush up his well-worn and antique regimentals, and to adjust his queue and the black cockade of his triple-cornered hat, as if preparing to depart.

As the time of that person's wished-for departure drew nigh, Ewen took courage, and shaking off the timidity with which the swearing and boisterous fury of Wooden-leg had impressed him, he ventured to expostulate a little on the folly and sin of his unmeaning oaths, and the atrocity of the crimes he boasted of having committed.

But the wicked old Wooden-leg laughed and swore more than ever, saying that a "true soldier was never a religious one."

"You are wrong, comrade," retorted the old Cameronian, taking fire at such an assertion; "religion is the lightest burden a poor soldier can carry; and, moreover, it hath upheld me on many a long day's march, when almost sinking under hunger and fatigue, with my pack, kettle, and sixty rounds of ball ammunition on my back. The duties of a good and brave soldier are no way imcompatible with those of a Christian man; and I never lay down to rest on the wet bivouac or bloody field, with my knapsack, or it might be a dead comrade, for a pillow, without thanking God—"

"Ha, ha, ha!"

"—The God of Scotland's covenanted Kirk for the mercies he vouchsafed to Ewen Mac Ewen, a poor grenadier of the 26th Regiment."

"Ho, ho, ho!"

The old Cameronian took off his bonnet and lifted up his eyes, as he spoke fervently, and with the simple reverence of the olden time; but Wooden-leg grinned and chuckled and gnashed his teeth as Ewen resumed.

"A brave soldier may rush to the cannon's mouth, though it be loaded with grape and cannister; or at a line of levelled bayonets—and rush fearlessly too—and yet he may tremble without shame, at the thought of hell, or of offended Heaven. It is not so, comrade? I shall never forget the words of our chaplain before we stormed the Isles of Saba and St Martin from the Dutch, with Admiral Rodney, in '81."

"Bah—that was after I was killed by the Cherokees. Well?"

"The Cameronians were formed in line, mid leg in the salt water, with bayonets fixed, the colors flying, the pipes playing and the drums beating 'Britons strike home,' and our chaplain, a reverend minister of God's word, stood beside the colonel with the shot and shell from the Dutch batteries flying about his old white head, but he was cool and calm, for he was the grandson of Richard Cameron, the glorious martyr of Airdsmoss.

" 'Fear not, my bairns,' cried he (he aye called us his bairns, having ministered unto us for fifty years and more)—'fear not; but remember that the eyes of the Lord are on every righteous soldier, and that His hand will shield him in the day of the battle!'

" 'Forward, my lads,' cried the colonel, waving his broad sword, while the musket shot shaved the curls of his old brigadier wig; 'forward, and at them with your bayonets'; and bravely we fell on—eight hundred Scotsmen, shoulder to shoulder—and in half an hour the British flag was waving over the Dutchman's Jack on the ramparts of St Martin."

But to all Ewen's exordiums, Wooden-leg replied by oaths, or mockery, or his incessant laugh, "Ha, ha, ha! Ho, ho, ho!"

At last came the long-wished for twenty-sixth of April!

The day was dark and louring. The pine woods looked black, and the slopes of the distant hills seemed close and near, and yet gloomy withal. The sky was veiled by masses of hurrying clouds, which seemed to chase each other across the Moray Firth. That estuary was flecked with foam, and the ships were riding close under the lee of the Highland shore, with topmasts struck, their boats secured, and both anchors out, for everything betokened a coming storm.

And with night it came in all its fury—a storm similar to that of the preceding year.

The fierce and howling wind swept through the mountain gorges, and levelled the lonely shielings, whirling their fragile roofs into the air, and uprooting strong pines and sturdy beeches; the water was swept up from the Loch of the Clans, and mingled with the rain which drenched the woods around it. The green and yellow lightning played in ghastly gleams about the black summit of Dun Daviot, and again the rolling thunder bellowed over the graves of the dead on the bleak, dark moor of Culloden. Attracted by the light in the windows of the tollhouse, the red deer came down from the hills in herds and cowered near the little dwelling; while the cries of the affrighted partridges, blackcocks, and even those of the gannets from the Moray Firth were heard at times, as they were swept past, with branches, leaves, and stones, on the skirts of the hurrying blast.

"It is just such a storm as we had this night twelve-months ago," said Meinie, whose cheek grew pale at the elemental uproar.

"There will be no one coming up the glen tonight," replied Ewen; "so I may as well secure the toll-bar, lest a gust should dash it to pieces."

It required no little skill or strength to achieve this in such a tempest; the gate was strong and heavy, but it was fastened at last, and Ewen retreated to his own fireside. Meanwhile, during all this frightful storm without, Wooden-leg was heard singing and carolling upstairs, stumping about in the lulls of the tempest, and rolling, pushing, and tumbling his chest from side to side; then he descended to get a fresh can of grog—for "grog, grog, grog," was ever his cry. His old withered face was flushed, and his excited eye shone like a baleful star. He was conscious that a great event would ensue.

Ewen felt happy in his soul that his humble home should no longer be the resting-place of this evil bird whom the last tempest had blown hither.

"So you leave us tomorrow, comrade?" said he.

"I'll march before daybreak," growled the other; " 'twas our old fashion in the days of Minden. Huske and Hawley always marched off in the dark."

"Before daybreak?"

"Fire and smoke, I have said so, and you shall see; for my friends are on the march already; but good night, for I shall have to parade betimes. They come; though far, far off as yet."

He retired with one of his diabolical leers, and Ewen and his wife ensconced themselves in the recesses of their warm box-bed; Meinie soon fell into a sound sleep, though the wind continued to howl, the rain to lash against the trembling walls of the little mansion, and the thunder to hurl peal after peal across the sky of that dark and tempestuous night.

The din of elements and his own thoughts kept Ewen long awake; but though the gleams of electric light came frequent as ever through the little window, the glow of the "gathering peat" sank lower on the hearth of hard-beaten clay, and the dull measured tick-tack of the drowsy clock as it fell on the drum of his ear, about midnight, was sending him to sleep, by the weariness of its intense monotony, when from a dream that the fierce hawk eye of his malevolent lodger was fixed upon him, he started suddenly to full consciousness. An uproar of tongue now rose and fell upon the gusts of wind without; and he heard an authoritative voice requiring the toll-bar to be opened.

Overhead rang the stumping of Wooden-leg, whose hoarse voice was heard bellowing in reply from the upper window.

"The Lord have a care of us!" muttered Mac Ewen, as he threw his kilt and plaid round him, thrust on his bonnet and brogues, and hastened to the door, which was almost blown in by the tempest as he opened it.

The night was as dark, and the hurricane as furious as ever; but how great was Ewen's surprise to see the advance guard of a corps of Grenadiers, halted at the toll-bar gate, which he hastened to unlock, and the moment he did so, it was torn off its iron hooks and swept up the glen like a leaf from a book, or a lady's handkerchief; as with an unearthly howling the wind came tearing along in fitful and tremendous gusts, which made the strongest forests stoop, and dashed the struggling coasters on the rocks of the Firth—the Æstuarium Vararis of the olden time.

As the levin brands burst in lurid fury overhead, they seemed to strike fire from the drenched rocks, the dripping trees, and the long line of flooded roadway, that wound through the pastoral glen towards Culloden.

The advance guard marched on in silence with arms slung; and Ewen, to prevent himself from being swept away by the wind, clung with both hands to a stone pillar of the bar gate, that he might behold the passage of this midnight regiment, which approached in firm and silent order in sections of twelve files abreast, all with muskets slung. The pioneers were in front, with their leather aprons, axes, saws, bill-hooks, and hammers; the band was at the head of the column; the drums, fifes, and colours were in the centre; the captains were at the head of their companies; the subalterns on the reverse flank, and the field-officers were all mounted on black chargers, that curvetted and pranced like shadows, without a sound.

Slowly they marched, but erect and upright, not a man of them seeming to stoop against the wind or rain, while overhead the flashes of the broad and blinding lightning were blazing like a ghastly torch, and making every musket-barrel, every belt-plate, sword-blade, and buckle, gleam as this mysterious corps filed through the barrier, with who? Wooden-leg among them!

By the incessant gleams Ewen could perceive that they were Grenadiers, and wore the quaint old uniform of George II's time; the sugar-loaf-shaped cap of red cloth embroidered with worsted; the great square-tailed red coat with its heavy cuffs and close-cut collar; the stockings rolled above the knee, and enormous shoe-buckles. They carried grenado-pouches; the officers had espontoons; the sergeants shouldered heavy halberds, and the coats of the little drum-boys were covered with fantastic lace.

It was not the quaint and antique aspect of this solemn battalion that terrified Ewen, or chilled his heart; but the ghastly expression of their faces, which were pale and hollow-eyed, being, to all appearance, the visages of spectres; and they marched past like a long and wavering panorama, without a sound; for though the wind was loud, and the rain was drenching, neither could have concealed the measured tread of so many mortal feet; but there was no footfall heard on the roadway, nor the tramp of a charger's hoof; the regiment defiled past, noiseless as a wreath of smoke.

The pallor of their faces, and the stillness which accompanied their march, were out of the course of nature; and the soul of Mac Ewen died away within him; but his eyes were riveted upon the marching phantoms—if phantoms, indeed, they were—as if by fascination; and, like one in a terrible dream, he continued to gaze until the last files were past; and with them rode a fat and full-faced officer, wearing a three-cocked hat, and having a star and blue ribbon on his breast. His face was ghastly like the rest, and dreadfully distorted, as if by mental agony and remorse. Two aides-de-camps accompanied him, and he rode a wild-looking black horse, whose eyes shot fire. At the neck of the fat specter—for a specter he really seemed—hung a card.

It was the Nine of Diamonds!

The whole of this silent and mysterious battalion passed in line of march up the glen, with the gleams of lightning flashing about them. One bolt more brilliant than the rest brought back the sudden flash of steel.

They had fixed bayonets, and shouldered arms!

And on, and on they marched, diminishing in the darkness and the distance, those ghastly Grenadiers, towards the flat bleak moor of Culloden, with the green lightning playing about them, and gleaming on the storm-swept waste.

The Wooden-leg—Ewen's unco' guest—disappeared with them, and was never heard of more in Strathnairn.

He had come with a tempest, and gone with one. Neither was any trace ever seen or heard of those strange and silent soldiers. No regiment had left Nairn that night, and no regiment reached Inverness in the morning; so unto this day the whole affair remains a mystery, and a subject of ridicule with some, although Ewen, whose story of the midnight march of a corps in time of war—caused his examination by the authorities in the Castle of Inverness—stuck manfully to his assertions, which were further corroborated by the evidence of his wife and children. He made a solemn affidavit of the circumstances I have related before the sheriff, whose court books will be found to confirm them in every particular; if not, it is the aforesaid sheriff's fault, and not mine.

There were not a few (but these were generally old Jacobite ladies of decayed Highland families, who form the gossiping tabbies and wall-flowers of the Northern Meeting) who asserted that in their young days they had heard of such a regiment marching by night, once a year to the field of Culloden; for it is currently believed by the most learned on such subjects in the vicinity of the "Clach na Cudden," that on the anniversary of the sorrowful battle, *a certain place*, which shall be nameless, opens, and that the restless souls of the murderers of the wounded clansmen march in military array to the green graves upon the purple heath, in yearly penance; and this story was thought to receive full corroboration by the apparition of a fat lubberly specter with the nine of diamonds chained to his neck; as it was on that card—since named the Curse of Scotland—the Duke of Cumberland hastily pencilled the savage order to "show no quarter to the wounded, but to slaughter all."

THE SPIRIT OF
SERGEANT DAVIES

Michael and Mollie Hardwick

When a war is over and won, the true reckoning begins. The Jacobite Rebellion of 1745 ended in total failure for the Stuart cause. Prince Charlie had fled back to France, leaving his faithful Highlanders to suffer unspeakable wrongs at the hands of the English victors, under their cruel leader "Butcher" Cumberland. Murder, rape, houseburning were the order of the day, and nothing was left undone that might break the spirit of the brave Clans. They might no longer wear their traditional tartans, nor carry swords—officially. But Highland blood is high, and the heaths and mountains hid as many broken and outlawed men as they did rabbits and foxes; each with some vestige of a knife or rusted gun, and each with hatred in his heart for the conquering Sassenach.

There is the tale of one Donald Ban and his wife, who were visited one night by a ghost, and sorely frightened. But the woman retained enough self-possession to beg the ghost to answer one question for her: "Will our Prince come again?" The phantom replied in the following lines:

> *The wind has left me bare indeed,*
> *And blawn my bonnet off my heid,*
> *But something's hid in Hieland brae—*
> *The wind's no' blawn my sword away!*

But this poetic spirit is not the ghost of our story.

By 1749, three years after the Rising was quelled, the English government was still uneasy about the Highlands. The feeling that "something's hid in Hieland brae" was only too strong upon them, and an Army of Occupation still kept a sharp watch on the territory. It was as popular as Armies of Occupation usually are.

But an exception to the general label of "bluidy redcoat" was Sergeant Arthur Davies, of Guise's regiment, who in the summer of 1749 was posted from Aberdeen to Dubrach in Braemar, eight miles away from the nearest guard-station at Glenshee. Between the two places stretched a wild waste of bog and mountain, rock and river. Sergeant Davies was not perturbed by the difference between this savage land and his own gentle countryside, and soon settled down. He was quickly accepted, for he was one of those men born to be liked by their fellow-men—kindly, honest, fair in his dealings, and in his private life devoted to his young wife and fond of children. This last must have been a remarkable attribute in a country where a second Slaughter of the Innocents had just taken place. His wife later testified that "he and she lived together in as great amity and love as any couple could do, and he never was in use to stay away a night from her."

The sergeant, who was comfortably off in England, and of saving disposition, must have appeared very wealthy to hungry Highland eyes. He wore a silver watch, and two gold rings—one with a peculiar knob on it. His brogues had silver buckles, and, like Bobbie Shafto, he wore "silver buckles at his knee." On his striped lute-string waistcoat were two dozen silver buttons; his coat was a cheerful bright blue, his hat, with his initials cut into the felt was silver-laced, and his dark brown hair was gathered into a silk ribbon. He had saved fifteen guineas and a half—a huge sum for those days—and was in the habit of carrying it in a green silk purse and innocently displaying it to those interested. He carried a gun—an envied possession in those parts. Such was Sergeant Davies, "a pretty man," every detail of his appearance and attire noted by those who saw him leave his lodgings at Michael Farquharson's in Dubrach on 28 September, early in the morning. His wife, in her cap and bed-gown, came down to kiss him good-bye at the door. Did her arms hold more tightly and long around him than usual? Or did she watch him out of sight, with the uneasy feeling that this was the beginning of a very long journey? Probably not; she was an English woman, not a Highland lass with "the sight." "Good-bye, Arthur—take good care of yourself," was more than likely to be all she said, before shutting the door and beginning her household tasks.

Sergeant Davies briskly collected four men, and set out towards Glenshee to meet the patrol which was coming from there. On the way he met a man called John Growar, and noticed that Growar was wearing a tartan coat—a thing forbidden by law. Instead of arresting him, as most English officers would have done, Davies kindly advised him to take it off and not to wear it again, and then let him go on his way. Davies was by this time alone, having left his men temporarily because he thought he would like to cross the hill and try to get a stag—he fancied himself as a sportsman. He promised to rejoin the men later on their way to the rendezvous with the patrol.

But when they met with the patrol, Sergeant Davies had not rejoined them. They gave him an hour or two, then went back and searched the route. They called, they shouted, but no voice answered, only the frightened moorland birds. The sun of a late summer was hot on their heads, and by the end of the day they gave up, exhausted.

For three days it was expected that Sergeant Davies would return of his own accord; on the fourth day a band of soldiers from the combined forces of Dubrach and Glenshee went out on an intensive search for him. But no trace of him was found; the substantial Sergeant Davies had vanished as if the fairies had taken him. Some simple folk believed they had; others had darker ideas.

The weeks passed, and the months. It was June, 1750, and the rooms where Sergeant Davies had lodged were occupied by his replacement. Poor Mrs. Davies had gone home to England; after waiting for months in Scotland for her lost husband to return, she had given up hope. Michael Farquharson's son, Donald, was at home when the servant came to tell him that there was a visitor asking for his father, one Alexander Macpherson. His father being away on business, Donald offered to see the man himself.

Alexander Macpherson was a middle-aged man who had so far stayed out of trouble with the English, and was living humbly but peacefully enough in a shephard's hut among the hills. The story he had to tell was a strange one. He had, he said, been visited repeatedly at night by the ghost of Sergeant Davies, looking exactly as he had done in life but with an anxious, troubled expression. The ghost had begged Macpherson to go and look for his bones, which were buried in a peat moss, about half a mile from the road taken by the patrols. Macpherson, afraid, refused to do this. "Bury my bones! bury my bones!" repeated the ghost over and over, despairingly. "I will not—I am afraid," returned Macpherson. "Then you will find one who will. Go to Michael and Donald Farquharson at my old lodgings, and tell them to bury my bones—bury my bones!"

Donald Farquharson listened to this recital incredulously. He was a level-headed person, and had heard many wild tales from his fellow-Highlanders. Frankly, he did not believe Macpherson, and said so.

"But at least come with me and see if the bones are there!" Macpherson pleaded. "If you could have seen and heard the ghost you would have believed!"

His insistence finally succeeded with Farquharson, who agreed to go with him. The next morning they set out, and within an hour or two arrived at the spot described by the ghost. They had brought spades, and now used them. Not far below the surface they turned up a shred of blue cloth. Deeper still they dug, until the peat yielded what the ghost had promised—the pathetic bones of Sergeant Davies, the brown hair still clinging to the skull, but the silk ribbon gone; the silk waistcoat almost intact, but without its silver buttons, and the buckles vanished from the bones of knee and foot. His murderers had torn the silver lacing from his hat and thrown the hat down beside him. There it lay, rotting, the initials "A.D." still clear.

Reverently, Farquharson and Macpherson dug a neat grave away from the peat moss, and in it they laid the poor bones, saying over them a service of prayer and committal; for they were both devout men. The rags and relics of clothing they collected and took back with them to Dubrach, as evidence of the murder that had been done.

A trial was held, and Alexander Macpherson was called upon to give evidence. His testimony differed substantially from the story he had told Donald Farquharson. According to what he now said, he had been visited late in May by a vision of a man clothed in blue, who said "I am Sergeant Davies!" At first he thought the figure was a real living man—a brother of Donald Farquharson's. He rose and followed the shape to the door, where it told him that its bones lay in a spot the direction of which it pointed out, and said that it wished them to be decently buried, and that Donald Farquharson would help to do this.

Next day Macpherson went out and found the bones, afterwards covering them up again. On his way back to his hut he met Growar, the man of the tartan coat whom Davies had encountered on his last day on earth. Growar said that if Macpherson did not keep quiet about the discovery, he himself would impeach Macpherson to Shaw of Daldownie, a magistrate. Macpherson, taking the wise course, went to Shaw himself and told his story; but Shaw told him to keep his mouth shut about the whole affair, and not give the district a bad name for harbouring rebels. Macpherson went home with a disturbed mind. That night the ghost again appeared to him, reproaching him, and once again commanding him to get Donald Farquharson to bury the bones. He also—and this caused a sensation in the court—revealed the names of the two men who had murdered him, Duncan Clerk and Alexander Bain Macdonald.

At this point the magistrate interrupted to ask in what language the ghost had spoken to Macpherson. "In the Gaelic," Macpherson replied. The magistrate wrote down his answer.

Then came an uncanny piece of evidence from Mistress Isobel MacHardie, for whom Macpherson worked as a shepherd. One night in June, 1750, she said, she had been sleeping in the sheiling (a hut for the use of shepherds) while Macpherson slept at the other end; a double watch was kept on the sheep. While she lay awake "she saw something naked come in at the door, which frightened her so much that she drew the clothes over her head. When it appeared it came in in a bowing posture, and next morning she asked Macpherson what it was that had troubled them in the night. He answered that she might be easy, for it would not trouble them any more."

Incredible as it may seem, no further inquiry was made into the doings of the men Clerk and Macdonald; the whole matter was suspended. Then, three years later, in September, 1753, they were suddenly arrested —on charges of rebellious behaviour, such as wearing the kilt! They were kept in Edinburgh's Tolbooth Prison until June, 1754, and then tried. At the trial it emerged that Clerk's wife wore Sergeant Davies's ring—the one with the characteristic knob—and that Clerk, after the murder, had suddenly become prosperous and had taken a farm. Witnesses came forward to swear that Clerk and Macdonald, armed, were on a hill in the neighbourhood of the murder on 18 September, 1749. And one Angus Cameron swore that he saw the murder committed, while he and another Cameron, now dead, had been hiding in a little hill-hollow all day, waiting for Donald Cameron, *who was afterwards hanged*, together with some of Donald's companions from Lochaber. The implication is that some underground Jacobite business was afoot. The watchers had seen Clerk and Macdonald strike and shoot a man in a blue coat and silver-laced hat, and then had run away.

The evidence impressed the court greatly. But, 142 years later, it was contradicted by the story told by a very old lady, a descendant of one of the witnesses at the trial. She said that her ancestor had been out stag-shooting on 28 September, 1749, with gun and deer-hound. He saw Clerk and Macdonald on the hill, and, thinking they had got a stag, went towards them, his dog running in front of him. As he drew nearer, he saw *what it was they had*. He called to the dog, and began to run away, but they fired a shot after him and the dog was wounded. Then he ran home as fast as he could.

Between the story of 1754 and that of 1896 it seems more than likely that Clerk and Macdonald were guilty. Their lawyers were certainly convinced of their guilt. And yet, when the jury of Edinburgh tradesmen returned to give their verdict, it was that of—Not Guilty. The reason for their acquittal was that the ghost had spoken to Alexander Macpherson in Gaelic, *a language it did not know in life*.

And so the unfortunate Sergeant Davies, who had struggled back through the gates of death to beg for Christian burial and to denounce his murderers, had made his journey in vain; for his bones were never interred in a kirkyard, and Clerk and Macdonald went free. They lived in prosperity, for those times, on the proceeds of the sergeant's guineas, watch and rings, and the silver buckles and buttons for which they had killed him. Small wonder if his forlorn blue-coated spirit walks the Braemar hills this day.

DEATH HOLDS THE POST

August Derleth

URGENT GOVERNMENT OF FRANCE ACTING ON ADVICE
FROM GERMANY ASKS ALL COMMANDERS OF ALGERIAN
POSTS TO WATCH FOR AND ARREST GERMAN SCIENTIST
DR OTTO PRETTWEG WHO ESCAPED FROM SANITARIUM
WITH IMPORTANT DOCUMENTS STOP BELIEVED HEAD-
ING FOR ALGERIA SINCE ALL OTHER AVENUES OF ES-
CAPE STOPPED SEEN ON FRENCH COAST STOP ARREST
THIS MAN IMMEDIATELY STOP DESCRIBED AS TALL THIN
MAN SUNKEN CHEEKS LIVID SCAR ON LEFT CHEEK BLACK
EYES GRAY HAIR URGENT RELAY

Eddie Cranston reread the dispatch he had just decoded and handed it to his companion in the stuffy
room. "They *would* spring that on us just when we're in
a hole about Mechar," he said in irritation.

His companion read the message, grunted perfuncto-
rily, and handed it back without comment. Cranston
went out into the deserted quadrangle where buildings
and ground alike baked in the mid-afternoon sun. He
was unpleasantly aware of the heavy, hot lifelessness of
the place. On the wall two guards were limned against
the parched blue of the African sky; in the shade of a
barracks doorway a native slept; there was no other sign
of life. Half a hundred men had marched from Surdez

to the post at Mechar two days before. The other half were finding relief from the heat in sleep.

Cranston went into the largest of the several buildings within the white walls of Surdez. Lieutenant Prageur, a big man with a troubled frown on his forehead, slept on his narrow untidy cot, snoring lightly, his boots on the floor, his blouse and shirt flung over the back of a chair. Cranston touched his superior's shoulder.

"Lieutenant," he said softly.

The officer awoke with a start, swinging his bare feet to the floor. "What d'you want? Anything happen?"

"Special dispatch, sir!"

Prageur took the message and read it. He shrugged irritably. "We won't have to worry much about that. Even a lunatic wouldn't hide in a god-forsaken hole like this. Now, what about Mechar? Still no contact?"

"Nothing, sir."

"Damned queer business. Those fellows should have been there a long while ago."

"Any orders, sir?"

"Stick at that wire. We can't do anything else."

Cranston left the building, thinking about Mechar. The trouble had started when news came from Mechar that a queer band of unidentified men—marauders, gipsies, Tuaregs, no one knew exactly—were occupying an old and deserted post near Mechar, the last outpost. Before Lieutenant D'Oblier at Mechar could send out an investigating party, the post had been surprised by a formidable army of men and, after a futile battle on the part of the Legionnaires, had been taken. Dispatches to Surdez had ceased in the middle of the sentence announcing Mechar's fall.

Orders had come from headquarters to dispatch fifty men to Mechar at once, and at the same time came the news that more men were being sent to Surdez from adjoining posts. Two days had passed since then, but no word had reached Surdez from Mechar, nor had any intelligence of the fifty men reached the post. Lieutenant Prageur and the remainder of the garrison had come to believe that D'Oblier had been deceived as to the number of men at the deserted post, for only a great number could have destroyed the garrison at Mechar, which, being the last outpost, had many more men than Surdez.

Cranston waited futilely at the telegraph, occasionally tapping out the code call for Mechar. Silence was his only answer. He slid down in his chair and dozed.

Half an hour later Cranston was shaken out of his sleep by the rough voice of a guard.

"Gasparri's come back," he said.

Cranston was instantly awake. Gasparri was one of the fifty dispatched to Mechar two days ago. "Gasparri!" he echoed. "Who else?"

"He's alone. Stumbling across the desert as if he were wounded. I saw him from a distance. He dropped from exhaustion just beyond the gates."

Gasparri lay at the door, stretched on the ground where the guard had put him. Cranston bent over the body. Gasparri's face was black with grime and sweat, his lips were cracked, and white with caked dust. His chest lifted and fell in heavy, disturbed breathing.

"Get him to bed. No wait—I'll get him in. You go for Lieutenant Prageur."

Cranston carried the unconscious man into the building, where he lowered him carefully to a cot. He sought and found some brandy, which he forced through Gasparri's parched lips. In a few moments the exhausted man's breathing eased up. Cranston was watching Gasparri's face when Prageur entered.

The lieutenant went over to the cot and looked down. He said nothing, but apprehension for the forty-nine men who had not returned was plainly written on his features. The Italian moved restlessly; he was coming around. Cranston and Prageur waited. Presently Gasparri opened his eyes. Immediately Cranston was at his side with a glass of water.

"Not too much, now," he said.

Gasparri gulped a few swallows with painful effort and sank back on the cot. His blood-shot eyes stared vacantly at the ceiling. His lips moved soundlessly. But in a moment blood flushed in his cheeks, crept back into his gray lips.

"Gasparri!" said Lieutenant Prageur.

Gasparri looked vacantly at him and said, "Not to Mechar!" That was all.

Prageur bent forward. "Where are the others, Gasparri?"

For a long moment Gasparri's face remained expressionless; then a look of unutterable horror crept over his features. His blood-shot eyes opened wide, his lips fell apart, his hands fumbled at his neck as if he were stifling. "*Dio!*" he gasped, "one of them—one had me by the neck!" Then he began to mutter incoherently.

Prageur held back his impatience.

It did not take Gasparri long to pull himself together. After his muttering subsided, he lay for almost a half-hour fully conscious, and at length pulled himself up into a sitting position and began to talk.

He told of the arrival of the fifty at Mechar. They had come to the post in eleven hours, for it was not a great distance from Surdez, and had found it apparently deserted. Yet the gates were locked on the inside. . . .

"We broke in after a while and waited for something to happen. Nothing did. Inside, everything was quiet and deserted. Then we went in. As soon as we were well inside, the firing began, from all sides, from doors and windows and roofs where *they* had been concealed. We answered their fire—but we didn't have a chance against an army like that!"

Gasparri shuddered, horror in his eyes.

"That army," he repeated. "*Dio!* it was no army. We shot, we struck home—but not one of them fell." His voice rose abruptly. "They were dead already! Some of them were skeletons, half-rotten corpses, and—*Dio!* —some were the men from Mechar—dead men, fighting!"

He fell back.

Prageur made a gesture of annoyance. "Sun's got him," he said irritably. "And he sounded all right."

He bent over the Italian, who was crouching back against the bed, covering his eyes with his hands, shuddering violently. "Look here, Gasparri!" he commanded sharply. "Forget that. We sent fifty good men to Mechar. They haven't come back, and we haven't had a word from them! What happened to them? You must know. *Tell me!*"

Gasparri raised his head, dropping his hands listlessly. Then he said, "I have told you, sir. They're dead. They were killed by those dead things at Mechar. I alone escaped." His voice was heavy and portentous with a calm, deadly hopelessness.

"You're delirious!" snapped Prageur. He sat down on the cot and grasped Gasparri's wrists roughly in a tight grip.

Gasparri made no protest; he only looked at the lieutenant out of fright-haunted eyes.

"Tell me!" Prageur ordered again, but his voice was less sure.

Gasparri repeated, "I have told you, sir. They were killed by dead men, and one who was not dead—a tall, thin old man, who directed their movements from the safety of the watch-tower, and he was like a ghost. But all the others are dead, I tell you, dead—and yet they moved, those dead ones."

"What happened to our men, Gasparri?"

"They're dead in Mechar." Then abruptly Gasparri's eyes flamed with a ghastly fear. *"Or perhaps they, too, are alive like those others."*

Prageur turned away, shrugging.

Cranston followed him to the door. "He's obviously mad, sir, but that doesn't explain his presence. Why is he here? He came alone on foot across the sand."

Lieutenant Prageur looked at him. *"Sand de Dieu!"* he exploded. "You don't put any faith in that tale, do you, Cranston?"

"No, sir," replied Cranston promptly. "But I don't understand his condition. He got a shock somewhere, because there's something more than imagination behind that story he's telling."

The whimpering voice of the Italian drifted out to

them. "My neck," Gasparri complained, "bones around my neck—rotted flesh—ahhrr. . . ."

Prageur jerked his head in the direction of the cot. "Look after him, and keep on trying to get Mechar," he said. Then he turned on his heel and walked out into the blazing quadrangle.

Cranston saluted smartly and went back into the building.

Gasparri's removal to his own quarters was but a matter of a few moments, and Cranston was soon attempting to contact Mechar, though he felt intuitively that this was hopeless. He had not been long at it when he was brought to his feet by a startled shout from the quadrangle. He ran quickly to the door, where he was assailed by a babble of voices and sight of a second guard running toward the lieutenant's quarters.

Someone saw Cranston and shouted, "Another coming across the sand wearing the uniform. From Mechar."

"How far out?"

"About a mile."

Lieutenant Prageur, who had heard, was already striding toward the walls. Cranston followed.

From the small turret surmounting the southwest corner of the walls, Prageur scanned the desert through his binoculars. Cranston, looking out, saw for a few moments nothing but a gleaming expanse of sand topped by undulating silver waves of heat, rising and falling into an endless sky, blue as the sea. Then his eyes focussed properly and he saw the oncoming man—a small figure, moving slowly but steadily across the golden expanse of sand.

"I don't recognize him," said the lieutenant doubtfully. "Can't make out his face for his *kepi*. But he's one of our men. Take a look."

As Cranston took the glasses, Prageur stepped out along the wall and shouted down. "Ourlet, ride out to meet him."

The glasses brought the man on the sand much closer. It was a white man in a private's uniform. But what instantly caught Cranston's eye was the ease with which the soldier was moving. He was coming in a straight line across the sands, heading obviously for the Surdez gates, never hesitating, never stumbling as a man in exhaustion might, just coming along at a steady though slow and mechanically awkward gait.

"Spot that walk?" asked Lieutenant Prageur.

Cranston nodded. "Funny, sir."

Prageur stood looking out across the sand, his hands moving nervously. "I don't like it," he said suddenly. "But he seems to be one of our men."

The two of them descended the stairs to the quadrangle. The gates had been thrown open, and Ourlet had ridden out to meet the oncoming Legionnaire. Cranston had the fleeting hope that from this one, at least, they might learn something.

Then abruptly a shot broke the tense stillness. It came from beyond the post, from the sand, from the weapon which had appeared in one hand of the advancing Legionnaire. And the shot had been fired at Ourlet!

It had happened in the space of a few seconds—the walking man suddenly producing a revolver and firing at Ourlet as Ourlet rode up, Ourlet hit, dropping on his horse, wheeling the animal about and riding furiously back toward the gates. Amid a babble of shouting from the men at the gates, a second shot rang out; a moment later Ourlet was safely within the walls.

Someone sprang forward to help him from the horse, while others moved to shut the gates.

"Wait!" ordered Prageur.

He was watching the oncoming figure, and there was a curious intentness in his gaze. But before he could give a further order, the abrupt silence that had fallen was again broken—this time from behind them.

Gasparri, aroused by the outcries and the shots, had come from his quarters and had crept unseen to the gates. Suddenly he began to scream, his horrified eyes fixed upon the figure looming out of the sand waste.

"It's one of those dead ones! *Dio!* We are lost if he gets in!"

At the same moment, Ourlet gasped, "Something queer—he's not one of us." Then he collapsed.

Prageur had stepped forward and was even now bending above Gasparri.

But Gasparri went on, his voice rising. "Lieutenant, sir, it is a dead man. He'll kill all of us, just as he was killed. We can't kill him—he's dead already! *Dio!* Close the gates before it is too late!"

Terror spoke mutely from the sick man's trembling lips, from his haunted eyes. The man from Mechar was less than a hundred feet from the gate now, but he had not once looked up to see what lay ahead of him. There was menace in the way he held on to his weapon.

"Hide, all of you," Prageur ordered. "Leave the gates wide. Some of you crouch to the wall. Some get on top and fall on him when he comes in. We'll take him alive!"

The men scrambled to obey, and in a few moments silence had fallen, all the men concealed, Cranston and Prageur close to the gate in order to be among the first to attack. The sand sounded under footsteps, and then the man from Mechar came through the opened gate.

Three Legionnaires who had been lying atop the wall launched themselves downward, one of them striking the intruder and carrying him to the sand with him. At the same moment men rushed at the man from Mechar from behind the gates and along the walls. The weapon he carried sounded only once; then it was wrenched from his grasp and he lay prone, unmoving, his *kepi* tipped off from his head.

It was over.

Then a long sob of horror rose from the men around the fallen Legionnaire, and there was a concerted backward movement. Cranston and Prageur pressed forward and saw. The face that had been hidden beneath the *kepi* was not a face. It was half exposed bone, half greenly rotting flesh! From it rose the odor of decaying flesh. The thing on the sand before them had been shot through the head a long time ago.

"*Mon Dieu!*" breathed Prageur, staring with wide

eyes, and abruptly turned away. "Tie it up and put it away somewhere—oh, bury it!"

Reluctantly, four of the men moved to obey.

Prageur looked uncertainly at Cranston. "Come along," he murmured.

He moved to where Gasparri was leaning weakly against the wall, shuddering at the memory this foul invasion had brought to fresh life.

"Come, Gasparri," said Prageur gently, taking him by the arm and leading the way to his quarters.

"All right," said Prageur without preliminary, "I'll grant you that story, Gasparri. Don't ask me what I think about it—I've got nothing to say. I want to ask you something."

He took a fragment of paper from his desk. Cranston recognized it as the paper upon which he had written the message from headquarters earlier in the day.

Prageur handed it to Gasparri. "Anything in that sound familiar to you?" he asked.

Gasparri took the paper wonderingly and read. Abruptly his expression changed. "*Dio*, yes!" he whispered harshly. "Tall thin man—sunken cheeks—livid scar on left cheek—gray hair," he read jerkingly, and looked up. "It's the man—the man who directs those dead ones!"

A mirthless smile appeared on Prageur's lips. "Get that, Cranston. Wire headquarters at once for detailed information on Prettweg and his documents."

Headquarters was vague. Their best was in a short wire that came two hours later:

PRETTWEG DANGEROUS LUNATIC WHO BELIEVES IN CERTAIN FORMULAE CONCERNING REANIMATION OF DEAD BODIES STOP ESCAPED SANITARIUM AND MADE FOR COAST BELIEVED IN ALGERIA SINCE HE HAD TALKED OF GOING TO COUNTRY WHERE CONFLICT WAS IN PROGRESS STOP GERMAN GOVERNMENT RELUCTANT TO RELAY MORE STOP SURETE BELIEVES PRETTWEG IS ON TO SOMETHING DEVELOPED IN GERMAN LABORATORIES

HAD ADDED DEVELOPMENTS FROM OWN DISEASED BRAIN STOP TAKE THIS MAN DEAD OR ALIVE.

The message gave scant satisfaction to Lieutenant Prageur. He studied it for a few moments in silence; then he dropped the paper with a mutter of impatience.

"Look here," he said, "reinforcements are due here almost any hour now, but we'll not wait. Forty of us march on Mechar tonight."

"Lieutenant, Sir!" protested Gasparri. "Those men go to something worse than death!"

"Leave that to me, Gasparri," snapped Prageur. "I'll lead them, and I'll lead most of them back here alive unless something goes seriously wrong. I don't think it will. Meanwhile, you keep a tight mouth about what you've told us; the men know that something's hitched up against them, and they're on edge.—You, Cranston, let Ellery take the telegraph; I've got a special use for you. Before you get ready, wire headquarters for three planes. We'll bomb Mechar, if necessary."

"But sir, why sacrifice your men?" asked Gasparri.

"There will be little sacrifice," said Prageur. "We'll fake an attack. As long as I'm not entirely convinced of what's going on at Mechar, I'm not taking chances either way. We'll lead them to attack us, and then retreat. One of us will have to get into the post, will have to fake death—and that may mean death, I don't know. But that's our only way of finding out what's going on in there, and we'll lose the least men that way."

Gasparri nodded.

"I've picked you for that, Cranston," said Prageur suddenly.

For a moment Cranston felt a sick feeling invade him. Then he dispelled it. "Very well, sir," he said.

"You know what it means?"

"Yes, sir."

"All right. You're the man. Granting Gasparri's story, your danger is two-fold—the directing genius, Prettweg, may discover that you're not really dead and may have you killed; and you may be trapped in the post when the bombing begins—if it becomes necessary to bomb. —All right, get ready. Send the wire for planes; I'll let the men know. Lehmann will be in charge until I come back—if I do."

The red globe of the sun was rising over the rim of the desert when the small troop of forty men sighted Mechar. A slight wind was blowing. Cranston and Prageur walked together at the side of the marching line.

"In case you don't come back?" asked the lieutenant soberly.

"Instructions for the disposal of what I own are in my quarters," replied Cranston curtly.

Prageur nodded. He took a small bottle from his pocket and gave it to Cranston. "Blood drawn just before we left," he said. "Spill it over your uniform and slit the cloth to resemble a bullet-hole. Take no more chances than you have to."

The lieutenant slowed up his men. Through his glasses he isolated a single figure high on the ramparts of Mechar, keeping carefully out of range.

"Prettweg, all right," he murmured, dropping his glasses. "I can make out the scar. Queer-looking devil."

Prageur ordered the men to break file, briefly repeated his earlier orders, spread them out, and ordered an advance. Cranston was well in the lead.

They were perhaps a hundred feet from the walls of Mechar when Prageur ordered them to fire. Prettweg had disappeared, and other figures had taken his place, carelessly exposing themselves to the fire of the Surdez men.

Immediately a volley of lead poured down on Lieutenant Prageur's men. And a second. But that was all, for at once the lieutenant ordered a retreat—indeed, some of the men had taken flight at the first volley, in accordance with Prageur's previous instructions. Cranston fell at the first volley, thinking fleetingly what supreme irony it would have been had he been shot and killed. Five other men fell with him. It was but the work of a few moments to uncork the bottle of blood and let it soak into his uniform, which he had split previously. Then he pushed the bottle deep into the sand.

From the corner of his eye he saw Prageur looking back; then he and the men were gone, and Cranston lay unmoving. He wondered what would happen now, warning himself not to move a muscle, to breathe shallowly. It seemed to him presently that hours were passing, but in a little while his ears caught the sound of activity behind the walls of the near-by post. The sun's heat had become terrific, and his hope that something would happen was intensified. Then he heard the gates of Mechar swing open.

From a carefully opened eye he saw a figure come forth alone, a revolver held menacingly in his hand. It was Doctor Prettweg. The old man was hatless, and his long white hair lent his face an air of benevolence, but nothing concealed the aura of diabolic evil about him—the crimson scar edged in blue and gray, the twisted mouth, the fierce, black eyes, loathsome and gloating. As Cranston watched, the doctor smiled at the sight of the dead men, his pleasure ghoulishly manifest. He turned and made irritable motions to someone beyond the gates.

The first corpse lay at a distance of twenty feet from Cranston. Against his better judgment, he continued to watch the mad doctor's approach. He saw him bend over the corpse, looking only casually at the body. Then Prettweg took a bottle from his pocket, opened it, and forced liquid into the dead man's mouth; he stood then, watching the corpse intently for a few moments, moving away only when he had seen—as Cranston, too, saw—*a faint, horrible movement from the dead man!*

Cranston restrained himself with a tremendous effort; he had seen something he knew to be impossible, yet it *was!* Prettweg came on to the second corpse, and Cranston, following him with his eyes, saw that the second Legionnaire was not dead, for he moved feebly at the doctor's approach. Could it be that the first of them had not been dead either?

But what doubts Cranston had were horribly, brutally dispelled; for the doctor, noticing the movement, hesitated, assured himself that the man was in no position to inflict injury, and then callously put a bullet through the Legionnaire's head. Cranston steeled himself to keep from giving voice to his fury and horror.

The bottle again, and once more liquid down a dead throat.

Inside him, Cranston was shuddering with loathing for this inhuman beast. But no emotion rose to the surface. He lay now with his lips fallen apart, his jaw hanging loosely agape, and despite the terrific strain, with his eyes wide and turned up against the sun. He was completely relaxed and motionless, his breathing restrained as much as possible.

Footsteps came toward him. He was aware suddenly of the doctor's hand grasping his neck, of long, clammy fingers touching his skin, and the strain of simulating death became almost unbearable. Then the bottle was at his mouth, and acrid liquid touching his tongue, and Prettweg's grip relaxed. Cranston's head fell against the sand, his one thought that his most difficult first stage was over, for the doctor had noticed nothing amiss. Cranston let the vile-tasting liquid in his mouth drool out upon the sand.

Prettweg was standing among the dead, his now malign face contemplating the nearest corpse, his hands clasped behind him much in the attitude of a physician in consultation. But his attitude underwent a subtle change—an unholy joy came into the old man's eyes, his mouth upcurved in evil triumph, and it seemed that psychic power flowed from his entire body. He extended his arms in an all-embracing gesture, and his hands beckoned. Now his eyes became hypnotic, his aspect momentarily benign, and in an almost suggestively benign voice, he spoke.

"Come now, my children. Rise and follow me."

If he had not been too concerned about his own safety, Cranston might have given himself away in his terror at what followed Prettweg's gentle words. For the dead began to move, stiffly, mechanically! One by one they rose and stood at attention, their dead faces turned expressionlessly toward the commanding figure whose medicine and mental magic had brought their bodies to ghastly life. Their arms hung limply at their sides, their heads were servilely bent, their eyes sought blankly for the directing force in the tall thin figure before them. Prettweg's gray hair, now ringed around by sunlight, lent him an ironical saintliness.

Cranston was the last to rise.

The doctor swept the six with his glance and looked back toward the fort.

Cranston felt deep within him the wish that the bombing planes might already be here. Let them come! he thought, but there was no sound in the air.

"Come," said Prettweg.

He strode away toward the open gates, and the incredibly animated dead moved after him, Cranston among them; he too, like those others, walking with the automatic precision of somnambulists. He suffered a momentary impulse to shoot the doctor as he walked along with his back to him, but a confused sense of honor, combined with the conviction that he must get inside Mechar as Prageur had ordered, to verify Gasparri's ghastly story, smothered his insane desire. His hands itched for the feel of his weapon, his entire body craved the maddening satisfying pleasure of shooting down this inhuman monster who had such terrible power over the dead.

But surely there was already enough verification? Or was it nightmare? Cranston was walking at the side of a Surdez Legionnaire, Franz Klast, a German whom he remembered as a good fellow. Cranston had seen him shot, had seen him fall—for an instant he fancied that he labored under a monstrous delusion, a mad dream from which he must shake himself; for Klast could not be dead, since he walked at his side, alive!

"Klast!" he whispered. "For God's sake, talk to me!"

There was no answer.

Cranston turned his head recklessly to the side and

looked at Klast, almost recoiling in horror at what he saw: the gaping hole in Klast's temple, torn by the fatal bullet fired by one of the dead from the walls of Mechar. The wound's black maw mocked Cranston.

Klast was walking sightlessly, animated by a ghastly force from beyond his body! A flash of intelligence gave sudden vision to Cranston—this madman Prettweg, controlling thousands upon thousands of dead, could ultimately sweep over the face of the earth, for his soldiers had conquered death, and were in themselves death. Death could sweep over the earth, could hold every fort, every outpost, every great city, could reign over all the country, directed by the cancerous brain of this madman! Far back, perhaps, some remote German scientist had manufactured this acrid elixir of life, but it took modern experimentation and the distorted mind of a madman to complete the frightful dreams of that earlier madman.

Cranston knew that every moment was vital. Prettweg must die, no matter what the cost.

Cranston looked guardedly ahead. Prettweg was just vanishing between the gates of Mechar. There was nothing to do but enter the post, and presently the shambling file of men passed through the gateway. Cranston heard the gates creaking shut behind him.

Prettweg must die! The thought drummed through his head. For without the doctor, the elixir was harmless—it needed the directing genius of this mad brain to complete the animation barely begun by the invention of a man now long forgotten. The font of this psychic power must be wiped out.

Now he stood, trapped within the walls of Mechar, he and a madman alone with a ghastly army of dead men. His companions had ceased to walk; they had stopped in their tracks, bodies wearily sagging. Cranston wondered whether Prettweg had removed that mysterious directing force. For a moment he allowed his lids to shut out the death around him, and strained his ears for the sound of motors humming in the sky.

There was nothing.

He looked cautiously around him. The quadrangle was cluttered with half-decayed bodies of living dead men, some of them skeletal remains of Tuaregs whose bodies had long lain exposed to the sun! They stood dumbly against the walls, they sat in doorways or on the sweltering sand, their arms dangling between their legs, they leaned on the ramparts, watching the sky through eyes destined soon to sink in decay into their sockets. And Cranston stood among them, isolated and alone.

Prettweg came suddenly from one of the doorways. He stood before them suddenly, and again Cranston was struck with the false saintliness lent him by the sun in his hair. The mad eyes were glowing again as from some inner vision, and presently the old man's lips parted and he began to speak, his voice slow and gentle, almost crooning, and yet alive with gloating power.

"Tomorrow, my children, we will take Surdez," he said. "There will be enough of us after that to move down the line upon post after post. This will be our country then. And afterward! I dream of what lies before us!"

The madness of him spoke from all his features. Once again Cranston conquered the desire to fire point-blank at the sinister face that seemed to hang in the arid heat of the quadrangle. For a moment Prettweg scanned their dead faces, and now his gaze lingered on Cranston. Could he suspect? Cranston wondered; or had he somehow seen Cranston's reckless movements of a few moments ago? But perhaps—more believable—he had in some way felt the mental force of another living mind! The thought froze Cranston with sudden fear; for surely this perceptive mind must have felt hate flowing toward him!

But Prettweg turned and began to walk away.

Instantly Cranston's fear broke into disorder. He whipped his revolver from its holster. But at the same instant, his dead comrades, galvanized into action by an unuttered command, flung themselves upon him. His revolver cracked, and a spurt of sand fanned into the air to show Cranston how far his bullet had gone from its mark. Then Mechar and Surdez dead were upon him, grappling with him, struggling clumsily for his weapon, and others were pouring toward him from all sides. He felt their rotting arms wrapped about his limbs, felt their decaying fingers and hardness of fleshless bones at his neck.

Revolvers cracked. He felt searing pains in his leg and shoulder, and went down under the mass of nauseating dead things. Still he fought. He had a momentary glimpse of Prettweg looking sardonically on, his mad face now afire with insane hatred, and saw that the doctor had a revolver ready to fire at Cranston's first appearance. With a pain-racking effort, he shifted under the struggling mass of dead, aimed wildly, and fired—once, twice, three times.

Abruptly the struggle ebbed away.

And died.

Cranston lay in the midst of a ghastly mound of dead flesh. He felt nausea assailing him, buried his face in his hands, and waited for death. Nothing happened. A moment passed and he looked up, pulling himself from the decaying flesh that pinned him down. He saw bodies fall from the ramparts like stones, saw the living dead in doorways sag and sprawl into the sand, saw the standing dead topple and collapse like empty sacks. And then he saw Doctor Prettweg against the wall of a near-by building sag gently and slide downward to the sand.

He writhed on the ground, shuddered, and died. Like a giant bird he lay, his white coat spread beneath his arms like the too feeble wings of some predatory creature, his long hair fanned away from his head, his arms outspread, his fingers twisted into the hot sand.

Cranston came unsteadily to his feet, his brain awhirl, the wounds in his leg and shoulder flaming with pain. It was over. The horror of living dead men had passed with Prettweg's death. Pray God it would never come again!

Abruptly he heard a familiar sound—the steady drone

of racing planes. His mind struggled to free itself from the horror of his surroundings. He must escape before the planes got there—but he alone could not open the gates in so short a time.

Then his mind cleared.

He began to run wildly toward the central building. Somewhere there must be the Foreign Legion flag. A glance told him it was no longer on the ramparts, the dead invaders having doubtless removed it. If he could find the flag or, failing to find it, if he could get to the roof and signal them—for they must know he was here. He could be certain they had first stopped at Surdez for instructions from Prageur.

He emerged on the roof to see the planes almost directly above, circling uncertainly about. At the same moment he caught sight of the flag, crumpled carelessly into a corner. He ran and gathered it up in his arms, mounted the highest wall, and there let the flag stream out behind him as he ran along the perilous rampart.

The leading plane banked and another dipped toward him. He had a sickening conviction that machine-gun fire would sweep him from the wall, but the plane veered away. They had seen and understood. Cranston jumped to the roof again and saw men from Surdez coming across the dunes beyond the gate. For a moment only he stood there; then he felt again the increasing pain of his wounds and he toppled forward, lost in an unfathomable sea of blackness.

Cranston was back at his telegraph next day when Lieutenant Prageur entered, in his hand a report to be dispatched to headquarters. As he left the room he turned.

"By the way, you may depend upon promotion," he said crisply, smiling. Then he was gone.

With grim lips Cranston tapped out the report to headquarters:

THE GARRISON AT MECHAR WAS WIPED OUT BY A SUR-
PRISE ATTACK OF TUAREGS STOP HELD FORT AND WIPED
OUT FIFTY-FOUR OF OUR MEN STOP SURPRISE ATTACK

BY REMAINDER OF OUR MEN YESTERDAY TOOK MECHAR
STOP TUAREGS FLED STOP DR OTTO PRETTWEG ABOUT
WHOM WIRE RECEIVED TWO DAYS AGO WAS KILLED
IN ACTION AT MECHAR STOP HAD JOINED AND WAS
LEADING TUAREG ATTACK STOP RELAY TO GERMAN
AUTHORITIES.

That was all. It did not need Lieutenant Prageur's
subsequent words to convince Cranston of the fitness of
the message. "You remember how I took Gasparri's
story at first. Can you imagine how they'd take it at
headquarters, Cranston?"

THE SOLID MULDOON

Rudyard Kipling

Did ye see John Malone, wid his shinin', brand-new
    hat?
Did ye see how he walked like a grand aristocrat?
There was flags an' banners wavin' high, an' dhress
    and shtyle were shown,
But the best av all the company was Misther John Ma-
    lone.

John Malone

There had been a royal dog-fight in the ravine at the
back of the rifle-butts, between Learoyd's *Jock* and
Ortheris's *Blue Rot*—both mongrel Rampur hounds,
chiefly ribs and teeth. It lasted for twenty happy, howling minutes, and then *Blue Rot* collapsed and Ortheris
paid Learoyd three rupees, and we were all very thirsty.
A dog-fight is a most heating entertainment, quite apart
from the shouting, because Rampurs fight over a couple
of acres of ground. Later, when the sound of belt-
badges clicking against the necks of beer-bottles had
died away, conversation drifted from dog to man-fights
of all kinds. Humans resemble red-deer in some respects. Any talk of fighting seems to wake up a sort of
imp in their breasts, and they bell one to the other,
exactly like challenging bucks. This is noticeable even
in men who consider themselves superior to Privates of

the Line: it shows the Refining Influence of Civilization and the March of Progress.

Tale provoked tale, and each tale more beer. Even dreamy Learoyd's eyes began to brighten, and he unburdened himself of a long history in which a trip to Malham Cove, a girl at Pateley Brigg, a ganger, himself and a pair of clogs were mixed in drawling tangle.

"An' so Ah coot's yead oppen from t' chin to t' hair, an' he was abed for t' matter o' a month," concluded Learoyd, pensively.

Mulvaney came out of a revery—he was lying down—and flourished his heels in the air. "You're a man, Learoyd," said he, critically, "but you've only fought wid men, an' that's an ivry-day expayrience; but I've stud up to a ghost, an' that was *not* an ivry-day expayrience."

"No?" said Ortheris, throwing a cork at him. "You get up an' address the 'ouse—you an' yer expayriences. Is it a bigger one nor usual?"

" 'Twas the livin' trut'!" answered Mulvaney, stretching out a huge arm and catching Ortheris by the collar. "Now where are ye, me son? Will ye take the wurrud av the Lorrd out av my mouth another time?" He shook him to emphasize the question.

"No, somethin' else, though," said Ortheris, making a dash at Mulvaney's pipe, capturing it and holding it at arm's length; "I'll chuck it acrost the ditch if you don't let me go!"

"You maraudin' hathen! 'Tis the only cutty I iver loved. Handle her tinder or I'll chuck *you* acrost the nullah. If that poipe was bruk—Ah! Give her back to me, sorr!"

Ortheris had passed the treasure to my hand. It was an absolutely perfect clay, as shiny as the black ball at Pool. I took it reverently, but I was firm.

"Will you tell us about the ghost-fight if I do?" I said.

"Is ut the shtory that's troublin' you? Av course I will. I mint to all along. I was only gettin' at ut my own way, as Popp Doggle said whin they found him thrying to ram a cartridge down the muzzle. Orth'ris, fall away!"

He released the little Londoner, took back his pipe, filled it, and his eyes twinkled. He has the most eloquent eyes of any one that I know.

"Did I iver tell you," he began, "that I was wanst the divil of a man?"

"You did," said Learoyd, with a childish gravity that made Ortheris yell with laughter, for Mulvaney was always impressing upon us his great merits in the old days.

"Did I iver tell you," Mulvaney continued, calmly, "that I was wanst more av a divil than I am now?"

"Mer—ria! You don't mean it?" said Ortheris.

"Whin I was Corp'ril—I was rejuced aftherward—but, as I say, *whin* I was Corp'ril, I was a divil of a man."

He was silent for nearly a minute, while his mind rummaged among old memories and his eye glowed. He bit upon the pipe-stem and charged into his tale.

"Eyah! They was great times. I'm ould now; me hide's wore off in patches; sinthrygo has disconceited me, an' I'm a married man tu. But I've had my day— I've had my day, an' nothin' can take away the taste av that! Oh my time past, whin I put me fut through ivry livin' wan av the Tin Commandmints between Revelly and Lights Out, blew the froth off a pewter, wiped me moustache wid the back av me hand, an' slept on ut all as quiet as a little child! But ut's over—ut's over, an' 'twill niver come back to me; not though I prayed for a week av Sundays. Was there *any* wan in the Ould Rig'mint to touch Corp'ril Terence Mulvaney whin that same was turned out for sedukshin? I niver met him. Ivry woman that was not a witch was worth the runnin' afther in those days, an' ivry man was my dearest frind or—I had stripped to him an' we knew which was the better av the tu.

"Whin I was Corp'ril I wud not ha' changed wid the Colonel—no, nor yet the Commandherin-Chief. I wud be a Sargint. There was nothin' I wud not be! Mother av Hivin, look at me! Fwhat am I *now*?

"We was quartered in a big cantonmint—'tis no manner av use namin' names, for ut might give the barricks disrepitation—an' I was the Imperor av the Earth to my own mind, an' wan or tu women thought the same. Small blame to thim. Afther we had lain there a year, Bragin, the Color Sargint av E Comp'ny, wint an' took a wife that was lady's maid to some big lady in the Station. She's dead now is Annie Bragin—died in child-bed at Kirpa Tal, or ut may ha' been Almorah—seven—nine years gone, an' Bragin he married agin. But she was a pretty woman whin Bragin inthrojuced her to cantonmint society. She had eyes like the brown av the butterfly's wing whin the sun catches ut, an' a waist no thicker than my arm, an' a little sof' button av a mouth I would ha' gone through all Asia bristlin' wid bay'nits to get the kiss av. An' her hair was as long as the tail av the Colonel's charger—forgive me mentionin' that blunderin' baste in the same mouthful with Annie Bragin—but 'twas all shpun gold, an' time was when ut was more than di'monds to me. There was niver pretty woman yet, an' I've had thruck wid a few, cud open the door to Annie Bragin.

" 'Twas in the Cath'lic Chapel I saw her first, me oi rolling round as usual to see fwhat was to be seen. 'You're too good for Bragin, my love,' thinks I to mesilf, 'but that's a mistake I can put straight, or my name is not Terence Mulvaney.'

"Now take my wurrd for ut, you Orth'ris there an' Learoyd, an' kape out av the Married Quarters—as I did not. No good iver comes av ut, an' there's always the chance av your bein' found wid your face in the dirt, a long picket in the back av your head, an' your hands playing the fifes on the tread av another man's doorstep. 'Twas so we found O'Hara, he that Rafferty killed six years gone, when he wint to his death wid his hair oiled, whistlin' *Larry O'Rourke* betune his teeth. Kape out av the Married Quarters, I say, as I did not. 'Tis onwholesim, 'tis dangerous an' 'tis ivrything else that's bad, but—O my sowl, 'tis swate while ut lasts!

"I was always hangin' about there whin I was off duty an' Bragin wasn't, but niver a sweet word beyon' ordinar' did I get from Annie Bragin. ' 'Tis the pervarsity av the sect,' sez I to mesilf, an' gave my cap another cock on my head an' straightened my back—'twas the back av a Dhrum Major in those days—an' wint off as tho' I did not care, wid all the women in the Married Quarters laughin'. I was persuaded—most bhoys *are* I'm thinkin' —that no women born uv woman cud stand against me av I hild up my little finger. I had reason for thinkin' that way—till I met Annie Bragin.

"Time an' agin whin I was blandandherin' in the dusk a man wud go past me as quiet as a cat. 'That's quare,' thinks I, 'for I am, or I should be, the only man in these parts. Now what divilment can Annie be up to?' Thin I called mysilf a blayguard for thinkin' such things; but I thought thim all the same. An' that, mark you, is the way av a man.

"Wan evenin' I said: 'Mrs. Bragin, manin' no disrespect to you, who is that Corp'ril man'—I had seen the stripes though I cud niver get sight av his face—'who is that Corp'ril man comes in always whin I'm goin' away?'

" 'Mother av God!' sez she, turnin' as white as my belt; 'have *you* seen him too?'

" 'Seen him!' sez I; 'av coorse I have. Did ye want me not to see him, for'—we were standin' talkin' in the dhark, outside the veranda av Bragin's quarters—'you'd betther tell me to shut me eyes. Onless I'm mistaken, he's come now.'

"An', sure enough, the Corp'ril man was walkin' to us, hangin' his head down as though he was ashamed av himsilf.

" 'Good-night, Mrs. Bragin,' sez I, very cool; ' 'tis not for me to interfere wid your *a-moors;* but you might manage some things wid more dacincy. I'm off to canteen,' I sez.

"I turned on my heel an' wint away, swearin' I wud give that man a dhressin' that wud shtop him messin' about the Married Quarters for a month an' a week. I had not tuk ten paces before Annie Bragin was hangin' on to my arm, an' I cud feel that she was shakin' all over.

" 'Stay wid me, Mister Mulvaney,' sez she; 'you're flesh an' blood, at the least—are ye not?'

" 'I'm *all* that,' sez I, an' my anger wint away in a flash. 'Will I want to be asked twice, Annie?'

"Wid that I slipped my arm round her waist, for, begad, I fancied she had surrendered at discretion, an' the honors av war were mine.

" 'Fwhat nonsinse is this?' sez she, dhrawin' hersilf up on the tips av her dear little toes. 'Wid the mother's milk not dhry on your impident mouth? Let go!' she sez.

" 'Did ye not say just now that I was flesh and blood?' sez I. 'I have not changed since,' I sez; an' I kep my arm where ut was.

" 'Your arms to yourself!' sez she, an' her eyes sparkild.

" 'Sure, 'tis only human nature,' sez I, an' I kep' my arm where ut was.

" 'Nature or no nature,' sez she, 'you take your arm away or I'll tell Bragin, an' he'll alter the nature av your head. Fwhat d'you take me for?' she sez.

" 'A woman,' sez I; 'the prettiest in barricks.'

" 'A *wife*,' sez she; 'the straightest in cantonmints!'

"Wid that I dropped my arm, fell back tu paces, an' saluted, for I saw that she mint fwhat she said."

"Then you know something that some men would give a good deal to be certain of. How could you tell?" I demanded in the interests of Science.

"Watch the hand," said Mulvaney; "av she shut her hand tight, thumb down over the knuckle, take up your hat an' go. You'll only make a fool av yoursilf av you shtay. But av the hand lies opin on the lap, or av you see her thryin' to shut ut, and she can't,—go on! She's not past reasonin' wid.

"Well, as I was sayin', I fell back, saluted, an' was goin' away.

" 'Shtay wid me,' she sez. 'Look! He's comin' again.'

"She pointed to the veranda, an' by the Hoight av Impartininnce, the Corp'ril man was comin' out av Bragin's quarters.

" 'He's done that these five evenin's past,' sez Annie Bragin. 'Oh, fwhat will I do!'

" 'He'll not do ut again,' sez I, for I was fightin' mad.

"Kape way from a man that has been a thrifle crossed in love till the fever's died down. He rages like a brute beast.

"I wint up to the man in the veranda, manin' as sure as I sit, to knock the life out av him. He slipped into the open. 'Fwhat are you doin' philanderin' about here, ye scum av the gutter?' sez I polite, to give him his warnin', for I wanted him ready.

"He never lifted his head, but sez, all mournful an' melancolius, as if he thought I wud be sorry for him: 'I can't find her,' sez he.

" 'My troth,' sez I, 'you've lived too long—you an' your seekin's an' findin's in a dacint married woman's quarters! Hould up your head, ye frozen thief av Genesis,' sez I, 'an' you'll find all you want an' more!'

"But he niver hild up, an' I let go from the shoulder to where the hair is short over the eyebrows.

" 'That'll do your business,' sez I, but it nearly did mine instid. I put my bodyweight behind the blow, but I hit nothing at all, an' near put my shouldther out. The Corp'ril man was not there, an' Annie Bragin, who had been watchin' from the veranda, throws up her heels, an' carries on like a cock whin his neck's wrung by the dhrummer-bhoy. I wint back to her, for a livin' woman, an' a woman like Annie Bragin, is more than a p'rade groun' full av ghosts. I'd never seen a woman faint before, an' I stud like a shtuck calf, askin' her whether she was dead, an' prayin' her for the love av me, an' the love av her husband, an' the love av the Virgin, to opin her blessed eyes again, an' callin' mesilf all the names undher the canopy av Hivin for plaguin' her wud my miserable *a-moors* whin I ought to ha' stud betune her an' this Corp'ril man that had lost the number av his mess.

"I misremember fwhat nonsinse I said, but I was not so far gone that I cud not hear a fut on the dirt outside. 'Twas Bragin comin' in, an' by the same token Annie was comin' to. I jumped to the far end av the veranda an' looked as if butter wudn't melt in my mouth. But Mrs. Quinn, the Quarter-Master's wife that was, had tould Bragin about my hangin' round Annie.

" 'I'm not pleased wid you, Mulvaney,' sez Bragin, unbucklin' his sword, for he had been on duty.

" 'That's bad hearin',' I sez, an' I knew that the pickets were dhriven in. 'What for, Sargint?' sez I.

" 'Come outside,' sez he, 'an' I'll show you why.'

" 'I'm willin',' I sez; 'but my stripes are none so ould that I can afford to lose thim. Tell me now, *who* do I go out wid?' sez I.

"He was a quick man an' just, an' saw fwhat I wud be afther. 'Wid Mrs. Bragin's husband,' sez he. He might ha' known by me askin' that favor that I had done him no wrong.

"We wint to the back av the arsenal, an' I stripped to him, an' for ten minutes 'twas all I cud do to prevent him killin' himself against my fistes. He was mad as a dumb dog—just frothing wid rage; but he had no chanst wid me in reach, or learnin', or anything else.

" 'Will ye hear reason?' sez I, whin his first wind was run out.

" 'Not whoile I can see,' sez he. Wid that I gave him both, one after the other smash through the low gyard that he'd been taught whin he was a boy, an' the eyebrow shut down on the cheek-bone like the wing av a sick crow.

" 'Will you hear reason now, ye brave man?' sez I.

" 'Not whoile I can speak,' sez he, staggerin' up blind as a stump. I was loath to do ut, but I wint round an' swung into the jaw side-on an' shifted ut a half pace to the lef'.

" 'Will ye hear reason now?' sez I; 'I can't keep my timper much longer, an' 'tis I will hurt you.'

" 'Not whoile I can stand,' he mumbles out av one corner av his mouth. So I closed an' threw him—blind, dumb, an' sick, an' jammed the jaw straight.

" 'You're an ould fool, *Mister* Bragin,' sez I.

" 'You're a young thief,' sez he, 'an' you've bruk my heart, you an' Annie betune you!'

"Thin he began cryin' like a child as he lay. I was sorry as I had niver been before. 'Tis an awful thing to see a strong man cry.

" 'I'll swear on the Cross!' sez I.

" 'I care for none av your oaths,' sez he.

" 'Come back to your quarters,' sez I, 'an' if you don't believe the livin', begad, you shall listen to the dead,' I sez.

"I hoisted him an' tuk him back to his quarters. 'Mrs. Bragin,' sez I, 'here's a man that you can cure quicker than me.'

" 'You've shamed me before my wife,' he whimpers.

" 'Have I so?' sez I. 'By the look on Mrs. Bragin's face I think I'm for a dhressin'-down worse than I gave you.'

"An' I was! Annie Bragin was woild wid indignation. There was not a name that a dacint woman cud use that was not given my way. I've had my Colonel walk roun' me like a cooper roun' a cask for fifteen minutes in Ord'ly room, bekaze I wint into the Corner Shop an' unstrapped lewnatic; but all that I iver tuk from his rasp of a tongue was ginger-pop to fwhat Annie tould me. An' that, mark you, is the way av a woman.

"Whin ut was done for want av breath, an' Annie was bendin' over her husband, I sez: ' 'Tis all thrue, an' I'm a blayguard an' you're an honest woman; but will you tell him of wan service that I did you?'

"As I finished speakin' the Corp'ril man came up to the veranda, an' Annie Bragin shquealed. The moon was up, an' we cud see his face.

" 'I can't find her,' sez the Corp'ril man, an' wint out like the puff av a candle.

" 'Saints stand betune us an' evil!' sez Bragin, crossin' himself; 'that's Flahy av the Tyrone.'

" 'Who was he?' I sez, 'for he has given me a dale av fightin' this day.'

"Bragin tould us that Flahy was a Corp'ril who lost his wife av cholera in those quarters three years gone, an' wint mad, an' *walked* afther they buried him, huntin' for her.

" 'Well,' sez I to Bragin, 'he's been hookin' out av Purgathory to kape company wid Mrs. Bragin ivry evenin' for the last fortnight. You may tell Mrs. Quinn, wid my love, for I know that she's been talkin' to you, an' you've been listenin', that she ought to ondherstand the differ 'twixt a man an' a ghost. She's had three husbands,' sez I, 'an' *you*'ve got a wife too good for you. Instid av which you lave her to be boddered by ghosts an'—an' all manner av evil spirruts. I'll niver go talkin' in the way av politeness to a man's wife again. Goodnight to you both,' sez I; an' wid that I wint away, havin' fought wid woman, man and Divil all in the heart av an hour. By the same token I gave Father Victor wan rupee to say a mass for Flahy's soul, me havin' discommoded him by shticking my fist into his systim."

"Your ideas of politeness seem rather large, Mulvaney," I said.

"That's as you look at ut," said Mulvaney, calmly; "Annie Bragin niver cared for me. For all that, I did not want to leave anything behin' me that Bragin could take hould av to be angry wid her about—whin an honust wurrd cud ha' cleared all up. There's nothing like opin-speakin'. Orth'ris, ye scutt, let me put me oi to that bottle, for my throat's as dhry as whin I thought I wud get a kiss from Annie Bragin. An' that's fourteen years gone! Eyah! Cork's own city an' the blue sky above ut—an' the times that was—the times that was!"

NIGHT ON
MISPEC MOOR

Larry Niven

In predawn darkness the battle began to take shape.
Helicopters circled, carrying newstapers and monitors.
Below, the two armies jockeyed for position. They dared
not meet before dawn. The monitors would declare a
mistrial and fine both sides heavily.

In the red dawn the battle began. Scout groups probed
each other's skills. The weapons were identical on both
sides: heavy swords with big basket hilts. Only the men
themselves differed in skill and strength.

By noon the battle had concentrated on a bare plain
strewn with white boulders and a few tight circles of
green Seredan vegetation. The warriors moved in little
clumps. Where they met, the yellow dirt was stained
red, and cameras in the helicopters caught it all for
public viewing.

Days were short in Sereda. For some, today was not
short enough.

As Sereda's orange dwarf sun dropped toward the
horizon, the battle had become a massacre with the
Greys at the wrong end. When Tomás Vatch could no
longer hold a sword, he ran. Other Greys had fled, and
Amber soldiers streamed after them, yelling. Vatch ran
with blood flowing down his sword arm and dripping
from his fingertips. He was falling behind, and the
Ambers were coming close.

He turned sharp left and kept running. The swarm moved north, toward the edge of Mispec Moor, toward civilization. Alone, he had a chance. The Ambers would not concern themselves with a single fleeing man.

But one did. One golden-skinned red-haired man shouted something, waved his sword in a circle over his head, and followed.

An ancient glacier had dropped blocks of limestone and granite all over this flat, barren region. The biggest rock in sight was twice the height of a man and wider than it was tall. Vatch ran toward it. He had not yet begun to wonder how he would climb it.

He moved in a quick unbalanced stumble now, his sword and his medical kit bouncing awkwardly at either side. He had dropped the sword once already, when a blade had sliced into him just under the armpit. The heavy-shouldered warrior had paused to gloat, and Vatch had caught the falling sword in his left hand and jabbed upward. Now he cradled his right arm in his left to keep it from flopping loose.

He'd reached the rock.

It was split wide open down the middle.

The red-haired Amber came on like an exuberant child. Vatch had noticed him early in the battle. He'd fought that way too, laughing and slashing about him with playful enthusiasm. Vatch thought this attitude inappropriate to so serious a matter as war.

Vatch stepped into the mammoth crack, set his back to one side and his feet to the other, and began to work his way up. Recent wounds opened, and blood flowed down the rock. Vatch went on, concentrating on the placement of his feet, trying not to wonder what would happen if the Amber caught him halfway up.

The red-haired man arrived, blowing and laughing, and found Vatch high above him. He reached up with his sword. Vatch, braced awkwardly between two lips of granite, felt the sharp tip poking him in the small of the back. The Amber was standing on tiptoe; he could reach no further.

The top was flat. Vatch rolled over on his belly and

rested. The world whirled around him. He had lost much blood.

And he couldn't afford this. He forced himself to sit up and look around. Where was the enemy?

A rock whizzed past his head. A voice bellowed, "Rammer! Give my regards to the nightwalkers!"

Vatch heard running footsteps, fading. He stood up.

Omicron 2 Eridani was a wide, distorted red blob on the flat horizon. Vatch could see far across Mispec Moor. He found his erstwhile enemy jogging north. Far ahead of him swarmed the army of the Ambers. Above them, the helicopters were bright motes.

Vatch smiled and dropped back to prone position. He was safe. No man, woman or child of Sereda would stay at night upon Mispec Moor.

On Sereda war is a heavily supervised institution. Battles are fought with agreed-upon weaponry. Strategy lies in getting the enemy to agree to the right weapons. This day the Greys had been out-strategied. The Ambers had the better swordsmen.

Seredan war set no limits to the use of medicine, provided that nothing in a medical kit could be used as a weapon, and provided that all medicines must be carried by fighting men. The convention was advantageous to an outworld mercenary.

Vatch fumbled the medical kit open, one-handed. He suspected that the gathering darkness was partly in his own eyes. But the Spectrum Cure was there: a soft plastic bottle, half-liter size, with a spray hypo and a pistol grip attached. Vatch pressure-injected himself, put the bottle carefully away and let himself roll over on his back.

The first effect was a tingling all through him.

Then his wounds stopped bleeding.

Then they closed.

His fatigue began to recede.

Vatch smiled up at the darkening sky. He'd be paid high for this day's work. His sword arm wasn't very good; he'd thought that Sereda's lower gravity would make a mighty warrior of him, but that hadn't worked out. But this Spectrum Cure was tremendous stuff! The biochemists of Miramon Lluagor had formulated it. It was ten years old there, and brand new on Sereda, and the other worlds of the Léshy circuit probably hadn't even heard of it yet. At the start of the battle he'd had enough to inject forty men, to heal them of any wound or disease, as long as their hearts still beat to distribute the stuff. The bottle was two-thirds empty now. He'd done a fair day's work, turning casualties back into fighting men while the battle raged about him.

The only adverse effect of Spectrum Cure began to show itself. Hunger. His belly was a yawning pit. Healing took metabolic energy. Tomás Vatch sat up convulsively and looked about him.

The damp air of Sereda was turning to mist around the foot of the rock.

He let himself over the lip, hung by his fingertips, and dropped. His belly was making grinding noises and sending signals of desperation. He had not eaten since early this morning. He set off at a brisk walk toward the nearest possible source of dinner; the battleground.

Twilight was fading rapidly. The mist crept over the ground like a soggy blanket. There were patches of grass-green on the yellow dirt, far apart, each several feet across and sharply bordered, each with a high yellow-tipped stalk springing from the center. The mist covered these too. Soon Vatch could see only a few blossoms like frilly yellow morels hovering at waist level, and shadowy white boulders looming like ghosts around him. His passage set up swirling currents.

Like most of the rammers, the men who travel the worlds of the Léshy circuit, Vatch had read the fantasies of James Branch Cabell. The early interstellar scout who discovered these worlds four hundred years ago had read Cabell. Toupan, Miramon Lluagor, Sereda, Horvendile, Koschei: the powerful though mortal Léshy of Cabell's fantasies had become five worlds circling five suns in a bent ring, with Earth and Sol making a sixth. Those who settled the Léshy worlds had followed tradition in the naming of names. A man who had read Cabell could guess the nature of a place from its name alone.

The Mispec Moor of Cabell's writings had been a place of supernatural mystery, a place where reality was vague and higher realities showed through.

Mispec Moor on Sereda had just that vague look, with darkness falling over waist-high mist and shadowy boulders looming above; and Vatch now remembered that this Mispec Moor had a complimentary set of legends. Sereda's people did not call them vampires or ghouls, but the fearsome nightwalkers of Mispec Moor seemed a combination of the two legends: things that had been men, whose bite would turn living or dead alike into more nightwalkers. They could survive ordinary weapons, but a silver bullet would stop them, especially if it had been dumdummed by a cross cut into its nose.

Naturally Tomás Vatch carried no silver bullets and no gun. He was lucky to be carrying a flashlight. He had not expected to be out at night, but the flashlight was part of his kit. He had often needed light to perform his secondary battlefield duties.

As he neared the place of the fallen soldiers he thought he saw motion in the mist. He raised the flashlight high over his head and drew his sword.

Thin shapes scampered away from the light. Tomás jumped violently—and then he recognized lopers, the doglike scavengers of Sereda. He kept his sword in hand. The lopers kept their distance, and he let them be. They were here for the same reason he was, he thought with no amusement at all.

Some soldiers carried bread or rolls of hard candy into battle.

Some of these never ate their provisions.

It was a repugnant task, this searching of dead men. He found the body of Robroy Tanner, who had come with him to Sereda aboard a Lluagorian ramship; and he cried, out here where nobody could see him. But he continued to search. He was savagely hungry.

The lopers had been at some of the bodies. More than once he was tempted to end his whimsical truce. The lopers still moved at the periphery of his vision. They seemed shy of the light, but would that last? Certainly the legends pointed to something dangerous on Mispec Moor. Could the lopers themselves be subject to something like rabies?

He found hard candy, and he found two canteens, both nearly empty. He sucked the candy a roll at a time, his cheeks puffed out like a squirrel's. Presently he found the slashed corpse of a man he had eaten breakfast with. *Jackpot.* He had watched Erwin Mudd take a block of stew from a freezer and double-wrap it in plastic bags, just before they entered the battlefield.

The stew was there. Vatch ate it as it was, cold, and was grateful for it.

Motion in the mist made him look up.

Two shadows were coming toward him. They were much bigger than lopers . . . and man-shaped.

Vatch stood up and called, "Hello?"

They came on, taking shape as they neared. A third blurred shadow congealed behind them. They had not answered. Annoyed, Vatch swung the flashlight beam toward them.

The light caught them full. Vatch held it steady, staring, not believing. Then, still not believing, he screamed and ran.

There is a way a healthy man can pace himself so that he can jog for hours across flat land, especially on a low-gravity world like Sereda. Tomás Vatch had that skill.

But now he ran like a mad sprinter, in sheer panic, his chest heaving, his legs burning. It was a minute or so before he thought to turn off the flashlight so that the things could not follow its glow. It was much longer before he could work up the courage to look back.

One of the things was following him.

He did not think to stand and fight. He had seen it too clearly. It was a corpse, weeks dead. He thought of turning toward the city, but the city was a good distance away; and now he remembered that they locked the gates at night. The first time he had seen them do that, he had asked why, and a native policeman had told him of the nightwalkers. He had had to hear the story from other sources before he knew that he was not being played for a gullible outworlder.

So he did not turn toward the city. He turned toward the rock that had been his refuge once before.

The thing followed. It moved at a fast walk; but, where Tomás Vatch had to stop and rest with his hands on his knees to catch his breath before he ran on, the nightwalker never stopped at all. It was a distant shadow when he reached the rock; but his haste was such that he skinned his shoulders working himself up the crack.

The top of the rock was still warm from daylight. Vatch lay on his back and felt the joy of breathing. The stars were clear and bright above him. There was no sound at all.

But when his breathing quieted he heard heavy, uneven footsteps.

He looked over the edge of the rock.

The nightwalker came wading through the mist in a wobbling shuffle. It walked like it would fall down at every step, and its feet fell joltingly hard. Yet it came fast. Its bulging eyes stared back into Vatch's flashlight.

Why should a nightwalker care if it sprained its ankles at every step? It was dead, dead and bloated. It still wore a soldier's kilt in green plaid, the sign of a commercial war now two weeks old. Above the broad belt a slashed belly wound gaped wide.

Vatch examined the corpse with self-conscious care. The only way he knew to quell his panic was to put his mind to work. He searched for evidence that this nightwalker was not what it seemed, that it was something else, a native life form, say, with a gift of mimickry.

It stood at the base of the rock, looking up with dull eyes and slack mouth. A walking dead man.

There was more motion in the mist . . . and two lopers came lurching up to stand near the nightwalker.

When Vatch threw the light on them they stared back unblinking. Presently Vatch realized why. They, too, were dead.

The policeman had told him that too: that nightwalkers could take the form of lopers and other things.

He had believed very little of what he had heard . . . and now he was trying frantically to remember details. They were not dangerous in daytime; hadn't he heard that? Then if he could hold out here till morning, he would be safe. He could return to the city.

But three more man-shapes were coming to join the first.

And the first was clawing at the side of the rock, trying to find purchase for its fingers. It moved along the base, scraping at the rough side. It entered the crack . . .

Three shadows came out of the mist to join their brother. One wore the familiar plaid kilt from the two-week-old battle. One wore a businessman's tunic; its white hair had come away in patches, taking scalp with it. The third had been a small, slender woman, judging from her dress and her long yellow hair.

They clawed at the rock. They began to spread out along the base.

And Vatch backed away from the edge and sat down.

What the hell was this? Legends like this had been left behind on Earth! Dead men did not walk, not without help. Ordinarily they just *lay* there. What was different about Sereda? What kind of biology could fit—? Vatch shook his head violently. The question was nonsense. This was fantasy, and he was in it.

Yet his mind clutched for explanations:

Costumes? Suppose a group of Seredans had something to hide out here. (What?) A guard of four in dreadful costumes might hold off a whole city, once the legend of the nightwalker was established. (But the legend was a century old. Never mind, the legend could have come first.) Anyone who came close enough to see the fraud could quietly disappear. (Costume and makeup? That gaping putrescent belly wound!)

Out of the crack in the rock came a fantasy arm, the bone showing through the forearm, the first joints missing on all the ragged fingers. Vatch froze. (*Costume?*) The other arm came up, and then a dead slack face. The smell reached him . . .

Vatch unfroze very suddenly, snatched up his sword and struck overhand. He split the skull to the chin.

The nightwalker was still trying to pull itself up.

Vatch struck at the arms. He severed one elbow, then the other, and the nightwalker dropped away without a cry.

Vatch began to shudder. He couldn't stop the spasms; he could only wait until they passed. He was beginning to understand how the fantasy would end. When the horror became too great, when he could stand it no longer, he would leap screaming to the ground and try to kill them all. And his sword would not be enough.

It was real! The dead forearms lay near his feet!

Fantasy!

Real!

Wait, wait. A fantasy was something that categorically could not happen. It was *always* a story, *always* something that originated in a man's mind. Could he be starring in somebody's fantasy?

This, a form of entertainment? Then it had holovision beat hands down. But Vatch knew of no world that had the technology to create such a total-experience entertainment, complete with what had to be ersatz memories! No world had that, let alone backward Sereda!

Wait. Was he really on Sereda? Was the date really 2731? Or was he living through some kind of Gothic historical?

Was he even Tomás Vatch the rammer? Rammer was a high-prestige career. Someone might well have paid for the illusion that he was a rammer . . . and if he had, someone had gotten more than he had bargained for. They'd pull him out of his total-environment cubical or theater in total catatonic withdrawal, if Tomás Vatch didn't get a grip on himself.

Wait. Was that motion in the mist, off toward the battlefield?

Or more of his runaway imagination? But no, the mist was a curdling, swirling line, aimed at his rock.

That almost did it. He almost leapt from the rock and ran. If the city gates were closed he'd run right up the walls . . . But he waited. In a minute he'd know for sure, one way or another.

Within the crack the one he had struck sat slumped with its head bowed, disconsolate or truly dead. The other three seemed to be accomplishing very little.

The dead men from the battlefield streamed toward Vatch's place of refuge. They wore kilts of grey and amber. Less than a hundred of them, casualties in a war between two medium-sized companies, a war which would not have been fought at all if the cost could not be partly defrayed by holovision rights. When they came close Vatch began to recognize individuals. There was Erwin Mudd, whose stew he had stolen. There was Roy Tanner the Lluagorian, the rammer, the medic. Death cancels all friendships. There—Enough. *Forget about costumes, Tomás.*

Enough, and too late. The nightwalkers swarmed around the rock and began trying to climb. Vatch stood above the crack, sword ready. The sword was all he had.

Hands came over the edge. He struck at them.

He looked around in time to see more hands coming up everywhere along the perimeter. He yelled and circled madly, striking, striking. They were not climbing the rock itself; they were climbing over each other to reach the top. And his sword, its edge dulled by repeated blows against rock and bone, was turning into a club . . .

Suddenly he stopped.

Fantasy? Real? What kind of biology . . . ?

He spilled his medical kit open and snatched at the bottle of Spectrum Cure. More than his life was at stake here. He was trying to save his sanity.

The pistol grip fitted his hand neatly. A nightwalker

pulled itself over the edge and tottered toward him, and he sprayed Spectrum Cure between its eyes. An eroded face appeared near his feet; he sprayed Spectrum Cure into its mouth. Then he stepped back and watched.

The first one dropped like a sack. The second let go and disappeared from view.

Nightwalkers were coming up all around him. Vatch moved among them in calm haste, spraying life into them, and they stopped moving. In his mind he gloated. It should have worked, and it had.

For if anything in this experience was real, then it had to be caused by the biology of Sereda. So: something could infect the dead, to make them move. Bacterium? Fungus? Virus? Whatever it was, it had to have evolved by using dead lopers and other native life forms to spread itself.

It would walk the infected corpse until there was no sugar or oxygen left in the blood or muscle tissues of the host. That alone could carry the disease further than it could travel by itself. And if it found another host to infect along the way, well and good.

But the first step in infection would be to restart the heart. It *had* to be, or the bacterium couldn't spread throughout the host.

And if the heart was going . . .

The Spectrum Cure seemed to be healing them right up. He'd cured about eight of them. They lay at the base of the rock and did not move. Other nightwalkers clustered around them. For the moment they had given up on Vatch's rock.

Vatch watched some of them bend over the bodies of those he had injected. They might have been nibbling at the flesh above the hearts. A minute of that, and then they fell over and lay as dead as the ones they had been trying to rescue.

Good enough, thought Vatch. He flashed the light on his bottle to check the supply of Spectrum Cure.

It was just short of dead empty.

Vatch sighed. The horde of dead men had drawn

away from the casualties—the *dead* dead ones—and gone back to trying to climb the rock. Some would make it. Vatch picked up his sword. An afterthought: he injected himself. Even if they got to him, they would not rouse him from death before morning.

The scrabbling of finger bones against rock became a cricket chorus.

Vatch stood looking down at them. Most of these had only been dead for hours. Their faces were intact, though slack. Vatch looked for Roy Tanner.

He circled the edge rapidly, striking occasionally at a reaching arm, but peering down anxiously. Where the blazes was Roy Tanner?

There, pulling himself over the lip of the crack.

In fact they were all swarming into the crack and climbing over each other. Their dead brains must be working to some extent. The smell of them was terrific. Vatch breathed through his mouth, closed his imagination tight shut, and waited.

The nightwalker remains of Roy Tanner pulled itself up on the rock. Vatch sprayed it in the face, turned the body over in haste, and found it: Roy Tanner's medical kit, still intact. He spilled out the contents and snatched up Roy's bottle of Spectrum Cure.

He sprayed it before him, and then into the crack, like an insecticide. He held his aim until they stopped moving . . . and then, finally, he could roll away from the choking smell. It was all right now. Roy had fallen early in the battle. His bottle had been nearly full.

For something like six hours they had watched each other: Tomás Vatch on the lip of the rock, seven nightwalkers below. They stood in a half circle, well out of range of Vatch's spray gun, and they stared unblinking into Vatch's flashlight.

Vatch was dreadfully tired. He had circled the rock several times, leaping the crack twice on each pass. "Cured" corpses surrounded the base and half filled the crack. He had seen none of them move. By now he was sure. There were only these seven left.

"I want to sleep," he told them. "Can't you understand? I won. You lost. Go away. I want to sleep." He had been telling them this for some time.

This time it seemed that they heard.

One by one they turned and stumbled off in different directions. Vatch watched, amazed, afraid to believe. Each nightwalker seemed to find a patch of level ground it liked. There it fell and did not move.

Vatch waited. The east was growing bright. It wasn't over yet, but it would be soon. With burning eyes he watched for the obvious dead to move again.

Red dawn touched the tops of glacier-spilled rocks. The orange dwarf sun made a cool light; he could almost look straight into it. He watched the shadows walk down the sides of the rocks to the ground.

When the light touched the seven bodies, they had become bright green patches, vaguely man-shaped.

Vatch watched until each patch had sprouted a bud of yellow in its center. Then he dropped to the ground and started walking north.

GOVERNOR MANCO
AND THE SOLDIER

Washington Irving

When Governor Manco, or "the one-armed," kept
up a show of military state in the Alhambra, he became
nettled at the reproaches continually cast upon his fortress, of being a nestling-place of rogues and contra-
bandistas. On a sudden, the old potentate determined
on reform; and setting vigorously to work, ejected whole
nests of vagabonds out of the fortress and the gipsy
caves with which the surrounding hills are honeycombed.
He sent out soldiers also, to patrol the avenues and
footpaths, with orders to take up all suspicious persons.

One bright summer morning, a patrol, consisting of
the testy old corporal who had distinguished himself in
the affair of the notary, a trumpeter, and two privates,
was seated under the garden-wall of the Generalife,
beside the road, which leads down from the Mountain
of the Sun, when they heard the tramp of a horse, and a
male voice singing in rough, though not unmusical tones,
an old Castilian campaigning song.

Presently they beheld a sturdy, sun-burnt fellow,
clad in the ragged garb of a foot-soldier, leading a
powerful Arabian horse, caparisoned in the ancient
Moresco fashion.

Astonished at the sight of a strange soldier, descending, steed in hand, from that solitary mountain, the
corporal stepped forth and challenged him.

"Who goes there?"

"A friend."

"Who and what are you?"

"A poor soldier just from the wars, with a cracked crown and empty purse for a reward."

By this time they were enabled to view him more narrowly. He had a black patch across his forehead which, with a grizzled beard, added to a certain dare-devil cast of countenance; while a slight squint threw into the whole an occasional gleam of roguish good humour.

Having answered the questions of the patrol, the soldier seemed to consider himself entitled to make others in return. "May I ask," he said, "what city is that which I see at the foot of the hill?"

"What city!" cried the trumpeter; "come, that's too bad. There's a fellow lurking about the Mountain of the Sun, and demands the name of the great city of Granada!"

"Granada! *Madre di Dios!* can it be possible?"

"Perhaps not!" rejoined the trumpeter; "and perhaps you have no idea that yonder are the towers of the Alhambra?"

"Son of a trumpet," replied the stranger, "do not trifle with me; if this be indeed the Alhambra, I have some strange matters to reveal to the governor."

"You will have an opportunity," said the corporal, "for we mean to take you before him." By this time the trumpeter had seized the bridle of the steed, the two privates had each secured an arm of the soldier, the corporal put himself in front, gave the word, "Forward—march!" and away they marched for the Alhambra.

The sight of a ragged foot-soldier and a fine Arabian horse, brought in captive by the patrol, attracted the attention of all the idlers of the fortress, and of those gossip groups that generally assemble about wells and fountains at early dawn. The wheel of the cistern paused in its rotations, and the slip-shod servant-maid stood gaping, with pitcher in hand, as the corporal passed by with his prize. A motley train gradually gathered in the rear of the escort.

Knowing nods and winks and conjectures passed from one to another. "It is a deserter," said one; "A contrabandista," said another; "A bandalero," said a third—until it was affirmed that a captain of a desperate band of robbers had been captured by the prowess of the corporal and his patrol. "Well, well," said the old crones, one to another, "captain or not, let him get out of the grasp of old Governor Manco if he can, though he is but one-handed."

Governor Manco was seated in one of the inner halls of the Alhambra, taking his morning's cup of chocolate in company with his confessor, a fat Franciscan friar, from the neighbouring convent. A demure, dark-eyed damsel of Malaga, the daughter of his housekeeper, was attending upon him. The world hinted that the damsel, who, with all her demureness, was a sly buxom baggage, had found out a soft spot in the iron heart of the old governor, and held complete control over him. But let that pass—the domestic affairs of these mighty potentates of the earth should not be too narrowly scrutinized.

When word was brought that a suspicious stranger had been taken lurking about the fortress, and was actually in the outer court, in durance of the corporal, waiting the pleasure of his excellency, the pride and stateliness of office swelled the bosom of the governor. Giving back his chocolate-cup into the hands of the demure damsel, he called for his basket-hilted sword, girded it to his side, twirled up his mustachios, took his seat in a large high-backed chair, assumed a bitter and forbidding aspect, and ordered the prisoner into his presence. The soldier was brought in, still closely pinioned by his captors, and guarded by the corporal. He maintained, however, a resolute self-confident air, and returned the sharp, scrutinizing look of the governor with an easy squint, which by no means pleased the punctilious old potentate.

"Well, culprit," said the governor, after he had regarded him for a moment in silence, "what have you to say for yourself—who are you?"

"A soldier, just back from the wars, who has brought away nothing but scars and bruises."

"A soldier—humph—a foot-soldier by your garb. I understand you have a fine Arabian horse. I presume you brought him too from the wars, beside your scars and bruises."

"May it please your excellency, I have something strange to tell about that horse. Indeed I have one of the most wonderful things to relate: something too that concerns the security of this fortress, indeed of all Granada. But it is a matter to be imparted only to your private ear, or in presence of such only as are in your confidence."

The governor considered for a moment, and then directed the corporal and his men to withdraw, but to post themselves outside the door, and be ready at a call. "This holy friar," said he, "is my confessor, you may say anything in his presence—and this damsel," nodding towards the handmaid, who had loitered with an air of great curiosity, "this damsel is of great secrecy and discretion, and to be trusted with anything."

The soldier gave a glance between a squint and a leer at the demure handmaid. "I am perfectly willing," said he, "that the damsel should remain."

When all the rest had withdrawn, the soldier commenced his story. He was a fluent, smooth-tongued varlet, and had a command of language above his apparent rank.

"May it please your excellency," said he, "I am, as I before observed, a soldier, and have seen some hard service, but my term of enlistment being expired, I was discharged, not long since, from the army at Valladolid, and set out on foot for my native village in Andalusia. Yesterday evening the sun went down as I was traversing a great dry plain of Old Castile."

"Hold," cried the governor, "what is this you say? Old Castile is some two or three hundred miles from this."

"Even so," replied the soldier coolly, "I told your excellency, I had strange things to relate; but not more strange than true; as your excellency will find, if you will deign me a patient hearing."

"Proceed, culprit," said the governor, twirling up his mustachios.

"As the sun went down," continued the soldier, "I cast my eyes about in search of some quarters for the night, but, far as my sight could reach, there were no signs of a habitation. I saw that I should have to make my bed on the naked plain, with my knapsack for a pillow; but your excellency is an old soldier, and knows that to one who has been in the wars, such a night's lodging is no great hardship."

The governor nodded assent, as he drew his pocket-handkerchief out of the basket-hilt, to drive away a fly that buzzed about his nose.

"Well, to make a long story short," continued the soldier, "I trudged forward for several miles until I came to a bridge over a deep ravine, through which ran a little thread of water, almost dried up by the summer heat. At one end of the bridge was a Moorish tower, the upper end all in ruins, but a vault in the foundation quite entire. Here, thinks I, is a good place to make a halt; so I went down to the stream, took a hearty drink, for the water was pure and sweet, and I was parched with thirst; then, opening my wallet, I took out an onion and a few crusts, which were all my provisions, and seating myself on a stone on the margin of the stream, began to make my supper, intending afterwards to quarter myself for the night in the vault of the tower; and capital quarters they would have been for a campaigner just from the wars, as your excellency, who is an old soldier, may suppose."

"I have put up gladly with worse in my time," said the governor, returning his pocket-handkerchief into the hilt of his sword.

"While I was quietly crunching my crust," pursued the soldier, "I heard something stir within the vault; I listened—it was the tramp of a horse. By and by, a man came forth from a door in the foundation of the tower, close by the water's edge, leading a powerful horse by the bridle. I could not well make out what he was, by the star-light. It had a suspicious look to be lurking among the ruins of a tower, in that wild solitary place. He might be a mere wayfarer, like myself; he might be a contrabandista; he might be a bandalero! what of that? thank Heaven and my poverty, I had nothing to lose; so I sat still and crunched my crusts.

"He led his horse to the water, close by where I was sitting, so that I had a fair opportunity of reconnoitring him. To my surprise he was dressed in a Moorish garb, with a cuirass of steel, and a polished skull-cup that I distinguished by the reflection of the stars upon it. His horse, too, was harnessed in the Moresco fashion, with great shovel-stirrups. He led him, as I said, to the side of the stream, into which the animal plunged his head almost to his eyes, and drank until I thought he would have burst.

" 'Comrade,' said I, 'your steed drinks well; it's a good sign when a horse plunges his muzzle bravely into the water.'

" 'He may well drink,' said the stranger, speaking with a Moorish accent, 'it is a good year since he had his last draught.'

" 'By Santiago,' said I, 'that beats even the camels that I have seen in Africa. But come, you seem to be something of a soldier, will you sit down and take part of a soldier's fare?' In fact, I felt the want of a companion in this lonely place, and was willing to put up with an infidel. Besides, as your excellency well knows, a soldier is never very particular about the faith of his company, and soldiers of all countries are comrades on peaceable ground."

The governor again nodded assent.

"Well, as I was saying, I invited him to share my supper, such as it was, for I could not do less in common hospitality. 'I have no time to pause for meat or drink,' said he, 'I have a long journey to make before morning.'

" 'In which direction?' said I.

" 'Andalusia,' said he.

" 'Exactly my route,' said I; 'so, as you won't stop and eat with me, perhaps you will let me mount and ride with you. I see your horse is of a powerful frame, I'll warrant he'll carry double.'

" 'Agreed,' said the trooper; and it would not have been civil and soldier-like to refuse, especially as I had offered to share my supper with him. So up he mounted, and up I mounted behind him.

" 'Hold fast,' said he, 'my steed goes like the wind.'

" 'Never fear me,' said I, and so off we set.

"From a walk the horse soon passed to a trot, from a trot to a gallop, and from a gallop to a harum scarum scamper. It seemed as if rocks, trees, houses, everything, flew hurry-scurry behind us.

" 'What town is this?' I said.

" 'Segovia,' said he; and before the word was out of his mouth, the towers of Segovia were out of sight. We swept up the Guadarama mountains, and down by the Escurial; and we skirted the walls of Madrid, and we scoured away across the plains of La Mancha. In this way we went up hill and down dale, by towers and cities, all buried in deep sleep, and across mountains, and plains, and rivers, just glimmering in the starlight.

"To make a long story short, and not to fatigue your excellency, the trooper suddenly pulled up on the side of a mountain. 'Here we are,' said he, 'at the end of our journey.' I looked about, but could see no habitation; nothing but the mouth of a cavern. While I looked I saw multitudes in Moorish dresses, some on horseback, some on foot, arriving as if borne by the wind from all points of the compass, and hurrying into the mouth of the cavern, like bees into a hive. Before I could ask a question, the trooper struck his long Moorish spurs into the horse's flanks and dashed in with the throng. We passed along a steep winding way, that descended into the very bowels of the mountain. As we pushed on, a light began to glimmer up, by little and little, like the first glimmerings of day, but what caused it I could not discern. It grew stronger and stronger, and enabled me to see everything around. I now noticed, as we passed along, great caverns, opening to the right and left, like halls in an arsenal. In some there were shields, and helmets, and cuirasses, and lances, and scimitars, hanging against the walls; in others there were great heaps of warlike munitions, and camp-equipage, lying upon the ground.

"It would have done your excellency's heart good, being an old soldier, to have seen such grand provision for war. Then, in other caverns, there were long rows of horsemen armed to the teeth, with lances raised and banners unfurled, all ready for the field; but they all sat motionless in their saddles like so many statues. In other halls were warriors sleeping on the ground beside their horses, and foot-soldiers in groups ready to fall into the ranks. All were in old-fashioned Moorish dress and armor.

"Well, your excellency, to cut a long story short, we at length entered an immense cavern, or I may say palace, of grotto-work, the walls of which seemed to be veined with gold and silver, and to sparkle with diamonds and sapphires and all kinds of precious stones. At the upper end sat a Moorish king on a golden throne, with his nobles on each side, and a guard of African blacks with drawn scimitars. All the crowd that continued to flock in, and amounted to thousands and thousands, passed one by one before his throne, each paying homage as he passed. Some of the multitude were dressed in magnificent robes without stain or blemish, and sparkling with jewels; others were in burnished and enamelled armor; while others were in mouldered and mildewed garments, and in armor all battered and dented and covered with rust.

"I had hitherto held my tongue, for your excellency well knows, it is not for a soldier to ask many questions when on duty, but I could keep silent no longer.

" 'Pr'ythee, comrade,' said I, 'what is the meaning of all this?'

" 'This,' said the trooper, 'is a great and fearful mystery. Know, O Christian, that you see before you the court and army of Boabdil the last king of Granada.'

" 'What is this you tell me?' cried I. 'Boabdil and his court were exiled from the land hundreds of years agone, and all died in Africa.'

" 'So it is recorded in your lying chronicles,' replied the Moor, 'but know that Boabdil and the warriors who made the last struggle for Granada were all shut up in the mountain by powerful enchantment. As for the king and army that marched forth from Granada at the time of the surrender, they were a mere phantom train, of spirits and demons permitted to assume those shapes to deceive the Christian sovereigns. And furthermore let me tell you, friend, that all Spain is a country under the power of enchantment. There is not a mountain cave, not a lonely watch-tower in the plains, nor ruined castle on the hills, but has some spellbound warriors sleeping from age to age within its vaults, until the sins are expiated for which Allah permitted the dominion to pass for a time out of the hands of the faithful. Once every year, on the eve of St John, they are released from enchantment from sunset to sunrise, and permitted to repair here to pay homage to their sovereign; and the crowds which you beheld swarming into the cavern are Moslem warriors from their haunts in all parts of Spain. For my own part, you saw the ruined tower of the bridge in Old Castile, where I have now wintered and summered for many hundred years, and where I must be back again by day-break. As to the battalions of horses and foot which you beheld drawn up in array in the neighbouring caverns, they are the spell-bound warriors of Granada. It is written in the book of fate, that when the enchantment is broken, Boabdil will descend from the mountain at the head of this army, resume his throne in the Alhambra and his sway of Granada, and gathering together the enchanted warriors from all parts of Spain, will reconquer the Peninsula and restore it to Moslem rule.'

" 'And when shall this happen?' said I.

" 'Allah alone knows; we had hoped the day of deliverance was at hand; but there reigns at present a vigilant governor in the Alhambra, a staunch old soldier, well known as Governor Manco. While such a warrior holds command of the very outpost, and stands ready to check the first irruption from the mountain, I fear Boabdil and his soldiery must be content to rest upon their arms.' "

Here the governor raised himself somewhat perpendicularly, adjusted his sword, and twirled up his mustachios.

"To make a long story short, and not to fatigue your excellency, the trooper, having given me this account, dismounted from his steed.

" 'Tarry here,' said he, 'and guard my steed while I go and bow the knee to Boabdil.' So saying, he strode away among the throng that pressed forward to the throne.

" 'What's to be done?' thought I, when thus left to myself; 'shall I wait here until this infidel returns to whisk me off on his goblin steed, the Lord knows where; or shall I make the most of my time and beat a retreat from this hobgoblin community?' A soldier's mind is soon made up, as your excellency well knows. As to the horse, he belonged to an avowed enemy of the faith and the realm, and was a fair prize according to the rules of war. So hoisting myself from the crupper into the saddle, I turned the reins, struck the Moorish stirrups into the sides of the steed, and put him to make the best of his way out of the passage by which he had entered. As we scoured by the halls where the Moslem horsemen sat in motionless battalions, I thought I heard the clang of armor and a hollow murmur of voices. I gave the steed another taste of the stirrups, and doubled my speed. There was now a sound behind me like a rushing blast; I heard the clatter of a thousand hoofs; a countless throng overtook me. I was borne along in the press, and hurled forth from the cavern, while thousands of shadowy forms were swept off in every direction by the four winds of heaven.

"In the whirl and confusion of the scene I was thrown senseless to the earth. When I came to myself I was lying on the brow of a hill with the Arabian steed standing beside me; for in falling, my arm had slipped within the bridle, which, I presume, prevented his whisking off to Old Castile.

"Your excellency may easily judge of my surprise on looking round, to behold hedges of aloes and Indian figs and other proofs of a southern climate, and to see a great city below me with towers and palaces, and a grand cathedral.

"I descended the hill cautiously, leading my steed, for I was afraid to mount him again, lest he should play me some slippery trick. As I descended I met with your patrol, who let me into the secret that it was Granada that lay before me; and that I was actually under the walls of the Alhambra, the fortress of the redoubted Governor Manco, the terror of all enchanted Moslems. When I heard this, I determined at once to seek your excellency, to inform you of all that I had seen, and to warn you of the perils that surround and undermine you, that you may take measures in time to guard your fortress, and the kingdom itself, from this intestine army that lurks in the very bowels of the land."

"And pr'ythee, friend, you who are a veteran campaigner, and have seen so much service," said the governor, "how would you advise me to proceed, in order to prevent this evil?"

"It is not for a humble private of the ranks," said the soldier modestly, "to pretend to instruct a commander of your excellency's sagacity, but it appears to me that your excellency might cause all the caves and entrances into the mountain to be walled up with solid masonwork, so that Boabdil and his army might be completely corked up in their subterranean habitation. If the good father, too," added the soldier, reverently bowing to the friar and devoutly crossing himself, "would consecrate the barricadoes with his blessing, and put up a few crosses and reliques and images of saints, I think they might withstand all the power of infidel enchantments."

"They doubtless would be of great avail," said the friar.

The governor now placed his arm akimbo, with his hand resting on the hilt of his toledo, fixed his eye upon the soldier, and gently wagged his head from one side to the other.

"So, friend," said he, "then you really suppose I am to be gulled with this cock-and-bull story about enchanted mountains and enchanted Moors? Hark ye, culprit!—not another word. An old soldier you may be, but you'll find you have an older soldier to deal with, and one not easily out-generalled. Ho! guards there! put this fellow in irons."

The demure handmaid would have put in a word in favor of the prisoner, but the governor silenced her with a look.

As they were pinioning the soldier, one of the guards felt something of bulk in his pocket, and drawing it forth, found a long leathern purse that appeared to be well filled. Holding it by one corner, he turned out the contents upon the table before the governor, and never did freebooter's bag make more gorgeous delivery. Out tumbled rings and jewels, and rosaries of pearls, and sparkling diamond crosses, and a profusion of ancient golden coin, some of which fell jingling to the floor and rolled away to the uttermost parts of the chamber.

For a time the functions of justice were suspended: there was a universal scramble after the glittering fugitives. The governor alone, who was imbued with true Spanish pride, maintained his stately decorum, though his eye betrayed a little anxiety until the last coin and jewel was restored to the sack.

The friar was not so calm; his whole face glowed like a furnace, and his eyes twinkled and flushed at sight of the rosaries and crosses.

"Sacrilegious wretch that thou art!" exclaimed he, "what church or sanctuary hast thou been plundering of these sacred relics?"

"Neither one nor the other, holy father. If they be sacrilegious spoils, they must have been taken in times long past, by the infidel trooper I have mentioned. I was just going to tell his excellency when he interrupted me, that on taking possession of the trooper's horse, I unhooked a leathern sack which hung at the saddle-bow, and which I presume contained the plunder of his campaignings in days of old, when the Moors overran the country."

"Mighty well; at present you will make up your mind to take up your quarters in a chamber of the vermilion tower, which, though not under a magic spell, will hold you as safe as any cave of your enchanted Moors."

"Your excellency will do as you think proper," said the prisoner coolly. "I shall be thankful to your excellency for any accommodation in the fortress. A soldier who has been in the wars, as your excellency well knows, is not particular about his lodgings: provided I have a snug dungeon and regular rations, I shall manage to make myself comfortable. I would only entreat that, while your excellency is so careful about me, you would have an eye to your fortress, and think on the hint I dropped about stopping up the entrances to the mountain."

Here ended the scene. The prisoner was conducted to a strong dungeon in the vermilion tower, and the Arabian steed was led to his excellency's stable, and the trooper's sack deposited in his excellency's strong-box. To the latter, it is true, the friar made some demur, questioning whether the sacred relics, which were evidently sacrilegious spoils, should not be placed in custody of the church; but as the governor was peremptory on the subject, and was absolute lord in the Alhambra, the friar discreetly dropped the discussion, but determined to convey intelligence of the fact to the church dignitaries in Granada.

To explain these prompt and rigid measures on the part of old Governor Manco, it is proper to observe, that about this time the Alpuxarra mountains in the neighbourhood of Granada were terribly infested by a gang of robbers, under the command of a daring chief named Manuel Borasco, who were accustomed to prowl about the country, and even to enter the city in various disguises, to gain intelligence of the departure of convoys of merchandise, or travellers with well-lined purses, whom they took care to way-lay in distant and solitary passes of their road. These repeated and daring outrages had awakened the attention of government, and the commanders of the various posts had received instructions to be on the alert and to take up all suspicious stragglers. Governor Manco was particularly zealous in consequence of the various stigmas that had been cast upon his fortress, and he now doubted not that he had entrapped some formidable desperado of this gang.

In the meantime the story took wind, and became the talk, not merely of the fortress, but of the whole city of Granada. It was said that the noted robber Manuel Borasco, the terror of the Alpuxarras, had fallen into the clutches of old Governor Manco, and been cooped up by him in a dungeon of the vermilion tower; and every one who had been robbed by him flocked to recognize the marauder. The vermilion towers, as is well known, stand apart from the Alhambra, on a sister hill, separated from the main fortress by the ravine down which passes the main avenue. There were no outer walls, but a sentinel patrolled before the tower. The window of the chamber in which the soldier was confined, was strongly grated, and looked upon a small esplanade. Here the good folks of Granada repaired to gaze at him, as they would at a laughing hyena, grinning through the cage of a menagerie. Nobody, however, recognized him for Manuel Borasco, for that terrible robber was noted for a ferocious physiognomy, and had by no means the good-humoured squint of the prisoner. Visitors came not merely from the city, but from all parts of the country; but nobody knew him, and there began to be doubts in the minds of the common people whether there might not be some truth in his story. That Boabdil and his army were shut up in the mountain, was an old tradition which many of the ancient inhabitants had heard from their fathers. Numbers went up to the mountain of the sun, or rather of St Elena, in search of the cave mentioned by the soldier; and saw and peeped into the deep dark pit, descending no one knows how far, into the mountain, and which remains there to this day—the fabled entrance to the subterranean abode of Boabdil.

By degrees the soldier became popular with the common people. A freebooter of the mountains is by no means the opprobrious character in Spain that a robber is in any other country: on the contrary, he is a kind of chivalrous personage in the eyes of the lower classes. There is always a disposition, also, to cavil at the conduct of those in command; and many began to murmur at the high-handed measures of old Governor Manco, and to look upon the prisoner in the light of a martyr.

The soldier, moreover, was a merry, waggish fellow, that had a joke for every one who came near his window, and a soft speech for every female. He had procured an old guitar also, and would sit by his window and sing ballads and love-ditties, to the delight of the women of the neighbourhood, who would assemble on the esplanade in the evenings and dance boleros to his music. Having trimmed off his rough beard, his sunburnt face found favour in the eyes of the fair, and the demure handmaid of the governor declared that his squint was perfectly irresistible. This kind-hearted damsel had from the first evinced a deep sympathy in his fortunes, and having in vain tried to mollify the governor, had set to work privately to mitigate the rigour of his dispensations. Every day she brought the prisoner some crumbs of comfort which had fallen from the governor's table, or been abstracted from his larder, together with, now and then, a consoling bottle of choice Val de Penas, or rich Malaga.

While this petty-treason was going on, in the very centre of the old governor's citadel, a storm of open war was brewing up among his external foes. The circumstances of a bag of gold and jewels having been found upon the person of the supposed robber, had been reported with many exaggerations, in Granada. A question of territorial jurisdiction was immediately started by the governor's inveterate rival, the captain-general. He insisted that the prisoner had been captured without the precincts of the Alhambra, and within the rules of his authority. He demanded his body therefore, and the *spolia opima* taken with him. Due information having been carried likewise by the friar to the grand Inquisitor of the crosses and rosaries, and other replicas contained in the bag, he claimed the culprit as having been guilty of sacrilege, and insisted that his plunder was due to the church, and his body to the next *auto da fé*. The feuds ran high, the governor was furious, and swore, rather than surrender his captive, he would hang him up within the Alhambra, as a spy caught within the purlieus of the fortress.

The captain-general threatened to send a body of soldiers to transfer the prisoner from the vermilion tower to the city. The grand Inquisitor was equally bent upon despatching a number of the familiars of the Holy Office. Word was brought late at night to the governor, of these machinations. "Let them come," said he, "they'll find me beforehand with them; he must rise bright and early who would take in an old soldier." He accordingly issued orders to have the prisoner removed at daybreak, to the donjon keep within the walls of the Alhambra. "And d'ye hear, child," said he to his demure handmaid, "tap at my door, and wake me before cockcrowing, that I may see to the matter myself."

The day dawned, the cock crowed, but nobody tapped at the door of the governor. The sun rose high above the mountain-tops, and glittered in at his casement, ere the governor was wakened from his morning dreams by his veteran corporal, who stood before him with terror stamped upon his iron visage.

"He's off! He's gone!" cried the corporal, gasping for breath.

"Who's off—who's gone?"

"The soldier—the robber—the devil for aught I know; his dungeon is empty, but the door locked, no one knows how he has escaped out of it."

"Who saw him last?"

"Your handmaid, she brought him his supper."

"Let her be called instantly."

Here was new matter of confusion. The chamber of the demure damsel was likewise empty, her bed had not been slept in: she had doubtless gone off with the culprit, as she had appeared, for some days past, to have frequent conversations with him.

This was wounding the old governor in a tender part, but he had scarce time to wince at it, when new misfortunes broke upon his view. On going into his cabinet he found his strong-box open, the leather purse of the trooper abstracted, and with it, a couple of corpulent bags of doubloons.

But how, and which way, had the fugitives escaped? An old peasant who lived in a cottage by the road-side, leading up to the Sierra, declared that he had heard the tramp of a powerful steed just before day-break, passing up into the mountains. He had looked out at his casement, and could just distinguish a horseman, with a female seated before him.

"Search the stables!" cried Governor Manco. The stables were searched; all the horses were in their stalls, excepting the Arabian steed. In his place was a stout cudgel tied to the manger, and on it a label bearing these words, "A gift to Governor Manco, from an Old Soldier."

THE SPECTRE GENERAL

Theodore Cogswell

I

"SERGEANT DIXON!" Kurt stiffened. He knew *that* voice.
Dropping the handles of the wooden plow, he gave a
quick "rest" to the private and a polite "by your
leave, sir" to the lieutenant who were yoked together in
double harness. They both sank gratefully to the ground
as Kurt advanced to meet the approaching officer.

Marcus Harris, the commander of the 427th Light
Maintenance Battalion of the Imperial Space Marines,
was an imposing figure. The three silver eagle feathers
of a full colonel rose proudly from his war bonnet and
the bright red of the flaming comet insignia of the
Space Marines that was painted on his chest stood out
sharply against his sun-blackened, leathery skin. As
Kurt snapped to attention before him and saluted, the
colonel surveyed the fresh-turned earth with an experienced eye.

"You plow a straight furrow, soldier!" His voice was
hard and metallic, but it seemed to Kurt that there was
a concealed glimmer of approval in his flinty eyes.
Dixon flushed with pleasure and drew back his broad
shoulders a little further.

The commander's eyes flicked down to the battle-ax

that rested snugly in its leather holster at Kurt's side. "You keep a clean sidearm, too."

Kurt uttered a silent prayer of thanksgiving that he had worked over his weapon before reveille that morning until there was a satin gloss to its redwood handle and the sheen of black glass to its obsidian head.

"In fact," said Colonel Harris, "you'd be officer material if—" His voice trailed off.

"If what?" asked Kurt eagerly.

"If," said the colonel with a note of paternal fondness in his voice that sent cold chills dancing down Kurt's spine, "you weren't the most completely unmanageable, undisciplined, overmuscled and underbrained knucklehead I've ever had the misfortune to have in my command. This last little unauthorized jaunt of yours indicates to me that you have as much right to sergeant's stripes as I have to have kittens. Report to me at ten tomorrow! I personally guarantee that when I'm through with you—if you live that long—you'll have a bare forehead!"

Colonel Harris spun on one heel and stalked back across the dusty plateau toward the walled garrison that stood at one end. Kurt stared after him for a moment and then turned and let his eyes slip across the wide belt of lush green jungle that surrounded the high plateau. To the north rose a great range of snow-capped mountains and his heart filled with longing as he thought of the strange and beautiful thing he had found behind them. Finally he plodded slowly back to the plow, his shoulders stooped and his head sagging. With an effort he recalled himself to the business at hand.

"Up on your aching feet, soldier!" he barked to the reclining private. "If you please, sir!" he said to the lieutenant. His calloused hands grasped the worn plow handles.

"Giddiup!" The two men strained against their collars and with a creak of harness the wooden plow started to move slowly across the arid plateau.

II

Conrad Krogson, Supreme Commander of War Base Three of Sector Seven of the Galactic Protectorate, stood at quaking attention before the visiscreen of his space communicator. It was an unusual position for the commander. He was accustomed to having people quake while *he* talked.

"The Lord Protector's got another hot tip that General Carr is still alive!" said the sector commander. "He's yelling for blood, and if it's a choice between yours and mine, you know who will do the donating!"

"But, sir," quavered Krogson to the figure on the screen, "I can't do anything more than I am doing. I've had double security checks running since the last time there was an alert, and they haven't turned up a thing. And I'm so shorthanded now that if I pull another random purge, I won't have enough techs left to work the base."

"That's your problem, not mine," said the sector commander coldly. "All I know is that rumors have got to the Protector that an organized underground is being built up and that Carr is behind it. The Protector wants action now. If he doesn't get it, heads are going to roll!"

"I'll do what I can, sir," promised Krogson.

"I'm sure you will," said the sector commander viciously, "because I'm giving you exactly ten days to produce something that is big enough to take the heat off me. If you don't, I'll break you, Krogson. If I'm sent to the mines, you'll be sweating right alongside me. That's a promise!"

Krogson's face blanched.

"Any questions?" snapped the sector commander.

"Yes," said Krogson.

"Well, don't bother me with them. I've got troubles of my own!" The screen went dark.

Krogson slumped into his chair and sat staring dully at the blank screen. Finally he roused himself with an effort and let out a bellow that rattled the windows of his dusty office.

"Schninkle! Get in here!"

A gnomelike little figure scuttled in through the door and bobbed obsequiously before him.

"Yes, commander?"

"Switch on your think tank," said Krogson. "The Lord Protector has the shakes again and the heat's on!"

"What is it this time?" asked Schninkle.

"General Carr!" said the commander gloomily, "the ex-Number Two."

"I thought he'd been liquidated."

"So did I," said Krogson, "but he must have slipped out some way. The Protector thinks he's started up an underground."

"He'd be a fool if he didn't," said the little man. "The Lord Protector isn't as young as he once was and his grip is getting a little shaky."

"Maybe so, but he's still strong enough to get us before General Carr gets him. The sector commander just passed the buck down to me. We produce or else!"

"We?" said Schninkle unhappily.

"Of course," snapped Krogson, "we're in this together. Now let's get to work! If you were Carr, where would be the logical place for you to hide out?"

"Well," said Schninkle thoughtfully, "if I were as smart as Carr is supposed to be, I'd find myself a hideout right on Prime Base. Everything's so fouled up there that they'd never find me."

"That's out for us," said Krogson. "We can't go rooting around in the Lord Protector's own back yard. What would Carr's next best bet be?"

Schninkle thought for a moment. "He might go out to one of the deserted systems," he said slowly. "There must be half a hundred stars in our own base area that haven't been visited since the old empire broke up. Our ships don't get around the way they used to and the chances are mighty slim that anybody would stumble on to him accidentally."

"It's a possibility," said the commander thoughtfully, "a bare possibility." His right fist slapped into his left palm in a gesture of sudden resolution. "But by the

Planets! at least it's something! Alert all section heads for a staff meeting in half an hour. I want every scout out on a quick check of every system in our area!"

"Beg pardon, commander," said Schninkle, "but half our light ships are red-lined for essential maintenance and the other half should be. Anyway it would take months to check every possible hideout in this area even if we used the whole fleet."

"I know," said Krogson, "but we'll have to do what we can with what we have. At least I'll be able to report to sector that we're doing *something!* Tell Astrogation to set up a series of search patterns. We won't have to check every planet. A single quick sweep through each system will do the trick. Even Carr can't run a base without power. Where there's power, there's radiation, and radiation can be detected a long way off. Put all electronic techs on double shifts and have all detection gear double-checked."

"Can't do that either," said Schninkle. "There aren't more than a dozen electronic techs left. Most of them were transferred to Prime Base last week."

Commander Krogson blew up. "How in the name of the Bloody Blue Pleiades am I supposed to keep a war base going without technicians? You tell me, Schninkle, you always seem to know all the answers."

Schninkle coughed modestly. "Well, sir," he said, "as long as you have a situation where technicians are sent to the uranium mines for making mistakes, it's going to be an unpopular vocation. And, as long as the Lord Protector of the moment is afraid that Number Two, Number Three, and so on have ideas about grabbing his job—which they generally do—he's going to keep his fleet as strong as possible and their fleets so weak they aren't dangerous. The best way to do that is to grab techs. If most of the base's ships are sitting around waiting repair, the commander won't be able to do much about any ambitions he may happen to have. Add that to the obvious fact that our whole technology has been on a downward spiral for the last three hundred years and you have your answer."

Krogson nodded gloomy agreement. "Sometimes I feel as if we were all on a dead ship falling into a dying sun," he said. His voice suddenly altered. "But in the meantime we have our necks to save. Get going, Schninkle!"

Schninkle bobbed and darted out of the office.

III

It was exactly ten o'clock in the morning when Sergeant Dixon of the Imperial Space Marines snapped to attention before his commanding officer.

"Sergeant Dixon reporting as ordered, sir!" His voice cracked a bit in spite of his best efforts to control it.

The colonel looked at him coldly. "Nice of you to drop in, Dixon," he said. "Shall we go ahead with our little chat?"

Kurt nodded nervously.

"I have here," said the colonel, shuffling a sheaf of papers, "a report of an unauthorized expedition made by you into *Off Limits* territory."

"Which one do you mean, sir?" asked Kurt without thinking.

"Then there has been more than one?" asked the colonel quietly.

Kurt started to stammer.

Colonel Harris silenced him with a gesture of his hand. "I'm talking about the country to the north, the tableland back of the Twin Peaks."

"It's a beautiful place!" burst out Kurt enthusiastically. "It's . . . it's like Imperial Headquarters must be. Dozens of little streams full of fish, trees heavy with fruit, small game so slow and stupid that they can be knocked over with a club. Why, the battalion could live there without hardly lifting a finger!"

"I've no doubt that they could," said the colonel.

"Think of it, sir!" continued the sergeant. "No more plowing details, no more hunting details, no more nothing but taking it easy!"

"You might add to your list of 'no mores,' no more

tech schools," said Colonel Harris. "I'm quite aware that the place is all you say it is, Sergeant. As a result I'm placing all information that pertains to it in a 'Top Secret' category. That applies to what is inside your head as well!"

"But, sir!" protested Kurt. "If you could only see the place—"

"I have," broke in the colonel, "thirty years ago."

Kurt looked at him in amazement. "Then why are we still on the plateau?"

"Because my commanding officer did just what I've just done, classified the information 'Top Secret.' Then he gave me thirty days' extra detail on the plows. After he took my stripes away that is." Colonel Harris rose slowly to his feet. "Dixon," he said softly, "it's not every man who can be a noncommissioned officer in the Space Marines. Sometimes we guess wrong. When we do we do something about it!" There was the hissing crackle of distant summer lightning in his voice and storm clouds seemed to gather about his head. "Wipe those chevrons off!" he roared.

Kurt looked at him in mute protest.

"You heard me!" the colonel thundered.

"Yes-s-s, sir," stuttered Kurt, reluctantly drawing his forearm across his forehead and wiping off the three triangles of white grease paint that marked him a sergeant in the Imperial Space Marines. Quivering with shame, he took a tight grip on his temper and choked back the angry protests that were trying to force their way past his lips.

"Maybe," suggested the colonel, "you'd like to make a complaint to the I.G. He's due in a few days and he might reverse my decision. It has happened before, you know."

"No, sir," said Kurt woodenly.

"Why not?" demanded Harris.

"When I was sent out as a scout for the hunting parties I was given direct orders not to range farther than twenty kilometers to the north. I went sixty." Suddenly his forced composure broke. "I couldn't help it, sir," he said. "There was something behind those peaks that kept pulling me and pulling me and"—he threw up his hands—"you know the rest."

There was a sudden change in the colonel's face as a warm human smile swept across it, and he broke into a peal of laughter. "It's a hell of a feeling, isn't it, son? You know you shouldn't, but at the same time there's something inside you that says you've got to know what's behind those peaks or die. When you get a few more years under your belt you'll find that it isn't just mountains that make you feel like that. Here, boy, have a seat." He gestured toward a woven wicker chair that stood by his desk.

Kurt shifted uneasily from one foot to the other, stunned by the colonel's sudden change of attitude and embarrassed by his request. "Excuse me, sir," he said, "but we aren't out on work detail, and—"

The colonel laughed. "And enlisted men not on work detail don't sit in the presence of officers. Doesn't the way we do things ever strike you as odd, Dixon? On one hand you'd see nothing strange about being yoked to a plow with a major, and on the other, you'd never dream of sitting in his presence off duty."

Kurt looked puzzled. "Work details are different," he said. "We all have to work if we're going to eat. But in the garrison, officers are officers and enlisted men are enlisted men and that's the way it's always been."

Still smiling, the colonel reached into his desk drawer, fished out something, and tossed it to Kurt.

"Stick this in your scalp lock," he said.

Kurt looked at it, stunned. It was a golden feather crossed with a single black bar, the insignia of rank of a second lieutenant of the Imperial Space Marines. The room swirled before his eyes.

"Now," said the older officer, "sit down!"

Kurt slowly lowered himself into the chair and looked at the colonel through bemused eyes.

"Stop gawking!" said Colonel Harris. "You're an officer now! When a man gets too big for his sandals, we give him a new pair—after we let him sweat a while!"

He suddenly grew serious. "Now that you're one of the family, you have a right to know why I'm hushing up the matter of the tableland to the north. What I have to say won't make much sense at first. Later I'm hoping it will. Tell me," he said suddenly, "where did the battalion come from?"

"We've always been here, I guess," said Kurt. "When I was a recruit, Granddad used to tell me stories about us being brought from some place else a long time ago by an iron bird, but it stands to reason that something that heavy can't fly!"

A faraway look came into the colonel's eyes. "Six generations," he mused, "and history becomes legend. Another six and the legends themselves become tales for children. Yes, Kurt," he said softly, "it stands to reason that something that heavy couldn't fly so we'll forget it for a while. We did come from some place else though. Once there was a great empire, so great that all the stars you see at night were only part of it. And then, as things do when age rests too heavily on them, it began to crumble. Commanders fell to fighting among themselves and the Emperor grew weak. The battalion was set down here to operate a forward maintenance station for his ships. We waited but no ships came. For five hundred years no ships have come," said the colonel somberly. "Perhaps they tried to relieve us and couldn't, perhaps the Empire fell with such a crash that we were lost in the wreckage. There are a thousand perhapses that a man can tick off in his mind when the nights are long and sleep comes hard! Lost . . . forgotten . . . who knows?"

Kurt stared at him with a blank expression on his face. Most of what the colonel had said made no sense at all. Wherever Imperial Headquarters was, it hadn't forgotten them. The I.G. still made his inspection every year or so.

The colonel continued as if talking to himself. "But our operational orders said that we would stand by to give all necessary maintenance to Imperial warcraft until properly relieved, and stand by we have."

The old officer's voice seemed to be coming from a place far distant in time and space.

"I'm sorry, sir," said Kurt, "but I don't follow you. If all these things did happen, it was so long ago that they mean nothing to us now."

"But they do!" said Colonel Harris vigorously. "It's because of them that things like your rediscovery of the tableland to the north have to be suppressed for the good of the battalion! Here on the plateau the living is hard. Our work in the fields and the meat brought in by our hunting parties give us just enough to get by on. But here we have the garrison and the Tech Schools—and vague as it has become—a reason for remaining together as the battalion. Out there where the living is easy we'd lose that. We almost did once. A wise commander stopped it before it went too far. There are still a few signs of that time left—left deliberately as reminders of what can happen if commanding officers forget why we're here!"

"What things?" asked Kurt curiously.

"Well, son," said the colonel, picking up his great war bonnet from the desk and gazing at it quizzically, "I don't think you're quite ready for that information yet. Now take off and strut your feather. I've got work to do!"

IV

At War Base Three nobody was happy. Ships that were supposed to be light-months away carrying on the carefully planned search for General Carr's hideout were fluttering down out of the sky like senile penguins, disabled by blown jets, jammed computers, and all the other natural ills that worn out and poorly serviced equipment is heir to. Technical maintenance was quietly going mad. Commander Krogson was being noisy about it.

"Schninkle!" he screamed. "Isn't anything happening anyplace?"

"Nothing yet, sir," said the little man.

"Well *make* something happen!" He hoisted his battered brogans onto the scarred top of the desk and chewed savagely on a frayed cigar. "How are the other sectors doing?"

"No better than we are," said Schninkle. "Commander Snork of Sector Six tried to pull a fast one but he didn't get away with it. He sent his STAP into a plantation planet out at the edge of the Belt and had them hypno the whole population. By the time they were through there were about fifteen million greenies running around yelling 'Up with General Carr!' 'Down with the Lord Protector!' 'Long Live the People's Revolution!' and things like that. Snork even gave them a few medium vortex blasters to make it look more realistic. Then he sent in his whole fleet, tipped off the press at Prime Base, and waited. Guess what the Bureau of Essential Information finally sent him?"

"I'll bite," said Commander Krogson.

"One lousy cub reporter. Snork couldn't back out then so he had to go ahead and blast the planet down to bedrock. This morning he got a three-line notice in *Space* and a citation as Third Rate Protector of the People's Space Ways, Eighth Grade."

"That's better than the nothing we've got so far!" said the commander gloomily.

"Not when the press notice is buried on the next to last page right below the column on 'Our Feathered Comrades'," said Schninkle, "and when the citation is posthumous. They even misspelled his name; it came out Snark!"

V

As Kurt turned to go, there was a sharp knock on Colonel Harris' door.

"Come in!" called the colonel.

Lieutenant Colonel Blick, the battalion executive officer, entered with an arrogant stride and threw his commander a slovenly salute. For a moment he didn't notice Kurt standing at attention beside the door.

"Listen, Harris!" he snarled. "What's the idea of pulling that clean-up detail out of my quarters?"

"There are no servants in this battalion, Blick," the older man said quietly. "When the men come in from work detail at night they're tired. They've earned a rest and as long as I'm C.O. they're going to get it. If you have dirty work that has to be done, do it yourself. You're better able to do it than some poor devil who's been dragging a plow all day. I suggest you check pertinent regulations!"

"Regulations!" growled Blick. "What do you expect me to do, scrub my own floors?"

"I do," said the colonel dryly, "when my wife is too busy to get to it. I haven't noticed that either my dignity or my efficiency have suffered appreciably. I might add," he continued mildly, "that staff officers are supposed to set a good example for their juniors. I don't think either your tone or your manner are those that Lieutenant Dixon should be encouraged to emulate." He gestured toward Kurt and Blick spun on one heel.

"*Lieutenant* Dixon!" he roared in an incredulous voice. "By whose authority?"

"Mine," said the colonel mildly. "In case you've forgotten I am still commanding officer of this battalion."

"I protest!" said Blick. "Commissions have always been awarded by decision of the entire staff."

"Which you now control," replied the colonel.

Kurt coughed nervously. "Excuse me, sir," he said, "but I think I'd better leave."

Colonel Harris shook his head. "You're one of our official family now, son, and you might as well get used to our squabbles. This particular one has been going on between Colonel Blick and me for years. He has no patience with some of our old customs." He turned to Blick. "Have you, Colonel?"

"You're right, I haven't!" growled Blick. "And that's why I'm going to change some of them as soon as I get the chance. The sooner we stop this Tech School nonsense and put the recruits to work in the fields where they belong, the better off we'll all be. Why should a plowman or a hunter have to know how to read wiring diagrams or set tubes? It's nonsense, superstitious nonsense. You!" he said, stabbing his finger into the chest of the startled lieutenant. "You! Dixon! You spent fourteen years in the Tech Schools just like I did when I was a recruit. What for?"

"To learn maintenance, of course," said Kurt.

"What's maintenance?" demanded Blick.

"Taking stuff apart and putting it back together and polishing jet bores with microplanes and putting plates in alignment and checking the meters when we're through to see the job was done right. Then there's class work in Direc calculus and subelectronics and—"

"That's enough!" interrupted Blick. "And now that you've learned all that, what can you do with it?"

Kurt looked at him in surprise.

"Do with it?" he echoed. "You don't *do* anything with it. You just learn it because regulations say you should."

"And this," said Blick, turning to Colonel Harris, "is one of your prize products. Fourteen of his best years poured down the drain and he doesn't even know what for!" He paused and then said in an arrogant voice, "I'm here for a showdown, Harris!"

"Yes?" said the colonel mildly.

"I demand that the Tech Schools be closed at once, and the recruits released for work details. If you want to keep your command, you'll issue that order. The staff is behind me on this!"

Colonel Harris rose slowly to his feet. Kurt waited for the thunder to roll, but strangely enough, it didn't. It almost seemed to him that there was an expression of concealed amusement playing across the colonel's face.

"Some day, just for once," he said, "I wish somebody around here would do something that hasn't been done before."

"What do you mean by that?" demanded Blick.

"Nothing," said the colonel. "You know," he continued conversationally, "a long time ago I walked into my C.O.'s office and made the same demands and the same threats that you're making now. I didn't get very far, though—just as you aren't going to—because I overlooked the little matter of the Inspector General's annual visit. He's due in from Imperial Headquarters Saturday night, isn't he, Blick?"

"You know he is!" growled the other.

"Aren't worried, are you? It occurs to me that the I.G. might take a dim view of your new order."

"I don't think he'll mind," said Blick with a nasty grin. "Now will you issue the order to close the Tech Schools or won't you?"

"Of course not!" said the colonel brusquely.

"That's final?"

Colonel Harris just nodded.

"All right," barked Blick, "you asked for it!"

There was an ugly look on his face as he barked, "Kane! Simmons! Arnett! The rest of you! Get in here!"

The door to Harris' office swung slowly open and revealed a group of officers standing sheepishly in the anteroom.

"Come in, gentlemen," said Colonel Harris.

They came slowly forward and grouped themselves just inside the door.

"I'm taking over!" roared Blick. "This garrison has needed a house-cleaning for a long time and I'm just the man to do it!"

"How about the rest of you?" asked the colonel.

"Beg pardon, sir," said one hesitantly, "but we think Colonel Blick's probably right. I'm afraid we're going to have to confine you for a few days. Just until after the I.G.'s visit," he added apologetically.

"And what do you think the I.G. will say to all this?"

"Colonel Blick says we don't have to worry about that," said the officer. "He's going to take care of everything."

A look of sudden anxiety played across Harris' face and for the first time he seemed on the verge of losing his composure.

"How?" he demanded, his voice betraying his concern.

"He didn't say, sir," the other replied. Harris relaxed visibly.

"All right," said Blick. "Let's get moving!" He walked behind the desk and plumped into the colonel's chair. Hoisting his feet on the desk he gave his first command.

"Take him away!"

There was a sudden roar from the far corner of the room. "No you don't!" shouted Kurt. His battle-ax leaped into his hand as he jumped in front of Colonel Harris, his muscular body taut and his gray eyes flashing defiance.

Blick jumped to his feet. "Disarm that man!" he commanded. There was a certain amount of scuffling as the officers in the front of the group by the door tried to move to the rear and those behind them resolutely defended their more protected positions.

Blick's face grew so purple that he seemed on the verge of apoplexy. "Major Kane," he demanded, "place that man under restraint!"

Kane advanced toward Kurt with a noticeable lack of enthusiasm. Keeping a cautious eye on the glittering ax head, he said in what he obviously hoped to be a placating voice, "Come now, old man. Can't have this sort of thing, you know." He stretched out his hand hesitantly toward Kurt. "Why don't you give me your ax and we'll forget that the incident ever occurred."

Kurt's ax suddenly leaped toward the major's head. Kane stood petrified as death whizzed toward him. At the last split second Kurt gave a practiced twist to his wrist and the ax jumped up, cutting the air over the major's head with a vicious whistle. The top half of his silver staff plume drifted slowly to the floor.

"You want it," roared Kurt, his ax flicking back and forth like a snake's tongue, "you come get it. That goes for the rest of you, too!"

The little knot of officers retreated still farther. Colonel Harris was having the time of his life.

"Give it to 'em, son!" he whooped.

Blick looked contemptuously at the staff and slowly

drew his own ax. Colonel Harris suddenly stopped laughing.

"Wait a minute, Blick!" he said. "This has gone far enough." He turned to Kurt.

"Give them your ax, son."

Kurt looked at him with an expression of hurt bewilderment in his eyes, hesitated for a moment, and then glumly surrendered his weapon to the relieved major.

"Now," snarled Blick, "take that insolent puppy out and feed him to the lizards!"

Kurt drew himself up in injured dignity. "That is no way to refer to a brother officer," he said reproachfully.

The vein in Blick's forehead started to pulse again. "Get him out of here before I tear him to shreds!" he hissed through clenched teeth. There was silence for a moment as he fought to regain control of himself. Finally he succeeded.

"Lock him up!" he said in an approximation to his normal voice. "Tell the provost sergeant I'll send down the charges as soon as I can think up enough."

Kurt was led resentfully from the room.

"The rest of you clear out," said Blick. "I want to talk with Colonel Harris about the I.G."

VI

There was a saying in the Protectorate that when the Lord Protector was angry, stars and heads fell. Commander Krogson felt his wobble on his neck. His far-sweeping scouts were sending back nothing but reports of equipment failure, and the sector commander had coldly informed him that morning that his name rested securely at the bottom of the achievement list. It looked as if War Base Three would shortly have a change of command. "Look, Schninkle," he said desperately, "even if we can't give them anything, couldn't we make a promise that would look good enough to take some of the heat off us?"

Schninkle looked dubious.

"Maybe a new five-year plan?" suggested Krogson.

The little man shook his head. "That's a subject we'd better avoid entirely," he said. "They're still asking nasty questions about what happened to the last one. Mainly on the matter of our transport quota. I took the liberty of passing the buck on down to Logistics. Several of them have been . . . eh . . . removed as a consequence."

"Serves them right!" snorted Krogson. "They got me into that mess with their 'if a freighter and a half flies a light-year and a half in a month and a half, ten freighters can fly ten light-years in ten months!' I knew there was something fishy about it at the time, but I couldn't put my finger on it."

VII

"Take off your war bonnet and make yourself comfortable," said Colonel Harris hospitably.

Blick grunted assent. "This thing is sort of heavy," he said. "I think I'll change uniform regulations while I'm at it."

"There was something you wanted to tell me?" suggested the colonel.

"Yeah," said Blick. "I figure that you figure the I.G.'s going to bail you out of this. Right?"

"I wouldn't be surprised."

"I would," said Blick. "I was up snoopin' around the armory last week. There was something there that started me doing some heavy thinking. Do you know what it was?"

"I can guess," said the colonel.

"As I looked at it, it suddenly occurred to me what a happy coincidence it is that the Inspector General always arrives just when you happen to need him."

"It is odd, come to think of it."

"Something else occurred to me, too. I got to thinking that if I were C.O. and I wanted to keep the troops whipped into line, the easiest way to do it would be to have a visible symbol of Imperial Headquarters appear in person once in a while."

"That makes sense," admitted Harris, "especially since the chaplain has started preaching that Imperial Headquarters is where good marines go when they die—*if* they follow regulations while they're alive. But how would you manage it?"

"Just the way you did. I'd take one of the old battle suits, wait until it was good and dark, and then slip out the back way and climb up six or seven thousand feet. Then I'd switch on my landing lights and drift slowly down to the parade field to review the troops." Blick grinned triumphantly.

"It might work," admitted Colonel Harris, "but I was under the impression that those rigs were so heavy that a man couldn't even walk in one, let alone fly."

Blick grinned triumphantly. "Not if the suit was powered. If a man were to go up into the tower of the arsenal and pick the lock of the little door labled 'Danger! Absolutely No Admittance,' he might find a whole stack of shiny little cubes that look suspiciously like the illustrations of power packs in the tech manuals."

"That he might," agreed the colonel.

Blick shifted back in his chair. "Aren't worried, are you?"

Colonel Harris shook his head. "I was for a moment when I thought you'd told the rest of the staff, but I'm not now."

"You should be! When the I.G. arrives this time, I'm going to be inside that suit. There's going to be a new order around here, and he's just what I need to put the stamp of approval on it. When the Inspector General talks, nobody questions!"

He looked at Harris expectantly, waiting for a look of consternation to sweep across his face. The colonel just laughed.

"Blick," he said, "you're in for a big surprise!"

"What do you mean?" said the other suspiciously.

"Simply that I know you better than you know yourself. You wouldn't be executive officer if I didn't. You know, Blick, I've got a hunch that the battalion is going to change the man more than the man is going to

change the battalion. And now if you'll excuse me—"
He started toward the door. Blick moved to intercept
him.

"Don't trouble yourself," chuckled the colonel, "I can
find my own way to the cell block." There was a broad
grin on his face. "Besides, you've got work to do."

There was a look of bewilderment in Blick's face as
the erect figure went out the door. "I don't get it," he
said to himself. "I just don't get it!"

VIII

Flight Officer Ozaki was unhappy. Trouble had started
two hours after he lifted his battered scout off War Base
Three and showed no signs of letting up. He sat glumly
at his controls and enumerated his woes. First there
was the matter of the air conditioner which had ac-
quired an odd little hum and discharged into the cabin
oxygen redolent with the rich, ripe odor of rotting fish.
Secondly, something had happened to the complex
insides of his food synthesizer and no matter what buttons he punched, all that emerged from the ejector
were quivering slabs of undercooked protein base
smeared with a raspberry-flavored goo.

Not last, but worst of all, the ship's fuel converter
was rapidly becoming more erratic. Instead of a slow,
steady feeding of the plutonite ribbon into the combus-
tion chamber, there were moments when the mechanism would falter and then leap ahead. The resulting
sudden injection of several square millimicrons of tape
would send a sudden tremendous flare of energy spout-
ing out through the rear jets. The pulse only lasted for a
fraction of a second, but the sudden application of several G's meant a momentary blackout and, unless he
was strapped carefully into the pilot seat, several new
bruises to add to the old.

What made Ozaki the unhappiest was that there was
nothing he could do about it. Pilots who wanted to stay
alive just didn't tinker with the mechanism of their
ships.

Glumly he pulled out another red-bordered IMME-DIATE MAINTENANCE card from the rack and began to fill it in.

Description of item requiring maintenance: "Shower thermostat, M7, Small Standard."

Nature of malfunction: "Shower will deliver only boiling water."

Justification for immediate maintenance: Slowly in large, block letters Ozaki bitterly inked in "Haven't had a bath since I left base!" and tossed the card into the already overflowing gripe box with a feeling of helpless anger.

"Kitchen mechanics," he muttered. "Couldn't do a decent repair job if they wanted to—and most of the time they don't. I'd like to see one of them three days out on a scout sweep with a toilet that won't flush!"

IX

It was a roomy cell as cells go but Kurt wasn't happy there. His continual striding up and down was making Colonel Harris nervous.

"Relax, son," he said gently, "you'll just wear yourself out."

Kurt turned to face the colonel who was stretched out comfortably on his cot. "Sir," he said in a conspiratorial whisper, "we've got to break out of here."

"What for?" asked Harris. "This is the first decent rest I've had in years."

"You aren't going to let Blick get away with this?" demanded Kurt in a shocked voice.

"Why not?" said the colonel. "He's the exec, isn't he? If something happened to me, he'd have to take over command anyway. He's just going through the impatient stage, that's all. A few days behind my desk will settle him down. In two weeks he'll be so sick of the job he'll be down on his knees begging me to take over again."

Kurt decided to try a new tack. "But, sir, he's going to shut down the Tech Schools!"

"A little vacation won't hurt the kids," said the colonel indulgently.

"After a week or so the wives will get so sick of having them underfoot all day that they'll turn the heat on him. Blick has six kids himself, and I've a hunch his wife won't be any happier than the rest. She's a very determined woman, Kurt, a very determined woman!"

Kurt had a feeling he was getting no place rapidly. "Please, sir," he said earnestly, "I've got a plan."

"Yes?"

"Just before the guard makes his evening check-in, stretch out on the bed and start moaning. I'll yell that you're dying and when he comes in to check, I'll jump him!"

"You'll do no such thing!" said the colonel sternly. "Sergeant Wetzel is an old friend of mine. Can't you get it through your thick head that I don't want to escape? When you've held command as long as I have, you'll welcome a chance for a little peace and quiet. I know Blick inside out, and I'm not worried about him. But, if you've got your heart set on escaping, I suppose there's no particular reason why you shouldn't. Do it the easy way, though. Like this." He walked to the bars that fronted the cell and bellowed, "Sergeant Wetzel! Sergeant Wetzel!"

"Coming, sir!" called a voice from down the corridor. There was a shuffle of running feet and a gray scalp-locked and extremely portly sergeant puffed into view.

"What will it be, sir?" he asked.

"Colonel Blick or any of the staff around?" questioned the colonel.

"No, sir," said the sergeant. "They're all upstairs celebrating."

"Good!" said Harris. "Unlock the door, will you?"

"Anything you say, colonel," said the old man agreeably and produced a large key from his pouch and fitted it into the lock. There was a slight creaking and the door swung open.

"Young Dixon here wants to escape," said the colonel.

"It's all right by me," replied the sergeant, "though

it's going to be awkward when Colonel Blick asks what happened to him."

"The lieutenant has a plan," confided the colonel. "He's going to overpower you and escape."

"There's more to it than just that!" said Kurt. "I'm figuring on swapping uniforms with you. That way I can walk right out through the front gate without anybody being the wiser."

"That," said the sergeant, slowly looking down at his sixty-three inch waist, "will take a heap of doing. You're welcome to try though."

"Let's get on with it then," said Kurt, winding up a roundhouse swing.

"If it's all the same with you, lieutenant," said the old sergeant, eyeing Kurt's rocklike fist nervously, "I'd rather have the colonel do any overpowering that's got to be done."

Colonel Harris grinned and walked over to Wetzel.

"Ready?"

"Ready!"

Harris' fist traveled a bare five inches and tapped Wetzel lightly on the chin.

"Oof!" grunted the sergeant cooperatively and staggered back to a point where he could collapse on the softest of the two cots.

The exchange of clothes was quickly effected. Except for the pants—which persisted in dropping down to Kurt's ankles—and the war bonnet—which with equal persistence kept sliding down over his ears—he was ready to go. The pants problem was solved easily by stuffing a pillow inside them. This Kurt fondly believed made him look more like the rotund sergeant than ever. The garrison bonnet presented a more difficult problem, but he finally achieved a partial solution. By holding it up with his left hand and keeping the palm tightly pressed against his forehead, it should appear to the casual observer that he was walking engrossed in deep thought.

The first two hundred yards were easy. The corridor was deserted and he plodded confidently along, the great war bonnet wobbling sedately on his head in spite of his best efforts to keep it steady. When he finally reached the exit gate, he knocked on it firmly and called to the duty sergeant.

"Open up! It's Wetzel."

Unfortunately, just then he grew careless and let go of his head-gear. As the door swung open, the great war bonnet swooped down over his ears and came to rest on his shoulders. The result was that where his head normally was there could be seen only a nest of weaving feathers. The duty sergeant's jaw suddenly dropped as he got a good look at the strange figure that stood in the darkened corridor. And then with remarkable presence of mind he slammed the door shut in Kurt's face and clicked the bolt.

"Sergeant of the guard!" he bawled. "Sergeant of the guard! There's a *thing* in the corridor!"

"What kind of a thing?" inquired a sleepy voice from the guard room.

"A horrible kind of a thing with wiggling feathers where its head ought to be," replied the sergeant.

"Get its name, rank, and serial number," said the sleepy voice.

Kurt didn't want to hear any more. Disentangling himself from the head-dress with some difficulty, he hurled it aside and pelted back down the corridor.

Lieutenant Dixon wandered back into the cell with a crestfallen look on his face. Colonel Harris and the old sergeant were so deeply engrossed in a game of "rockets high" that they didn't even see him at first. Kurt coughed and the colonel looked up.

"Change your mind?"

"No, sir," said Kurt. "Something slipped."

"What?" asked the colonel.

"Sergeant Wetzel's war bonnet. I'd rather not talk about it." He sank down on his bunk and buried his head in his hands.

"Excuse me," said the sergeant apologetically, "but if the lieutenant's through with my pants I'd like to have them back. There's a draft in here."

Kurt silently exchanged clothes and then moodily walked over to the grille that barred the window and stood looking out.

"Why not go upstairs to officers' country and out that way?" suggested the sergeant, who hated the idea of being overpowered for nothing. "If you can get to the front gate without one of the staff spotting you, you can walk right out. The sentry never notices faces, but just checks for insignia."

Kurt grabbed Sergeant Wetzel's plump hand and wrung it warmly. "I don't know how to thank you," he stammered.

"Then it's about time you learned," said the colonel. "The usual practice in civilized battalions is to say 'thank you.'"

"Thank you!" said Kurt.

"Quite all right," said the sergeant. "Take the first stairway to your left. When you get to the top, turn left again and the corridor will take you straight to the exit."

Kurt got safely to the top of the stairs and turned right. Three hundred feet later the corridor ended in a blank wall. A small passageway angled off to the left and he set off down it. It also came to a dead end in a small anteroom whose farther wall was occupied by a set of great bronze doors. He turned and started to retrace his steps. He had almost reached the main corridor when he heard angry voices sounding from it. He peeked cautiously around the corridor. His escape route was blocked by two officers engaged in acrimonious argument. Neither was too sober and the captain obviously wasn't giving the major the respect that a field officer usually commanded.

"I don't care what she said!" the captain shouted. "I saw her first."

The major grabbed him by the shoulder and pushed him back against the wall. "It doesn't matter who saw her first. You keep away from her or there's going to be trouble!"

The captain's face flushed with rage. With a snarl he

tore off the major's breechcloth and struck him in the face with it.

The major's face grew hard and cold. He stepped back, clicked his calloused heels together and bowed slightly.

"Axes or fists?"

"Axes," snapped the captain.

"May I suggest the armory anteroom?" said the major formally. "We won't be disturbed there."

"As you wish, sir," said the captain with equal formality. "Your breechcloth, sir." The major donned it with dignity and they started down the hall toward Kurt. He turned and fled back down the corridor.

In a second he was back in the anteroom. Unless he did something quickly was he trapped. Two flaming torches were set in brackets on each side of the great bronze door. As flickering pools of shadow chased each other across the worn stone floor, Kurt searched desperately for some other way out. There was none. The only possible exit was through the bronze portals. The voices behind him grew louder. He ran forward, grabbed a projecting handle, and pulled. One door creaked open slightly and with a sigh of relief Kurt slipped inside.

There were no torches here. The great hall stood in half darkness, its only illumination the pale moonlight that streamed down through the arching skylight that formed the central ceiling. He stood for a moment in awe, impressed in spite of himself by the strange unfamiliar shapes that loomed before him in the half-darkness. He was suddenly brought back to reality by the sound of voices in the anteroom.

"Hey! The armory door's open!"

"So what? That place is off limits to everybody but the C.O."

"Blick won't care. Let's fight in there. There should be more room."

Kurt quickly scanned the hall for a safe hiding place. At the far end stood what looked like a great bronze statue, its burnished surface gleaming dimly in the moonlight. As the door swung open behind him, he slipped cautiously through the shadows until he reached it. It looked like a coffin with feet, but to one side of it there was a dark pool of shadow. He slipped into it and pressed himself close against the cold metal. As he did so his hipbone pressed against a slight protrusion and with a slight clicking sound, a hinged middle section of the metallic figure swung open, exposing a dark cavity. The thing was hollow!

Kurt had a sudden idea. "Even if they do come down here," he thought, "they'd never think of looking inside this thing!" With some difficulty he wiggled inside and pulled the hatch shut after him. There were legs to the thing—his own fit snugly into them—but no arms.

The two officers strode out of the shadows at the other end of the hall. They stopped in the center of the armory and faced each other like fighting cocks. Kurt gave a sigh of relief. It looked as if he were safe for the moment.

There was a sudden wicked glitter of moonlight on ax-heads as their weapons leaped into their hands. They stood frozen for a moment in a murderous tableau and then the captain's ax hummed toward his opponent's head in a vicious slash. There was a shower of sparks as the major parried and then with a quick wrist twist sent his own weapon looping down toward the captain's midriff. The other pulled his ax down to ward the blow, but he was only partially successful. The keen obsidian edge raked his ribs and blood dripped darkly in the moonlight.

As Kurt watched intently, he began to feel the first faint stirrings of claustrophobia. The Imperial designers had planned their battle armor for efficiency rather than comfort and Kurt felt as if he were locked away in a cramped dark closet. His malaise wasn't helped by a sudden realization that when the men left they might very well lock the door behind them. His decision to change his hiding place was hastened when a bank of dark clouds swept across the face of the moon. The flood of light poured down through the skylight suddenly dimmed until Kurt could barely make out the pirouetting forms of the two officers who were fighting in the center of the hall.

This was his chance. If he could slip down the darkened side of the hall before the moon lighted up the hall again, he might be able to slip out of the hall unobserved. He pushed against the closed hatch through which he entered. It refused to open. A feeling of trapped panic started to roll over him, but he fought it back. "There must be some way to open this from the inside," he thought.

As his fingers wandered over the dark interior of the suit looking for a release lever, they encountered a bank of keys set just below his midriff. He pressed one experimentally. A quiet hum filled the armor and suddenly a feeling of weightlessness came over him. He stiffened in fright. As he did so one of his steel shod feet pushed lightly backwards against the floor. That was enough. Slowly, like a child's balloon caught in a light draft, he drifted toward the center of the hall. He struggled violently, but since he was now several inches above the floor and rising slowly it did him no good.

The fight was progressing splendidly. Both men were master axmen, and in spite of being slightly drunk, were putting on a brilliant exhibition. Each was bleeding from a dozen minor slashes, but neither had been seriously axed as yet. Their flashing strokes and counters were masterful, so masterful that Kurt slowly forgot his increasingly awkward situation as he became more and more absorbed in the fight before him. The blond captain was slightly the better axman, but the major compensated for it by occasionally whistling in cuts that to Kurt's experienced eye seemed perilously close to fouls. He grew steadily more partisan in his feelings until one particularly unscrupulous attempt broke down his restraint altogether.

"Pull down your guard!" he screamed to the captain. "He's trying to cut you below the belt!" His voice reverberated within the battle suit and boomed out with strange metallic overtones.

Both men whirled in the direction of the sound. They

could see nothing for a moment and then the major caught sight of the strange menacing figure looming above him in the murky darkness.

Dropping his ax he dashed frantically toward the exit shrieking: "It's the Inspector General!"

The captain's reflexes were a second slower. Before he could take off, Kurt poked his head out of the open faceport and shouted down, "It's only me, Dixon! Get me out of here, will you?"

The captain stared up at him goggle-eyed. "What kind of a contraption is that?" he demanded. "And what are you doing in it?"

Kurt by now was floating a good ten feet off the floor. He had visions of spending the night on the ceiling and he wasn't happy about it. "Get me down now," he pleaded. "We can talk after I get out of this thing."

The captain gave a leap upwards and tried to grab Kurt's ankles. His jump was short and his outstretched fingers gave the weightless armor a slight shove that sent it bobbing up another three feet.

He cocked his head back and called up to Kurt. "Can't reach you now. We'll have to try something else. How did you get into that thing in the first place?"

"The middle section is hinged," said Kurt. "When I pulled it shut, it clicked."

"Well, unclick it!"

"I tried that. That's why I'm up here now."

"Try again," said the man on the floor. "If you can open the hatch, you can drop down and I'll catch you."

"Here I come!" said Kurt, his fingers selecting a stud at random. He pushed. There was a terrible blast of flame from the shoulder jets and he screamed skywards on a pillar of fire. A microsecond later, he reached the skylight. Something had to give. It did!

At fifteen thousand feet the air pressure dropped to the point where the automatics took over and the face plate clicked shut. Kurt didn't notice that. He was out like a light. At thirty thousand feet the heaters cut in. Forty seconds later he was in free space. Things could have been worse though; he still had air for two hours.

X

Flight Officer Ozaki was taking a catnap when the alarm on the radiation detector went off. Dashing the sleep out of his eyes, he slipped rapidly into the control seat and cut off the gong. His fingers danced over the controls in a blur of movement. Swiftly the vision screen shifted until the little green dot that indicated a source of radiant energy was firmly centered. Next he switched on the pulse analyzer and watched carefully as it broke down the incoming signal into components and sent them surging across the scope in the form of sharp-toothed sine waves. There was an odd peak to them, a strength and sharpness that he hadn't seen before.

"Doesn't look familiar," he muttered to himself, "but I'd better check to make sure."

He punched the comparison button and while the analyzer methodically began to check the incoming trace against the known patterns stored up in its compact little memory bank, he turned back to the vision screen. He switched on high magnification and the system rushed toward him. It expanded from a single pinpoint of light into a distinct planetary system. At its center a giant dying sun expanded on the plate like a malignant red eye. As he watched, the green dot moved appreciably, a thin red line stretching out behind it to indicate its course from point of first detection. Ozaki's fingers moved over the controls and a broken line of white light came into being on the screen. With careful adjustments he moved it up toward the green track left by the crawling red dot. When he had an exact overlay, he carefully moved the line back along the course that the energy emitter had followed prior to detection.

Ozaki was tense. It looked as if he might have something. He gave a sudden whoop of excitement as the broken white line intersected the orange dot of a planetary mass. A vision of the promised thirty-day leave and six months' extra pay danced before his eyes as he waited for the pulse analyzer to clear.

"Home!" he thought ecstatically. "Home and un-plugged plumbing!"

With a final whir of relays the analyzer clucked like a contented chicken and dropped an identity card out of its emission slot. Ozaki grabbed it and scanned it eagerly. At the top was printed in red, "Identity. Unknown," and below in smaller letters, "Suggest check of trace pattern on base analyzer." He gave a sudden whistle as his eyes caught the energy utilization index. 927! That was fifty points higher than it had any right to be. The best tech in the Protectorate considered himself lucky if he could tune a propulsion unit so that it delivered a thrust of forty-five per cent of rated maximum. Whatever was out there was hot! Too hot for one man to handle alone. With quick decision he punched the transmission key of his space communicator and sent a call winging back to War Base Three.

XI

Commander Krogson stormed up and down his office in a frenzy of impatience.

"It shouldn't be more than another fifteen minutes, sir," said Schninkle.

Krogson snorted. "That's what you said an hour ago! What's the matter with those people down there? I want the identity of that ship and I want it now."

"It's not Identification's fault," explained the other. "The big analyzer is in pretty bad shape and it keeps jamming. They're afraid that if they take it apart they won't be able to get it back together again."

The next two hours saw Krogson's blood pressure steadily rising toward the explosion point. Twice he ordered the whole identification section transferred to a labor battalion and twice he had to rescind the command when Schninkle pointed out that scrapings from the bottom of the barrel were better than nothing at all. His fingernails were chewed down to the quick when word finally came through.

"Identification, sir," said a hesitant voice on the intercom.

"Well?" demanded the commander.

"The analyzer says—" The voice hesitated again.

"The analyzer says what?" shouted Krogson in a fury of impatience.

"The analyzer says that the trace pattern is that of one of the old Imperial drive units."

"That's impossible!" sputtered the commander. "The last Imperial base was smashed five hundred years ago. What of their equipment was salvaged has long since been worn out and tossed on the scrap heap. The machine must be wrong!"

"Not this time," said the voice. "We checked the memory bank manually and there's no mistake. It's an Imperial all right. Nobody can produce a drive unit like that these days."

Commander Krogson leaned back in his chair, his eyes veiled in deep thought. "Schninkle," he said finally, thinking out loud, "I've got a hunch that maybe we've stumbled on something big. Maybe the Lord Protector is right about there being a plot to knock him over, but maybe he's wrong about who's trying to do it. What if all these centuries since the Empire collapsed a group of Imperials have been hiding out waiting for their chance?"

Schninkle digested the idea for a moment. "It could be," he said slowly. "If there is such a group, they couldn't pick a better time than now to strike; the Protectorate is so wobbly that it wouldn't take much of a shove to topple it over."

The more he thought about it, the more sense the idea made to Krogson. Once he felt a fleeting temptation to hush up the whole thing. If there were Imperials and they did take over, maybe they would put an end to the frenzied rat race that was slowly ruining the galaxy—a race that sooner or later entangled every competent man in the great web of intrigue and power politics that stretched through the Protectorate and forced him in self-defense to keep clawing his way toward the top of the heap.

Regretfully he dismissed the idea. This was a matter of his own neck, here and now!

"It's a big IF, Schninkle," he said, "but if I've guessed right, we've bailed ourselves out. Get hold of that scout and find out his position."

Schninkle scooted out of the door. A few minutes later he dashed back in. "I've just contacted the scout!" he said excitedly. "He's closed in on the power source and it isn't a ship after all. It's a man in space armor! The drive unit is cut off, and it's heading out of the system at fifteen hundred per. The pilot is standing by for instructions."

"Tell him to intercept and capture!" Schninkle started out of the office. "Wait a second; what's the scout's position?"

Schninkle's face fell. "He doesn't quite know, sir."

"He *what?*" demanded the commander.

"He doesn't quite know," repeated the little man. "His astrocomputer went haywire six hours out of base."

"Just our luck!" swore Krogson. "Well, tell him to leave his transmitter on. We'll ride in on his beam. Better call the sector commander while you're at it and tell him what's happened."

"Beg pardon, commander," said Schninkle, "but I wouldn't advise it."

"Why not?" asked Krogson.

"You're next in line to be sector commander, aren't you, sir?"

"I guess so," said the commander.

"If this pans out, you'll be in a position to knock him over and grab his job, won't you?" asked Schninkle shyly.

"Could be," admitted Krogson in a tired voice. "Not because I want to, though—but because I have to. I'm not as young as I once was, and the boys below are pushing pretty hard. It's either up or out—and out is always feet first."

"Put yourself in the sector commander's shoes for a

minute," suggested the little man. "What would you do if a war base commander came through with news of a possible Imperial base?"

A look of grim comprehension came over Krogson's face. "Of course! I'd ground the commander's ships and send out my own fleet. I must be slipping; I should have thought of that at once!"

"On the other hand," said Schninkle, "you might call him and request permission to conduct routine maneuvers. He'll approve as a matter of course and you'll have an excuse for taking out the full fleet. Once in deep space, you can slap on radio silence and set course for the scout. If there is an Imperial base out there, nobody will know anything about it until it's blasted. I'll stay back here and keep my eyes on things for you."

Commander Krogson grinned. "Schninkle, it's a pleasure to have you in my command. How would you like me to make you Devoted Servant of the Lord Protector, Eighth Class? It carries an extra shoe ration coupon!"

"If it's all the same with you," said Schninkle, "I'd just as soon have Saturday afternoons off."

XII

As Kurt struggled up out of the darkness, he could hear a gong sounding in the faint distance. *Bong!* BONG! *BONG!* It grew nearer and louder. He shook his head painfully and groaned. There was light from some place beating against his eyelids. Opening them was too much effort. He was in some sort of a bunk. He could feel that. But the gong. He lay there concentrating on it. Slowly he began to realize that the beat didn't come from outside. It was his head. It felt swollen and sore and each pulse of his heart sent a hammer thud through it.

One by one his senses began to return to normal. As his nose reassumed its normal acuteness, it began to quiver. There was a strange scent in the air, an unpleasant sickening scent as of—he chased the scent down his aching memory channels until he finally had it cornered—rotting fish. With that to anchor on, he slowly began to reconstruct reality. He had been floating high above the floor in the armory and the captain had been trying to get him down. Then he had pushed a button. There had been a microsecond of tremendous acceleration and then a horrendous crash. That must have been the skylight. After the crash was darkness, then the gongs, and now fish—dead and rotting fish.

"I must be alive," he decided. "Imperial Headquarters would never smell like this!"

He groaned and slowly opened one eye. Wherever he was he hadn't been there before. He opened the other eye. He was in a room. A room with a curved ceiling and curving walls. Slowly, with infinite care, he hung his head over the side of the bunk. Below him in a form-fitting chair before a bank of instruments sat a small man with yellow skin and blue-black hair. Kurt coughed. The man looked up. Kurt asked the obvious question.

"Where am I?"

"I'm not permitted to give you any information," said the small man. His speech had an odd slurred quality to Kurt's ear.

"Something stinks!" said Kurt.

"It sure does," said the small man gloomily. "It must be worse for you. I'm used to it."

Kurt surveyed the cabin with interest. There were a lot of gadgets tucked away here and there that looked familiar. They were like the things he had worked on in Tech School except that they were cruder, and simpler. They looked as if they had been put together by an eight-year-old recruit who was doing the first trial assembly. He decided to make another stab at establishing some sort of communication with the little man.

"How come you have everything in one room? We always used to keep different things in different shops."

"No comment," said Ozaki.

Kurt had a feeling he was butting his head against a stone wall. He decided to make one more try.

"I give up," he said, wrinkling his nose, "where'd you hide it?"

"Hide what?" asked the little man.

"The fish," said Kurt.

"No comment."

"Why not?" asked Kurt.

"Because there isn't anything that can be done about it," said Ozaki. "It's the air conditioner. Something's haywire inside."

"What's an air conditioner?" asked Kurt.

"That square box over your head."

Kurt looked at it, closed his eyes, and thought for a moment. The thing did look familiar. Suddenly a picture of it popped into his mind. Page 318 in the "Manual of Auxiliary Mechanisms."

"It's fantastic!" he said.

"What is?" said the little man.

"This," Kurt pointed to the conditioner. "I didn't know they existed in real life. I thought they were just in books. You got a first echelon kit?"

"Sure," said Ozaki. "It's in the recess by the head of the bunk. Why?"

Kurt pulled the kit out of its retaining clips and opened its cover, fishing around until he found a small screwdriver and a pair of needle-nose pliers.

"I think I'll fix it," he said conversationally.

"Oh, no you won't!" howled Ozaki. "Air with fish is better than no air at all." But before he could do anything, Kurt had pulled the cover off the air conditioner and was probing into the intricate mechanism with his screwdriver. A slight thumping noise came from inside. Kurt cocked his ear and thought. Suddenly his screwdriver speared down through the maze of whirring parts. He gave a slow quarter turn and the internal thumping disappeared.

"See," he said triumphantly, "no more fish!"

Ozaki stopped shaking long enough to give the air a tentative sniff. He had got out of the habit of smelling in self-defense and it took him a minute or two to detect the difference. Suddenly a broad grin swept across his face.

"It's going away! I do believe it's going away!"

Kurt gave the screwdriver another quarter of a turn and suddenly the sharp spicy scent of pines swept through the scout. Ozaki took a deep ecstatic breath and relaxed in his chair. His face lost its pallor.

"How did you do it?" he said finally.

"No comment," said Kurt pleasantly.

There was silence from below. Ozaki was in the throes of a brainstorm. He was more impressed by Kurt's casual repair of the air conditioner than he liked to admit.

"Tell me," he said cautiously, "can you fix other things besides air conditioners?"

"I guess so," said Kurt, "if it's just simple stuff like this." He gestured around the cabin. "Most of the stuff here needs fixing. They've got it together wrong."

"Maybe we could make a dicker," said Ozaki. "You fix things, I answer questions—some questions that is," he added hastily.

"It's a deal," said Kurt, who was filled with a burning curiosity as to his whereabouts. Certain things were already clear in his mind. He knew that wherever he was he'd never been there before. That meant evidently that there was a garrison on the other side of the mountains whose existence had never been suspected. What bothered him was how he had got there.

"Check," said Ozaki. "First, do you know anything about plumbing?"

"What's plumbing?" asked Kurt curiously.

"Pipes," said Ozaki. "They're plugged. They've been plugged for more time than I like to think about."

"I can try," said Kurt.

"Good!" said the pilot and ushered him into the small cubicle that opened off the rear bulkhead. "You might tackle the shower while you're at it."

"What's a shower?"

"That curved dingbat up there," said Ozaki pointing. "The thermostat's out of whack."

"Thermostats are kid stuff," said Kurt, shutting the door.

Ten minutes later Kurt came out. "It's all fixed."

"I don't believe it," said Ozaki, shouldering his way past Kurt. He reached down and pushed a small curved handle. There was the satisfying sound of rushing water. He next reached into the little shower compartment and turned the knob to the left. With a hiss a needle spray of cold water burst forth. The pilot looked at Kurt with awe in his eyes.

"If I hadn't seen it, I wouldn't have believed it! That's two answers you've earned."

Kurt peered back into the cubicle curiously. "Well, first," he said, "now that I've fixed them, what are they *for?*"

Ozaki explained briefly and a look of amazement came over Kurt's face. Machinery he knew, but the idea that it could be used for something was hard to grasp.

"If I hadn't seen it, I wouldn't have believed it!" he said slowly. This would be something to tell when he got home. Home! The pressing question of location popped back into his mind.

"How far are we from the garrison?" he asked.

Ozaki made a quick mental calculation.

"Roughly two light-seconds," he said.

"How far's that in kilometers?"

Ozaki thought again. "Around six hundred thousand. I'll run off the exact figures if you want them."

Kurt gulped. No place could be that far away. Not even Imperial Headquarters! He tried to measure out the distance in his mind in terms of days' marches, but he soon found himself lost. Thinking wouldn't do it. He had to see with his own eyes where he was.

"How do you get outside?" he asked.

Ozaki gestured toward the air lock that opened at the rear of the compartment. "Why?"

"I want to go out for a few minutes to sort of get my bearings."

Ozaki looked at him in disbelief. "What's your game, anyhow?" he demanded.

It was Kurt's turn to look bewildered. "I haven't any

game. I'm just trying to find out where I am so I'll know which way to head to get back to the garrison."

"It'll be a long, cold walk." Ozaki laughed and hit the stud that slid back the ray screens on the vision ports. "Take a look."

Kurt looked out into nothingness, a blue-black void marked only by distant pinpoints of light. He suddenly felt terribly alone, lost in a blank immensity that had no boundaries. *Down* was gone and so was *up*. There was only this tiny lighted room with nothing underneath it. The port began to swim in front of his eyes as a sudden, strange vertigo swept over him. He felt that if he looked out into that terrible space for another moment he would lose his sanity. He covered his eyes with his hands and staggered back to the center of the cabin.

Ozaki slid the ray screens back in place. "Kind of gets you first time, doesn't it?"

Kurt had always carried a little automatic compass within his head. Wherever he had gone, no matter how far afield he had wandered, it had always pointed steadily toward home. Now for the first time in his life the needle was spinning helplessly. It was an uneasy feeling. He had to get oriented.

"Which way is the garrison?" he pleaded.

Ozaki shrugged. "Over there some place. I don't know whereabouts on the planet you come from. I didn't pick up your track until you were in free space."

"Over where?" asked Kurt.

"Think you can stand another look?"

Kurt braced himself and nodded. The pilot opened a side port to vision and pointed. There, seemingly motionless in the black emptiness of space, floated a great greenish-gray globe. It didn't make sense to Kurt. The satellite that hung somewhat to the left did. Its face was different, the details were sharper than he'd ever seen them before, but the features he knew as well as his own. Night after night on scouting detail for the hunting parties while waiting for sleep he had watched the silver sphere ride through the clouds above him.

He didn't want to believe but he had to!

His face was white and tense as he turned back to Ozaki. A thousand sharp and burning questions milled chaotically through his mind.

"Where am I?" he demanded. "How did I get out here? Who are you? Where did you come from?"

"You're in a spaceship," said Ozaki, "a two-man scout. And that's all you're going to get out of me until you get some more work done. You might as well start on this microscopic projector. The thing burned out just as the special investigator was about to reveal who had blown off the commissioner's head by wiring a bit of plutonite into his autoshave. I've been going nuts ever since trying to figure out who did it!"

Kurt took some tools out of the first echelon kit and knelt obediently down beside the small projector.

Three hours later they sat down to dinner. Kurt had repaired the food machine and Ozaki was slowly masticating synthasteak that for the first time in days tasted like synthasteak. As he ecstatically lifted the last savory morsel to his mouth, the ship gave a sudden leap that plastered him and what remained of his supper against the rear bulkhead. There was darkness for a second and then the ceiling lights flickered on, then off, and then on again. Ozaki picked himself up and gingerly ran his fingers over the throbbing lump that was beginning to grow out of the top of his head. His temper wasn't improved when he looked up and saw Kurt still seated at the table calmly cutting himself another piece of pie.

"You should have braced yourself," said Kurt conversationally. "The converter's out of phase. You can hear her build up for a jump if you listen. When she does you ought to brace yourself. Maybe you don't hear so good?" he asked helpfully.

"Don't talk with your mouth full, it isn't polite," snarled Ozaki.

Late that night the converter cut out altogether. Ozaki was sleeping the sleep of the innocent and didn't find out about it for several hours. When he did awake, it was to Kurt's gentle shaking.

"Hey!" Ozaki groaned and buried his face in the pillow.

"Hey!" This time the voice was louder. The pilot yawned and tried to open his eyes.

"Is it important if all the lights go out?" the voice queried. The import of the words suddenly struck home and Ozaki sat bolt upright in his bunk. He opened his eyes, blinked, and opened them again. The lights *were* out. There was a strange unnatural silence about the ship.

"Good Lord!" he shouted and jumped for the controls. "The power's off."

He hit the starter switch but nothing happened. The converter was jammed solid. Ozaki began to sweat. He fumbled over the control board until he found the switch that cut the emergency batteries into the lighting circuit. Again nothing happened.

"If you're trying to run the lights on the batteries, they won't work," said Kurt in a conversational tone.

"Why not?" snapped Ozaki as he punched savagely and futilely at the starter button.

"They're dead," said Kurt. "I used them all up."

"You what?" yelled the pilot in anguish.

"I used them all up. You see, when the converter went out, I woke up. After a while the sun started to come up, and it began to get awfully hot so I hooked the batteries into the refrigeration coils. Kept the place nice and cool while they lasted."

Ozaki howled. When he swung the shutter of the forward port to let in some light, he howled again. This time in dead earnest. The giant red sun of the system was no longer perched off to the left at a comfortable distance. Instead, before Ozaki's horrified eyes was a great red mass that stretched from horizon to horizon.

"We're falling into the sun!" he screamed.

"It's getting sort of hot," said Kurt. "Hot" was an understatement. The thermometer needle pointed at a hundred and ten and was climbing steadily.

Ozaki jerked open the stores compartment door and grabbed a couple of spare batteries. As quickly as his trembling fingers would work, he connected them to the emergency power line. A second later the cabin lights flickered on and Ozaki was warming up the space communicator. He punched the transmitter key and a call went arcing out through hyperspace. The vision screen flickered and the bored face of a communication tech, third class, appeared.

"Give me Commander Krogson at once!" demanded Ozaki.

"Sorry, old man," yawned the other, "but the commander's having breakfast. Call back in half an hour, will you?"

"This is an emergency! Put me through at once!"

"Can't help it," said the other, "nobody can disturb the Old Man while he's having breakfast!"

"Listen, you knucklehead," screamed Ozaki, "if you don't get me through to the commander as of right now, I'll have you in the uranium mines so fast that you won't know what hit you!"

"You and who else?" drawled the tech.

"Me and my cousin Takahashi!" snarled the pilot. "He's Reclassification Officer for the Base STAP."

The tech's face went white. "Yes, sir!" he stuttered. "Right away, sir! No offense meant, sir!" He disappeared from the screen. There was a moment of darkness and then the interior of Commander Krogson's cabin flashed on.

The commander was having breakfast. His teeth rested on the white tablecloth and his mouth was full of mush.

"Commander Krogson!" said Ozaki desperately.

The commander looked up with a startled expression. When he noticed his screen was on, he swallowed his mush convulsively and popped his teeth back into place.

"Who's there?" he demanded in a neutral voice in case it might be somebody important.

"Flight Officer Ozaki," said Flight Officer Ozaki.

A thundercloud rolled across the commander's face. "What do you mean by disturbing me at breakfast?" he demanded.

"Beg pardon, sir," said the pilot, "but my ship's falling into a red sun."

"Too bad," grunted Commander Krogson and turned back to his mush and milk.

"But, sir," persisted the other, "you've got to send somebody to pull me off. My converter's dead!"

"Why tell me about it?" said Krogson in annoyance. "Call Space Rescue, they're supposed to handle things like this."

"Listen, Commander," wailed the pilot, "by the time they've assigned me a priority and routed the paper through proper channels, I'll have gone up in smoke. The last time I got in a jam it took them two weeks to get to me; I've only got hours left!"

"Can't make exceptions," snapped Krogson testily. "If I let you skip the chain of command, everybody and his brother will think he has a right to."

"Commander," howled Ozaki, "we're frying in here!"

"All right. All right!" said the commander sourly. "I'll send somebody after you. What's your name?"

"Ozaki, sir. Flight Officer Ozaki."

The commander was in the process of scooping up another spoonful of mush when suddenly a thought struck him squarely between the eyes.

"Wait a second," he said hastily, "you aren't the scout who located the Imperial base, are you?"

"Yes, sir," said the pilot in a cracked voice.

"Why didn't you say so?" roared Krogson. Flipping on his intercom he growled, "Give me the Exec." There was a moment's silence.

"Yes, sir?"

"How long before we get to that scout?"

"About six hours, sir."

"Make it three!"

"Can't be done, sir."

"It will be done!" snarled Krogson and broke the connection.

The temperature needle in the little scout was now pointing to a hundred and fifteen.

"I don't think we can hold on that long," said Ozaki.

"Nonsense!" said the commander and the screen went blank.

Ozaki slumped into the pilot chair and buried his face in his hands. Suddenly he felt a blast of cold air on his neck. "There's no use in prolonging our misery," he said without looking up. "Those spare batteries won't last five minutes under this load."

"I knew that," said Kurt cheerfully, "so while you were doing all the talking, I went ahead and fixed the converter. You sure have mighty hot summers out here!" he continued, mopping his brow.

"You what?" yelled the pilot, jumping half out of his seat. "You couldn't even if you did have the know-how. It takes half a day to get the shielding off so you can get at the thing!"

"Didn't need to take the shielding off for a simple job like that," said Kurt. He pointed to a tiny inspection port about four inches in diameter. "I worked through there."

"That's impossible!" interjected the pilot. "You can't even see the injector through that, let alone get to it to work on!"

"Shucks," said Kurt, "a man doesn't have to see a little gadget like that to fix it. If your hands are trained right, you can feel what's wrong and set it to rights right away. She won't jump on you anymore either. The syncromesh thrust baffle was a little out of phase so I fixed that, too, while I was at it."

Ozaki still didn't believe it, but he hit the controls on faith. The scout bucked under the sudden strong surge of power and then, its converter humming sweetly, arced away from the giant sun in a long sweeping curve.

There was silence in the scout. The two men sat quietly, each immersed in an uneasy welter of troubled speculation.

"That was close!" said Ozaki finally. "Too close for comfort. Another hour or so and—!" He snapped his fingers.

Kurt looked puzzled. "Were we in trouble?"

"Trouble!" snorted Ozaki. "If you hadn't fixed the converter when you did, we'd be cinders by now!"

Kurt digested the news in silence. There was something about this super-being who actually made machines work that bothered him. There was a note of bewilderment in his voice when he asked: "If we were really in danger, why didn't you fix the converter instead of wasting time talking on that thing?" He gestured toward the space communicator.

It was Ozaki's turn to be bewildered. "Fix it?" he said with surprise in his voice. "There aren't a half a dozen techs on the whole base who know enough about atomics to work on a propulsion unit. When something like that goes out, you call Space Rescue and chew your nails until a wrecker can get to you."

Kurt crawled into his bunk and lay back staring at the curved ceiling. He had thinking to do, a lot of thinking!

Three hours later, the scout flashed up alongside the great flagship and darted into a landing port. Flight Officer Ozaki was stricken by a horrible thought as he gazed affectionately around his smoothly running ship.

"Say," he said to Kurt hesitantly, "would you mind not mentioning that you fixed this crate up for me? If you do, they'll take it away from me sure. Some captain will get a new rig, and I'll be issued another clunk from Base Junkpile."

"Sure thing," said Kurt.

A moment later the flashing of a green light on the control panel signaled that the pressure in the lock had reached normal.

"Back in a minute," said Ozaki. "You wait here."

There was a muted hum as the exit hatch swung slowly open. Two guards entered and stood silently beside Kurt as Ozaki left to report to Commander Krogson.

XIII

The battle fleet of War Base Three of Sector Seven of the Galactic Protectorate hung motionless in space twenty thousand kilometers out from Kurt's home planet. A hundred tired detection techs sat tensely before their screen, sweeping the globe for some sign of energy radiation. Aside from the occasional light spatters caused by space static, their scopes remained dark. As their reports filtered into Commander Krogson he became more and more exasperated.

"Are you positive this is the right planet?" he demanded of Ozaki.

"No question about it, sir."

"Seems funny there's nothing running down there at all," said Krogson. "Maybe they spotted us on the way in and cut off power. I've got a hunch that—" He broke off in mid sentence as the red top-priority light on the communication panel began to flash. "Get that," he said. "Maybe they've spotted something at last."

The executive officer flipped on the vision screen and the interior of the flagship's communication room was revealed.

"Sorry to bother you, sir," said the tech whose image appeared on the screen, "but a message just came through on the emergency band."

"What does it say?"

The tech looked unhappy. "It's coded, sir."

"Well, decode it!" barked the executive.

"We can't," said the technician diffidently. "Something's gone wrong with the decoder. The printer is pounding out random groups that don't make any sense at all."

The executive grunted his disgust. "Any idea where the call's coming from?"

"Yes, sir; it's coming in on a tight beam from the direction of Base. Must be from a ship emergency rig, though. Regular hyperspace transmission isn't directional. Either the ship's regular rig broke down or the operator is using the beam to keep anybody else from picking up his signal."

"Get to work on that decoder. Call back as soon as you get any results." The tech saluted and the screen went black.

"Whatever it is, it's probably trouble," said Krogson morosely. "Well, we'd better get on with this job. Take the fleet into atmosphere. It looks as if we are going to have to make a visual check."

"Maybe the prisoner can give us a lead," suggested the executive officer.

"Good idea. Have him brought in."

A moment later Kurt was ushered into the master control room. Krogson's eyes widened at the sight of scalp lock and paint.

"Where in the name of the Galactic Spirit," he demanded, "did you get that rig?"

"Don't you recognize an Imperial Space Marine when you see one?" Kurt answered coldly.

The guard that had escorted Kurt in made a little twirling motion at his temple with one finger. Krogson took another look and nodded agreement.

"Sit down, son," he said in a fatherly tone. "We're trying to get you home, but you're going to have to give us a little help before we can do it. You see, we're not quite sure just where your base is."

"I'll help all I can," said Kurt.

"Fine!" said the commander, rubbing his palms together. "Now just where down there do you come from?" He pointed out the vision port to the curving globe that stretched out below.

Kurt looked down helplessly. "Nothing makes sense, seeing it from up here," he said apologetically.

Krogson thought for a moment. "What's the country like around your base?" he asked.

"Mostly jungle," said Kurt. "The garrison is on a plateau though and there are mountains to the north."

Krogson turned quickly to his exec. "Did you get that description?"

"Yes, sir!"

"Get all scouts out for a close sweep. As soon as the base is spotted, move the fleet in and hover at forty thousand!"

Forty minutes later a scout came streaking back.

"Found it, sir!" said the exec. "Plateau with jungle all

around and mountains to the north. There's a settle-
ment at one end. The pilot saw movement down there,
but they must have spotted us on our way in. There's
still no evidence of energy radiation. They must have
everything shut down."

"That's not good!" said Krogson. "They've probably
got all their heavy stuff set up waiting for us to sweep
over. We'll have to hit them hard and fast. Did they
spot the scout?"

"Can't tell, sir."

"We'd better assume that they did. Notify all gunnery officers to switch their batteries over to central
control. If we come in fast and high and hit them with
simultaneous fleet concentration, we can vaporize the
whole base before they can take a crack at us."

"I'll send the order out at once, sir," said the executive officer.

The fleet pulled into tight formation and headed
toward the Imperial base. They were halfway there when
the fleet gunnery officer entered the control room and
said apologetically to Commander Krogson, "Excuse
me, sir, but I'd like to suggest a trial run. Fleet concentration is a tricky thing, and if something went haywire—
we'd be sitting ducks for the ground batteries."

"Good idea," said Krogson thoughtfully. "There's
too much at stake to have anything to go wrong. Select
an equivalent target, and we'll make a pass."

The fleet was now passing over a towering mountain
chain.

"How about that bald spot down there?" said the
Exec, pointing to a rocky expanse that jutted out from
the side of one of the towering peaks.

"Good enough," said Krogson.

"All ships on central control!" reported the gunnery
officer.

"On target!" repeated the tech on the tracking screen.
"One. Two. Three. Four—"

Kurt stood by the front observation port watching the
ground far below sweep by. He had been listening
intently, but what had been said didn't make sense.

There had been something about *batteries*—the term
was alien to him—and something about the garrison.
He decided to ask the commander what it was all
about, but the intentness with which Krogson was watching the tracking screen deterred him. Instead he gazed
moodily down at the mountains below him.

"Five. Six. Seven. Ready. FIRE!"

A savage shudder ran through the great ship as her
ground-pointed batteries blasted in unison. Seconds went
by and then suddenly the rocky expanse on the shoulder
of the mountain directly below twinkled as blinding
flashes of actinic light danced across it. Then as Kurt
watched, great masses of rock and earth moved slowly
skyward from the center of the spurting nests of tangled
flame. Still slowly, as if buoyed up by the thin mountain air, the debris began to fall back again until it was
lost from sight in quick rising mushrooms of jet-black
smoke. Kurt turned and looked back toward Commander
Krogson. *Batteries* must be the things that had torn the
mountains below apart. And *garrison*—there was only
one garrison!

"I ordered fleet fire," barked Krogson. "This ship was
the only one that cut loose. What happened?"

"Just a second, sir," said the executive officer, "I'll
try and find out." He was busy for a minute on the
intercom system. "The other ships were ready, sir," he
repeated finally. "Their guns were all switched over to
our control, but no impulse came through. Central fire
control must be on the blink!" He gestured toward a
complex bank of equipment that occupied one entire
corner of the control room.

Commander Krogson said a few appropriate words.
When he reached the point where he was beginning to
repeat himself, he paused and stood in frozen silence
for a good thirty seconds.

"Would you mind getting a fire control tech in here
to fix that obscenity bank?" he asked in a voice that put
everyone's teeth on edge.

The other seemed to have something to say, but he
was having trouble getting it out.

"Well?" said Krogson.

"Prime Base grabbed our last one two weeks ago. There isn't another left with the fleet."

"Doesn't look like much to me," said Kurt as he strolled over to examine the bank of equipment.

"Get away from there!" roared the commander. "We've got enough trouble without you making things worse."

Kurt ignored him and began to open inspection ports.

"Guard!" yelled Krogson. "Throw that man out of here!"

Ozaki interrupted timidly. "Beg pardon, Commander, but he can fix it if anybody can."

Krogson whirled on the flight officer. "How do you know?"

Ozaki caught himself just in time. If he talked too much, he was likely to lose the scout that Kurt had fixed for him.

"Because he . . . he . . . talks like a tech," he concluded lamely.

Krogson looked at Kurt dubiously. "I guess there's no harm in giving it a trial," he said finally. "Give him a set of tools and turn him loose. Maybe for once a miracle will happen."

"First," said Kurt, "I'll need the wiring diagrams for this thing."

"Get them!" barked the commander and an orderly scuttled out of the control, headed aft.

"Next you'll have to give me a general idea of what it's supposed to do," continued Kurt.

Krogson turned to the gunnery officer. "You'd better handle this."

When the orderly returned with the circuit diagrams, they were spread out on the plotting table and the two men bent over them.

"Got it!" said Kurt at last and sauntered over to the control bank. Twenty minutes later he sauntered back again.

"She's all right now," he said pleasantly.

The gunner officer quickly scanned his testing board. Not a single red trouble light was on. He turned to Commander Krogson in amazement.

"I don't know how he did it, sir, but the circuits are all clear now."

Krogson stared at Kurt with a look of new respect in his eyes. "What were you down there, chief maintenance tech?"

Kurt laughed. "Me? I was never chief anything. I spent most of my time on hunting detail."

The commander digested that in silence for a moment. "Then how did you become so familiar with fire-control gear?"

"Studied it in school like everyone else does. There wasn't anything much wrong with that thing anyway except a couple of sticking relays."

"Excuse me, sir," interrupted the executive officer, "but should we make another trial run?"

"Are you sure the bank is in working order?"

"Positive, sir!"

"Then we'd better make straight for that base. If this boy here is a fair example of what they have down there, their defenses may be too tough for us to crack if we give them a chance to get set up!"

Kurt gave a slight start which he quickly controlled. Then he had guessed right! Slowly and casually he began to sidle toward the semi-circular bank of controls that stood before the great tracking screen.

"Where do you think you're going!" barked Krogson.

Kurt froze. His pulses were pounding within him, but he kept his voice light and casual.

"No place," he said innocently.

"Get over against the bulkhead and keep out of the way!" snapped the commander. "We've got a job of work coming up."

Kurt injected a note of bewilderment into his voice.

"What kind of work?"

Krogson's voice softened and a look approaching pity came into his eyes. "It's just as well you don't know about it until it's over," he said gruffly.

"There she is!" sang out the navigator, pointing to a tiny brown projection that jutted up out of the green jungle in the far distance. "We're about three minutes out, sir. You can take over at any time now."

The fleet gunnery officer's fingers moved quickly over the keys that welded the fleet into a single instrument of destruction, keyed and ready to blast a barrage of ravening thunderbolts of molecular disruption down at the defenseless garrison at a single touch on the master fire-control button.

"Whenever you're ready, sir," he said deferentially to Krogson as he vacated the controls. A hush fell over the control room as the great tracking screen brightened and showed the compact bundle of white dots that marked the fleet crawling slowly toward the green triangle of the target area.

"Get the prisoner out of here," said Krogson. "There's no reason why he should have to watch what's about to happen."

The guard that stood beside Kurt grabbed his arm and shoved him toward the door.

There was a sudden explosion of fists as Kurt erupted into action. In a blur of continuous movement, he streaked toward the gunnery control panel. He was halfway across the control room before the pole-axed guard hit the floor. There was a second of stunned amazement, and then before anyone could move to stop him, he stood beside the controls, one hand poised tensely above the master stud that controlled the combined fire of the fleet.

"Hold it!" he shouted as the moment of paralysis broke and several of the officers started toward him menacingly. "One move, and I'll blast the whole fleet into scrap!"

They stopped in shocked silence, looking to Commander Krogson for guidance.

"Almost on target, sir," called the tech on the tracking screen.

Krogson stalked menacingly toward Kurt. "Get away from those controls!" he snarled. "You aren't going to blow anything to anything. All that you can do is let off a premature blast. If you are trying to alert your base, it's no use. We can be on a return sweep before they have time to get ready for us."

Kurt shook his head calmly. "Wouldn't do you any good," he said. "Take a look at the gun ports on the other ships. I made a couple of minor changes while I was working on the control bank."

"Quit bluffing," said Krogson.

"I'm not bluffing," said Kurt quietly. "Take a look. It won't cost you anything."

"On target!" called the tracking tech.

"Order the fleet to circle for another sweep," snapped Krogson over his shoulder as he stalked toward the forward observation port. There was something in Kurt's tone that had impressed him more than he liked to admit. He squinted out toward the nearest ship. Suddenly his face blanched!

"The gunports! They're closed!"

Kurt gave a whistle of relief. "I had my fingers crossed," he said pleasantly. "You didn't give me enough time with the wiring diagrams for me to be sure that cutting out that circuit would do the trick. Now . . . guess what the results would be if I should happen to push down on this stud."

Krogson had a momentary vision of several hundred shells ramming their sensitive noses against the thick chrome steel of the closed gun ports.

"Don't bother trying to talk," said Kurt, noticing the violent contractions of the commander's Adam's apple. "You'd better save your breath for my colonel."

"Who?" demanded Krogson.

"My colonel," repeated Kurt. "We'd better head back and pick him up. Can you make these ships hang in one place or do they have to keep moving fast to stay up?"

The commander clamped his jaws together sullenly and said nothing.

Kurt made a tentative move toward the firing stud.

"Easy!" yelled the gunnery officer in alarm. "That thing has hair-trigger action!"

"Well?" said Kurt to Krogson.

"We can hover," grunted the other.

"Then take up a position a little to one side of the plateau." Kurt brushed the surface of the firing stud with a casual finger. "If you make me push this, I don't want a lot of scrap iron falling down on the battalion. Somebody might get hurt."

As the fleet came to rest above the plateau, the call light on the communication panel began to flash again.

"Answer it," ordered Kurt, "but watch what you say."

Krogson walked over and snapped on the screen.

"Communications, sir."

"Well?"

"It's that message we called you about earlier. We've finally got the decoder working—sort of, that is." His voice faltered and then stopped.

"What does it say?" demanded Krogson impatiently.

"We still don't know," admitted the tech miserably. "It's being decoded all right, but it's coming out in a North Vegan dialect that nobody down here can understand. I guess there's still something wrong with the selector. All that we can figure out is that the message has something to do with General Carr and the Lord Protector."

"Want me to go down and fix it?" interrupted Kurt in an innocent voice.

Krogson whirled toward him, his hamlike hands clenching and unclenching in impotent rage.

"Anything wrong, sir?" asked the technician on the screen.

Kurt raised a significant eyebrow to the commander.

"Of course not," growled Krogson. "Go find somebody to translate that message and don't bother me until it's done."

A new face appeared on the screen.

"Excuse me for interrupting sir, but translation won't be necessary. We just got a flash from Detection that they've spotted the ship that sent it. It's a small scout heading in on emergency drive. She should be here in a matter of minutes."

Krogson flipped off the screen impatiently. "Whatever it is, it's sure to be more trouble," he said to nobody in particular. Suddenly he became aware that the fleet was no longer in motion. "Well," he said sourly to Kurt, "we're here. What now?"

"Send a ship down to the garrison and bring Colonel Harris back up here so that you and he can work this thing out between you. Tell him that Dixon is up here and has everything under control."

Krogson turned to the executive officer. "All right," he said, "do what he says." The other saluted and started toward the door.

"Just a second," said Kurt. "If you have any idea of telling the boys outside to cut the transmission leads from fire control, I wouldn't advise it. It's a rather lengthy process, and the minute a trouble light blinks on that board, up we go! Now on your way!"

XIV

Lieutenant Colonel Blick, acting commander of the 427th Light Maintenance Battalion of the Imperial Space Marines, stood at his office window and scowled down upon the whole civilized world, all twenty-six square kilometers of it. It had been a hard day. Three separate delegations of mothers had descended upon him demanding that he reopen the Tech Schools for the sake of their sanity. The recruits had been roaming the company streets in bands composed of equal numbers of small boys and large dogs creating havoc wherever they went. He tried to cheer himself up by thinking of his forthcoming triumph when he in the guise of the Inspector General would float magnificently down from the skies and once and for all put the seal of final authority upon the new order. The only trouble was that he was beginning to have a sneaking suspicion that maybe that new order wasn't all that he had planned it to be. As he thought of his own six banshees screaming through quarters, his suspicion deepened almost to certainty.

He wandered back to his desk and slumped behind it

gloomily. He couldn't backwater now, his pride was at stake. He glanced at the water clock on his desk, and then rose reluctantly and started toward the door. It was time to get into battle armor and get ready for the inspection.

As he reached the door, there was a sudden slap of running sandals down the hall. A second later, Major Kane burst into the office, his face white and terrified.

"Colonel," he gasped, "the I.G.'s here!"

"Nonsense," said Blick. "I'm the I.G. now!"

"Oh yeah?" whimpered Kane. "Go look out the window. He's here, and he's brought the whole Imperial fleet with him!"

Blick dashed to the window and looked up. High above, so high that he could see them only as silver specks, hung hundreds of ships.

"Headquarters *does* exist!" he gasped.

He stood stunned. What to do . . . what to do . . . what to do— The question swirled around in his brain until we was dizzy. He looked to Kane for advice, but the other was as bewildered as he was.

"Don't stand there, man," he stormed. "Do something!"

"Yes, sir," said Kane. "What?"

Blick thought for a long, silent moment. The answer was obvious, but there was a short, fierce inner struggle before he could bring himself to accept it.

"Get Colonel Harris up here at once. He'll know what we should do."

A stubborn look came across Kane's face. "We're running things now," he said angrily.

Blick's face hardened and he let out a roar that shook the walls. "Listen, you pup, when you get an order, you follow it. Now get!"

Forty seconds later, Colonel Harris stormed into the office. "What kind of mess have you got us into this time?" he demanded.

"Look up there, sir," said Blick leading him to the window.

Colonel Harris snapped back into command as if he'd never left it.

"Major Kane!" he shouted.

Kane popped into the office like a frightened rabbit.

"Evacuate the garrison at once! I want everyone off the plateau and into the jungle immediately. Get litters for the sick and the veterans who can't walk and take them to the hunting camps. Start the rest moving north as soon as you can."

"Really, sir," protested Kane, looking to Blick for a cue.

"You heard the colonel," barked Blick. "On your way!" Kane bolted.

Colonel Harris turned to Blick and said in a frosty voice: "I appreciate your help, colonel, but I feel perfectly competent to enforce my own orders."

"Sorry, sir," said the other meekly. "It won't happen again."

Harris smiled. "O.K., Jimmie," he said, "let's forget it. We've got work to do!"

XV

It seemed to Kurt as if time was standing still. His nerves were screwed up to the breaking point and although he maintained an air of outward composure for the benefit of those in the control room of the flagship, it took all his will power to keep the hand that was resting over the firing stud from quivering. One slip and they'd be on him. Actually it was only a matter of minutes between the time the scout was dispatched to the garrison below and the time it returned, but to him it seemed as if hours had passed before the familiar form of his commanding officer strode briskly into the control room.

Colonel Harris came to a halt just inside the door and swept the room with a keen penetrating gaze.

"What's up, son?" he asked Kurt.

"I'm not quite sure. All that I know is that they're here to blast the garrison. As long as I've got control of this," he indicated the firing stud, "I'm top dog, but you'd better work something out in a hurry."

The look of strain on Kurt's face was enough for the colonel.

"Who's in command here?" he demanded.

Krogson stepped forward and bowed stiffly. "Commander Conrad Krogson of War Base Three of the Galactic Protectorate."

"Colonel Marcus Harris, 427th Light Maintenance Battalion of the Imperial Space Marines," replied the other briskly. "Now that the formalities are out of the way, let's get to work. Is there some place here where we can talk?"

Krogson gestured toward a small cubicle that opened off the control room. The two men entered and shut the door behind them.

A half hour went by without agreement. "There may be an answer somewhere," Colonel Harris said finally, "but I can't find it. We can't surrender to you, and we can't afford to have you surrender to us. We haven't the food, facilities, or anything else to keep fifty thousand men under guard. If we turn you loose, there's nothing to keep you from coming back to blast us—except your word, that is, and since it would obviously be given under duress, I'm afraid that we couldn't attach much weight to it. It's a nice problem. I wish we had more time to spend on it, but unless you can come up with something workable during the next five minutes, I'm going to give Kurt orders to blow the fleet."

Krogson's mind was operating at a furious pace. One by one he snatched at possible solutions, and one by one he gave them up as he realized that they would never stand up under the scrutiny of the razor-sharp mind that sat opposite him.

"Look," he burst out finally, "your empire is dead and our Protectorate is about to fall apart. Give us a chance to come down and join you and we'll chuck the past. We need each other and you know it!"

"I know we do," said the colonel soberly, "and I rather think you are being honest with me. But we just can't take the chance. There are too many of you for us to digest and if you should change your mind—" He threw up his hands in a helpless gesture.

"But I wouldn't," protested Krogson. "You've told me what your life is like down there and you know what kind of a rat race I've been caught up in. I'd welcome the chance to get out of it. All of us would!"

"You might to begin with," said Harris, "but then you might start thinking what your Lord Protector would give to get his hands on several hundred trained technicians. No, Commander," he said, "we just couldn't chance it." He stretched his hand out to Krogson and the other after a second's hesitation took it.

Commander Krogson had reached the end of the road and he knew it. The odd thing about it was that now he found himself there, he didn't particularly mind. He sat and watched his own reactions with a sense of vague bewilderment. The strong drive for self-preservation that had kept him struggling ahead for so long was petering out and there was nothing to take its place. He was immersed in a strange feeling of emptiness and though a faint something within him said that he should go out fighting, it seemed pointless and without reason.

Suddenly the moment of quiet was broken. From the control room came a muffled sound of angry voices and scuffling feet. With one quick stride, Colonel Harris reached the door and swung it open. He was almost bowled over by a small disheveled figure who darted past him into the cubicle. Close behind came several of the ship's officers. As the figure came to a stop before Commander Krogson, one of them grabbed him and started to drag him back into the control room.

"Sorry, sir," the officer said to Krogson, "but he came busting in demanding to see you at once. He wouldn't tell us why and when we tried to stop him, he broke away."

"Release him!" ordered the commander. He looked sternly at the little figure. "Well, Schninkle," he said sternly, "what is it this time?"

"Did you get my message?"

Krogson snorted. "So it was you in that scout! I might

have known it. We got it all right, but Communication still hasn't got it figured out. What are you doing out here? You're supposed to be back at base keeping knives out of my back!"

"It's private, sir," said Schninkle.

"The rest of you clear out!" ordered Krogson. A second later, with the exception of Colonel Harris, the cubicle stood empty. Schninkle looked questioningly at the oddly uniformed officer.

"Couldn't put him out if I wanted to," said Krogson, "now go ahead."

Schninkle closed the door carefully and then turned to the commander and said in a hushed voice, "There's been a blowup at Prime Base. General Carr was hiding out there after all. He hit at noon yesterday. He had two-thirds of the Elite Guard secretly on his side and the Lord Protector didn't have a chance. He tried to run but they chopped him down before he got out of the atmosphere."

Krogson digested the news in silence for a moment. "So the Lord Protector is dead." He laughed bitterly. "Well, long live the Lord Protector!" He turned slowly to Colonel Harris. "I guess this lets us both off. Now that the heat's off me, you're safe. Call off your boy out there, and we'll make ourselves scarce. I've got to get back to the new Lord Protector to pay my respects. If some of my boys get to Carr first, I'm apt to be out of a job."

Harris shook his head. "It isn't as simple as that. Your new leader needs technicians as much as your old one did. I'm afraid we are still back where we started."

As Krogson broke into an impatient denial, Schninkle interrupted him. "You can't go back, Commander. None of us can. Carr has the whole staff down on his 'out' list. He's making a clean sweep of all possible competition. We'd all be under arrest now if he knew where we were!"

Krogson gave a slow whistle. "Doesn't leave me much choice, does it?" he said to Colonel Harris. "If you don't turn me loose, I get blown up; if you do, I get shot down."

Schninkle looked puzzled. "What's up, sir?" he asked.

Krogson gave a bitter laugh. "In case you didn't notice on your way in, there is a young man sitting at the fire controls out there who can blow up the whole fleet at the touch of a button. Down below is an ideal base with hundreds of techs, but the colonel here won't take us in, and he's afraid to let us go."

"I wouldn't," admitted Harris, "but the last few minutes have rather changed the picture. My empire has been dead for five hundred years and your Protectorate doesn't seem to want you around any more. It looks like we're both out of a job. Maybe we both ought to find a new one. What do you think?"

"I don't know what to think," said Krogson. "I can't go back and I can't stay here, and there isn't any place else. The fleet can't keep going without a base."

A broad grin came over the face of Colonel Harris. "You know," he said, "I've got a hunch that maybe we can do business after all. Come on!" He threw open the cubicle door and strode briskly into the control room, Krogson and Schninkle following close at his heels. He walked over to Kurt who was still poised stiffly at the fire-control board.

"You can relax now, lad. Everything is under control."

Kurt gave a sigh of relief and pulling himself to his feet, stretched luxuriantly. As the other officers saw the firing stud deserted, they tensed and looked to Commander Krogson questioningly. He frowned for a second and then slowly shook his head.

"Well?" he said to Colonel Harris.

"It's obvious," said the other, "you've a fleet, a darn good fleet, but it's falling apart for lack of decent maintenance. I've got a base down there with five thousand lads who can think with their fingers. This knucklehead of mine is a good example." He walked over to Kurt and slapped him affectionately on the shoulder. "There's nothing on this ship that he couldn't tear down and put back together blindfolded if he was given a little time to think about it. I think he'll enjoy having some real work to do for a change."

"I may seem dense," said Krogson with a bewildered expression on his face, "but wasn't that the idea that I was trying to sell you?"

"The idea is the same," said Harris, "but the context isn't. You're in a position now where you have to cooperate. That makes a difference. A big difference!"

"It sounds good," said Krogson, "but now you're overlooking something. Carr will be looking for me. We can't stand off the whole galaxy!"

"You're overlooking something too, sir," Schninkle interrupted. "He hasn't the slightest idea where we are. It will be months before he has things well enough under control to start an organized search for us. When he does, his chances of ever spotting the fleet are mighty slim if we take reasonable precautions. Remember that it was only by a fluke that we ever happened to spot this place to begin with."

As he talked a calculating look came into his eyes. "A year of training and refitting here, and there wouldn't be a fleet in the galaxy that could stand against us." He casually edged over until he occupied a position between Kurt and the fire-control board. "If things went right, there's no reason why you couldn't become Lord Protector, Commander."

A flash of the old fire stirred within Krogson and then quickly flickered out. "No, Schninkle," he said heavily. "That's all past now. I've had enough. It's time to try something new."

"In that case," said Colonel Harris, "let's begin! Out there a whole galaxy is breaking up. Soon the time will come when a strong hand is going to be needed to piece it back together and put it in running order again. You know," he continued reflectively, "the name of the old empire still has a certain magic to it. It might not be a bad idea to use it until we are ready to move on to something better."

He walked silently to the vision port and looked down on the lush greenness spreading far below. "But whatever we call ourselves," he continued slowly, half talking to himself, "we have something to work for now." A quizzical smile played over his lips and his wise old eyes seemed to be scanning the years ahead. "You know, Kurt; there's nothing like a visit from the Inspector General once in a while to keep things in line. The galaxy is a big place, but when the time comes, we'll make our rounds!"

XVI

On the parade ground behind the low buildings of the garrison, the 427th Light Maintenance Battalion of the Imperial Space Marines stood in rigid formation, the feathers of their war bonnets moving slightly in the little breeze that blew in from the west and their war paint glowing redly in the slanting rays of the setting sun.

A quiver ran through the hard surface soil of the plateau as the great mass of the fleet flagship settled down ponderously to rest. There was a moment of expectant silence as a great port clanged open and a gangplank extended to the ground. From somewhere within the ship a fanfare of trumpets sounded. Slowly and with solemn dignity, surrounded by his staff, Conrad Krogson, Inspector General of the Imperial Space Marines, advanced to review the troops.

THE BELLS
OF SHOREDAN

Roger Zelazny

No living thing dwelled in the land of Rahoringhast.

Since an age before this age had the dead realm been empty of sound, save for the crashing of thunders and the *spit-spit* of raindrops ricocheting from off its stonework and the stones. The towers of the Citadel of Rahoring still stood; the great archway from which the gates had been stricken continued to gape, like a mouth frozen in a howl of pain and surprise, of death; the countryside about the place resembled the sterile landscape of the moon.

The rider followed the Way of the Armies, which led at last to the archway, and on through into the Citadel. Behind him lay a twisted trail leading downward, downward, and back, toward the south and the west. It ran through chill patterns of morning mist that clung, swollen, to dark and pitted ground, like squadrons of gigantic leeches. It looped about the ancient towers, still standing only by virtue of enchantments placed upon them in foregone days. Black and awesome, high rearing, and limned in nightmare's clarity, the towers of the Citadel were the final visible extensions of the character of their dead maker: Hohorga, King of the World.

The rider, the green-booted rider who left no footprints when he walked, must have felt something of the dark power that still remained within the place, for he halted and sat silent, staring for a long while at the broken gates and the high battlements. Then he spoke a word to the black, horselike thing he rode upon, and they pressed ahead.

As he drew near, he saw that something was moving in the shadows of the archway.

He knew that no living thing dwelled in the land of Rahoringhast . . .

The battle had gone well, considering the number of the defenders.

On the first day, the emissaries of Lylish had approached the walls of Dilfar, sought parley, requested surrender of the city, and been refused. There followed a brief truce to permit single combat between Lance, the Hand of Lylish, and Dilvish called the Damned, Colonel of the East, Deliverer of Portaroy, scion of the Elvish House of Selar and the human House that hath been stricken.

The trial lasted but a quarter of an hour, until Dilvish, whose wounded leg had caused his collapse, did strike upward from behind his buckler with the point of his blade. The armor of Lance, which had been deemed invincible, gave way then, when the blade of Dilvish smote at one of the two devices upon the breastplate— those that were cast in the form of cloven hoof marks. Men muttered that these devices had not been present previously and an attempt was made to take the colonel prisoner. His horse, however, which had stood on the sidelines like a steel statue, did again come to his aid, bearing him to safety within the city.

The assault was then begun, but the defenders were prepared and held well their walls. Well fortified and well provided was Dilfar. Fighting from a position of strength, the defenders cast down much destruction upon the men of the West.

After four days the army of Lylish had withdrawn with the great rams that it had been unable to use. The men of the West commenced the construction of helepoles, while they awaited the arrival of catapults from Bildesh.

Above the walls of Dilfar, high in the Keep of Eagles, there were two who watched.

"It will not go well, Lord Dilvish," said the king, whose name was Malacar the Mighty, though he was short of stature and long of year. "If they complete the towers-that-walk and bring catapults, they will strike us from afar. We will not be able to defend against this. Then the towers will walk when we are weakened from the bombardment."

"It is true," said Dilvish.

"Dilfar must not fall."

"No."

"Reinforcements have been sent for, but they are many leagues distant. None were prepared for the assault of Lord Lylish, and it will be long before sufficient troops will be mustered and be come here to the battle."

"That is also true, and by then may it be too late."

"You are said by some to be the same Lord Dilvish who liberated Portaroy in days long gone by."

"I am that Dilvish."

"If so, that Dilvish was of the House of Selar of the Invisible Blade."

"Yes."

"Is it also true, then—what is told of the House of Selar and the bells of Shoredan in Rahoringhast?"

Malacar looked away as he said it.

"This thing I do not know," said Dilvish. "I have never attempted to raise the cursed legions of Shoredan. My grandmother told me that only twice in all the ages of Time has this been done. I have also read of it in the Green Books of Time at the keep of Mirata. I do not *know*, however."

"Only to one of the House of Selar will the bells respond. Else they swing noiseless, it is said."

"So is it said."

"Rahoringhast lies far to the north and east, and distressful is the way. One with a mount such as yours might make the journey, might ring there the bells, might call forth the doomed legions, though. It is said they will follow such a one of Selar to battle."

"Aye, this thought has come to me, also."

"Willst essay this thing?"

"Aye, sir. Tonight. I am already prepared."

"Kneel then and receive thou my blessing, Dilvish of Selar. I knew thou wert he when I saw thee on the field before these walls."

And Dilvish did kneel and receive the blessing of Malacar, called the Mighty, Liege of the Eastern Reach, whose realm held Dilfar, Bildesh, Maestar, Mycar, Portaroy, Princeaton, and Poind.

The way was difficult, but the passage of leagues and hours was as the movement of clouds. The western portal to Dilfar had within it a smaller passing-place, a man-sized door studded with spikes and slitted for the discharge of bolts.

Like a shutter in the wind, this door opened and closed. Crouched low, mounted on a piece of the night, the colonel passed out through the opening and raced across the plain, entering for a moment the outskirts of the enemy camp.

A cry went up as he rode, and weapons rattled in the darkness.

Sparks flew from unshod steel hooves.

"All the speed at thy command now, Black, my mount!"

He was through the campsite and away before arrow could be set to bow.

High on the hill to the east, a small fire throbbed in the wind. Pennons, mounted on tall poles, flopped against the night, and it was too dark for Dilvish to read the devices thereon, but he knew that they stood before the tents of Lylish, Colonel of the West.

Dilvish spoke the words in the language of the damned, and as he spoke them the eyes of his mount glowed like embers in the night. The small fire on the hilltop leapt, one great leaf of flame, to the height of four men. It did not reach the tent, however. Then there was no fire at all, only the embers of all the fuels consumed in a single moment.

Dilvish rode on, and the hooves of Black made lightning on the hillside.

They pursued him a small while only. Then he was away and alone.

All that night did he ride through places of rock. Shapes reared high above him and fell again, like staggering giants surprised in their drunkenness. He felt himself launched, countless times, through empty air, and when he looked down on these occasions, there was only empty air beneath him.

With the morning, there came a leveling of his path, and the far edge of the Eastern Plain lay before him, then under him. His leg began to throb beneath its dressing, but he had lived in the Houses of Pain for more than the lifetimes of Men, and he put the feeling far from his thoughts.

After the sun had raised itself over the jagged horizon at his back, he stopped to eat and to drink, to stretch his limbs.

In the sky then he saw the shapes of the nine black doves that must circle the world forever, never to land, seeing all things on the earth and on the sea, and passing all things by.

"An omen," he said. "Be it a good one?"

"I know not," replied the creature of steel.

"Then let us make haste to learn."

He remounted.

For four days did he pass over the plain, until the yellow and green waving grasses gave way and the land lay sandy before him.

The winds of the desert cut at his eyes. He fixed his scarf as a muffle, but it could not stop the entire assault. When he would cough and spit, he needed to lower it, and the sand entered again. He would blink and his face would burn, and he would curse, but no spell he knew could lay the entire desert like yellow tapestry, smooth and unruffled below him. Black was an opposing wind, and the airs of the land rushed to contest his passage.

On the third day in the desert, a mad wight flew invisible and gibbering at his back. Even Black could not outrun it, and it ignored the foulest imprecations of Mabrahoring, language of the demons and the damned.

The following day, more joined with it. They would not pass the protective circle in which Dilvish slept, but they screamed across his dreams—meaningless fragments of a dozen tongues—troubling his sleep.

He left them when he left the desert. He left them as he entered the land of stone and marches and gravel and dark pools and evil openings in the ground from which the fumes of the underworld came forth.

He had come to the border of Rahoringhast.

It was damp and gray, everywhere.

It was misty in places, and the water oozed forth from the rocks, came up from out of the ground.

There were no trees, shrubs, flowers, grasses. No birds sang, no insects hummed. . . . No living thing dwelled in the land of Rahoringhast.

Dilvish rode on and entered through the broken jaws of the city.

All within was shadow and ruin.

He passed up the Way of the Armies.

Silent was Rahoringhast, a city of the dead.

He could feel this, not as the silence of nothingness now, but as the silence of a still presence.

Only the steel cloven hooves sounded within the city.

There came no echoes.

Sound . . . Nothing. Sound . . . Nothing. Sound . . .

It was as though something unseen moved to absorb every evidence of life as soon as it noised itself.

Red was the palace, like bricks hot from the kiln and flushed with the tempers of their making. But of one piece were the walls. No seams, no divisions were there in the sheet of red. It was solid, was imponderable, broad of base, and reached with its thirteen towers higher than any building Dilvish had ever seen, though he had dwelled in the high keep of Mirata itself, where the Lords of Illusion hold sway, bending space to their will.

Dilvish dismounted and regarded the enormous stairway that lay before him. "That which we seek lies within."

Black nodded and touched the first stair with his hoof. Fire rose from the stone. He drew back his hoof and smoke curled about it. There was no mark upon the stair to indicate where he had touched.

"I fear I cannot enter this place and preserve my form," he stated. "At the least, my form."

"What compels thee?"

"An ancient enchantment to preserve this place against the assault of any such as I."

"Can it be undone?"

"Not by any creature which walks this world or flies above it or writhes beneath it or I'm a horse. Though the seas some day rise and cover the land, this place will exist at their bottom. This was torn from Chaos by Order in the days when those principles stalked the land, naked, just beyond the hills. Whoever compelled them was one of the First, and powerful even in terms of the Mighty."

"Then I must go alone."

"Perhaps not. One is approaching even now with whom you had best wait and parley."

Dilvish waited, and a single horseman emerged from a distant street and advanced upon them.

"Greetings," called the rider, raising his right hand, open.

"Greetings." Dilvish returned the gesture.

The man dismounted. His costume was deep violet in color, the hood thrown back; the cloak all engulfing. He bore no visible arms.

"Why stand you here before the Citadel of Rahoring?" he asked.

"Why stand you here to ask me, priest of Babrigore?" said Dilvish, and not ungently.

"I am spending the time of a moon in this place of

death, to dwell upon the ways of evil. It is to prepare myself as head of my temple."

"You are young to be head of a temple."

The priest shrugged and smiled.

"Few come to Rahoringhast," he observed.

"Small wonder," did Dilvish reply. "I trust I shall not remain here long."

"Were you planning on entering this—place?" He gestured.

"I was, and am."

The man was half a head shorter than Dilvish, and it was impossible to guess at his form beneath the robes he wore. His eyes were blue and he was swarthy of complexion. A mole on his left eyelid danced when he blinked.

"Let me beg you reconsider this action," he stated. "It would be unwise to enter this building."

"Why is that?"

"It is said that it is still guarded within by the ancient warders of its lord."

"Have you ever been inside?"

"Yes."

"Were you troubled by any ancient wardens?"

"No, but as a priest of Babrigore I am under the protection of—of—Jelerak."

Dilvish spat.

"May his flesh be flayed from his bones and his life yet remain."

The priest dropped his eyes.

"Though he fought the creature which dwelled within this place," said Dilvish, "he became as foul himself afterward."

"Many of his deeds do lie like stains upon the land," said the priest, "but he was not always such a one. He was a white wizard who matched his powers against the Dark One, in days when the world was young. He was not sufficient. He fell. He was taken as servant by the Maleficent. For centuries he endured this bondage, until it changed him, as such must. He, too, came to glory in the ways of darkness. But then when Selar of the Unseen Blade bought the life of Hohorga with his own, Jel—he fell as if dead and lay as such for the space of a week. Near delirious, when he awakened, he worked with counterspell at one last act of undoing: to free the cursed legions of Shoredan. He essayed that thing. He did. He stood upon this very stairway for two days and two nights, until the blood mingled with perspiration on his brow, but he could not break the hold of Hohorga. Even dead, the dark strength was too great for him. Then he wandered mad about the countryside, until he was taken in and cared for by the priests of Babrigore. Afterward he lapsed back into the ways he had learned, but he has always been kindly disposed toward the Order which cared for him. He has never asked anything more of us. He has sent us food in times of famine. Speak no evil of him in my presence."

Dilvish spat again.

"May he thrash in the darkness of the darknesses for the ages of ages, and may his name be cursed forever."

The priest looked away from the sudden blaze in his eyes.

"What want you in Rahoring?" he asked finally.

"To go within—and do a thing."

"If you must, then I shall accompany you. Perhaps my protection shall also extend to yourself."

"I do not solicit your protection, priest."

"The asking is not necessary."

"Very well. Come with me then."

He started up the stairway.

"What is that thing you ride?" asked the priest, gesturing back. "—Like a horse in form, but now it is a statue."

Dilvish laughed.

"I, too, know something of the ways of darkness, but my terms with it are my own."

"No man may have special terms with darkness."

"Tell it to a dweller in the Houses of Pain, priest. Tell it to a statue. Tell it to one who is all of the race of Men! Tell it not to me."

"What is your name?"

"Dilvish. What is yours?"

"Korel. I shall speak to you no more of darkness then, Dilvish, but I will still go with you into Rahoring."

"Then stand not talking." Dilvish turned and continued upward.

Korel followed him.

When they had gone halfway, the daylight began to grow dim about them. Dilvish looked back. All he could see was the stairway leading down and down, back. There was nothing else in the world but the stairs. With each step upward, the darkness grew.

"Did it happen thus when last you entered this place?" he asked.

"No," said Korel.

They reached the top of the stairs and stood before the dim portal. By then it was as though night lay upon the land.

They entered.

A sound, as of music, came far ahead and there was a flickering light within. Dilvish laid his hand upon the hilt of his sword. The priest whispered to him: "It will do you no good."

They moved up the passageway and came at length into a vacant hall. Braziers spewed flame from high sockets in the walls. The ceiling was lost in shadow and smoke.

They crossed that hall to where a wide stair led up into a blaze of light and sound.

Korel looked back.

"It begins with the light," said he, "all this newness"—gesturing. "The outer passage bore only rubble and . . . dust . . ."

"What else is the matter?" Dilvish looked back.

Only one set of footprints led into the hall through the dust. Dilvish then laughed, saying: "I tread lightly."

Korel studied him. Then he blinked and his mole jerked across his eye.

"When I entered here before," he said, "there were no sounds, no torches. Everything lay empty and still, ruined. Do you know what is happening?"

"Yes," said Dilvish, "for I read of it in the Green Books of Time at the keep of Mirata. Know, O priest of Babrigore, that within the hall above the ghosts do play at being ghosts. Know, too, that Hohorga dies again and again so long as I stand within this place."

As he spoke the name of Hohorga a great cry was heard within the high hall. Dilvish raced up the stairs, the priest rushing after him.

Now within the halls of Rahoring there came up a mighty wailing.

They stood at the top of the stairs, Dilvish like a statue, blade half drawn from its sheath; Korel, hands within his sleeves, praying after the manner of his order.

The remains of a great feast were strewn about the hall; the light came down out of the air from colored globes that circled like planets through the great heaven-design within the vaulted ceiling; the throne on the high dais beside the far wall was empty. That throne was too large for any of this age to occupy. The walls were covered all over with ancient devices, strange, on alternate slabs of white and orange marble. In the pillars of the wall were set gems the size of doubled fists, burning yellow and emerald, infraruby and ultrablue, casting a fire radiance, transparent and illuminating, as far as the steps to the throne. The canopy of the throne was wide and all of white gold, worked in the manner of mermaids and harpies, dolphins and goat-headed snakes; it was supported by wyvern, hippogriff, firedrake, chimera, unicorn, cockatrice, griffin, and pegasus, sejant erect. It belonged to the one who lay dying upon the floor.

In the form of a man, but half again as large, Hohorga lay upon the tiles of his palace and his intestines filled his lap. He was supported by three of his guard, while the rest attended to his slayer. It had been said in the Books of Time that Hohorga the Maleficent was indescribable. Dilvish saw that this was both true and untrue.

He was fair to look upon and noble of feature; but so blindingly fair was he that all eyes were averted from that countenance now lined with pain. A faint bluish halo was diminishing about his shoulders. Even in the death pain he was as cold and perfect as a carved gemstone, set upon the red-green cushion of his blood; his was the hypnotic perfection of a snake of many colors. It is said that eyes have no expression of their own, and that one could not reach into a barrel of eyes and separate out those of an angry man or those of one's beloved. Hohorga's eyes were the eyes of a ruined god: infinitely sad, as proud as an ocean of lions.

One look and Dilvish knew this thing, though he could not tell their color.

Hohorga was of the blood of the First.

The guards had cornered the slayer. He fought them, apparently empty-handed, but parrying and thrusting as though he gripped a blade. Wherever his hand moved, there were wounds.

He wielded the only weapon that might have slain the King of the World, who permitted none to go armed in his presence save his own guard.

He bore the Invisible Blade.

He was Selar, first of the Elvish house of that name, great-gone-sire of Dilvish, who at that moment cried out his name.

Dilvish drew his blade and rushed across the hall. He cut at the attackers, but his blade passed through them as through smoke.

They beat down Selar's guard. A mighty blow sent something unseen ringing across the hall. Then they dismembered him, slowly, Selar of Shoredan, as Dilvish wept, watching.

And then Hohorga spoke, in a voice held firm though soft, without inflection, like the steady beating of surf or the hooves of horses:

"I have outlived the one who presumed to lay hands upon me, which is as it must be. Know that it was written that eyes would never see the blade that could slay me. Thus do the powers have their jokes. Much of what I have done shall never be undone, O children of Men and Elves and Salamanders. Much more than you know do I take with me from this world into the silence. You have slain that which was greater than yourselves, but do not be proud. It matters no longer to me. Nothing does. Have my curses."

Those eyes closed and there was a clap of thunder.

Dilvish and Korel stood alone in the darkened ruins of a great hall.

"Why did this thing appear today?" asked the priest.

"When one of the blood of Selar enters here," said Dilvish, "it is reenacted."

"Why have you come here, Dilvish, son of Selar?"

"To ring the bells of Shoredan."

"It cannot be."

"If I am to save Dilfar and redeliver Portaroy it *must* be."

"I go now to seek the bells," he said.

He crossed through the near blackness of night without stars, for neither were his eyes the eyes of Men, and he was accustomed to much dark.

He heard the priest following after him.

They circled behind the broken bulk of the Earth Lord's throne. Had there been sufficient light as they passed, they would have seen darkened spots upon the floor turning to stain, then crisp sand-brown, and then to red-green blood, as Dilvish moved near them, and vanishing once again as he moved away.

Behind the dais was the door to the central tower. Fevera Mirata, Queen of Illusion, had once shown Dilvish this hall in a mirror the size of six horsemen riding abreast, and broidered about with a frame of golden daffodils that hid their heads till it cleared of all save their reflections.

Dilvish opened the door and halted. Smoke billowed forth, engulfing him. He was seized with coughing but he kept his guard before him.

"It is the Warden of the Bells!" cried Korel. "Jelerak deliver us!"

"Damn Jelerak!" said Dilvish. "I'll deliver myself."

But as he spoke, the cloud swirled away and spun itself into a glowing tower that held the doorway, illuminating the throne and the places about the throne. Two red eyes glowed within the smoke.

Dilvish passed his blade through and through the cloud, meeting with no resistance.

"If you remain incorporeal, I shall pass through you," he called out. "If you take a shape, I shall dismember it. Make your choice," and he said it in Mabrahoring, the language spoken in Hell.

"Deliverer, Deliverer, Deliverer," hissed the cloud, "my pet Dilvish, little creature of hooks and chains. Do you not know your master? Is your memory so short?" And the cloud collapsed upon itself and coalesced into a bird-headed creature with the hindquarters of a lion and two serpents growing up from its shoulders, curling and engendering about its high crest of flaming quills.

"Cal-den!"

"Aye, your old tormentor, Elf man. I have missed you, for few depart my care. It is time you returned."

"This time," said Dilvish, "I am not chained and unarmed, and we meet in my world," and he cut forward with his blade, striking the serpent head from Cal-den's left shoulder.

A piercing bird cry filled the hall and Cal-den sprang forward.

Dilvish struck at his breast but the blade was turned aside, leaving only a smallish gash from which a pale liquor flowed.

Cal-den struck him then backward against the dais, catching his blade in a black claw, shattering it, and he raised his other arm to smite him. Dilvish did then stab upward with what remained of the sword, nine inches of jagged length.

It caught Cal-den beneath the jaw, entering there and remaining, the hilt torn from Dilvish's hand as the tormentor shook his head, roaring.

Then was Dilvish seized about the waist so that his bones did sigh and creak within him. He felt himself raised into the air, the serpent tearing at his ear, claws piercing his sides. Cal-den's face was turned up toward him, wearing the hilt of his blade like a beard of steel.

Then did he hurl Dilvish across the dais, so as to smash him against the tiles of the floor.

But the wearer of the green boots of Elfland may not fall or be thrown to land other than on his feet.

Dilvish did recover him then, but the shock of his landing caused pain in the thigh wound he bore. His leg collapsed beneath him, so that he put out his hand to the side.

Cal-den did then spring upon him, smiting him sorely about the head and shoulders. From somewhere Korel hurled a stone that struck upon the demon's crest.

Dilvish came scrambling backward, until his hand came upon a thing in the rubble that drew the blood from it.

A blade.

He snatched at the hilt and brought it up off the floor with a side-armed cut that struck Cal-den across the back, stiffening him into a bellow that near burst the ears to hear. Smoke rose from the wound.

Dilvish stood, and saw that he held nothing.

Then did he know that the blade of his ancestor, which no eyes may look upon, had come to him from the ruins, where it had lain across the ages, to serve him, scion of the House of Selar, in this moment of his need.

He directed it toward the breast of Cal-den.

"My rabbit, you are unarmed, yet you have cut me," said the creature. "Now shall we return to the Houses of Pain."

They both lunged forward.

"I always knew," said Cal-den, "that my little Dilvish was something special," and he fell to the floor with an enormous crash and the smokes arose from his body.

Divish placed his heel upon the carcass and wrenched free the blade outlined in steaming ichor.

"To you, Selar, do I owe this victory," he said, and raised a length of smouldering nothingness in salute. Then he sheathed the sword.

Korel was at his side. He watched as the creature at their feet vanished like embers and ice, leaving behind a stench that was most foul to smell.

Dilvish turned him again to the door to the tower and entered there, Korel at his side.

The broken bellpull lay at his feet. It fell to dust when he touched it with his toe.

"It is said," he told Korel, "that the bellpull did break in the hands of the last to ring it, half an age ago."

He raised his eye, and there was only darkness above him.

"The legions of Shoredan did set forth to assault the Citadel of Rahoring," said the priest, as though reading it from some old parchment, "and word of their movement came soon to the King of the World. Then did he lay upon three bells cast in Shoredan a weird. When these bells were rung, a great fog came over the land and engulfed the columns of marchers and those on horseback. The fog did disperse upon the second ringing of the bells, and the land was found to be empty of the troop. It was later written by Merde, Red Wizard of the South, that somewhere still do these marchers and horsemen move, through regions of eternal fog. 'If these bells be rung again by a hand of that House which dispatched the layer of the weird, then will these legions come forth from a mist to serve that one for a time in battle. But when they have served, they will vanish again into the places of gloom, where they will continue their march upon a Rahoringhast which no longer exists. How they may be freed to rest, this thing is not known. One mightier than I has tried and failed.' "

Dilvish bowed his head a moment, then he felt the walls. They were not like the outer walls. They were cast of blocks of that same material, and between those blocks were scant crevices wherein his fingers found purchase.

He raised himself above the floor and commenced to climb, the soft green boots somehow finding toe-holds wherever they struck.

The air was hot and stale, and showers of dust descended upon him each time he raised an arm above his head.

He pulled himself upward, until he counted a hundred such movements and the nails of his hands were broken. Then he clung to the wall like a lizard, resting, and felt the pains of his last encounter burning like suns within him.

He breathed the fetid air and his head swam. He thought of the Portaroy he had once delivered, long ago, the city of friends, the place where he had once been feted, the land whose need for him had been strong enough to free him from the Houses of Pain and break the grip of stone upon his body; and he thought of that Portaroy in the hands of the Colonel of the West, and he thought of Dilfar now resisting that Lylish who might sweep the bastions of the East before him.

He climbed once again.

His head touched the metal lip of a bell.

He climbed around it, bracing himself on the crossbars that now occurred.

There were three bells suspended from a single axle.

He set his back against the wall and clung to the crossbars, placing his feet upon the middle bell.

He pushed, straightening his legs.

The axle protested, creaking and grinding within its sockets.

But the bell moved, slowly. It did not return, however, but stayed in the position into which it had been pushed.

Cursing, he worked his way through the crossbars and over to the opposite side of the belfry.

He pushed it back and it stuck on the other side. All the bells moved with the axle, though.

Nine times more did he cross over in darkness to push at the bells.

Then they moved more easily.

Slowly they fell back as he released the pressure of his legs. He pushed them out again and they returned again. He pushed them again, and again.

A click came from one of the bells as the clapper struck. Then another. Finally one of them rang.

He kicked out harder and harder, and then did the

bells swing free and fill the tower about him with a pealing that vibrated the roots of his teeth and filled his ears with pain. A storm of dust came down over him and his eyes were full of tears. He coughed and closed them. He let the bells grow still.

Across some mighty distance he thought he heard the faint winding of a horn.

He began the downward climb.

"Lord Dilvish," said Korel, when he had reached the floor, "I have heard the blowing of horns."

"Yes," said Dilvish.

"I have a flask of wine with me. Drink."

Dilvish rinsed his mouth and spat, then drank three mighty swallows.

"Thank you, priest. Let us be gone from here now."

They crossed through the hall once more and descended the inner stairs. The smaller hall was now unlighted and lay in ruin. They made their way out, Dilvish leaving no tracks to show where he had gone; and halfway down the stairs the darkness departed from them.

Through the bleak day that now clung to the land, Dilvish looked back along the Way of the Armies. A mighty fog filled the air far beyond the broken gates, and from within that fog there came again the notes of the horn and the sounds of the movements of troops. Almost, Dilvish could see the outlines of the columns of marchers and riders, moving, moving, but not advancing.

"My troops await me," said Dilvish upon the stair. "Thank you, Korel, for accompanying me."

"Thank you, Lord Dilvish. I came to this place to dwell upon the ways of evil. You have shown me much that I may meditate upon."

They descended the final stairs. Dilvish brushed dust from his garments and mounted Black.

"One thing more, Korel, priest of Babrigore," he said. "If you ever meet with your patron, who should provide you much more evil to meditate upon than you have seen here, tell him that, when all the battles have been fought, his statue will come to kill him."

The mole danced as Korel blinked up at him.

"Remember," he replied, "that once he wore a mantle of light."

Dilvish laughed, and the eyes of his mount glowed red through the gloom.

"There!" he said, gesturing. "There is your sign of his goodness and light!"

Nine black doves circled in the heavens.

Korel bowed his head and did not answer.

"I go now to lead my legions."

Black reared on steel hooves and laughed along with his rider.

Then they were gone, up the Way of the Armies, leaving the Citadel of Rahoring and the priest of Babrigore behind them in the gloom.

GHOSTS OF THE MUTINY

Michael and Mollie Hardwick

The Indian Mutiny, that great revolt of the Bengal native army in 1857, was a bloody and treacherous business undertaken by violent men, and involving the brutal murder of many harmless civilians. So many women and children were horribly slaughtered that the reputation of Herod pales beside that of some of the mutineers.

It is not surprising—especially in a country noted for legends and mysticism—that supernatural echoes of the Mutiny were heard for long after it was over. Nearly all involved haunting. Such was the case of the Haunted Palace, visited about 1890 by a government official, Mr. Gerard, and his wife. The Gerards had reached the town of Hissar, where, on behalf of the Government, they exchanged hospitality with the Europeans living there.

Their visit coincided with Christmas. On Christmas Day they were invited to dinner by Colonel Robinson, an officer holding a staff appointment. The party was small—the Gerards, Colonel and Mrs. Robinson, their elder and younger sons, and the Civil Surgeon of the station. The Palace, where the Robinsons lived, had once been the residence of the Rajahs of Hissar; but after the Mutiny the then Rajah was removed and the Palace taken over by the British Government.

Mr. and Mrs. Gerard were struck by the strange approach to the Robinsons' apartments, which were in the upper part of the Palace. The huge doors on the ground-floor level were boarded up and had obviously not been used for a very long time. An iron staircase like a fire-escape, attached to the outside wall, led up to a long, high hall, running along the front of the building, and containing many high windows. Parallel with this was a similar room, used by the Robinsons as a dining room. Next to this came the drawing-room, and at the far end of it a door led into the bedroom, and another from the bedroom into the bathroom.

Dinner was a pleasant, informal affair, and Mrs. Gerard remarked to her host that they must have an excellent cook. She was surprised when he replied that this treasure was shortly leaving them, in spite of raised wages and other inducements. A new one, he sighed, would have to be recruited from somewhere outside the district.

This struck Mrs. Gerard as very odd, and she inquired why a local servant would not do. "Because nobody for miles around would take service here," answered Colonel Robinson. "We were told so when we came, but we didn't believe it." Mrs. Gerard expressed great surprise that such a pleasant couple could not keep their servants. The Colonel, smiling, told her that it was not their employers the servants did not like—it was the Palace. "It's haunted, you see," he explained.

Mrs. Gerard raised her eyebrows, and replied that it was just like superstitious native servants to believe such nonsense. *She* didn't believe in such things, and she hoped Colonel Robinson did not, either. He raised his eyebrows and smiled at her; and Mrs. Gerard, slightly annoyed, called across the table to Mrs. Robinson that the Colonel was teasing her with a stupid ghost-story.

Mrs. Robinson, who had been chatting away gaily enough to the Surgeon, immediately stopped, and looked nervously at her little boy, who, at the mention of ghost stories, had become all eyes and attention.

"It's true enough, unfortunately," she said, "but I'll tell you about it later, if you don't mind."

Mrs. Gerard instantly turned to Colonel Robinson and apologized for mistaking his intention. "It would not be the first time I've been disbelieved!" he told her.

After dinner, Mrs. Robinson and Mrs. Gerard, the only ladies of the party, moved into the drawing-room, while the gentlemen remained to smoke and drink their port. Mrs. Robinson's small son was taken to bed by his ayah, though he would obviously have preferred to stay and listen to whatever fascinating story his mother was going to tell. As soon as the ladies were seated by the drawing-room fire, Mrs. Robinson offered to tell her guest the truth about the manifestations that made it impossible for her to keep servants; and Mrs. Gerard, sipping her coffee, listened attentively.

The Robinsons had moved to Hissar fifteen years before. They were pleased with the appointment, but less pleased to find that no arrangements had been made about quarters for them. At last they decided to move into part of the old Palace, now shut up and deserted. It was well-built and weather-tight, and only wanted thorough cleaning and airing. The Robinsons could make themselves a splendid flat from the four large parallel rooms, and the smaller ones would easily adapt into bedroom and bathroom.

So far so good. The cleaning and refurbishing of their apartments proceeded, and they were able to move in very speedily. But, they were told, they would never keep servants—the place was badly haunted—"wicked things had been done there"—and nobody who knew the Palace would work in it. Like most Europeans of their day and age, Colonel and Mrs. Robinson were not prepared to take this seriously. They imagined that somebody wanted them to stay away from the Palace—perhaps somebody who wanted to use it as a headquarters for some nefarious undertaking. So they laughed, and moved in.

Rumour proved all too true. No native of Hissar

would agree to join their staff; and the old servants they had brought with them soon left, with feeble excuses. Undefeated, and still healthily sceptical, the Robinsons recruited servants from other districts, and paid them well. The household at the old Palace settled down into a well-organized routine, and the Robinsons were very content with their dwelling. "You see, dear, it's all nonsense about this haunting," said the Colonel to his wife.

Then came an unpleasant surprise. One night Mrs. Robinson had gone to bed as usual, and was just hovering between waking and sleep when she heard what she thought to be her husband fumbling about with her bunch of keys at the locked wardrobe. She remembered, sleepily, that she had put her keys and watch under her pillow before going to bed, as she always did—her husband must have got up and removed them while she was dozing. Hardly bothering to open her eyes, she called to ask him what he was doing.

There was no answer; the rattling noise continued. Mrs. Robinson roused herself and sat up—to see her husband, not at the wardrobe, but beside her in bed, staring at her. He, too, had heard the noise, and had thought it was his wife, rattling her keys. To prove that he had been wrong, she put her hand under the pillow, and withdrew the keys. The Robinsons stared blankly at each other.

Meanwhile, the sound grew louder. It seemed to them now more like the rattling of chains than of keys. Nor did they hear it alone—their two great dogs, who always slept in their room, had stirred, risen, and were now growling in their corner. The noise was certainly alarming, for to the rattling was now added a dragging sound, like metal trailing on stone, and a heavy, ominous thudding like gigantic footsteps.

"What on earth can it be?" said Colonel Robinson. "Someone's playing tricks—that's it. I told you they wanted to keep us out of this place. Well, I'm getting up to find out."

Slipping out of bed, he turned up the lamp, put on

his dressing-gown and placed his loaded revolver in the pocket of it. His wife began to reach for her dressing-gown.

"I must come with you! Don't leave me alone in here, George!"

Gently he pushed her back, telling her that if there was going to be a physical struggle, and perhaps shooting, she would be better out of it. She remained sitting on the edge of the bed, trembling violently, and watching her husband as he took up his hurricane-lamp and opened the door, calling the dogs to come with him. But there was no need. As soon as the door was opened they rushed past him and out of the room, growling deeply. Then Mrs. Robinson was alone in the room.

It seemed to her that she had been there for hours, though in fact it was not more than a few minutes, when a remarkable thing happened—the strange sounds stopped, suddenly, after drawing so near and growing so loud that Mrs. Robinson felt she would be deafened by them. There was absolute silence, and she felt this to be as frightening as the previous noises.

Then, through the open door, came the dogs; not the bold creatures that had rushed out ahead of the Colonel, but beaten, crawling things, dragging themselves along, their eyes rolling and their bodies shaking with fear. Mrs. Robinson had never seen them look like that before. They appeared to have had a terrible shock, which had sent them almost out of their minds. She approached them and tried to comfort them; but they crawled out of her reach and hid under the bed, where they crouched, whining. Then Colonel Robinson returned.

"Whatever has happened?" asked his wife. "What have you seen?"

"These two poor dogs have seen something," he replied, "but I haven't. I can't understand it. As I walked from room to room the sounds seemed to come nearer and nearer—"

"Just as they did in here," she put in.

"—until when I came to the dining-room they stopped, all in a moment. Before I got to it I met the dogs coming back—as you see them now, poor things. I don't know what all this means, Mary, but I intend to find out."

And he lost no time in calling up the servants to make a thorough search of the Palace. All night the Robinsons and the staff tramped up and down with lanterns, through great empty rooms, up and down winding staircases, into cellars and dungeons. Not one trace of the night's activity rewarded them—not a single footprint in the dust. Eventually they gave up the search and went, exhausted, to bed.

When they woke next morning, hardly believing in the strange events of the night, a dreadful confirmation met their eyes. Under their bed lay the two beautiful dogs, cold and dead. They had died of sheer fright.

The Robinsons' distress was great. They had hardly taken in the tragedy when the first of their servants gave notice. After him came another, and another—all with excuses involving sick parents or family troubles. By the end of the day not one was left.

Now that the Robinsons were alone in the Palace, the noises of the night returned with a regularity that amounted to persecution. Always they were the same— beginning softly, with a light metallic rattling, and increasing to a dreadful clashing and tramping. It seemed to occur always on a festival or holiday, whether native or English. The Robinsons became partly resigned to it, though they never ceased to cling to each other in apprehension when the terrible crescendo began. One night, Mrs. Robinson, who had been lying with the bedclothes over her head, trying to shut out the sound, suddenly sat up and clutched her husband's arm.

"Elephants!" she exclaimed. "George, it's elephants!"

Her husband stared. "How on earth can it be elephants? Where?"

"How do I know where? Phantom ones, I suppose. But it *is* elephants, dragging chains and tramping. Can't you hear it?"

He listened, and finally agreed.

It was not long before Mrs. Robinson's guess was confirmed. A native who was not too frightened to talk to them told them the dreadful legend of the man who had been Rajah of Hissar at the time of the Mutiny. An inhumanly cruel man, in the tradition of the terrible Indian rulers of the eighteenth century, he had elephants specially trained to destroy people. If any of his many wives angered him, he would have them shut into the underground dungeons of the Palace; then the elephants were admitted to them, and either trampled them to death or caught them up and dashed out their brains against the dungeon walls.

When the Mutiny broke out, the Rajah prepared to treat the hated British as he had treated his own people. As the rebellious troops swept in from Delhi, many Europeans fled. But those who were unable to escape were seven men and their wives, with fifteen small children and two Eurasian native servants.

Desperate, they risked the Rajah's evil reputation and begged him for help. He would give it, he said; they should be safe. Let them only take refuge with him in the Palace and nobody should touch them. Thankfully they came, the pathetic little band, babies in arms, small children led by the hand, expectant mothers and anxious husbands. They were brought up to the apartments later used by the Robinsons, and shut into the room at the end—the Robinsons' future bathroom. Then the Rajah's soldiers burst in and hacked them to pieces, leaving not a single one alive.

The British relief troops, when they arrived, found the room ankle-deep in blood, corpses heaped on top of one another, the walls sticky with brains and blood; and—almost worst of all—sixteen of the corpses were headless, and the heads, in a graded line, were placed mockingly on the mantelpiece of the room to be used by the Robinsons as a drawing-room.

Mrs. Robinson ended her story. Her guest, who had been listening in appalled silence, looked up at the mantelpiece, now cheerful with flowers and family photographs.

"And do you still hear the sounds now?" she asked.

"No. It seemed as though, having got us on our own

and nearly frightening us to death, they had served their purpose. But none of the servants will believe that, of course."

"I wonder why it was only the elephants you heard, and not—the other sounds?"

"We don't know. But I thank God we were spared those."

Mrs. Gerard remembered the great barred doors that had led to the basement—and the dungeons—glanced up again at the mantelpiece, and shuddered deeply. The door opened, and she looked towards it in fear; but it was only the gentlemen who entered, rosy and good-tempered from their port.

Another strange story of the Mutiny concerned Mrs. Torrens, widow of General Torrens. In 1856 she was living at Southsea, Hampshire. Her daughter had married a Captain Hayes and gone out to India with him. Mrs. Torrens naturally regretted that she was so far away, but knew her to be happy and had no fears for her future.

One night, however, her attitude was abruptly changed. She dreamed, vividly, that she was in India, in the town where her daughter's husband was stationed. There seemed to be something like a revolution in progress. Dark-faced natives were surging in the streets, shouting and waving guns and other weapons—some of which, Mrs. Torrens noticed with horror, had blood on them.

As is the way of dreams, she was not particularly surprised that nobody seemed to notice her presence or to offer to molest her in any way. Nor did it seem strange to her that she knew by instinct how to get to Captain Hayes's barracks, though the situation had never been described to her. In a few minutes she was there. The building was encircled by a mass of yelling natives, all apparently bent on murdering those within. And yet Mrs. Torrens passed unharmed through them, entered the building, and found herself guided to the quarters of Captain Hayes.

To her intense horror, she found the Captain and her daughter had already been attacked by the insurgents, and were struggling wildly in the grasp of five or six savage-looking Sepoys. Now came the most terrible part of her dream. She found herself quite helpless to move, to call out, or to make any sort of impression on the attackers or the attacked. She could only stand there, paralysed by her dream-state, and watch the indescribably horrible death of her daughter and son-in-law. So ghastly was it that she awoke, trembling and in a cold sweat.

So dreadfully vivid had been the dream that she could not feel the usual relief of a sleeper waking from nightmare. The terrible impression remained with her, and prompted her to sit down and write to her daughter, urging her to come home at once. Posts in those days were slow, and it was some weeks before the reply came. To her disappointment, it was to say that Mrs. Hayes felt she could not leave her husband in India on such slight grounds; but she took her mother's warning seriously enough to promise to send her children to England. Before very long they arrived, and Mrs. Torrens's mind was relieved on their account, at least, although she had not seen them in her dream.

1857 came, and with it the outbreak of the Indian Mutiny. When Captain Hayes and his young wife were reported to have been brutally murdered, Mrs. Torrens's distress held no quality of shock, for she already knew too well the manner of their death. The supernatural warning had been true in every particular.

Presumably the dream of Mrs. Torrens had been sent to her by the forces responsible with kindly intentions. An equally good spirit operated in the case of a Captain's wife whose fate was happier than that of Mrs. Hayes. She had been warned, at her husband's quarters in Meerut, of the approach of the mutineers, and was packing, ready for flight. Suddenly the door of her bedroom flew open, and there entered a terrible figure—a huge, wild-faced Sepoy, waving a blood-stained axe. Mrs. X, like Mrs. Torrens in her dream, was rooted to the spot; but with fear, not with the helpless immobility of the dreamer. She managed to pray, however, for the habit of prayer was strong in her and she knew that she stood more in need of help now than ever before.

Time was suspended as they faced each other—the giant Sepoy, a dreadful genie-figure drunk with bloodlust, and the small Englishwoman, half-dressed, her pathetic possessions strewn at her feet. Then an extraordinary thing happened. The floor-board beneath her shook and creaked, as though somebody tremendously heavy had stepped in front of her, and she felt something brush against the front of her skirt. The Sepoy's grinning face changed. If it were possible for a brown face to turn pale, his paled in an instant, and his eyes widened with horror. For a moment he faced his ghostly antagonist; then turned and fled from the room.

Mrs. X fell on her knees and prayed once more. But this time it was a prayer of deep thankfulness.

THE ROLL-CALL OF THE REEF

Sir Arthur Quiller-Couch

"Yes, sir," said my host the quarryman, reaching
down the relics from their hook in the wall over the
chimneypiece; "they've hung there all my time, and
most of my father's. The women won't touch 'em; they're
afraid of the story. So here they'll dangle, and gather
dust and smoke, till another tenant comes and tosses
'em out o' doors for rubbish. Whew! 'tis coarse weather."

He went to the door, opened it, and stood studying
the gale that beat upon his cottage-front, straight from
the Manacle Reef. The rain drove past him into the
kitchen aslant like threads of gold silk in the shine of
the wreckwood fire. Meanwhile by the same firelight I
examined the relics on my knee. The metal of each was
tarnished out of knowledge. But the trumpet was evidently an old cavalry trumpet, and the threads of its
parti-colored sling, though frayed and dusty, still hung
together. Around the side-drum, beneath its cracked
brown varnish, I could hardly trace a royal coat-of-arms
and a legend running, *Per mare per Terram*—the motto
of the Marines. Its parchment, though colored and
scented with wood-smoke, was limp and mildewed; and
I began to tighten up the straps—under which the
drumsticks had been loosely thrust—with the idle purpose of trying if some music might be got out of the old
drum yet.

But as I turned it on my knee, I found the drum attached to the trumpet-sling by a curious barrel-shaped padlock, and paused to examine this. The body of the lock was composed of half a dozen brass rings, set accurately edge to edge; and, rubbing the brass with my thumb, I saw that each of the six had a series of letters engraved around it.

I knew the trick of it, I thought. Here was one of those word padlocks, once so common; only to be opened by getting the rings to spell a certain word, which the dealer confides to you.

My host shut and barred the door and came back to the hearth.

" 'Twas just such a wind—east by south—that brought in what you've got between your hands. Back in the year 'nine it was; my father has told me the tale a score o' times. You're twisting round the rings, I see. But you'll never guess the word. Parson Kendall, he made the word, and knocked down a couple o' ghosts in their graves with it; and when his time came, he went to his own grave and took the word with him."

"Whose ghosts, Matthew?"

"You want the story, I see, sir. My father could tell it better than I can. He was a young man in the year 'nine, unmarried at the time, and living in this very cottage just as I be. That's how he came to get mixed up with the tale."

He took a chair, lit a short pipe, and unfolded the story in a low, musing voice, with his eyes fixed on the dancing violet flames.

"Yes, he'd ha' been about thirty years old in January of the year 'nine. The storm got up in the night o' the twenty-first o' that month. My father was dressed and out long before daylight; he never was one to 'bide in bed, let be that the gale by this time was pretty near lifting the thatch over his head. Besides which, he'd fenced a small 'taty-patch that winter, down by Lowland Point, and he wanted to see if it stood the night's work. He took the path across Gunner's Meadow—where they buried most of the bodies afterward. The wind was

right in his teeth at the time, and once on the way (he's
told me this often) a great strip of oreweed came flying
through the darkness and fetched him a slap on the
cheek like a cold hand. But he made shift pretty well
till he got a Lowland, and then had to drop upon his
hands and knees and crawl, digging his fingers every
now and then into the shingle to hold on, for he declared to me that the stones, some of them as big as a
man's head, kept rolling and driving past till it seemed
the whole foreshore was moving westward under him.
The fence was gone, of course; not a stick left to show
where it stood; so that, when first he came to the place,
he thought he must have missed his bearings. My father, sir, was a very religious man; and if he reckoned
the end of the world was at hand—there in the great
wind and night, among the moving stones—you may
believe he was certain of it when he heard a gun fired,
and, with the same, saw a flame shoot up out of the
darkness to windward, making a sudden fierce light in
all the place about. All he could find to think or say
was, 'The Second Coming—The Second Coming! The
Bridegroom cometh, and the wicked He will toss like a
ball into a large country!' and being already upon his
knees, he just bowed his head and 'bided, saying this
over and over.

"But by'm-by, between two squalls, he made bold to
lift his head and look, and then by the light—a bluish
color 'twas—he saw all the coast clear away to Manacle
Point, and off the Manacles, in the thick of the weather,
a sloop-of-war with top-gallants housed, driving stern
foremost toward the reef. It was she, of course, that was
burning the flare. My father could see the white streak
and the ports of her quite plain as she rose to it, a little
outside the breakers, and he guessed easy enough that
her captain had just managed to wear ship, and was
trying to force her nose to the sea with the help of her
small bower anchor and the scrap or two of canvas that
hadn't yet been blown out of her. But while he looked,
she fell off, giving her broadside to it foot by foot, and
drifting back on the breakers about Carn dû and the

Varses. The rocks lie so thick thereabouts, that 'twas a toss up which she struck first; at any rate, my father couldn't tell at the time, for just then the flare died down and went out.

"Well, sir, he turned then in the dark and started back for Coverack to cry the dismal tidings—though well knowing ship and crew to be past any hope; and as he turned, the wind lifted him and tossed him forward 'like a ball,' as he'd been saying, and homeward along the foreshore. As you know, 'tis ugly work, even by daylight, picking your way among the stones there, and my father was prettily knocked about at first in the dark. But by this 'twas nearer seven than six o'clock, and the day spreading. By the time he reached North Corner, a man could see to read print; hows'ever he looked neither out to sea nor toward Coverack, but headed straight for the first cottage—the same that stands above North Corner to-day. A man named Billy Ede lived there then, and when my father burst into the cottage bawling, 'Wreck! wreck!' he saw Billy Ede's wife, Ann, standing there in her clogs, with a shawl over her head, and her clothes wringing wet.

" 'Save the chap!' says Billy Ede's wife, Ann. 'What d' 'ee mean by crying stale fish at that rate?'

" 'But 'tis a wreck, I tell 'ee. I've a-zeed'n!'

" 'Why, so 'tis,' says she, 'and I've a-zeed'n, too; and so has every one with an eye in his head.'

"And with that she pointed straight over my father's shoulder, and he turned; and there, close under Dolor Point, at the end of Coverack town, he saw another wreck washing, and the Point black with people, like emmets, running to and fro in the morning light. While he stood staring at her, he heard a trumpet sounded on board, the notes coming in little jerks, like a bird rising against the wind; but faintly, of course, because of the distance and the gale blowing—though this had dropped a little.

" 'She's a transport,' said Billy Ede's wife, Ann, 'and full of horse soldiers, fine long men. When she struck they must ha' pitched the hosses over first to lighten the ship, for a score of dead hosses had washed in afore I left, half an hour back. An' three or four soldiers, too—fine long corpses in white breeches and jackets of blue and gold. I held the lantern to one. Such a straight young man.'

"My father asked her about the trumpeting.

"'That's the queerest bit of all. She was burnin' a light when me an' my man joined the crowd down there. All her masts had gone; whether they were carried away, or were cut away to ease her, I don't rightly know. Anyway, there she lay 'pon the rocks with her decks bare. Her keelson was broke under her and her bottom sagged and stove, and she had just settled down like a sitting hen—just the leastest list to starboard; but a man could stand there easy. They had rigged up ropes across her, from bulwark to bulwark, an' beside these the men were mustered, holding on like grim death whenever the sea made a clean breach over them, an' standing up like heroes as soon as it passed. The captain an' the officers were clinging to the rail of the quarter-deck, all in their golden uniforms, waiting for the end as if 'twas King George they expected. There was no way to help, for she lay right beyond cast of line, though our folk tried it fifty times. And beside them clung a trumpeter, a whacking big man, an' between the heavy seas he would lift his trumpet with one hand, and blow a call; and every time he blew the men gave a cheer. There (she says)—hark 'ee now—there he goes agen! But you won't hear no cheering any more, for few are left to cheer, and their voices weak. Bitter cold the wind is, and I reckon it numbs their grip o' the ropes, for they were dropping off fast with every sea when my man sent me home to get his breakfast. Another wreck, you say? Well, there's no hope for the tender dears, if 'tis the Manacles. You'd better run down and help yonder; though 'tis little help that any man can give. Not one came in alive while I was there. The tide's flowing, an' she won't hold together another hour, they say.'

"Well, sure enough, the end was coming fast when

my father got down to the Point. Six men had been cast up alive, or just breathing—a seaman and five troopers. The seaman was the only one that had breath to speak; and while they were carrying him into the town, the word went round that the ship's name was the *Despatch*, transport, homeward bound from Corunna with a detachment of the 7th Hussars, that had been fighting out there with Sir John Moore. The seas had rolled her farther over by this time, and given her decks a pretty sharp slope; but a dozen men still held on, seven by the ropes near the ship's waist, a couple near the break of the poop, and three on the quarter-deck. Of these three my father made out one to be the skipper; close by him clung an officer in full regimentals—his name, they heard after, was Captain Duncanfield; and last came the tall trumpeter; and if you'll believe me, the fellow was making shift there, at the very last, to blow 'God Save the King.' What's more, he got to 'Send us victorious' before an extra big sea came bursting across and washed them off the deck—every man but one of the pair beneath the poop—and *he* dropped his hold before the next wave; being stunned, I reckon. The others went out of sight at once, but the trumpeter—being, as I said, a powerful man as well as a tough swimmer—rose like a duck, rode out a couple of breakers, and came in on the crest of the third. The folks looked to see him broke like an egg at their feet; but when the smother cleared, there he was, lying face downward on a ledge below them; and one of the men that happened to have a rope round him—I forget the fellow's name, if I ever heard it—jumped down and grabbed him by the ankle as he began to slip back. Before the next big sea, the pair were hauled high enough to be out of harm, and another heave brought them up to grass. Quick work; but master trumpeter wasn't quite dead; nothing worse than a cracked head and three staved ribs. In twenty minutes or so they had him in bed, with the doctor to tend him.

"Now was the time—nothing being left alive upon the transport—for my father to tell of the sloop he'd

seen driving upon the Manacles. And when he got a
hearing, though the most were set upon salvage, and
believed a wreck in the hand, so to say, to be worth half
a dozen they couldn't see, a good few volunteered to
start off with him and have a look. They crossed Lowland Point; no ship to be seen on the Manacles, nor
anywhere upon the sea. One or two was for calling my
father a liar. 'Wait till we come to Dean Point,' said he.
Sure enough, on the far side of Dean Point, they found
the sloop's mainmast washing about with half a dozen
men lashed to it—men in red jackets—every mother's
son drowned and staring; and a little farther on, just
under the Dean, three or four bodies cast up on the
shore, one of them a small drummer-boy, side-drum
and all; and, near by, part of a ship's gig, with 'H. M. S.
Primrose' cut on the sternboard. From this point on,
the shore was littered thick with wreckage and dead
bodies—the most of them marines in uniform; and in
Godrevy Cove in particular, a heap of furniture from
the captain's cabin, and among it a water-tight box, not
much damaged, and full of papers, by which, when it
came to be examined next day, the wreck was easily
made out to be the *Primrose* of eighteen guns, outward
bound from Portsmouth, with a fleet of transports for
the Spanish War, thirty sail, I've heard, but I've never
heard what became of them. Being handled by mer-
chant skippers, no doubt they rode out the gale and
reached the Tagus safe and sound. Not but what the
captain of the *Primrose* (Mein was his name) did quite
right to try and club-haul his vessel when he found
himself under the land; only he never ought to have got
there if he took proper soundings. But it's easy talking.

"The *Primrose*, sir, was a handsome vessel—for her
size, one of the handsomest in the King's service—and
newly fitted out at Plymouth Dock. So the boys had
brave pickings from her in the way of brass-work, ship's
instruments, and the like, let alone some barrels of
stores not much spoiled. They loaded themselves with
as much as they could carry, and started for home,
meaning to make a second journey before the preven-

tive men got wind of their doings and came to spoil the
fun. But as my father was passing back under the Dean,
he happened to take a look over his shoulder at the
bodies there. 'Hullo,' says he, and dropped his gear, 'I
do believe there's a leg moving!' And, running fore, he
stooped over the small drummer-boy that I told you
about. The poor little chap was lying there, with his
face a mass of bruises and his eyes closed; but he had
shifted one leg an inch or two, and was still breathing.
So my father pulled out a knife and cut him free from
his drum—that was lashed on to him with a double turn
of manila rope—and took him up and carried him along
here, to this very room that we're sitting in. He lost a
good deal by this, for when he went back to fetch his
bundle the preventive men had got hold of it, and were
thick as thieves along the foreshore; so that 'twas only
by paying one or two to look the other way that he
picked up anything worth carrying off; which you'll
allow to be hard, seeing that he was the first man to
give news of the wreck.

"Well, the inquiry was held, of course, and my father
gave evidence, and for the rest they had to trust to the
sloop's papers, for not a soul was saved besides the
drummer-boy, and he was raving in a fever, brought on
by the cold and the fright. And the seamen and the five
troopers gave evidence about the loss of the *Despatch*.
The tall trumpeter, too, whose ribs were healing, came
forward and kissed the Book; but somehow his head had
been hurt in coming ashore, and he talked foolish-like,
and 'twas easy seen he would never be a proper man
again. The others were taken up to Plymouth, and so
went their ways; but the trumpeter stayed on in
Coverack; and King George, finding he was fit for nothing, sent him down a trifle of a pension after a while—
enough to keep him in board and lodging, with a bit of
tobacco over.

"Now the first time that this man—William Tallifer,
he called himself—met with the drummer-boy, was
about a fortnight after the little chap had bettered enough
to be allowed a short walk out of doors, which he took,

if you please, in full regimentals. There never was a
soldier so proud of his dress. His own suit had shrunk a
brave bit with the salt water; but into ordinary frock an'
corduroys he declared he would not get—not if he had
to go naked the rest of his life; so my father, being a
good-natured man and handy with the needle, turned
to and repaired damages with a piece or two of scarlet
cloth cut from the jacket of one of the drowned Marines. Well, the poor little chap chanced to be standing,
in this rig-out, down by the gate of Gunner's Meadow,
where they had buried twoscore and over of his comrades. The morning was a fine one, early in March
month; and along came the cracked trumpeter, likewise
taking a stroll.

"'Hullo!' says he; 'good-mornin'! And what might
you be doin' here?'

"'I was a-wishin',' says the boy, 'I had a pair o'
drumsticks. Our lads were buried yonder without so
much as a drum tapped or a musket fired; and that's not
Christian burial for British soldiers.'

"'Phut!' says the trumpeter, and spat on the ground;
'a parcel of Marines!'

"The boy eyed him a second or so, and answered up:
'If I'd a tab of turf handy, I'd bung it at your mouth,
you greasy cavalryman, and learn you to speak respect-
ful of your betters. The Marines are the handiest body
of men in the service.'

"The trumpeter looked down on him from the height
of six foot two, and asked: 'Did they die well?'

"'They died very well. There was a lot of running to
and fro at first, and some of the men began to cry, and a
few to strip off their clothes. But when the ship fell off
for the last time, Captain Mein turned and said something to Major Griffiths, the commanding officer on
board, and the Major called out to me to beat to quarters. It might have been for a wedding, he sang it out so
cheerful. We'd had word already that 'twas to be parade
order, and the men fell in as trim and decent as if they
were going to church. One or two even tried to shave at
the last moment. The Major wore his medals. One of

the seamen, seeing that I had hard work to keep the drum steady—the sling being a bit loose for me and the wind what you remember—lashed it tight with a piece of rope; and that saved my life afterward, a drum being as good as a cork until it's stove. I kept beating away until every man was on deck; and then the Major formed them up and told them to die like British soldiers, and the chaplain read a prayer or two—the boys standin' all the while like rocks, each man's courage keeping up the other's. The chaplain was in the middle of a prayer when she struck. In ten minutes she was gone. That was how they died, cavalryman.'

" 'And that was very well done, drummer of the Marines. What's your name?'

" 'John Christian.'

" 'Mine's William George Tallifer, trumpeter, of the 7th Light Dragoons—the Queen's Own. I played *God Save the King* while our men were drowning. Captain Duncanfield told me to sound a call or two, to put them in heart; but that matter of *God Save the King* was a notion of my own. I won't say anything to hurt the feelings of a Marine, even if he's not much over five foot tall; but the Queen's Own Hussars is a tearin' fine regiment. As between horse and foot 'tis a question o' which gets the chance. All the way from Sahagun to Corunna 'twas we that took and gave the knocks—at Mayorga and Rueda and Bennyventy.' (The reason, sir, I can speak the names so pat is that my father learnt 'em by heart afterward from the trumpeter, who was always talking about Mayorga and Rueda and Bennyventy.) 'We made the rear-guard, under General Paget, and drove the French every time; and all the infantry did was to sit about in wine-shops till we shipped 'em out, an' steal an' straggle an' play the tom-fool in general. And when it came to a stand-up fight at Corunna, 'twas we that had to stay seasick aboard the transports, an' watch the infantry in the thick o' the caper. Very well they behaved, too; 'specially the 4th Regiment, an' the 42d Highlanders, an' the Dirty Half Hundred. Oh, ay; they're decent regiments, all three. But the Queen's

Own Hussars is a tearin' fine regiment. So you played on your drum when the ship was goin' down? Drummer John Christian, I'll have to get you a new pair o' drumsticks for that.'

"Well, sir, it appears that the very next day the trumpeter marched into Helston, and got a carpenter there to turn him a pair of box-wood drumsticks for the boy. And this was the beginning of one of the most curious friendships you ever heard tell of. Nothing delighted the pair more than to borrow a boat of my father and pull out to the rocks where the *Primrose* and the *Despatch* had struck and sunk; and on still days 'twas pretty to hear them out there off the Manacles, the drummer playing his tattoo—for they always took their music with them—and the trumpeter practising calls, and making his trumpet speak like an angel. But if the weather turned roughish, they'd be walking together and talking; leastwise, the youngster listened while the other discoursed about Sir John's campaign in Spain and Portugal, telling how each little skirmish befell; and of Sir John himself, and General Baird and General Paget, and Colonel Vivian, his own commanding officer, and what kind men they were; and of the last bloody stand-up at Corunna, and so forth, as if neither could have enough.

"But all this had to come to an end in the last summer, for the boy, John Christian, being now well and strong again, must go up to Plymouth to report himself. 'Twas his own wish (for I believe King George had forgotten all about him), but his friend wouldn't hold him back. As for the trumpeter, my father had made an arrangement to take him on as a lodger as soon as the boy left; and on the morning fixed for the start he was up at the door here by five o'clock; with his trumpet slung by his side, and all the rest of his belongings in a small valise. A Monday morning it was, and after breakfast he had fixed to walk with the boy some way on the road toward Helston, where the coach started. My father left them at breakfast together, and went out to meat the pig, and do a few odd morning jobs of that sort. When he came back, the boy was still at table, and the trumpeter standing here by the chimney-place with the drum and trumpet in his hands, hitched together just as they be at this moment.

" 'Look at this,' he says to my father, showing him the lock; 'I picked it up off a starving brass-worker in Lisbon, and it is not one of your common locks that one word of six letters will open at any time. There's *janius* in this lock; for you've only to make the ring spell any six-letter word you please, and snap down the lock upon that, and never a soul can open it—not the maker, even—until somebody comes along that knows the word you snapped it on. Now, Johnny here's goin', and he leaves his drum behind him; for, though he can make pretty music on it, the parchment sags in wet weather, by reason of the sea-water getting at it; an' if he carries it to Plymouth, they'll only condemn it and give him another. And as for me, I shan't have the heart to put lip to the trumpet any more when Johnny's gone. So we've chosen a word together, and locked 'em together upon that; and, by your leave, I'll hang 'em here together on the hook over your fireplace. Maybe Johnny'll come back; maybe not. Maybe, if he comes, I'll be dead and gone, an' he'll take 'em apart an' try their music for old sake's sake. But if he never comes, nobody can separate 'em; for nobody besides knows the word. And if you marry and have sons, you can tell 'em that here are tied together the souls of Johnny Christian, drummer, of the Marines, and William George Tallifer, once trumpeter of the Queen's Own Hussars. Amen.'

"With that he hung the two instruments 'pon the hook there; and the boy stood up and thanked my father and shook hands; and the pair went forth of the door, toward Helston.

"Somewhere on the road they took leave of one another; but nobody saw the parting, nor heard what was said between them. About three in the afternoon the trumpeter came walking back over the hill; and by the time my father came home from the fishing, the cottage was tidied up and the tea ready, and the whole place shining like a new pin. From that time for five years he lodged here with my father, looking after the house and tilling the garden; and all the while he was steadily failing, the hurt in his head spreading, in a manner, to his limbs. My father watched the feebleness growing on him, but said nothing. And from first to last neither spake a word about the drummer, John Christian; not did any letter reach them, nor word of his doings.

"The rest of the tale you'm free to believe, sir, or not, as you please. It stands upon my father's words, and he always declared he was ready to kiss the Book upon it before judge and jury. He said, too, that he never had the wit to make up such a yarn; and he defied any one to explain about the lock, in particular, by any other tale. But you shall judge for yourself.

"My father said that about three o'clock in the morning, April fourteenth of the year 'fourteen, he and William Tallifer were sitting here, just as you and I, sir, are sitting now. My father had put on his clothes a few minutes before, and was mending his spiller by the light of the horn lantern, meaning to set off before daylight to haul the trammel. The trumpeter hadn't been to bed at all. Toward the last he mostly spent his nights (and his days, too) dozing in the elbow-chair where you sit at this minute. He was dozing then (my father said), with his chin dropped forward on his chest, when a knock sounded upon the door, and the door opened, and in walked an upright young man in scarlet regimentals.

"He had grown a brave bit, and his face was the color of woodashes; but it was the drummer, John Christian. Only his uniform was different from the one he used to wear, and the figures '38' shone in brass upon his collar.

"The drummer walked past my father as if he never saw him, and stood by the elbow-chair and said:

" 'Trumpeter, trumpeter, are you one with me?'

"And the trumpeter just lifted the lids of his eyes and answered, 'How should I not be one with you, drummer Johnny—Johnny boy? The men are patient, Till you come, I count; you march, I mark time until the discharge comes.'

" 'The discharge has come to-night,' said the drummer, 'and the word is Corunna no longer'; and stepping to the chimney-place, he unhooked the drum and trumpet, and began to twist the brass rings of the lock, spelling the word aloud, so—C-O-R-U-N-A. When he had fixed the last letter, the padlock opened in his hand.

" 'Did you know, trumpeter, that when I came to Plymouth they put me into a line regiment?'

" 'The 38th is a good regiment,' answered the old Hussar, still in his dull voice. 'I went back with them from Sahagun to Corunna. At Corunna they stood in General Fraser's division, on the right. They behaved well.'

" 'But I'd fain see the Marines again,' says the drummer, handing him the trumpet, 'and you—you shall call once more for the Queen's Own. Matthew,' he says, suddenly, turning on my father—and when he turned, my father saw for the first time that his scarlet jacket had a round hole by the breast-bone, and that the blood was welling there—'Matthew, we shall want your boat.'

"Then my father rose on his legs like a man in a dream, while they two slung on, the one his drum, and t'other his trumpet. He took the lantern, and went quaking before them down to the shore, and they breathed heavily behind him; and they stepped into his boat, and my father pushed off.

" 'Row you first for Dolor Point,' says the drummer. So my father rowed them out past the white houses of Coverack to Dolor Point, and there, at a word, lay on his oars. And the trumpeter, William Tallifer, put his trumpet to his mouth and sounded the *Revelly*. The music of it was like rivers running.

" 'They will follow,' said the drummer. 'Matthew, pull you now for the Manacles.'

"So my father pulled for the Manacles, and came to an easy close outside Carn dû. And the drummer took his sticks and beat a tattoo, there by the edge of the reef; and the music of it was like a rolling chariot.

" 'That will do,' says he, breaking off, 'they will follow. Pull now for the shore under Gunner's Meadow.'

"Then my father pulled for the shore, and ran his boat in under Gunner's Meadow. And they stepped out, all three, and walked up to the meadow. By the gate the drummer halted and began his tattoo again, looking out toward the darkness over the sea.

"And while the drum beat, and my father held his breath, there came up out of the sea and the darkness a troop of many men, horse and foot, and formed up among the graves; and others rose out of the graves and formed up—drowned Marines with bleached faces, and pale Hussars riding their horses, all lean and shadowy. There was no clatter of hoofs or accoutrements, my father said, but a soft sound all the while, like the beating of a bird's wing and a black shadow lying like a pool about the feet of all. The drummer stood upon a little knoll just inside the gate, and beside him the tall trumpeter, with hand on hip, watching them gather; and behind them both my father, clinging to the gate. When no more came the drummer stopped playing, and said, 'Call the roll.'

"Then the trumpeter stepped toward the end man of the rank and called, 'Troop-Sergeant-Major Thomas Irons,' and the man in a thin voice answered, 'Here!'

" 'Troop-Sergeant-Major Thomas Irons, how is it with you?'

"The man answered, 'How should it be with me? When I was young, I betrayed a girl; and when I was grown, I betrayed a friend, and for these things I must pay. But I died as a man ought. God save the King!'

"The trumpeter called to the next man, 'Trooper Henry Buckingham,' and the next man answered, 'Here!'

" 'Trooper Henry Buckingham, how is it with you?'

" 'How should it be with me? I was a drunkard, and I stole, and in Lugo, in a wine-shop, I knifed a man. But I died as a man should. God save the King!'

"So the trumpeter went down the line; and when he

had finished, the drummer took it up, hailing the dead Marines in their order. Each man answered to his name, and each man ended with 'God save the King!' When all were hailed, the drummer stepped back to his mound, and called:

" 'It is well. You are content, and we are content to join you. Wait yet a little while.'

"With this he turned and ordered my father to pick up the lantern, and lead the way back. As my father picked it up, he heard the ranks of dead men cheer and call, 'God save the King!' all together, and saw them waver and fade back into the dark, like a breath fading off a pane.

"But when they came back here to the kitchen, and my father set the lantern down, it seemed they'd both forgot about him. For the drummer turned in the lantern-light—and my father could see the blood still welling out of the hole in his breast—and took the trumpet-sling from around the other's neck, and locked drum and trumpet together again, choosing the letters on the lock very carefully. While he did this he said:

" 'The word is no more Corunna, but Bayonne. As you left out an "n" in Corunna, so must I leave out an "n" in Bayonne.' And before snapping the padlock, he spelt out the word slowly—'B-A-Y-O-N-E.' After that, he used no more speech; but turned and hung the two instruments back on the hook; and then took the trumpeter by the arm; and the pair walked out into the darkness, glancing neither to right nor left.

"My father was on the point of following, when he heard a sort of sigh behind him; and there, sitting in the elbow-chair, was the very trumpeter he had just seen walk out by the door! If my father's heart jumped before, you may believe it jumped quicker now. But after a bit, he went up to the man asleep in the chair, and put a hand upon him. It was the trumpeter in flesh and blood that he touched; but though the flesh was warm, the trumpeter was dead.

"Well, sir, they buried him three days after; and at

first my father was minded to say nothing about his dream (as he thought it). But the day after the funeral, he met Parson Kendall coming from Helston market; and the parson called out: 'Have 'ee heard the news the coach brought down this mornin'?' 'What news?' says my father. 'Why, that peace is agreed upon.' 'None too soon,' says my father. 'Not soon enough for our poor lads at Bayonne,' the parson answered. 'Bayonne!' cries my father with a jump. 'Why, yes'; and the parson told him all about a great sally the French had made on the night of April 13th. 'Do you happen to know if the 38th regiment was engaged?' my father asked. 'Come, now,' said Parson Kendall, 'I didn't know you was so well up in the campaign. But, as it happens, I *do* know that the 38th was engaged, for 'twas they that held a cottage and stopped the French advance.'

"Still my father held his tongue; and when, a week later, he walked into Helston and bought a 'Mercury' off the Sherborne rider, and got the landlord of the Angel to spell out the list of killed and wounded, sure enough, there among the killed was Drummer John Christian, of the 38th Foot.

"After this there was nothing for a religious man but to make a clean breast. So my father went up to Parson Kendall and told the whole story. The parson listened, and put a question or two, and then asked:

" 'Have you tried to open the lock since that night?'

" 'I ha'n't dared to touch it,' says my father.

" 'Then come along and try.' When the parson came to the cottage here, he took the things off the hook and tried the lock. 'Did he say "*Bayonne*"? The word has seven letters.'

" 'Not if you spell it with one "n" as *he* did,' says my father.

"The parson spelt it out—B-A-Y-O-N-E. 'Whew!' says he, for the lock had fallen open in his hand.

"He stood considering it a moment, and then he says, 'I tell you what. I shouldn't blab this all round the parish, if I was you. You won't get no credit for truth-telling, and a miracle's wasted on a set of fools. But if you like, I'll shut down the lock again upon a holy word that no one but me shall know, and neither drummer nor trumpeter, dead nor alive, shall frighten the secret out of me.'

" 'I wish to gracious you would, parson,' said my father.

"The parson chose the holy word there and then, and shut the lock back upon it, and hung the drum and trumpet back in their place. He is gone long since, taking the word with him. And till the lock is broken by force, nobody will ever separate those twain."

COMMANDER IN THE MIST

Sterling Lanier

It was a rather normal day, or actually, afternoon, for New York. In November, that is. Crowds were moving along Fifth Avenue in a cold sleeting rain. Traffic was blaring horns and cab drivers were yelling obscenities at jaywalkers, other hapless motorists and each other. The brown-uniformed Traffic Police, including a few women, with the aid of the standard men in blue, were trying to make sense out of it all and, true to the reputation of New York's police over the Earth, were doing so, with terse, barking commands of "Move along there," and "Can't you see the color of a stop light, goddammit?"

I was standing against the solid stone wall of Central Park, in the low Sixties, which was some protection against the cold wind and wet. The wind was out of the west, over the Hudson River and coming over the few leaves on the park trees with some force. The thin, cold drops of water were apt to be driven down one's neck while walking. Still, I had only two blocks to go. Then the park would end and I could easily cross to my destination.

I was looking downtown and about to move on when I was startled by a voice from my other flank.

"Like the thunder of the city, old chap?" A man stood beside me, his Burberry belted and his slouch hat, some natty Italian make, maybe a Borsalino, slanted over one blue eye. A grin cut across the ruddy, smooth-shaven face, and I wondered again at the absence of lines on it. The Brigadier, as Ffellowes preferred to be called, had been everywhere in the world and not only done most known things, but seemed to have been mixed up in a whole bunch of things no one else had not only never done, most people had never conceived of them being remotely possible. His years of service to the British Crown had dumped him in every branch of their army I had ever heard of, and then some! If he's truthful, and I think he is, it would hardly take me by surprise to have him state calmly that he had com-manded a battle-cruiser at Jutland or been leader of the much later air strike on Dresden. What a man, and how quietly and unobtrusively he could move! A long period in some intelligence branch or branches, that had taught him this trick, or so he claimed. Now he spoke again, the clipped, even tones cutting through street noise like a knife through butter.

"Don't recognize the quote, do you?" His smile broad-ened. "It was said to, or thought by, a hero, if you like. Fictional, I'm afraid." He saw from my puzzled look that I had no idea what he was talking about, which was not rare, and went on with his joke. "It was said about this town to one Simon Templar. That ring a bell? Said by or inspired by a lovely girl though, not an aging hack of the Empire."

My memory raced and finally came up with reading long past but still memorable. "For Christ's sake! The Saint! Didn't know you liked that kind of thing, Briga-dier. What's the story called?"

"If my recollection serves, very simple. *The Saint in New York*, by that chap, Leslie Charteris. Damned good book, too. You ought to try it. Maybe it's in the club library, hmm?"

"Let's go and look. I was headed there anyway. There's no sun, to put it mildly, and it's getting dark. This park has muggers, you know."

My answer didn't make him turn a hair. As a matter

of fact, I would have feared for any mugger who tried on Ffellowes, unless he had a team headed by a large tank, to help him.

He was going to the same place I was, and we strolled quickly along the rain-swept street in the growing dark, chatting away together. In no time we were in our club and had shucked our coats and settled down with drinks in the library. He had, not tea, which might have been what he was raised on, but a large cup of black coffee, fresh-ground as the club does it.

There were three or four of our acquaintances in the big room, and they quickly stopped whatever they were gabbing about and drew near to us and around the fire. I knew what they were hoping for, but I could hardly blame them. Any time I got Ffellowes at his ease by a fire, or just relaxed, I hoped for one of his incredible stories. They were rare but fantastic. We all felt the same way, but none of us wanted to beg to put the man at a disadvantage. If we had, we all felt, he might stop coming around at all. Better an occasional tale from the Brigadier, than none at all.

We were simply having a chat, about nothing in particular though, and I was about to give up hope of any of his bizarre reminiscences, when we were saved and by a most unlikely person, not to say an improbable one.

A voice like a rusty foghorn sounded from the stairs, and the sound of heavy, clumping shoes. We all straightened in our chairs and even Ffellowes stopped talking. "This God-awful town! I ought to go down to Florida and check on my horses at that stud place, north of Tampa. I got a lot of dough in them things, and IRS ought to be easy on my trips down there. Nobody knows what a real horse-lover has to put out and the work he's got to do. Besides, any excuse to get the hell outta this shit-hole of a town and this weather, will do me." Mason Williams was in full cry and sounded as unpleasant as ever. So much for peace and quiet in the library, was my thought as I watched his bulky shape thudding over our way, red face and bulbous nose under a thinning mop of greying hair. I had forgot our secret weapon, and the incisive syllables stirred me as they always did.

"You seem a trifle out of shape, Williams. Going to put in some time as an exercise-boy? Nothing like it for a horse-lover such as yourself, is there?"

Williams' nasty face turned an even redder hue and verged on the purple in places. He hated Ffellowes anyway and was maddened by the cold contempt which was all he ever got from him. The Englishman fascinated him, more or less the way a cobra is supposed to petrify a bird, though, and he could never stay away from those cold eyes and the gelid tones, when they were about. Now he slouched into one vacant leather armchair and scowled in anger.

"I suppose you British know all about horses, pal," was his opening gun. "No crummy Yank can hold a candle to you jerks and your Grando National jazz. Jeez, why don't you give us a break, Genarul!" (he knew well that Ffellowes did not care for this title) "and let the Amurrican peasants play with their toys in a back room, huh?"

As often he had done before, Brigadier Ffellowes smiled politely. It might have been a parrot squawking or a dog yapping at him. Williams could say nothing that even slightly ruffled him, then or ever. But the next words made us all, and that includes the unspeakable Williams, sit up straighter and also, shut up.

"Why I'm only a fair rider, old man. Hardly know one end of a filly from another. Equine, that is." He smiled gently, and I cast my mind back to other stories which gave the lie to this statement. I held my breath.

"Frankly, I think there may be too much trouble, hunting for horses, you know. Can be fraught with peril and all that sort of thing. To say nothing of experiences that one really doesn't care to recall. I remember the banks of the Danube in '45, now. Very odd and, d'you know, men, rather unsettling. Not at this time of year but just this sort of weather. Colder perhaps. No heat pipes running along the *Donau* banks, though once there was some decent heating. In *Palaestrum,* that is. Any of you know it?"

We shook our heads in silence and no one opened his mouth. I don't know about the others, but for me the windy and wet eve of outside Manhattan was totally gone. I wanted to hear this one as I always did, more than anything I could think of. The high, curtained windows of the club library made a good sound barrier and the roar of the city outside was dim and far away.

Ffellowes smiled gently and looked up and off into space for a second. No one opened his yap, and the Brigadier knew, I think, that we were waiting.

"Well, if it would not bore you, it's a vaguely interesting tale. *Palaestrum* is, or was, one of the old Roman bases on the Danube frontier. Got Roman cemeteries and the remains of amphitheaters, even a broken-down HQ or something, which might have had the structure of a palace. I think they're still rooting about there and even finding things now and again. Off in a field, there's some sort of big triumphal arch or something. The Russkies left it alone, though it was in their zone, which seems odd, but perhaps they had other things on their mind. More complexity in the Slav mentality than they often get credit for, you know."

This was more than Williams could take. His anger overcame his fascination, but it did no harm. "Very funny, my dear Genarul. All them Romans and their lousy Empire. Like you Limeys, they ain't around no more, are they? So what has any of this got to do with your Grando National winners? Nothing, right?"

We all held our breath, and I vowed once again to try and find out how Williams had ever got by the Election Committee. But it did no harm.

"Quite right, my dear man. Nothing at all to do with Aintree. But there are other steeds in the world, you know. And I was looking for some. Never found 'em though. To find these horses, it took an old cavalryman. I suppose you've heard of George Patton? Ever hear of the Lippizaners?"

We were all mute again. At the mention of a great

American general, even Williams had to clam up. It was very deft, as it always was. And it went calmly on, with no more interruptions.

"As I say, we were looking for horses. At the time, they were far north and east of our location. The Allies, all of us, had swung wide of Vienna and Austria and kept driving north into Germany, quickly, with a sharp lookout being kept. Plenty of Kraut stragglers and broken units about. A lot of 'em wanted to surrender, but not all, not by any means. Several die-hard SS units were in our neighborhood, and God knows what else. The main army, ours, was U.S. and French.

"We ourselves were a special small unit. We had three American half-tracks though and more than a few bazookas. I was in command and had three officers and a half-company of other ranks. All volunteers and good men. Let me see, I seem to think they were Gloucesters. All combat-proofed and veterans. Some of them went back a long time, to the Western Desert and similar places.

"My Second was a Major Broke, and there were two lieutenants, named Garvin and Embey. A couple of good sergeants, too. All in all, a good, self-contained group.

"We'd been sent south, alone, to find the whereabouts of the famous Spanish Riding School of Vienna and above all, its mounts, the Lippizaners. What, or who, they were destined for, I have no idea. They're back in Austria now, of course, or their descendants are. Your Third Army leader saw to that. As I said, an old cavalryman. Ever know he designed the last saber ever thought of for issue to your mounted troops? Never used, but I've got one somewhere. Very good design, I always thought.

"Anyhow, some Intelligence wallah, probably in London, thought or heard that the damn horses had or were coming by a certain route. We were going to place ourselves, a lost company, on or across said route. Snaffle the animals and bring off a great coup for the British Army. It was all wrong, but so were a lot of efforts of that sort and many a lot more important. Not the intention, that was all right. But the dope we'd been given was very late and way off anyway. We were miles from any of our own troops, let alone allies.

"So, as it happens, we found ourselves very close to the Blue Danube. Well, it may have been blue to Strauss, but I've seen a lot of it at one time or another, and it always looked brown and turgid as hell to me. Especially on a cold, spring afternoon, with the bare trees dripping with rain and patches of fog at low points. That, my friends, is how we got to *Palaestrum*. There's a town there, built in the 16th Century or so, just about the time that Spanish School got going, or even earlier. Called *Sankt Udo* or close to it, as I recall. There was a ruined baroque *Schloss,* or castle, the seat of a family named Antenstein, I think. We avoided the town altogether, which was common sense. Anyone or anything could have been in those old houses. But by the castle, which seemed more or less gutted and empty, there ran a narrow dirt track, which, if our info was correct, actually ran down to the river itself. Here, the horses were supposed to cross, on makeshift barges or some gear of that sort or other. And there, if all went well, we would nab them."

He paused and again his eyes went far away. "Wish you all could have seen what we did. Might even put Williams off on his devotion to rare equines. As we went left off a battered main highway, with gutted vehicles and ruins all about, it was around fourish in the afternoon of very early spring. The lines of tall trees on either side of our dirt track were bare and dripping wet. There was no wind and only that dank and sodden sound of water dripping. One could hear nothing else when our vehicles had to break their progress and the rumble of their engines fell silent.

"Then, there was a break in the trees. We stopped, for the road or excuse for a road, led out into an open space, largish, with more trees on the far side. All the while the track, by the way, had been running downhill at a slight angle.

"It was Broke, sitting beside me in the back of the lead vehicle, who put a thought into speech. 'Someone destroyed something here, by God. Looks as if it had happened a long time ago, though.'

"Before us, through the thin rain, we could see a vast hole in the ground, bowl-shaped and shallow, grading down to a level and rounded center. There were serrated lines sort of cut all around the rim, actually cut level, into the earth. Here and there, other, deeper cuts made what seemed to be openings or even entrances, which led down ramped earth into the level at the bottom. At a couple of the gaps, battered columns of greyish stone lifted themselves out of the dark soil to about ten or so feet. It brought some memories back, of jaunts in southern Europe long before.

"I laughed, for all our men were swiveling their rocket launchers and machine guns about as they peered off into the obscurity. 'It was a long time ago, Major,' I said, 'I had a briefing by some of the Intell. brass that you missed. But tell the men not to worry, though not to relax. You're looking at some remnants of an old war indeed. We're at *Palaestrum*, friend, and this is a dug-up Roman amphitheater in front of us. Lions and Christians might have come through those gates, or chariots. But the last time troops had to be alerted here was against the Marcomanni or some other beginners at the *Völkerwanderung*. It's their descendants, and remote ones, we have to guard ourselves from. Especially if they have SS badges on the collar.'

"Word was passed through the line back to the other two vehicles, and I could hear a refreshing ripple of amusement when they heard what they were goggling at. But they were too much on the alert to relax entirely. Before I could order it, three men with Stens were out in front of us on foot, just in case something modern was lying in wait somewhere in the ruins of the past. We all waited patiently for an 'All Clear' signal. Far off, through the silence, I now could hear the drone of planes, either ours or Russian we felt sure. The *Luftwaffe* was mostly gone by now. Presently, our scouts came back to my half-track. But they had a surprise with them, our first prisoner. She was not very menacing.

"She must have been seventy at least and was a nice-looking old thing, though in ragged and much patched clothes with a ratty scarf covering grey locks from the cold and wet. She was gabbling away at a great rate, her squint orbs darting from one to the other of us in fright. My German is passable, but I could only make out an occasional word or two. I had had an instructor of the Potsdam variety, and the slurred patois of Austrian peasants was beyond me. But, my luck was in, as usual. From beside me, Broke took over. Turned out he'd spent summers in Austria as a boy, and it was nothing to him. He told the men to let go of the poor old thing and was soon chattering away happily with her, while she began to smile and wave her arthritic paws as she prattled at him. He turned to me at length with a smile on his face.

" 'Can I tell the men to let her go, sir? She lives not far away and was only gathering herbs. She knows what we are and has no use for Germans or even her own folk in the German ranks. I think she'll keep her mouth shut.'

"I had a few questions, which he put and she was prompt to answer. She had seen no sign of armor, wagons, horses or uniformed men, save for occasional stragglers in the past weeks. She was delighted to see us, as a matter of fact, since we were not what she was dreading from over the Volga. But as I waved her politely away and the men all smiled at her kindly, she burst out in a torrent of expostulations, pointing ahead in the direction we were going.

"I turned to Broke and he was smiling even more broadly. He bowed and waved the poor thing off and she went, often looking back at us, until she disappeared into the side woods and the gathering mist. Then she was gone and I turned to my companion.

" 'Well, sir,' he explained, his teeth showing, 'seems we are still in danger, at least if we push on to the river. There are dread spirits down there, on my word, *hexerei* of the most nasty sort. They've always been there by the river, and she meant that too, having been warned by a great-grandfather or somesuch, when a kid herself. Think we dare risk it? We mustn't camp there at night, was an emphasis in that chatter.'

"I laughed. I told him I thought that we could manage that sort of thing, and the men near us laughed as well. So we signaled the others and all of us in our truncated column started engines and we went on past the amphitheater of a lost empire and entered the woods again at the other side. I had sent word that no one was to slack off and all were quite on the *qui vive*.

"It was now getting very dark and gloomy, though we could still hold the track without lights, though just. The rain had stopped and we went on through a cold and windless dark under the tall shining dark tree trunks, still down a long and gentle slope.

"The man sitting by the driver up front gave us a hand signal then and we all saw it. We had come to great willows, whose dripping branches, still with many small leaves, hung down all about us. But this was not why we had stopped. There in front was dark water, smooth and almost silent in the gathering night, save for a chuckle where a log broke the surface and caused the great river to ripple about it. We were on the Danube, that ancient waterway of races since time began.

"Swirling mists lay on the water's surface also, but not constant any more than they had been in the woods on the slope above. They veiled the waters but only in patches and shifted slowly to reveal new and shadowy vistas and then closed again and reformed anon some way off. In one opening of the white fog, I had seen a thing quite close to us and only a little way upstream, a couple of hundred feet. It had intrigued me for very obvious reasons, since dark was now coming fast. I gave orders and the wagons, all three, were put in a half-circle with the water at our backs. Sentries were posted at good points and silence imposed. I told the men to eat their combat rations cold and keep mum and lightless. Then I took Broke and a couple of well-armed men and all went to what I had spotted. When we got there, I got out a hooded flash and used it on what lay on the ground and also went out into the water.

"It was nothing more than a broad jetty or the shore portion of one. I looked it over carefully and so did the other three. A very thin layer of soil and leaves did not hide what lay underneath. I was struck silent by it. There were massive blocks of some stone or other, rough and worn yet still strong and solid. The chief wear was logically on our left side, the upstream side. The whole mass thrust out into the Danube for some fifty or so feet and then came to a stop.

" 'Not built yesterday, men,' I said at length. 'This is part of ancient Rome, if I'm not wrong, and was one of their piers. Probably been used by fishers and such, since the 4th Century, and still has uses. I rather think that what we're looking for will be coming this way. Good place to tie up to, and a riverman, coming from the other side, would not have too much trouble finding it. Even at night and a night like this one.'

"So that was all. We went back and sent the same two men with one of the veteran sergeants back to the pier we had found. They were to stay low and keep a sharp lookout. We were deep in enemy country. We were winning but not here or yet.

"The rest of us, having arranged watches and checked all the posts where the inland advance guard was to keep watch, ate and turned in. I chatted for a bit with the three officers and then curled up in my waterproof under a blanket on one of the half-tracks. The night was very silent, save for the burble of the river and the steady drip from the trees, which blended with it. Every so often, planes would hum in the distance and once I heard a far-off thud which may have been a major explosion. But that was all, and I soon fell into an easy slumber, having satisfied myself that I had taken all precautions and done the best I could. I had a quiet smile as I dropped off. Even the ghosts the old girl had been so afraid of, wherever they were, were good and quiet."

Outside the big, high-ceilinged room, the thunder of one of man's great cities seemed very far away. Save for our breathing and an occasional crackle from the fire, all was silent about us. I saw more than one mouth stay open as we waited for the next words of that silent, far-off night in an alien land.

"It was one of the younger officers who woke me up. I flicked a glance at my watch and it was two a.m. on a very dark morning. I could hear nothing and the night was silent, save for the splash of water and the fainter drip of that on the trees.

" 'Don't know what's up, sir,' was the low-voiced message. 'The sergeant sent one of his watch back a second ago, from the bridgehead you found. They've heard some sound they don't like, I gather.'

"I was on my feet quickly. I hissed at him to alert all hands and that I would go over and check myself on whatever it was. I drew my Webley from its holster and, at a crouch, eeled over to where the sergeant was waiting for me, in the shadow of a willow trunk by the ancient pier. I could feel his tension, even in the dark, and I could not even see his face clearly. The fog was heavier now and, with the night as well, we were in a lightless shroud.

" 'We have heard something, sir,' came his hoarse whisper. 'Maybe it's what we're expecting. Very quiet and the sound of a few men marching. But I heard metal clink and so did the other three.' He paused. 'Something else, too. What might have been a couple of horses, maybe unshod or walking on them leaves and stuff. That could be for us, now, right, sir?'

"I patted his arm and we listened intently. For some time, I heard only the usual night noise and the river. Once an owl hooted, faintly and a long piece off. Then when I was beginning to wonder if the men had bad dreams, I heard it myself.

"It was the sound of soft but regular footsteps, more than one, as if in that utter dark, some folk could actually keep in step. Too, just as the man had said, there came a clink of metal and now a creaking as well, which might have been leather or something like that. I held my breath and sure enough, there came the other sound. It was heavy and caused by some weight, but even muffled and hard to make out, it was quite close and the sound of more than two feet.

"I told him to get his men facing out and stay with them. I would stay hid at the pier's foot and meet whatever it was. The others were on alert and ready to chip in if needed. He faded from my side and I crept over to a tree bole where I had said. Then we all waited in that dark and soggy night. Not even the hum of a plane was heard, as we all faced away from the river to the black wall of the wood.

"The sound of the muffled but regular pace, of both man and beast, came even closer. And, suddenly, I saw what I was listening to, or at least part of it. And what a sight it was!

"There in front of me, perhaps ten yards off, was a man and he held in one hand a kind of rude torch. I had heard no sound of its being lit; it was suddenly on and illumined what lay under it to my startled eye. I stood up and stepped forward, and a voice, that of the man in front of me, cried out something. I held up my empty left hand, palm outward, so he could see it. He stared at me, his jaw set, and then he spoke to me.

" 'Who are you?' he began, 'and what do you here on our side? You are on the lands of the Empire, Barbarian, and what do you here at night? It is death to be here and a ban exists. Do you understand me?'

"He was a short swarthy man, smooth-faced, and must have been given a short haircut, for none showed below his helmet. But he was no youth and his strong jaw had white scar lines. The eyes were dark and sharp and there were many wrinkles at the corners. I stood, frozen by a paralysis strong enough to melt bones. And suddenly the cold of the night went through my very soul, as if the wavering aura of torchlight around the figure before me had some malign and invisible miasma of its own. I could only stare, mouth wide open at what I saw.

"First, there was the helmet, of what looked like battered brass, dented and with verdigris over some of it. It was rounded, with a tail coming down the back of the neck and flaring around the sides. A ridge of smooth metal crowned it, also dented. He wore a tunic of stained leather, and on his breast was the brass of a *pectorale* which screened the chest. His brownish kilt came to his knees, and his boots were soft leather but with greave armor on their fronts. The *gladius*, the two-edged Spanish or Celtiberian short sword, was hung from a shoulder belt. Tucked into this belt was what looked like a switch or crop.

"Then and for the first time I realized what tongue I had been hearing. My Sixth Form at school came back with a rush to me. The barking voice was in Latin! I could understand it perfectly well, save for an occasional word. But something old and cold had come into my spirit. Time had stood still and all thought of the present was gone, as if it were some ephemeral cloud.

"I heard the voice of the sergeant over my shoulder and close by as if it were from another world. All I heard was, 'Are you all right . . . ' and then the figure in front of me barked a command.

"There was a sudden movement in the dark behind him, and something whizzed past my head. There was a sharp sound like a branch being broken, and I felt, rather than saw, a figure slump to the ground on my right and rear.

" 'Tell those *Massagetae* of yours to stay back,' rapped the voice from the front, 'and stand still yourself, even if you are their Prince!'

"I did not move and it was not voluntary. My hand was still raised and now even higher. Had Adolf seen me, he would have been proud, save that it was the wrong hand. I knew why that open hand was raised too, and terror crept through me. Was this a bad dream or the end of the world? The silent, fog-ensorcelled night had eaten all sounds but what I heard, and now I heard a new sound.

"It was the earthy sound of a horse pacing and it was

coming out of the blackness behind the man before me, straight for me. Its head appeared in the light and I saw the gleam of silvery and gilt chains across its brow. A man, a very dark man, whose eyeballs flashed in the torchlight, was leading it. I hardly looked at him, but got the idea that he was swathed in white robes and had a hood pulled back of the same hue.

"It was the mounted man, whose mount he was leading; it was he whom I watched as my arm grew even stiffer. I could no longer even feel the Webley in my right fist.

"This new appearance was striking. His *lorica*, the cuirass on his chest, gleamed with a yellow light, and I knew gold when I saw it. It was ornate, too, and I saw scrollwork and the glitter of gems on his breast. He too wore a helmet but his was of finely wrought gold, and surmounting its gleaming ridge was a higher, great ridge of scarlet, running from the front to the rear, upright and narrow. The helmet had a slight bill over the dark eyes, and—oh, yes—thrown back over his shoulders was a heavy and shimmering cloak, whose golden fringe accented the deeper purple of the main body of the garment.

"His face, that of a mature and stern man, as hairless as the first man's, gripped my gaze. It was commanding, that face, and yet, somehow, it was weary, with an unutterable tiredness. A thrill of ice went through me as I met those dark, weary eyes. Then he spoke, though not to me, and I flinched inside as I heard the voice of a doomed and mighty shade, for it contained all the weariness of the ages, mingled with its great authority. Tears came unbidden to my eyes and yet I stood frozen, held in that fog and dark by some mindbending, tragic power.

"'What have we here, Legate? More incursions of the hordes of the East? They look strange enough to have come from the far, strange land of silks, on which our women will always waste our substance.' His horse turned slightly and he addressed me, myself.

"His speech was plain, his voice of a deep timbre.

'*Principes Barbarii*, this place and this river are forbid
when *Noctens* rules. Not even the *Foederati* in my pay
can come here then, not if they wish to live. My priests
and some of ancient Set from the far-off *Nilus*, they
have all laid this ban, and the dark powers will enforce
it as did my own slinger from *Balearica*. Should you
wish to take service, this is done only when Apollo
himself is high in the Heavens. Otherwise, get you
gone or the Powers of Darkness will hold you forever. I
guard *Vindobonum* yet and always will and these are
approaches that no one can cross the mighty river upon
and live without an eternal price upon them.' "

Ffellowes fell silent and the room stayed that way
too. The thunder of New York was a far-distant murmur, and only a glow of remaining coals lit the high,
dark of the big room. We were all a long way off, in
time and space and only breathing was audible. At
length, he spoke once more and finished his tale.

"We were, you fellows see, trapped by a thing that
had emerged from the ages and the mists, not only of
the river but the mists of time. In the next morning,
after I had quietly nursed the sergeant, whose skull, for
he'd taken off his helmet, was not cracked but badly
gashed, I told everyone else that I had seen two stray
nags, lost from some farm, and nothing else. The sergeant, who was concussed, looked at me but did not
give me the lie. No one else had seen anything but the
flicker of a light, which I explained as St. Elmo's fire
and quite natural. Before we went back to work and
retraced our steps northwest, I gave the sergeant a
smooth black pebble. It was apparently lava, and I have
seen thousands on the Majorca or Ibizan beaches before
and since.

"When I came back to myself lying on the ground in
the still, cold glimmer of early day and amid the first
piping of birds, I had a great deal of thought pass
through my dazed head. Was *Vindobonum* which is the
ancient name for Vienna, still sacrosanct and if so, how?
Well, if it were, I knew how, deep in my heart. The
last of the great stoic emperors, the Divine Marcus

Aurelius, had died there. You'll find his maxims in this room if you care to look for them. We two had seen and one had felt the effect of a Balearic slinger, a picked man from one of what amounted to the machine-gun units of the oldest army to ever guard the Danube frontier.

"And who was the man who had spoken to me from the back of his own charger? Well, I just gave you his name, my friends."

The room was so silent that no breath could be heard as Ffellowes spoke his last words. I can hear them still.

"The mists were all about us, gentlemen. In the forest, out on the river, and I had them forever in my mind. For I had spoken to something awesome and of great and unconquerable dignity, from a far-away past and a duty unflagging through the mists of time. For, you see, in search of those rare horses, I had found something rare and far more tragic and yet, you know, still mighty. I had heard the voice of a self-imposed guard to all he held sacred. I had heard the Commander in the Mist."

The vast room was silent as seldom before. We had all been given a glimpse into the long-lost ages. We too had heard the words of . . . the Commander in the Mist.

An excerpt from MAN-KZIN WARS II, created by *Larry Niven*:

The Children's Hour

Chuut-Riit always enjoyed visiting the quarters of his male offspring.

"What will it be this time?" he wondered, as he passed the outer guards.

The household troopers drew claws before their eyes in salute, faceless in impact-armor and goggled helmets, the beam-rifles ready in their hands. He paced past the surveillance cameras, the detector pods, the death-casters and the mines; then past the inner guards at their consoles, humans raised in the household under the supervision of his personal retainers.

The retainers were males grown old in the Riit family's service. There had always been those willing to exchange the uncertain rewards of competition for a secure place, maintenance, and the odd female. Ordinary kzin were not to be trusted in so sensitive a position, of course, but these were families which had served the Riit clan for generation after generation. There was a natural culling effect; those too ambitious left for the Patriarchy's military and the slim chance of advancement, those too timid were not given opportunity to breed.

Perhaps a pity that such cannot be used outside the household, Chuut-Riit thought. Competition for rank was far too intense and personal for that, of course.

He walked past the modern sections, and into an area that was pure Old Kzin; maze-walls of reddish sandstone with twisted spines of wrought-iron on their tops, the tips glistening razor-edged. Fortress-architecture from a world older than this, more massive, colder and drier; from a planet harsh enough that a plains carnivore had changed its ways, put to different use an upright posture designed to place its head above savanna grass, grasping paws evolved to climb rock. Here the modern features were reclusive, hidden in wall and buttress. The door was a hammered slab graven with the faces of night-hunting beasts, between towers five times the height of a kzin. The air smelled of wet rock and the raked sand of the gardens.

Chuut-Riit put his hand on the black metal of the outer portal, stopped. His ears pivoted, and he blinked; out of the corner of his eye he saw a pair of tufted eyebrows glancing through the thick twisted metal on the rim of the ten-meter battlement. *Why, the little sthondats,* he thought affectionately. *They managed to put it together out of reach of the holo pickups.*

The adult put his hand to the door again, keying the locking sequence, then bounded backward four times his own length from a standing start. Even under the lighter gravity of Wunderland, it was a creditable feat. And necessary, for the massive panels rang and toppled as the rope-swung boulder slammed forward. The children had hung two cables from either tower, with the rock at the point of the V and a third rope to draw it back. As the doors bounced wide he saw the blade they had driven into the apex of the egg-shaped granite rock, long and barbed and polished to a wicked point.

Kittens, he thought. *Always going for the dramatic.* If that thing had struck him, or the doors under its impetus had, there would have been no need of a blade. *Watching too many historical adventure holos.* "Errorowwww!" he shrieked in mock-rage, bounding through the shattered portal and into the interior court, halting atop the kzin-high boulder. A round dozen of his older sons were grouped behind the rock, standing in a defensive clump and glaring at him; the crackly scent of their excitement and fear made the fur bristle along his spine. He glared until they dropped their eyes, continued it until they went down on their stomachs, rubbed their chins along the ground and then rolled over for a symbolic exposure of the stomach.

"Congratulations," he said. "That was the closest you've gotten. Who was in charge?"

More guilty sidelong glances among the adolescent males crouching among their discarded pull-rope, and then a lanky youngster with platter-sized feet and hands came squatting-erect. His fur was in the proper flat posture, but the naked pink of his tail still twitched stiffly.

"I was," he said, keeping his eyes formally down. "Honored Sire Chuut-Riit," he added, at the adult's warning rumble.

"Now, youngling, what did you learn from your first attempt?"

"That no one among us is your match, Honored Sire Chuut-Riit," the kitten said. Uneasy ripples went over the black-striped orange of his pelt.

"And what have you learned from this attempt?"

"That all of us together are no match for you, Honored Sire Chuut-Riit," the striped youth said.

"That we didn't locate all of the cameras," another muttered. "You idiot, Spotty." That to one of his siblings; they snarled at each other from their crouches, hissing past barred fangs and making striking motions with unsheathed claws.

"No, you did locate them all, cubs," Chuut-Riit said. "I presume you stole the ropes and tools from the workshop, prepared the boulder in the ravine in the next courtyard, then rushed to set it all up between the time I cleared the last gatehouse and my arrival?"

Uneasy nods. He held his ears and tail stiffly, letting his whiskers quiver slightly and holding in the rush of love and pride he felt, more delicious than milk heated with bourbon. *Look at them!* he thought. At the age when most young kzin were helpless prisoners of instinct and hormone, wasting their strength ripping each other up or making fruitless direct attacks on their sires, or demanding to be allowed to join the Patriarchy's service *at once* to win a Name and house hold of their own . . . *His* get had learned to *cooperate* and use their minds!

"Ah, Honored Sire Chuut-Riit, we set the ropes up beforehand, but made it look as if we were using them for tumbling practice," the one the others called Spotty said. Some of them glared at him, and the adult raised his hand again.

"No, no, I am *moderately* pleased." A pause. "You did not hope to take over my official position if you had disposed of me?"

"No, Honored Sire Chuut-Riit," the tall leader said. There had been a time when any kzin's holdings were the prize of the victor in a duel, and the dueling rules were interpreted more leniently for a young subadult. Everyone had a sentimental streak for a successful youngster; every male kzin remembered the intolerable stress of being physically mature but remaining under dominance as a child.

Still, these days affairs were handled in a more civilized manner. Only the Patriarchy could award military and political office. And this mass assassination attempt was ... unorthodox, to say the least. Outside the rules more because of its rarity than because of formal disapproval. . . .

A vigorous toss of the head. "Oh, no, Honored Sire Chuut-Riit. We had an agreement to divide the private possessions. The lands and the, ah, females." Passing their own mothers to half-siblings, of course. "Then we wouldn't each have so much we'd get too many challenges, and we'd agreed to help each other against outsiders," the leader of the plot finished virtuously.

"Fatuous young scoundrels," Chuut-Riit said. His eyes narrowed dangerously. "You haven't been communicating outside the household, have you?" he snarled.

"Oh, *no*, Honored Sire Chuut-Riit!"

"Word of honor! May we die nameless if we should do such a thing!"

The adult nodded, satisfied that good family feeling had prevailed. "Well, as I said, I am somewhat pleased. If you have been keeping up with your lessons. Is there anything you wish?"

"Fresh meat, Honored Sire Chuut-Riit," the spotted one said. The adult could have told him by the scent, of course, a kzin never forgot another's personal odor, that was one reason why names were less necessary among their species. "The reconstituted stuff from the dispensers is always ... so ... *quiet.*"

Chuut-Riit hid his amusement. Young Heroes-to-be were always kept on an inadequate diet, to increase their aggressiveness. A matter for careful gauging, since too much hunger would drive them into mindless cannibalistic frenzy.

"And couldn't we have the human servants back? They were nice." Vigorous gestures of assent. Another added: "They told good stories. I miss my Clothilda-human."

"Silence!" Chuut-Riit roared. The youngsters flattened stomach and chin to the ground again. "Not until you can be trusted not to injure them; how many times do I have to tell you, it's dishonorable to attack household servants! Until you learn self-control, you will have to make do with machines."

This time all of them turned and glared at a mottled youngster in the rear of their group; there were half-healed scars over his head and shoulders. "It bared its *teeth* at me," he said sulkily. "All I did was swipe at it, how was I supposed to know it would die?" A chorus of rumbles, and this time several of the covert kicks and clawstrikes landed.

"Enough," Chuut-Riit said after a moment. *Good, they have even learned how to discipline each other as a unit.* "I will consider it, when all of you can pass a test on the interpretation of human expressions and body-language." He drew himself up. "In the meantime, within the next two eight-days, there will be a formal hunt and meeting in the Patriarch's Preserve; kzinti homeworld game, the best Earth animals, and even some feral-human outlaws, perhaps!"

He could smell their excitement increase, a mane-crinkling musky odor not unmixed with the sour whiff of fear. Such a hunt was not without danger for adolescents, being a good opportunity for hostile adults to cull a few of a hated rival's offspring with no possibility of blame. *They will be in less danger than most,* Chuut-Riit thought judiciously. *In fact, they may run across a few of my subordinates' get and mob them. Good.*

"And if we do well, afterwards a feast and a visit to the Sterile Ones." That had them all quiveringly alert, their tails held rigid and tongues lolling; nonbearing females were kept as a rare privilege for Heroes whose accomplishments were not *quite* deserving of a mate of their own. Very rare for kits still in the household to be granted such, but Chuut-Riit thought it past time to admit that modern society demanded a prolonged adolescence. The day when a male kit could be given a spear, a knife, a rope and a bag of salt and kicked out the front gate at puberty were long gone. Those were the wild, wandering years in the old days, when survival challenges used up the superabundant energies. Now they must be spent learning history, technology, xenology, none of which burned off the gland-juices saturating flesh and brain.

He jumped down amid his sons, and they pressed around him, purring throatily with adoration and fear and respect;

his presence and the failure of their plot had reestablished his personal dominance unambiguously, and there was no danger from them for now. Chuut-Riit basked in their worship, feeling the rough caress of their tongues on his fur and scratching behind his ears. *Together*, he thought. *Together we will do wonders.*